Remember the Shadow

Table of Contents

The Dream

It was the end of summer and the beginning of fall. The days were still warm, and the nights brought a slight chill. It was a cool night and Mark Martinez, for the first time in a long time, slept comfortably in his bed. It has been three years since his wife, Janet, passed. Mark had always slept on his own side of the bed, careful not to disturb his wife's side. However, tonight he felt as if he had permission to sleep in the middle of the bed and all felt right in the world.

Mark had a smile, as if Janet had kissed him and he hugged all the pillows and took all the blankets. A cool night with a soft and comfy bed, it was the recipe for a good dream.

Mark remembered such nights snuggling with Janet. Sometimes he could hear his kids through the walls, making all kinds of noises, as most kids do, but tonight he knew the house was empty. Mark and Janet had three children, all of them are grown and out of the house.

Thomas, his eldest son, and Alyssa, his only daughter, had families of their own. His youngest, Jeremy, was off in Australia, working for a marketing firm or something like that, making videos to post on the internet. Deep into slumber, Mark remembered the time he first met Janet. It was at an Austin City Limits concert; Norah Jones was playing one of her sultry songs.

Magic is real.

Mark always knew that magic was real. It takes different forms as we grow older. That night, he found magic again when he made eye contact with a beautiful woman with soft brown hair and almond-colored eyes. It was love at first sight: his heart skipped several beats that night. Mark found the courage to talk to her, and while it took time and effort to win Janet's attention and later her affection, it all started that wonderful night.

Years later, when Janet told their children about the night they met, her story was similar yet different. One thing she said made Mark fall deeper in love with her: she told them that the night they met was the night she discovered magic. Mark smiled and felt the warmth of the blankets and for a second, he could feel Janet's embrace.

"Please stay" he said in his sleep.

Then, the image of Janet disappeared. Mark felt a cold draft, a strong gust of wind with a stinging coldness with it. "No" Mark mumbled. He was tossing and turning, he felt the warmth leaving the bed and the room. "Please stay or let me go with you".

Mark saw himself as an 8-year-old boy, in his pajamas chasing after his brother Francisco, or Frankie as everyone called him. Frankie was 11 years old and he was going outside after bedtime. Frankie's friends were outside on their bikes. "No Markie, you gotta stay here! I told you, it's too dangerous. Go back to bed." He said while gathering a few things and shoving them into a backpack. A strange crystal was wrapped up in an old pillowcase.

Mark refused and insisted he go with his big brother. He knew that Frankie needed him. Dale, one of Frankie's friends, came up to them. "We got to go before it's too late." Frankie nodded and mounted his bike. Mark chased after him. Frankie stopped and looked at his brother. "It'll be alright, I promise you. I will be back before mom and dad find out. I need you to stay here and keep your mouth shut. Okay? Brothers look out for brothers, you understand?" Mark nodded and handed Frankie a slingshot with some marbles. "Take this, it will protect you. Take it and I'll go back to bed." Frankie took the slingshot and marbles. He put them in his backpack. He gave his little brother a hug. "Go back to bed, it will be alright, I promise". The wind shifted and got louder like a roar. Truth be told, Mark did not realize that was going to be the last time he saw his brother alive.

Mark tried to go to sleep but his mind was cluttered with scary images. He saw himself being dragged underneath his bed by a creature with long arms and sharp talons. He cried out for help, but no one came to help. Older Mark was tossing in the center of the bed, the blankets felt heavy, the air colder, stinging still.

The memories came back, all of them, but shattered like broken glass. It was Halloween 1990; his brother and his friends went out on some big adventure. Sometimes, Mark would wander in his brother's room and hear him talking to his friends about monsters, demons, ghosts and warlocks that drank the blood of children.

November 1, 1990. The morning came with a sense of dread. Frankie was not in his room; he did not come home. Mark thought if he kept quiet then his brother would come back home but if he said something then Frankie would be mad and never come back.
Hours drifted into days and Frankie didn't come home. Nobody knew where he was or seen him around town. Mark's parents called around, Frankie and his friends were nowhere to be found. Eventually, the police came and talked to everyone, including Mark.

Mark remembered his mom crying for hours. She did not cook or clean the house. His father never slept and kept searching everywhere for Frankie. On November 11th, Veteran's Day, the Martinez family got a phone call: Frankie was found. The police received an anonymous tip that five bikes and an old truck were found outside Miller's Quarry. Deep in the quarry, an underground passage was found along with the bodies of five children, and two elderly adults were found dead trying to leave the tunnel.

Mark saw himself as a little boy again, walking into the tunnel and hearing a wicked howl. Something pulled him in and he saw the bodies of five creatures, short with greenish-yellow skin, dark brown hair and yellow eyes. They were fighting over something, one of them tried to take an object wrapped in an old pillowcase when something in the dark killed them. One of the strange creatures dropped the object down a dark crevice.

Mark heard Frankie and his friends! They were trying to escape from the tunnels. Mark tried to call out to them; he wanted to warn them and maybe get Frankie to come and help him. He heard Frankie's voice "Mark? Hang on, I'm coming!" and then the strange power that pulled Mark into the tunnel pinned him against the wall. He saw a strange, inhuman shape pull the skin and muscles from the five dead creatures into a makeshift bodysuit and run down the tunnels towards Frankie. "AHHHHH!"

Mark woke up, no longer eight but sixty-eight. He was soaked in a pool of sweat and tears. He got up to close the window, the chilly stinging air was still around him, to his surprise, the windows were closed.

He couldn't go back to sleep now; he went to the bathroom to freshen up. He splashed water on his face.

He was awake but he knew that the dream was real. Mark knew it was a reminder and deep down, he knew, it was also a warning.

Mark stared into the mirror for a while as if he was staring down some dark abyss and before anything else can stare back…. he made the *"Zoolander"* face and moved his cheeks from side to side, as if he was inspecting the merchandise. This was something he did when he was younger, when he wanted to tease his wife while shaving, or when he wanted to make one of his kids or grandkids laugh. Mark went downstairs and began turning on the lights. He turned on the TV and began to make coffee.

The house was so quiet this early in the morning. Mark looked around his empty kitchen and remembered a time when there was always something happening in the house. He remembered the sounds of children and animals. The animals also passed on a few years ago and all his children are out of the house.

He remembered when he and his late wife wished for a quieter house and now it is. Only the faint glow of the living room night light kept the house from looking cold. Mark sat down and waited for the coffee machine to brew his first cup. The TV was on some random news station, and he didn't pay attention to what was going on. It's always some tragedy or weather event, nothing uplifting. Mark kept the TV on, just to hear some noise. He didn't know why he had the dreams he had but today, he felt alone.

"Come on down to Betty's Kitchen for some real home cooking! Now serving Breakfast".

Wait, what? Mark thought to himself. It was a commercial for a restaurant close by the museum district in downtown Coralyn Bay. Mark had just poured himself a cup of coffee and his mind wandered around the house. Many thoughts were racing in his mind, and he decided that he needed a distraction to take his mind off the memories, the visions he had. *Perhaps I will go and check out Betty's Kitchen*, he told himself.

Before the Storm

Downtown Coralyn Bay

Bruce Brixby arrived at the Coralyn Bay Museum of Natural History two hours before opening, earlier than usual. Field Trip Day always demanded extra preparation, but today he woke up at 5 AM with restless energy that he couldn't explain.

He parked in the employee lot and paused before getting out, looking toward the port a few blocks away. Ships moved in and out of the harbor, their lights still visible in the pre-dawn sky. The museum sat at the intersection of everything: downtown, the financial district, the port, the beach. A perfect location for a perfect institution.

Someday, Bruce told himself as he locked his car, *I'll have a museum of my own to run. Hell, to own.*

The sea breeze hit him as he crossed the parking lot, carrying that familiar salt-and-fish smell that worked better than coffee. He walked past the xeriscape garden to the side entrance, already mentally cataloging the day's tasks. The employee lounge was mundane and musky at this hour, but Bruce didn't mind. It was when he walked to the museum floor that he felt that sense of traveling through time, each fossil a treasure, each display a story. The entire place was a testament to human history and achievement.

And sometimes, late at night when he was closing, Bruce wondered about the stories the museum didn't tell. The artifacts in storage that didn't quite fit. The specimens with notations like "origin uncertain" or "classification pending." He shook off the thought and headed to the break room for coffee.

By 8:30am, the staff had assembled in Dr. Shelley's office. The chief curator stood at her desk with her usual clipboard, looking more frazzled than normal. "Alright everyone, quick briefing," she said. "We have three schools today: Sam Houston Elementary at 9 AM, Sadie Hawkins Middle at 10, and Jim Davis High around 11. The guest lecturer from Stonewall University will do a presentation on the new asteroid exhibit for all three groups."

Bruce raised an eyebrow. "Three schools, almost back-to-back? That's tight."

"The schedule had to compress," Gilbert, the assistant director, cut in. "We needed to accommodate the professor's availability. Students come in, hear the lecture, then explore on their own. Standard field trip protocol."

"Asteroids from Mars, Venus, and Europa," Dr. Shelley added, trying to inject enthusiasm.

"Very exciting for the kids."

"Should've had them last week when the Trimond was here," Lester the janitor muttered. Dr. Shelley's smile tightened slightly. "The Trimond was a private exhibition, Lester. Today is about education." She clapped her hands together. "Alright everyone: stations. Let's make this a magical day." Bruce caught Cindy's eye as they dispersed. "Did she just say, 'magical day'?" Cindy, a student volunteer from Tri-Coastal Community College, shrugged. "First time for everything." Bruce made his rounds through the exhibits, checking displays and lighting. He paused at the prehistoric wing: the museum's pride and joy, though it was smaller than it should be due to funding issues.

The massive, fossilized dragonfly wing caught his eye as it always did. Beautiful specimen. He'd helped

install it two years ago. The notation card read: Meganeura monyi. Carboniferous Period. Approximately 300 million years old.
Bruce stared at it for a moment. Something about the wing had always bothered him, though he couldn't put his finger on what. The shape was right, the size was right for a Meganeura, but...

He checked his watch. 8:55. The first bus would arrive any minute. Bruce headed back to the entrance, pushing the thought aside. Today was about managing chaos, not pondering curiosities. Still, as he positioned himself near the doors, he felt that same restless energy from this morning. Like something was about to shift.
The first yellow bus pulled into the lot.
"Here we go," Cindy said beside him. Bruce smiled. "Here we go."

The doors opened and an army of eight-to-ten-year-olds poured in, full of barely contained energy. Their teacher, a young woman in her twenties, tried to organize them into some semblance of order while parent volunteers looked already exhausted.
"Welcome to the Coralyn Bay Museum of Natural History!" Bruce announced with practiced enthusiasm. "If everyone will follow me to the auditorium, we have a very special presentation this morning."

The students bunched together, chattering excitedly. Bruce caught fragments of conversation: "I hope we see dinosaurs!" "My mom said there's space rocks!" "Can we go to the gift shop?" As they filed into the auditorium, Bruce noticed Lester lingering near the entrance, straightening his custodian's uniform. The teacher passed by, and Lester muttered under his breath, "Damn, where were teachers like that when I was in school?"

Bruce shook his head and focused on getting the kids seated. The auditorium filled quickly, students claiming the back rows first until the teacher herded them forward. Dr. Shelley took the stage. "Good morning, everyone! We have a special guest today: all the way from Neon City, a professor of space science from Stonewall University. Please welcome Dr. John Eagle!"

The kids perked up immediately. Bruce saw eyes widen, whispers spread. John Eagle? The famous pro-wrestler-astronaut-celebrity? A middle-aged man in a plaid blazer with elbow patches shuffled onto the stage. "You ain't John Eagle!" a boy called out.

"I assure you, I am Professor John Eagle," the man said in a dry, academic tone. "And I'm here to discuss the fascinating asteroid specimens you'll see shortly. But first, a brief lesson on asteroidal composition and orbital mechanics."

Bruce sighed and found a spot against the back wall. This was going to be a long lecture. The worst part? He'd have to hear it two more times today. Halfway through Dr. Eagle's explanation of silicate-based mineral structures, Bruce's attention drifted. He scanned the auditorium: some kids were paying attention, most were fidgeting, a few were outright asleep. His walkie-talkie crackled. Gilbert's voice came through: "Bruce, heads up. Second bus just pulled in early. Driver says the third bus broke down: they're combining trips." Bruce's eyes widened. He keyed the walkie. "All three schools at once?"

"Affirmative. Code Overflow."

Bruce invented Code Overflow last year: code for "all hell's breaking loose, all hands-on deck." He slipped out of the auditorium and found Dr. Shelley in her office, already on the phone. "I understand, but we weren't prepared for…yes, yes, of course we'll accommodate them." She hung up and looked at Bruce with barely controlled panic. "The second bus arrived forty minutes early, and the third had mechanical issues. We're going to have approximately two hundred students in the museum simultaneously."

"We can handle it," Bruce said, more confidently than he felt. "I'll coordinate with Cindy and the volunteers. We'll split them into groups, stagger the exhibit access…"

"Just keep them from destroying anything," Gilbert interjected, rushing past with an armful of museum maps. "And for God's sake, confiscate any silly string before they get inside." By 10:30, the museum was controlled chaos. Elementary students mixed with middle schoolers and high schoolers. Bruce waded through crowds, confiscating contraband such as silly string, poppers, markers that weren't supposed to leave the classroom.

He was breaking up a minor scuffle near the marine biology exhibit when he noticed an older man at the entrance, talking to the ticket attendant. The man looked to be in his late sixties, moving with the careful deliberation of someone whose body didn't quite keep up with his mind anymore. The attendant was smiling. "No way you're over fifty!"

The old man grinned. "If my hips were better and I was a hundred years younger, I'd race you to the buffet." Bruce watched the man accept his senior ticket and a museum map. Something about him stood out: not his age, but the way he carried himself. Alert. Purposeful. Like he was here for something specific.

Then a high schooler nearly knocked over a display case, and Bruce's attention snapped back to crisis management. The afternoon blurred into a cycle of questions, redirections, and minor emergencies. Bruce barely noticed when the old man appeared in the prehistoric wing, studying the exhibits with unusual intensity. By the time the last bus pulled away at 2:30, Bruce felt like he'd survived a small war.

"That," Cindy said, slumping against the information desk, "was insane."

"That was Wednesday," Bruce replied, surveying the damage. Candy wrappers, scattered brochures, a few questionable stains on the carpet that Lester would not be happy about. Dr. Shelley emerged from her office looking shell-shocked but relieved. "Well. We survived. And the district paid in advance, so..." She managed a weak smile. "Silver linings."

Bruce nodded absently. His mind was already drifting back to that nagging feeling from this morning. The dragonfly wing. Those "classification pending" artifacts in storage. That old man who'd shown up alone on field trip day...

"Bruce?" Cindy waved a hand in front of his face. "You, okay?"

"Yeah," he said. "Just tired."

But that wasn't quite true. He wasn't tired. He was restless. Like something had started today that wasn't finished yet.

The Meeting

Mark Martinez had learned long ago that museums were good places to think. The quiet reverence, the weight of history, the sense that time moved differently within these walls: it all helped settle his mind. Today, he needed settling.

The dream from last night still clung to him. The tunnel. The creatures. Frankie's voice calling out in the dark. After breakfast at Betty's Kitchen and a phone call with his granddaughter, he'd almost gone home. But the museum advertisement had felt like a sign.

Free admission for seniors on Wednesdays.

So here he was, wandering exhibits while trying to outpace his memories. The field trip chaos had mostly cleared out with only a few stragglers finishing up some assignments or waiting for their parents to pick them up. Mark appreciated the relative quiet. He'd already spent an hour in the maritime history wing, then moved through geology, and now found himself in the prehistoric section.

He stopped in front of a massive, fossilized wing mounted on the wall. The placard read: Meganeura monyi. Carboniferous Period. Approximately 300 million years old. Mark stared at it for a long moment, then shook his head slightly. "That's not right," he murmured. "Excuse me?"

Mark turned around to find a younger man in museum staff attire: probably late twenties or early thirties, friendly face, name tag that read "Bruce." "I'm sorry," Mark said. "Just thinking out loud."

"No, I'm curious." Bruce stepped closer, studying the wing. "What's not right about it?" Mark hesitated.

He'd spent decades keeping certain things to himself. But something about this young man's genuine curiosity made him reconsider. "The dating and the classification. This isn't from the Carboniferous Period," Mark said carefully. Bruce's eyebrows rose. "You're saying our specimen is mislabeled?"

"I'm saying it's not a Meganeura at all." Mark met the younger man's eyes. "That's a Nogwyn wing. I'd guess it's less than two hundred years old." For a moment, Bruce just stared at him. Then a slow smile spread across his face, not mocking, but fascinated. "A Nogwyn?" he repeated. "Right. Because those are real."

"As real as you or me," Mark said quietly. "Or they were, anyway. Most of them are gone now." Bruce should have walked away. Should have politely excused himself and reported the eccentric old man to security. Instead, he found himself leaning against the wall, arms crossed, studying this stranger who'd just casually claimed that a 300-million-year-old fossil was a wing from a make-believe creature.
"Let me guess," Bruce said. "You're here to tell me Bigfoot is real too?"

"Sasquatch," Mark corrected. "And yes, though the West Coast populations are functionally extinct. The Pacific Northwest logging industry saw to that in the 1970s." He said it matter-of-factly, like he was discussing the weather. "Uh-huh." Bruce glanced around. A few students were still in the wing, but none paying attention or causing any trouble. "And you know this because...?"

"Because I grew up around them." Mark returned his attention to the wing. "Not sasquatch; forest-folk. Fairies, brownies, pixies. Various species. They lived in the forests, caves and hollow places. My brother and his friends used to explore the woods looking for pixie nests." The way he said "my brother" made Bruce pause. There was weight there. Old grief. "Used to?" Bruce asked quietly.

Mark's jaw tightened. "He died when I was eight. Halloween 1990. He and five other kids, along with an elderly couple." He turned to face Bruce fully. "They went into Miller's Quarry looking for something. They found it. And something else found them." Bruce felt a chill running down his spine. The old man's voice had gone flat, distant. This wasn't some eccentric making up stories. This was someone speaking from experience. "I'm sorry," Bruce said. "That's…I'm sorry for your loss."

Mark nodded once, acknowledging the condolence. Then he seemed to shake himself slightly, coming back to the present. "Anyway. That wing. You should check your archives. Someone at this museum knew what it really was. There's probably documentation buried in your files."

"How would you know that?" Bruce raised an eyebrow.

"Because institutions like this used to catalog everything, even the things they didn't want to admit existed." Mark pulled a small notebook from his jacket pocket and scribbled something. He tore out the page and handed it to Bruce. "My number. If you find anything interesting, I'd appreciate a call. I'm trying to… document some things. Before it's all forgotten."

Bruce took the paper. The handwriting was neat, precise. "Mark Martinez," he read aloud. "That's me." Mark extended his hand. "And you're Bruce. Good to meet you." They shook hands. Mark's grip was firm despite his age. "I should get going," Mark said. "Long day. But seriously, check your archives. You might be surprised at what you find."

Bruce looked up to the exhibit and thought to himself; *a Nogwyn wing*. It was absurd. Completely absurd. And yet.

Mark walked up to the 'Nogwyn' wing and positioned himself behind it. From this angle, Bruce could see the wing clearly belonged to a creature with human-like features. Mark nodded once, then left the museum. Bruce pulled out his phone and took several photos of the wing from different angles. Then he photographed the placard, the mounting, and the lighting setup. He'd been bothered by this exhibit for two years. That vague sense that something was off. He'd always dismissed it as perfectionism, or maybe imposter syndrome; the feeling that he didn't know enough to be working in a real museum.

But what if it was something else? What if his instincts had been trying to tell him something? Bruce glanced toward the exit where Mark had disappeared, then back at the wing. "Code Overflow," he muttered to himself. All hell's breaking loose. He just didn't know it yet. Gilbert found Bruce still standing in front of the dragonfly wing twenty minutes later.

"You good?" the assistant director asked. "You've been staring at that thing like it insulted your mother."

"Gil," Bruce said slowly, "where do we keep the old acquisition files? The original documentation for specimens?"

"Central filing. Two levels down." Gilbert gave him a curious look. "Why?"

"Just curious about something." Bruce checked his watch. 4:30. Still time before closing. "You mind if I do some digging?"

"Knock yourself out. Keys are in my office." Gilbert started to walk away, then paused. "You know,

Dr. Shelley's old advisor; the one who donated a bunch of stuff in the '90s, he used to tell stories about that wing. Said it came from some private collection in Appalachia. Real weird circumstances."

Bruce's pulse quickened. "Yeah? What kind of circumstances?"

"Hell, if I know. Ancient history." Gilbert shrugged. "Filing cabinet M-N should have the original intake forms. Have fun with the dust bunnies." The basement level that staff called "the Bat Cave" smelled like old paper and stale air. Bruce unlocked the filing room and flicked on the lights. Rows of metal cabinets stretched into the shadows.

He found cabinet M-N and started pulling drawers. Mammoth tooth. Marlboro Formation sample. Meteorite fragment. He was about to give up when his fingers landed on a thick folder simply labeled: Meganeura — Specimen 1997-042.

Bruce pulled it out and carried it to the nearest desk lamp. The first few pages were standard acquisition forms.

Donor: "Private collection, estate of Elias Thornwood." Location: "Blue Ridge Mountains, North Carolina." Date: "March 1997." Then Bruce found a page with handwritten notes in the margin. The writing was small, cramped, worried: "Preliminary analysis inconclusive. Trace elements of living tissue present (HOW??). Wing structure does not match known Meganeura specimens. Morphology suggests either fabrication or... alternative origin. Possible supernatural classification: mountain fairy, woodland sprite, or similar entity. Recommend further study before public display. — Dr. Helena Finch, 3/15/97"

At the bottom of the page, someone else had written in red ink: "Display as Meganeura. Do not pursue

'supernatural' angle. Museum credibility at stake. —
Director's Office"

Bruce read it three times. Then he pulled out his
phone and photographed every page. When he finally
emerged from the basement ninety minutes later, the
museum was closed. The evening custodial staff were
making their rounds. Bruce found his way to his car in a
daze. He sat in the driver's seat, staring at the photos on
his phone. A Nogwyn.
The old man had been right.

Bruce pulled up a browser and typed:
"supernatural creatures and forest." The results flooded
in. An hour later, Bruce decided to leave his car there and
walk over to meet his friends at a nearby bar and grill.
While he walked, Bruce started to think that everything
had changed. He just didn't know how much yet.

Opening the Door

Crystal Valley, Texas. Two miles from Miller's Quarry.
Dr. Veronica Chalmers was lost. She'd left Coralyn Bay an hour ago with printed directions, but the expedition site was deeper into the valley than she'd anticipated. Her phone's GPS kept cycling between "searching for signal" and complete failure. Should've bought a truck, she thought, wincing as her sedan bottomed out on another pothole.

Then she saw them: three vehicles parked in a clearing ahead. One bore the Texas Parks and Wildlife seal. Another displayed Coralyn Bay University's logo. The third was a personal truck, covered in road dust. Dr. Chalmers pulled up beside them and stepped out.

A young man in his late twenties was deep in conversation with a ranger, gesturing animatedly at a tablet screen. Several undergraduates were unloading equipment while experienced cave divers checked their gear.
The young man looked up and waved. "Dr. Chalmers! Perfect timing."

Jake Dawson crossed the clearing with easy confidence. "Jake." She shook his hand, then turned to the ranger. "And you must be Deputy Riley."
"Ma'am." Deputy Riley touched his hat brim. "I was just explaining to Mr. Dawson here that once you're underground, I can't guarantee we'll be able to get anyone out if something goes wrong."

"We appreciate your concern, Deputy." Dr. Chalmers pulled a folder from her bag. "That's why we're using CaveScan drones for initial exploration. We can map significant portions of the system without putting anyone at risk."

"Drones." Deputy Riley's expression suggested he wasn't convinced expensive toys were a substitute for common sense. "And if your drone finds something interesting?"

"Then we assess the risk and proceed carefully." Dr. Chalmers smiled. "This isn't our first expedition, Deputy."

It wasn't. But something about this site made her uneasy in ways she couldn't articulate. Jake gathered the team while Dr. Chalmers set up her field office: a folding table, two laptops, and a portable power station. Three years ago, Jake had been one of her students. Bright, athletic, destined for professional sports until an Achilles injury changed everything. He'd switched his focus from Liberal Arts to Geology and worked harder than anyone else in class. Then Grant Kingsley got involved.

Kingsley was a local tycoon who'd built his fortune on oil, real estate, and an uncanny ability to be in the right place at the right time. He sponsored young athletes but usually dropped them when they failed or suffered an injury. He hadn't dropped Jake. He'd funded this expedition instead. *Why?*

The question had nagged at Dr. Chalmers for weeks. Kingsley didn't fund academic research out of charity. "Alright everyone, listen up." Jake stood on an outcropping, the cave entrance visible behind him: a dark slash in the limestone hillside. "We're here because ground-penetrating radar showed an extensive system beneath Crystal Valley. Preliminary scans suggest chambers, possibly multiple levels." One of the undergraduates raised her hand. "Is this connected to Miller's Quarry?"

"Potentially." Jake pulled up a map on his tablet. "Miller's Quarry is two miles east. The geological formations are similar. But that system was deemed too unstable for exploration after the incident in 1990."

Dr. Chalmers noticed how carefully he said, "*the incident.*" Everyone local knew the story. Five kids and two adults found dead in the tunnels. The official report cited toxic gas and structural collapse. The unofficial stories were darker.

"Our job today," Jake continued, "is to send the CaveScan drones in, map what we can, and determine if it's safe for human exploration. Dr. Chalmers will monitor from base camp. Any questions?" Deputy Riley stepped forward. "Just one piece of advice. I've been doing search and rescue in these hills for twenty years. Caves don't care about your equipment or your degrees. You respect them, or they'll kill you."

The team fell silent.
"Noted," Jake said quietly. "Let's get to work."

The first drone went in at 10:47 AM.
Dr. Chalmers watched the feed from her laptop. The entrance passage was narrow, angling downward at roughly fifteen degrees. Limestone walls, moisture slicked. After fifty meters, the passage opened into a larger chamber.

"Temperature's dropping," Jake reported from the cave entrance, monitoring the telemetry. "High humidity." The drone's lights swept the chamber. Stalactites hung from the ceiling like teeth. The floor was uneven, scattered with rock and other unidentified shards. "There." One of the undergraduates pointed at the screen. "Lower left." Another passage. This one descended more steeply. Jake piloted the drone deeper.

The second chamber was larger. Cathedral-sized. The drone's lights couldn't reach the far walls.

"My God," Dr. Chalmers whispered. The walls were covered in markings. Not natural formations. Symbols and figures etched into the stone. Some looked ancient, weathered, barely visible. Others were sharper, more recent. "Are those hieroglyphics?" someone asked. "No." Dr. Chalmers leaned closer to the screen. "I don't recognize the script. It's not any known language."

Jake adjusted the drone's camera, panning across the wall. More symbols. And then: A figure. Humanoid but wrong. Too tall, limbs too long, head tilted at an unnatural angle. Around it, smaller figures. Some prostrate. Others fleeing. And in the center of the chamber, carved larger than the rest: A door. Not a physical door. A carving of one. Massive, ornate, covered in the same strange script. And around its edges, symbols that made Dr. Chalmers' eyes hurt to look at. "Pull back," she said.
"What?" Jake asked. But he was already staring past the monitor, toward the cave entrance. "Do you hear that?" Dr. Chalmers stopped. Listened. A low vibration. Not quite sound. More like a pressure in the air. The drone's feed flickered. Dr. Chalmers said, "Jake, bring it back."

"I'm trying. It's not responding." On screen, the drone's camera spun wildly. The carved door filled the frame, those symbols burning into Dr. Chalmers' vision. Then the feed cut to static. And in the static, for just a moment, she could have sworn she saw something moving. Something that had been waiting.
Downtown Coralyn Bay 6:45 PM

Julie's Bar & Grill sat three blocks from the museum, close enough that Bruce could walk. After the chaos of Field Trip Day, he needed a drink and familiar faces.

The sun was setting over the port, casting orange light across the water. Bruce paused at the corner, letting the sea breeze clear his head. His phone buzzed. A text from Chris: *Already here. Grabbed our usual table. Roxy's running late (shocking).*

The restaurant was busy but not packed. Wednesday night regulars. Julie herself was behind the bar, a woman in her fifties with silver-streaked hair and the kind of smile that made everyone feel welcome. "Bruce!" She called out. "Rough day?"

"You have no idea."

"First drink's on me, honey. You look like you need it."

Bruce spotted Chris in the back corner booth, already halfway through a beer. Chris Trotter had the look of someone who'd spent too many years staring at computer screens before deciding life was too short. Hence the career change from I.T. to law school. He was in his second year now, perpetually exhausted but somehow thriving on it. "There he is." Chris raised his bottle in salute. "Survivor of the field trip massacre." Bruce slid into the booth. "Three schools. Simultaneously. It was like watching piranhas discover a buffet."

"Jesus." Chris signaled the server. "Jake bailed, by the way. Said the expedition ran long and he's dead on his feet."

"Can't blame him. Cave exploring sounds exhausting."

"Right?" Chris took a sip. "He texted something about 'interesting discoveries' but didn't elaborate. You know how he gets when he's in research mode." Bruce ordered a whiskey, neat. The server brought it quickly, along with a basket of chips and salsa. "So how bad was it really?" Chris asked.

"Code Overflow."

"Oh damn." Chris knew the museum staff lingo. "Casualties?"

"Just my sanity." Bruce took a sip of whiskey; felt it burn pleasantly. "But that wasn't even the weirdest part of my day."

"Yeah?" Chris took a bite out of salsa dipped chip. "So, this old guy comes into the museum during all the chaos. Late sixties, moves like he's got some miles on him." Bruce grabbed a chip. "He walks straight to the dragonfly wing in Hall B and just stares at it for like twenty minutes."

"Okay...?" Chris shrugged.

"Then he tells me it's not a dragonfly wing at all." Bruce leaned forward. "He says it's a fairy wing. A mountain fairy, from the Appalachian range. Maybe two hundred years old."

Chris stared at him for a moment, then burst out laughing. "A fairy wing. Right. Because those are real."

"That's what I thought." Bruce pulled out his phone. "But then I went down to central filing and checked the original acquisition records." He pulled up the photos he'd taken and handed his phone to Chris. "Look at this. The original researcher in 1997, Dr. Helena Finch, wrote that the specimen had 'trace elements of living tissue' and the morphology didn't match known Meganeura fossils. She recommended classifying it as 'possible supernatural origin.'" Chris squinted at the screen, scrolling through the images. "Okay, but that just means she had a weird theory. Doesn't mean she was right."

"Look at the next note. Red ink. The director's office shut down any further investigation. Told them to display it as Meganeura and forget the 'supernatural angle' because it would hurt the museum's credibility."

"So, they covered up bad science. That's not exactly shocking." Chris leaned back on his chair while stretching for another chip. "But what if it wasn't bad science?" Bruce took his phone back. "What if she was right?" The door chimed and Roxy walked in.

Roxalyn Dominguez was impossible to miss. She had the kind of presence that turned heads. Brown curly hair fell past her shoulders, and she wore a leather jacket over a fitted classic rock band t-shirt that left little to the imagination. She moved with a slight hitch in her step, barely noticeable unless you knew to look for it. Bruce knew. They all did.

Two years ago, Roxy had been a rising star in the Coralyn Bay Police Department. During a routine traffic stop, another distracted driver who was glued to their phone struck Roxy, practically running over her. The doctors said she'd never walk again. Chris had helped Roxy prove them wrong. Roxy was always strong and now she was back in school, studying forensic examination, and kicking ass with the best of them. Bruce had never seen her quit on anything. "Gentlemen." Roxy slid into the booth next to Chris, wincing slightly as she adjusted her position. "Sorry I'm late. What's the drama? You both look way too serious for a Wednesday."

"Bruce met a crazy old man who thinks the museum has a fairy wing," Chris said, grinning. Roxy's eyebrows shot up. "I'm sorry, what?" Bruce sighed and went through the story again. The old man, the mountain fairy claim, the archive documents. He showed Roxy the photos on his phone. She studied them more carefully than Chris had. "Okay, so you've got a researcher from the '90s who had an unconventional theory that got shut down by administration. That happens. Academic politics are brutal."

"But what if…"

"Bruce." Roxy handed his phone back. "I love you, but fairies or whatever that thing is aren't real."

"How do you know?" Bruce scoffed.

"Because I spent two years as a cop. You know how many 'supernatural' cases I investigated? Dozens. You know how many turned out to be supernatural? Zero." She flagged down the server and ordered a margarita. "Every single one had a rational explanation."

"But the tissue samples…" Bruce tried to defend his doubts.

"Could be contamination. Misidentification. Hell, for all you know, that researcher was trying to make a name for herself with a controversial theory." Roxy's drink arrived and she took a sip. "Look, I get it. It's a fun mystery. But supernatural creatures don't exist." Chris nodded. "She's right, man. There's probably a perfectly normal explanation for why that wing doesn't quite match the fossil record. Maybe it's a related species, or maybe the classification system changed since 1997."

Bruce sat back, feeling deflated. He knew how it sounded. He knew how crazy it was. But he couldn't shake the certainty in Mark Martinez's voice. The way he looked at that wing like he knew exactly what it was. "So, what did this old guy say when you asked for proof?" Roxy asked.

"He gave me his number. Said I should call him if I found anything interesting in the archives." Bruce pulled out the piece of paper Mark had given him. "Mark Martinez."

"And are you going to call him?" Roxy asked while sipping her drink.

Bruce hesitated. "I don't know. Maybe."
"Dude." Chris leaned forward. "You know that's a bad idea, right? Best case scenario, he's a harmless eccentric who's really into folklore. Worst case, he's trying to scam the museum somehow."

"He didn't seem like a scammer." Bruce retorted.
"They never do," Roxy said gently. "Look, if you're really curious about the wing, why don't you just do some legitimate research? Contact paleontology departments, see if anyone can explain the discrepancy. But chasing after some old man's fairy tales?" She shook her head. "That's not going to lead anywhere good."

Bruce knew they were right. Of course they were right. But a part of him, the part that had always felt like something was off about that exhibit, wanted to call Mark Martinez anyway. They stayed at Julie's until almost nine. The conversation drifted to safer topics. Chris's impossible contracts professor, Roxy's thesis research on forensic documentation, weekend plans that probably wouldn't happen.

But Bruce couldn't fully engage. His mind kept circling back to the dragonfly wing. To Mark's matter-of-fact tone when he'd said as real as you or me. To the archive note: Possible supernatural classification. When he finally headed home, walking through the quiet streets near the museum, Bruce pulled out the piece of paper with Mark's number.
He stared at it for a long moment.

Chris and Roxy thought he was chasing a fantasy. Maybe they were right. Maybe Mark Martinez was just an old man with an overactive imagination. But what if he wasn't? Bruce folded the paper carefully and put it back in his pocket. Not tonight. But soon. He needed to

know what Mark Martinez knew. And why it felt so
important.

Echoes in the Dark

Mark got home after seven, later than he'd intended. He'd taken the long way back from the museum, walking along Oceanview Drive past City Beach. The pier stretched into the bay, and Mark paused there for a while, remembering. He'd brought Janet here when they were dating. Later, with the kids. He used to skip stones while she collected seashells.

Mark's chest tightened. He turned away from the water and headed home. The house was dark when he opened the door. He didn't bother turning on lights as he walked to the kitchen. Too tired for coffee, he poured himself a glass of coconut rum instead. Just a little, but enough to take the edge off.

As he lifted the glass, he caught the faint scent of guava flowers and honey. He smiled. KayKay had been here. The note on the refrigerator confirmed it:

Abuelito - Sorry I missed you! Brought you some tamales from Jeri's Kitchen (in the fridge). Please eat them and take your meds. Love you! - K

"I'll make it up to you, KayKay," Mark murmured. "I promise." He found the container in the fridge but wasn't hungry. He took his rum to the living room, turned on the TV without really watching it, and let the noise fill the empty space. The house felt hollow tonight.

Mark remembered when it had been full. Children running through rooms, the dog going crazy every time someone came home, the cat dragging toys to his office demanding playtime. Be careful what you wish for. He finished the rum, feeling it warm up his chest but not quite reaching the ache deeper down. He didn't want to go upstairs yet. Didn't want to face the empty bed, the dark hallways, the rooms that used to hold life.

Mark settled into his recliner instead, listening to the quiet. The ticking clock. The soft hum of the refrigerator. The whisper of air through the vents. His eyes grew heavy. He told himself he'd just rest for a minute. Just a minute. Something was not right.

Mark was running through woods, branches tearing at his face and hands. His heart hammered against his ribs. His breathing came in ragged gasps. Someone was missing. One of his kids? One of his grandkids? He couldn't remember, but the panic was real, visceral, choking.

The woods grew thicker. Spiny branches clawed at him as he pushed forward. Behind him, fog rolled through the trees. Not natural fog, but something wrong. It glowed with a sickly yellow light, and wherever it touched, things withered. He had to keep moving. Voices ahead. Children's voices, crying for help. "Hang on!" Mark shouted, his throat raw. "I'm coming!"

He didn't know them, but it didn't matter. They were in danger. He would help them. No matter the cost. His hands bled as he tore through the underbrush, palms shredded by thorns. He could barely feel it. He just had to reach them. There. A small clearing. Three boys and a girl huddled together, lost and terrified. "It's okay," Mark gasped, stumbling into the clearing. "I'm going to help you. How did you get here?" The children stared at him with wide, frightened eyes. Too scared to speak.

"It's okay. Follow me." Mark extended his bleeding hand. "Everybody hold hands. Stay close." They obeyed, forming a chain. The smallest boy gripped Mark's hand so tightly it hurt. The yellow fog crept closer, oozing between the trees like something alive and hungry. "Come on. Keep up." Mark pushed forward, trying to retrace his path. His hands were cut so deep he could barely make a fist, but he held onto the boy, pulling them all forward. He glanced back to check on them. One of the boys was gone. Mark stopped. "Where…"

Another boy vanished. Then the girl. Just gone, swallowed by the fog without a sound. "No, no, no…" Mark knelt beside the last remaining boy, the one still gripping his hand. "What's happening? Where did they…" The ground exploded. An arm punched through the earth. Not flesh, but something worse. Obsidian bone wrapped in decaying skin that pulsed with orange light like flowing magma.

The hand seized the boy's ankle. "HANG ON!" Mark grabbed the child's shoulders, trying to pull him free. But the arm was impossibly strong. It dragged the boy downward, the earth opening like a mouth, swallowing him whole. The boy's scream cut off abruptly. Mark lunged forward, reaching into the hole. His hands closed on nothing. The ground sealed itself. The boy was gone.

"ARGGHH!"

Mark woke with a strangled cry, clutching his chest. His hands. He stared at them in the dim light. They were covered in scabs. Old wounds, weeks healed, crisscrossing his palms and fingers. But that was impossible. His hands were fine when he fell asleep. Mark's heart hammered. He looked around the living room. Everything seemed normal. The TV had gone to a blue screen. The clock read 3:47 AM. But the house felt wrong. Too warm. The air thick, almost humid, despite the cool night outside. And there was something else. A presence. Mark couldn't see it, but he felt it. Something in the room with him. Watching. Waiting.

As he sat frozen in the recliner, the unnatural heat began to fade. The presence withdrew, sliding away like a shadow peeling off a wall. Whatever it was, it was leaving.

Mark waited until his breathing steadied, then got up and walked to the window. The sky was beginning to lighten. Not dawn yet, but that deep blue that comes before. He'd been asleep for hours, but he felt exhausted. Drained.

Unrestful sleep was a sign of distress. Either from the person trying to sleep...or from something close to them that needed help. Mark looked at his scarred hands again.

The dream had been different from the one about Frankie. That nightmare was memory. Trauma resurfacing. This was something else. This was a warning.

Something changed today. Something had opened. And whatever darkness had been sleeping was awake now, reaching out, testing. Finding the vulnerable. Finding children. Mark's jaw tightened. He walked to his study and pulled out an old notebook; one he hadn't touched in years. The pages were yellowed, filled with notes and sketches from decades ago. Things his brother had told him. Things he'd learned himself.

Things he'd tried to forget. He couldn't forget anymore. Something was awakening and it wanted to hunt. Everyone was in danger; men, women, children...even nature itself. Mark sat down at his desk and began to write, pouring out knowledge that he had almost forgotten about, but it needed to be saved.

The Atrox

Crystal Valley, Texas Thursday Morning

"Careful, everyone" Jake said as he led his group through one of the corridors leading down to one of the antechambers. It was dark and unusually warm for an underground passage. Normally, temperatures would be lower in a cave, but Jake suspected that something is causing the temperature to rise.

He wiped the sweat from his brow and made sure to mind his feet. The floor was wet and uneven. Nancy and Blaine, two of Jake's classmates, followed closely. "Is it me or does it feel like the passageway is getting narrow?" Nancy asked as she steadied herself by touching the cavern walls.

Jake removed his backpack to make himself fit through the narrow corridors. "Blaine, can you check the readings, are we headed in the right direction?" Blaine pulled out his CaveScan tablet and checked their heading. "Yeah, if the readings are correct, the antechamber should just be up ahead".

Deeper they went and suddenly a gush of cool wind as Jake began to reach the end of the corridor but as soon as Jake entered the antechamber, it became narrower for Nancy and Blaine. "WOW!" Jake said as he observed the antechamber. For a moment, it looked like he stepped into outer space, and the antechamber was made of sparkling gems. He saw distant stars and a purplish nebula of some sort.

"Guys, you should check this out" Jake stepped further into the antechamber. The ground felt steadier and something was calling to him, telling him to move closer when suddenly "YHOW!". Jake turned around to see Nancy and Blaine as they forced their way through the narrow passage into the antechamber.

"Incredible, look at this, the thermal readings are higher, and the source is somewhere in the center for that area, over there" Blaine said while pointing in Jake's direction. Jake and his team used their flashlights and set up some temporary glow sticks to provide some more light. "What is that?" Blaine said as he looked towards the wall.

"Probably some fossilized plants or insect, can't make it out" Nancy said while trying to use her flashlight to look around while giving Blaine enough time to snap a few pictures with the CaveScan tablet. Jake kept walking towards the center of the antechamber. He stumbled and landed forward on his left knee: the bad one. "Are you okay?" Nancy asked.

"Yeah, fine" Jake answered and then felt it, a geode of some kind. It felt smooth yet leathery. He picked it up and could feel traces of heat coming from it. *Put it down.* The voice in his head told him but something else convinced him to take it. Jake reached for his flashlight to see the geode more closely when he heard "What was that!". He turned around and he could hear Nancy and Blaine in near panic mode.

"I felt something trying to go up my leg!" Nancy said. Blaine used the night vision scanner to see if there was any movement. "Nothing, there's nothing down here" Blaine scanned the room and then he pointed his device towards Jake. "What is that?". Jake immediately put the geode into his backpack. "What was what?" Jake answered. Blaine took a step closer to him and turned off the night vision and used the remaining power cell to light up the immediate area. "Oh my god!". Bones and pieces of flesh with some cartilage were on the ground as if some subterranean predator had forgotten to eat the rest of its lunch. "I don't know but let's get out of here" Jake said while motioning for his team to leave.

Dr. Veronica Chalmers was finishing her daily report when she heard boots on gravel. Her team was coming up from the cave system earlier than expected. Jake Dawson led the group, and something in his posture made her straighten. He moved with purpose, his jaw set. Jake removed his backpack and held it by its straps.

"Dr. Chalmers." Jake glanced at the Kingsmen Technology representative standing near the equipment. "Can we talk somewhere private?" She followed his gaze. The corporate observer had been a thorn in her side all week, watching everything, reporting back to Grant Kingsley. Whatever Jake had found, he didn't want the Kingsmen rep to know.

"Take a break, everyone," Dr. Chalmers called out. She waited until the representative wandered toward his truck before turning back to Jake. "This is as good as it gets. What is it? Are you okay? It looks like you've seen a ghost".

Jake took a deep breath and then pulled out his tablet. "The mapping data. Look at the preliminary scans from last week." Dr. Chalmers studied the screen. A network of passages leading to various chambers, with a faint outline of what might be the main antechamber. "Now look at these." Jake swiped through screenshots. Nancy's data, Blaine's, his own from different days including today's activity. "The main passages stay consistent. But the smaller tunnels..." He zoomed in. "They're changing. Opening and contracting."

Dr. Chalmers felt her stomach tighten. "Computer hallucination. The equipment..."

"That's what I thought too. But we felt as if the corridors were narrowing on purpose. We detected a heat source, not sure of the cause but I think it has something to do with this."

Jake unwrapped the cloth. The object looked like a geode at first. Rough calcification covering something crystalline. But as Dr. Chalmers took it, she felt as if something knocked the air of her lungs.

The outer layer resembled diseased skin, gray and tubercular. Beneath it, a dark purple crystal pulsed with inner light. Not reflected light. Light from within, like magma trapped in stone. As she held it, the calcification seemed to peel back slightly, revealing more of the crystal beneath. Polished. Cut. Deliberately shaped. And in its depths, something moved. "Where did you find this?" Her voice came out hoarse.

"Deep in the antechamber. There's a section we haven't fully mapped yet. We have some partial images but something about that place made everyone feel uneasy. There were bones littered all over the place. Some fossilized patterns of possible prehistoric creatures on the walls. We didn't stay long enough to complete the scans. We got out of there before the passageways got any tighter." Jake was doing his best to remain calm.

Jake's eyes were fixed on the stone. "Dr. Chalmers, I've been thinking about it since we came up. I can't stop thinking about it. Whatever it is, I've never seen or heard anything like it." Dr. Chalmers looked up sharply. Jake's pupils were dilated, his breathing shallow.
And there, just for a moment, Dr. Chalmers saw something that made her blood run cold.

A wisp of smoke, darker than shadow, curling from the stone toward Jake's face. It touched his forehead like a caress before dissipating. Jake didn't react. Didn't seem to notice.

"Did you tell anyone else about this?" Dr. Chalmers wrapped the stone quickly, breaking whatever connection it had. Jake blinked, seeming to come back to himself. "Blaine and Nancy know I found something. I told them it was just a geode."

"Good." Dr. Chalmers placed the wrapped stone in her briefcase. Her hands were shaking. "That's what it is. Just a geode. Interesting mineral formation, nothing more."

"But…" Jake began to reach out for the geode but then stopped.

"Jake." She met his eyes. "If anyone asks, that's the story. I'm taking this for analysis. The grant stipulates we notify Kingsmen of significant finds, but this isn't significant. Understand?" She watched him struggle with it. Jake was honest to his core, uncomfortable with even small deceptions. But finally, he nodded. "If you or anyone else finds something similar, use the code word 'beetle stone.' I'll know what you mean." Dr. Chalmers closed her briefcase. "Don't touch it directly. Don't let anyone else touch it. Are we clear?"

"Yes, ma'am."

But as Jake turned to rejoin the team, Dr. Chalmers saw him touch his forehead. Right where the smoke had caressed him. He didn't know he was doing it. That night, Dr. Chalmers sat alone in her home office, the stone on her desk. She'd wrapped it in three layers of cloth, placed it in a sealed container, and still, she could feel it. A pressure behind her eyes. A whisper at the edge of hearing.

She pulled out her phone and searched: Miller's Quarry 1990 supernatural creatures

The results were mostly conspiracy sites and folklore blogs. But buried among them, she found old newspaper archives.

Five Children, Two Adults Found Dead in Quarry Tunnels Police Recover "Unusual Biological Evidence" Sheriff's Office: No Satanic Cult Involvement, Despite Rumors

She clicked through to a scanned article from the Coralyn Bay Tribune, November 1990:

"Among the evidence recovered were skeletal remains of unknown origin. Dr. Helena Finch of Coralyn Bay University and formerly of Coralyn Bay Museum of Natural History has stated the remains showed characteristics inconsistent with known wildlife. However, state officials have determined the remains to be fraudulent, likely planted by parties unknown..."

Dr. Chalmers sat back. Helena Finch. The same researcher from the museum archives. The one whose findings had been suppressed. She tried to warn us, Dr. Chalmers thought. And someone made sure no one would listen. The museum had some of those remains. She'd seen them in passing. A wing, some bone fragments, things labeled as "misidentified specimens" or "fraudulent evidence."

What if they weren't fraudulent? What if Miller's Quarry had held something real?

And what if they'd just opened a passage that connected to it? Dr. Chalmers looked at the stone again. In the dim light of her office, the inner glow was brighter. Pulsing. Like a heartbeat. She picked up her phone again, this time searching for a different number. Someone who might know the truth about what happened in 1990. Someone who'd survived it.

No luck. Dr. Chalmers was at her wit's end when she instinctively picked up one of her books to see if she could find something the old-fashioned way. Her eyes were scanning various pages, and nothing seemed to pop out. She picked out another book, an older book in her collection about local wildlife when she saw a dogeared page with faded yellow highlights that reminded her of something from a long time ago. In fact, as Veronica's mind started to drift, it was something from her own life that she couldn't believe that she buried so deeply.

Elisa and Ronnie

Late September 1985, in the Crystal Valley forest, close to the Devil's Maw.

Veronica always loved the outdoors. The crisp, clear air rushing through her hair. The sunlight touched her cheeks and surrounded by cedar, lots of cedar. The Texas Hill Country is notorious for its cedar trees. Cedar fever is real and many native Texans had to deal with it. However, Veronica, or Ronnie as her friends and family called her, will not let the cedar ruin a beautiful fall day.

Ronnie was walking through the forest trails with her dad. Her dad was making a map of all the trails in the Tri-Coastal area in hopes of selling them to tourists and maybe to a few government agencies as well. Ronnie's dad had a homemade map and some thick map pencils as he carefully tracked the trails. Sometimes, he would let Ronnie come up with the names.

Today, Ronnie and her dad were walking the "Lucky Star" trail. The forests were thick and the branches seemed to lower themselves as if they wanted to take off their hats. Ronnie's biggest worry was not getting lost but catching fleas and ticks, especially ticks. She wore a long sleeve shirt, and knee-high socks underneath her blue jeans. Her dad was more worried about their path as Lucky Star seemed to go on and on.

"We might cut this hike short today, Ronnie!" he said as he checked his compass and noted how far they walked. Ronnie had her own map, and she made little ticks on her map to indicate any landmarks or unusual trees. The forest was quiet but suddenly, they heard something off in the distance. Something or someone was running towards them.

Ronnie and her dad could hear the snapping of twigs and branches, the pounding of bare feet on the rough terrain. Suddenly, a woman appeared in front of them. She was over five feet tall with short brown hair, green eyes and a burlap dress that barely reached the top of her knees. She stopped in front of them. Ronnie instinctively went to her father's side. "Are you okay?" he asked.

This strange woman, her lips trembling and her hands shaking, was running from something or someone. She wanted to speak but kept looking over her shoulders. Ronnie's dad took a step back and held on to Ronnie. "It's okay. Ma'am, if you need help. We can take you to a ranger station. Are you lost?"

Ronnie's dad looked around and could not see or hear anything else, but he could feel an awful presence. "I think we better go now" he said. He looked at the strange woman. "My name is Leonard and this is my daughter Veronica. You are welcome to join us on our way back to the edge of the trail."

The woman nodded and followed them at a distance. Leonard and Ronnie walked at a brisk pace. Leonard did not know what was going on but he knew they had to get out of there. The stranger kept looking over her shoulders and kept up with her guides. Ronnie would look back and swore she heard something following them.

Three miles later, the group was clear of the forest and back towards the parking area where many locals would leave their cars while exploring the forest. Ronnie could see a pickup truck with deer antlers on the hood. *Hunters.* She thought to herself. It was the season after all. Perhaps this lady had a bad encounter with some hunters or worse, poachers. Leonard turned around to speak with their lost follower. "Are you sure? We can give you a ride to Hornet's Nest or Coralyn Bay. I hate to leave you out here by yourself, Ms.?" Leonard raised an eyebrow.

"Elisa" she responded. Elisa seemed more relaxed. "My name is Elisa".

Ronnie noticed the strong accent. Elisa must not be from around here. The back of Elisa's dress seemed to have two slits behind her shoulder blades. Ronnie was filled with questions, but she knew it was not her place to ask but she also felt uncomfortable leaving her behind by herself. "Dad, we should give her a ride. Coralyn Bay is not too far away".

Leonard unlocked his little truck and opened the passenger door. "Ma'am, you can take the passenger seat by the door. Ronnie can sit in the middle that way you can always step out whenever you want but I don't think we can just leave you here." Elisa looked around and took a deep breath. "I will be okay. I was just lost tis'all". Ronnie jumped in the truck and made herself comfortable in the middle of the bench. Then she heard a faint but metallic click-click.

Two men in camouflage stepped out of the forest. Both had shotguns pointed at Elisa. "Get away from her! She's a witch with devil wings. We saw her performing witchcraft over our deer. She is coming with us!" One of them had a trucker hat and other had dirty blond hair. Trucker Hat moved in closer to Elisa who shrieked as he got within arm's reach.

"I can't let you do that" Leonard said. "I didn't see her do any witchcraft or commit any crime. She is coming with me". Leonard looked into the cab of his little truck and saw that Ronnie had made herself small.

Leonard raised his hands in the air as gesture of good faith. "Ma'am, please get in the truck".

Trucker Hat reached over and ripped off Elisa's burlap dress "She's not going anywhere!" and suddenly two dragonfly-like wings sprung open from her back. Elisa used her arms to cover herself. Dirty Hair investigated the truck and noticed some movement. Dirty Hair started to point his shotgun towards the cab when Leonard span into action. He took out a can of bear mace from the back of his utility belt and sprayed both men.

"AWWW SHIT! I CAN'T SEE!"

Leonard quickly punched Dirty Hair, threw his vest towards Elisa and then tackled Trucker Hat. Trucker Hat dropped his shotgun and fighting back the pain, he held on to Leonard and started punching him. Elisa quickly put on the vest and kicked Trucker Hat in the face and immediately kicked Dirty Hair in the balls, shattering them. Dirty Hair dropped to his knees screaming out in incredible pain.

Trucker Hat's lower jaw was dislocated and the bear mace soaked deeper in his eyes. All the fight left him as he rolled around in pain as Dirty Hair stayed on his knees crying his eyes out. "MY NUTS! MY NUTS! BITCH BROKE MY NUTS!". Leonard and Elisa jumped into the truck. Leonard started it up and backed into the other guys' pickup truck with the deer antlers behind them, smashing up their front end. Then Leonard hit the gas and took off as fast as he could.

Ronnie could see the tree branches fly by them as her dad drove away as fast as possible. "OH GOD! OH MY GOD!" he said again as he gripped the wheel tightly. After a few miles, Leonard asked "Ma'am, what was that about?" he said as he tried to regain his composure. "You're not going to hurt us? Are you?"

Elisa looked out the passenger window. Her wings had folded themselves flat on her back, but it made the vest feel tight, so she was holding the front of the vest closed with her hands. "I didn't mean any harm. I found a doe and her fawn, shot by some strange weapon. I was blessing them so they may enter the next realm together. I didn't mean any harm. No harm to anyone."

"I believe you" Ronnie said. She looked at the woman's green eyes. Green like the leaves of the forest. She looked like a woman, but her skin tone was more dark peach with a light violet hue. "What are you?"

Elisa stopped to think for a moment. "I am a Nogwyn. Shepherd of the land and all its creatures. It's my job to retain balance". Elisa was shivering from the trauma and exposure. "Don't worry, we will take you somewhere to get some fresh clothes. We can't have you, Nogwyn or otherwise running around without something to wear, its indecent" Leonard said. He was thinking how he would tell his wife that he came across a naked "fairy" and brought her home.

Ronnie looked at her dad. Leonard made eye contact with his daughter and knew that no matter what happened, she would back him up. Leonard kept checking his rearview mirror and thankfully nobody was following them. He drove back home as fast as he could without getting the attention of the cops. He pulled up to his driveway and saw his wife's car was gone. Great, maybe she stepped out for a minute.

"Sweetie. Go upstairs and get some of your mom's old clothes in the cardboard box by bathroom. Ma'am, if you would follow me, I will show you where you can change into something more presentable." He pointed to the side door, and Ronnie ran ahead with her keys. Ronnie entered the house with Elisa close by when Leonard heard his nosy neighbor saying, "Hey Lenny, who's the young lady?".

"Earl, how ya doing?" Leonard said while grinding his teeth. "My niece is in town. You know teenagers nowadays. Spandex with bracelets up to their armpits. Don't get me started with all the gunk in their hair, am I right?"

"How come I never seen her before?" Earl said while trying to get a look at the mysterious young lady wearing a man's vest and apparently no underwear. Leonard made sure to stand in the way so Earl couldn't see clearly. "Dad! I can't find the box". Leonard took a deep breath "Gotta go, say hi to Mary Lou for me" and quickly entered the house. Leonard rushed upstairs and saw that Ronnie had indeed found the box. She called out to her dad to get him out of that sticky situation with Earl.

"I owe you one sweetie" he said.

A few minutes later, Elisa was wearing a complete outfit, nothing fancy, just an oversized flannel shirt with sweatpants and a slightly worn pair of sandals as she refused to wear closed toe shoes. Leonard measured and cut two long slits in the back of the shirt so Elisa can slip her wings out when needed. Leonard heard a car pull up.

"Mom's home!" Ronnie called out.

No need to panic, we've done nothing wrong. Leonard looked out the window. *Aw shit! Doesn't Earl got anything better to do.* Mrs. Chalmers was chatting with Earl and Leonard could tell from Earl's gestures that he was talking about Elisa. Leonard tried to come up with a new plan. Maybe Elisa can hide or walk out the back door. The side door began to open. *Oh shit! Elisa!*

Elisa walked out on her own and met up with Mrs. Chalmers and Earl. "My name is Elisa; I am Leonard's niece. I was visiting my cousin and now I am going home". The voice sounded hypnotic like a siren. Mrs. Chalmers and Earl looked at this strange young lady and nodded. Together they repeated the story "Hi Elisa, Ronnie's cousin. Good to see you again. Tell your mom we said hi". Elisa looked back towards the side door/kitchen area and winked at Leonard and Ronnie. "Do you think we will see her again?" Ronnie asked.

"I don't know sweetie. I really don't know." Leonard said. He still was trying to put together the events of the day. "Ronnie, do not tell your mother what happened today".

"Why not?" Ronnie asked. She knew they did nothing wrong.

Leonard tried to think of a good reason. Nothing came to mind so the truth will have to do. "If we tell mommy what happened, do you think she will believe us?".

Ronnie thought about it for a second "probably not".

"Exactly. It's our little secret." Leonard looked back out the window and there was no trace of Elisa. She just vanished. Later that night, Ronnie sat by the side of her bed and looked out her bedroom window. The night sky was clear. She saw a shooting star pass by and immediately closed her eyes to make a wish. She wished for a big sister. The following morning, Ronnie went downstairs and told her parents about an elaborate dream she had that involve lush forests filled with wonders and strange creatures. She told them about her guide, a big sister, that showed her the beauty of a hidden world that is only a dream away.

Ronnie's mom just dismissed it as childhood fantasy. Leonard on the other hand recognized Elisa from Ronnie's description. He later told Ronnie that it was okay to have dreams or make up stories but to not believe in them. Ronnie took out a small necklace made of jade and emeralds "then explain this?" she asked her daddy.

"Where did you get that? From your mom's jewelry box! You know how she doesn't like it when you go through her stuff without permission" he said. "I didn't go to mom's jewelry, honest!" Ronnie protested. Leonard held on to the necklace and examined it carefully. It doesn't look like one of his wife's necklaces. He doesn't remember Ronnie going up to his bedroom lately, but kids often sneak around when parents aren't looking but the necklace had this aura, this kind of glow.

He handed it back to Ronnie "Keep it safe. Don't wear it outside, to school, nowhere, you understand me?"

"Yes daddy" Ronnie took back the necklace and lowered her head, almost in shame.

Leonard knelt. "Listen, I am not mad and I am not saying you did something bad, okay? Just put that necklace away for a while. If your mom comes looking for it, I will handle it. Otherwise, just keep it safe. There are a lot of good and bad things in the world. We must protect the good whenever we can. There will always be bad things out there, people, especially people and other things."

Ronnie nodded as she listened. "Okay, put your necklace away and get ready for school". Leonard watched as his daughter went back upstairs. Ronnie put the necklace away in a shoebox under her bed. Each night, she had dreams about going on amazing adventures, each one more vivid than the last. Each time she found treasure, she was allowed to keep something as a souvenir. In time, that little shoe box became filled with small treasures.

Despite all the treasure she found, the only one that Ronnie truly valued was the relationship she had with her parents and her new big sister, who promised her that one day she would teach her to fly.

Losing Control

Coralyn Bay Museum of Natural History Friday Afternoon
Bruce was reorganizing the maritime exhibit when Dr. Shelley found him. "Bruce, do you have a moment?" She looked excited, almost girlish. "I have someone I'd like you to meet. Well, re-meet." Mark Martinez stood in the lobby, dressed in khakis and a button-down shirt, looking more formal than he had the last time he was there.

"Mr. Martinez and I had a lovely conversation yesterday," Dr. Shelley said. "He taught me in high school; can you believe it? And when I mentioned we could use help with our archives, particularly reclassification of some older specimens, he volunteered!"
Bruce tried to hide his surprise. "That's... that's great."

"We can't offer pay right now," Dr. Shelley continued, "but if the arrangement works out, we might manage a part-time position or consulting fee down the road." Mark smiled. "I have plenty of time on my hands. One of the benefits of retirement."

"Wonderful! Bruce, can you show Mr. Martinez around? Get him oriented to our filing systems?" Dr. Shelley checked her watch. "I have a donor call in ten minutes, but we'll talk more next week." As she hurried off, Bruce turned to Mark. "You're volunteering? Here?"
"Seemed like a good way to help." Mark's expression was mild, but his eyes held purpose. "And to keep an eye on things." They walked through the exhibits, Bruce explaining the organization system, where different specimens were stored, how the database worked.

But Mark seemed distracted, his attention drifting to certain displays. He stopped in front of a case containing bone fragments. The placard read: Miller's Quarry, 1990. Specimens determined to be fraudulent.
"These aren't fraudulent," Mark said quietly.
"What are they?" Bruce asked.

"Proof." Mark moved on before Bruce could ask more. "Listen, I know this is sudden, but I wanted to extend an invitation. How about you come over to my place Sunday? We can grill some steaks, talk more about... all of this. Somewhere less public."
"Yeah, I'd like that." Bruce nodded.

"Bring your friends if you want. The more the merrier." Mark's face brightened. "I haven't had people over in a long time. It'd be nice." Bruce thought of Chris and Roxy. "I know a couple of hungry knuckleheads who'd love a good steak."
"Perfect." Mark wrote his address on a museum business card. "Sunday afternoon, around two?"

"We'll be there."

As Mark headed to the archives, Bruce stood in front of the bone fragments display. Fraudulent. What if the real fraud was the label itself? What if the truth had been sitting here all along, dismissed as lies? Bruce pulled out his phone and texted the group chat:

BBQ at my new friend's place Sunday. Steaks involved. You in?

Chris replied immediately: *Free food? I'm there.*

Roxy's response took longer: *Who's the friend?*

Bruce hesitated, then typed: *The guy from the museum. The one who knew about the fairy wing. Long story. I'll explain Sunday, so are you in?* Roxy texted back: *Sure, can I bring a +1?*

Bruce smiled and replied "Sure, the more the merrier".

Roxy: *K, great, see you then, send me the details.*
Jake's Apartment Friday Night

Roxy wasn't sure what had come over Jake. They had plans. Dinner and a movie, nothing special. But the moment she'd walked through his door, he'd been on her. Hungry. Almost desperate. It wasn't like him. Jake was usually gentle, considerate, the kind of guy who asked permission. But tonight, he'd torn her clothes off like a man starving, his hands everywhere, his mouth demanding. She'd gone with it at first. The intensity was exciting. Different. But now, lying in his bed while he traced patterns on her skin, Roxy felt uneasy.

"Jake," she said softly. "You, okay?"

"Never better." His voice was rough, distracted. His fingers continued their path across her stomach, up her ribs. "You've seemed a little off this week. Like you're a thousand miles away or something" Roxy said while fighting back temptation. Jake looked at her with hungry eyes and said. "Just stressed. You know because of the expedition." His hand slid higher. His hands had this roughness like sandpaper.

"Jake...."

He kissed her, cutting off the question. When he pulled back, his eyes were dark. Wrong. For just a moment, Roxy could have sworn she saw something behind his gaze. Something looking out through him. Then he blinked, and it was gone. "I should go," Roxy said, sitting up. "Stay." His hand caught her wrist. Not hard, but firm. "Please."

She looked at his hand on her wrist, then at his face. Jake had never held her like that before. Never asked with quite that edge of command. "I have an early class tomorrow," she lied, pulling free. "I'll text you." As she dressed, she felt his eyes on her. Watching. Assessing. Like a predator deciding whether to let prey escape.

Roxy left quickly, her cop instincts screaming that something was deeply wrong. Jake lay in bed after Roxy left, staring at the ceiling. Enough, he told himself. ENOUGH. He'd felt it again. That thing inside him, pushing, demanding. The hunger that had nothing to do with his own desires and everything to do with something else wearing his skin.

He forced himself to stay still. To not follow Roxy. To not…

Darkness.

Suddenly he wasn't in bed anymore. He was walking downwards like in the cave, jagged and uneven. It wasn't just dark, but he felt the absence of light and sound, as if he was walking towards a void, a wound in the universe itself. Water rose around his ankles, cold and thick — not water exactly, but something that moved like it had intention, like it was aware of him. Something pulled him deeper. Above, a point of light burst like a dying star. In its illumination, Jake saw an underground lake. And rising from it, a mountain. But wrong. Crooked. Twisted at impossible angles.

The mountain called to him.

He tried to resist, but the pull was inexorable. His feet moved without permission, carrying him toward….

Jake woke up and he was behind the wheel of his car. He was driving. Hands at ten and two, eyes on the road. Streetlights passed overhead in regular intervals. He had no memory of getting dressed. No memory of leaving his apartment. No memory of starting the car. But here he was, driving through empty streets at 2:47

AM according to the dashboard. His hands turned the wheel without his input. His foot pressed the accelerator. Jake tried to force his hands to stop. Nothing. Something else had the wheel now.

Saturday Morning

Gloria Shelley woke to her phone buzzing on the coffee table. She'd fallen asleep on the sofa again, wrapped in her favorite blanket, Netflix still playing on the TV. The screen showed an incoming call: Ronnie C. "Hello?" Gloria's voice was rough with sleep. "Hi Gloria, it's Ronnie."

"Ronnie?" Gloria sat up, stretching her stiff back. Pale light seeped through the blinds. Dawn, or close to it. "What's going on? What time is it?"

"Early. I'm sorry. But I have something I need you to look at today if possible." The urgency in Veronica Chalmers' voice cut through Gloria's grogginess. They'd known each other since graduate school, and Ronnie didn't panic easily. "Okay. Give me an hour."

Gloria drove through almost empty streets toward the museum, nursing herself on drive-through coffee. Mist rolled in from the bay, making the morning feel dreamlike and uncertain. A dirty SUV sat alone in the visitor's lot. Gloria had called ahead to security; told them she was meeting someone to receive a late shipment. The security guard waved her on without question. Ronnie waited by the side entrance, clutching a worn leather briefcase like it might escape. Her hair was pulled back messily, and she looked like she hadn't slept. "Thank you for coming." Ronnie glanced around the empty lot. "Let's talk inside."

They took the stairs down to the basement level. Offices, storage, the small laboratory the museum used for specimen analysis. The Coralyn Bay Museum of

Natural History had been built with an underground level despite being so close to the water. Locals joked it was either deep magic or dumb luck that had kept it from flooding in eighty years. Gloria unlocked the lab and flipped on the lights. "Alright, Ronnie. You dragged me out of bed before six on a Saturday morning. What is this about?"

Ronnie didn't answer. She opened her briefcase and placed something on the examination table. Gloria stepped closer. At first glance, it looked like a dark purple geode. Rough, unremarkable. But as Gloria picked it up, the calcified exterior seemed to flake away slightly, revealing something beneath. A crystal. Deep purple, polished smooth, with what looked like magma trapped inside. Glowing faintly. Pulsing. "What is this?" Gloria whispered.

"That's why I brought it to you." Ronnie's voice was tight. "I was hoping you could tell me."
"Where did you find it?"

"Crystal Valley. One of my students pulled it from one of the deeper chambers." Gloria turned the object in her hands. It was cool and warm at the same time, radiating a strange energy. Not exactly heat but something else. The crystal had small cracks running through it, and what looked like deliberate repair work. Someone had mended this thing.

Help me...
Gloria froze.

Help me and I will give you everything... anything or nothing...
The voice was barely audible. More a feeling than sound. A whisper at the edge of thought. "Gloria?" Ronnie's hand touched her shoulder. "You, okay?" Gloria set the crystal down quickly. "Yeah. I'm fine." She stepped back,

putting distance between herself and the object. "Ronnie, whatever this is, it's not just a geological specimen."

"I know." Ronnie wrapped it again carefully. "I've been hearing it too. Since Jake found it Thursday. I thought maybe I was going crazy, but..."
"You're not crazy." Gloria stared at the wrapped bundle. "We need to test this. Carefully. And we need to figure out what it's connected to."
"Connected to?"

Gloria thought about the specimens in storage upstairs. The evidence from Miller's Quarry. The dragonfly wing that Mark Martinez had questioned. "I think," she said slowly, "this might be connected to something that happened here a long time ago. Something people tried to warn us about. And something we've been ignoring ever since." Veronica's heartbeat started increasing as if she was freefalling without a parachute.

The Devil's Maw Site Office Saturday Afternoon
The man called Mr. Suit reviewed the latest surveillance footage for the third time, his jaw tight with irritation. His associate, a security analyst named Finn who'd been hired from an overseas firm, sat beside him, pulling up comparison scans on dual monitors.

"The images aren't fabricated," Finn said, zooming in on the cave mapping data. "Look at the root collection string here." He pointed to lines of code in the GIS software. "No alterations. These readings are genuine."

"So, what are we looking at?" Mr. Suit asked. "A living geological system?"
"In a manner of speaking. The passages are... responsive. Shifting."

Mr. Suit hated vague answers. He preferred yes or no, black or white. "What about the antechamber?" Finn brought up a combined 3D projection of the cave system. "The proposed tourist route is here. Perfectly safe. But the deeper sections?" He used a laser pointer. "Too unstable. Passages that contract, dead ends, structural risks. We've lost four drones already."

"I don't care about tourist routes. Is there anything valuable in the antechamber?" Finn hesitated. "Possibly. We detected an energy variance three days ago. But it's gone now." Mr. Suit pulled up the equipment logs on his tablet, cross-referencing with the surveillance feeds. There. A CaveScan drone entering the chamber detecting the strange signature and then went offline. Later, one of them is carrying the strange signal back with them.

He switched to Dr. Chalmers' workstation feed. The audio was patchy, but he caught enough: "...found something... don't trust that suit... keep it quiet..." Mr. Suit's expression didn't change, but his fingers tightened on the tablet. He stood, adjusted his collar, and pulled out a specialized phone. The blue line. "I need to make a call."

Neon City Kingsley Tower, Penthouse Level

Grant Kingsley was pouring himself scotch when the blue line phone buzzed. He picked it up immediately, pressed his thumb to the biometric scanner. "Talk to me, Suit."

"Sir, as suspected, there are access routes available to the destination, but not for commercial traffic. However, the situation has changed. The quarterback took the ball to a different stadium." Kingsley's eyes narrowed. They used sports metaphors for sensitive calls. "Is the game still on the same channel?"

"No. The game moved to a public arena with historical value." A public arena. The museum. "That's unfortunate," Kingsley said quietly. "I really wanted that game ball for my trophy case. Do whatever is necessary. I must have it."

He ended the call and walked slowly through his penthouse to the trophy room. Floor-to-ceiling displays held his most prized acquisitions: the sword of Charlemagne, Churchill's hat, a signed first edition of On the Origin of Species, and mounted in the center of the room, the head of the last North American Unicorn.

Most people thought unicorns were myth. Grant Kingsley knew better. And if there was something in the cave with real power, something from the old world before humanity. A relic from a forgotten era then he would be the one to own it.

Coralyn Bay Museum of Natural History

"Are you sure about this?" Veronica asked. "I hate to find out this thing is radioactive or toxic." Gloria looked up at her friend with a droopy scowl. "If this thing was radioactive, I'm sure your corporate sponsor would have picked it up by now, after all, if somebody got sick because of exposure to something toxic or radioactive, imagine the PR nightmare it would cause."

"Yeah, Miller's Quarry is not too far away. The press would have a field day." Veronica said. Her heart started to beat more slowly and naturally now. "Alright, be careful and let me know whatever you find out as soon as possible." Gloria took the geode and locked it up in a secure container and put it in her office. She left a note on her monitor to tell Gilbert to analyze the specimen first thing on Monday.

Veronica got back in her car and left. Her mind was racing with so many thoughts. She wanted to vent to someone, anyone. This was getting heavy and she had no one to turn to since her father died a few years ago.

Veronica took the long way home, letting her thoughts stray.

In the hills overlooking Crystal Valley, in the deep forest.

The local wildlife started migrating away from The Devil's Maw. No birds, squirrels, foxes or crickets. They all left as fast as they could. The only movement belonged to the employees of Kingsmen Enterprises and in the distance, a lone figure set up camp to keep an eye on the activity. She wore a camouflage outfit with an orange vest. The tag inside the back of the vest read: *Property of Leonard Chalmers.*

The Soft Sofa

Barney's Bargain Barn Saturday Afternoon

"Thanks for the company," Chris said, pushing the shopping cart through the produce section. "I hate shopping alone." Roxy tossed lettuce and potatoes into the cart. "No problem. Besides, I needed to pick up a few things anyway."

"I'm making potato salad for tomorrow." Chris checked his list. "Capers, green olives, eggs... So, do you know anything about Bruce's new friend?"
"Nope. But he's the same guy Bruce met at the museum the other day." Roxy scanned the aisles absently. "Supposed to know a lot about history or something." Chris grabbed a jar of mayonnaise. "Bruce has been weird all week. All excited about this dragonfly wing mystery."

"Yeah, he texted me about it." Roxy paused by the deli counter. "Think there's actually something to it?"
"Knowing Bruce? Probably just got caught up in some old museum paperwork drama." Chris shrugged. "But hey, the man's offering free steaks, so I'm not complaining." They moved through the store, Chris collecting ingredients while Roxy grabbed wine and chips. As they turned down the condiment aisle, Chris noticed something on Roxy's neck when her hair shifted.

A bruise. And what looked like scratches, partially healed.
"What's that?" He gestured toward her neck. Roxy touched it self-consciously, pulling her hair back over it. "It's nothing. Jake's been under a lot of pressure. I've been helping him relax." Chris's expression tightened. "Roxy..."

"It's not what you think. We're both adults." But her tone was defensive. "Jake's just been... different lately. More intense." Chris didn't push it. He knew when Roxy had made up her mind about something. They continued shopping in silence for a few minutes before Roxy spoke again but more softly this time. "He called me something weird. A nickname he's never used before." Chris looked up. "What?"

Roxy hesitated, then shrugged. "He keeps calling me his ornament." She said it like it was nothing. A quirky endearment. But something about the word made Chris's skin crawl.

Mark's House, Sunday Afternoon

Mark heard the doorbell just past noon. He wiped his hands on a dish towel and opened the door to find Bruce grinning like a kid on Christmas morning. "Bruce and friends, welcome, welcome!" Mark stepped aside, gesturing them in. "I hope you brought your appetites." Bruce stepped forward and without thinking, hugged Mark like he'd known him for years. Mark returned the embrace. Warm, firm, paternal. The kind of hug that said you're safe here. "This is Jake," Bruce said as a massive figure ducked through the doorway carrying a case of soda in one hand and beer in the other. "Wasn't sure if you drank, so I hedged my bets."

Mark's eyebrows rose. "Wow. You're a big guy, aren't you? Protein bars and barbell plates?" He gave Jake's midsection a gentle nudge. "You can put those on the table. I'll get them cold. Don't worry, big man. Plenty of steaks for you."

Jake smiled, but something about it didn't quite reach his eyes. He moved past Mark toward the kitchen. Chris came next, nearly tripping over a small decorative pile of stones near the front garden. He caught himself, clutching a covered dish like his life depended on it. "The graceful one over here is Chris," Bruce said with a grin. "And behind him," Bruce continued as the final guest appeared, "is Roxy. The muscle of the group."

Roxy stepped through the door carrying a glass bowl of mixed green salad. "Hi, Mark," she said warmly. "We've heard so much about you."
"The pleasure's all mine." Mark pointed toward the kitchen. "You can set those on the counter. I've got the grill going out back."

Chris and Jake were already arguing by the time Mark joined them in the kitchen. "For the last time, I didn't put raisins in potato salad!" Chris defended his creation. "Those are capers!" Mark peered into the bowl and scooped up a small taste. "Mmmm…Soft potatoes, mustard with a hint of mayo, olives with some juices, and capers. This is a fine dish. Thank you, Chris." Chris shot Jake a I told you so look.

"Come on, everyone! Grab a plate. I've got chicken breasts, steaks, and fajitas over here. T-bones, burgers, hot dogs. I'm putting shrimp on the grill next with those little skewers. Don't be shy. My house is your house." While the others fixed their plates, Roxy wandered into the living room. Family photos covered the walls. Graduations, weddings, birthday parties. Decades of love captured in frames. She sank onto the big brown sofa and felt something she hadn't felt in months.
Peace.

All her worries drifted away. Jake's strange behavior, occasional flare ups due to her back, school stress, the uncertainty of her future. The cushions embraced her like a warm hug. "Watch out now, young lady." Mark sat down beside her. "This sofa is under a spell. If you sit here long enough, you will fall asleep."

Roxy smiled, her body relaxing deeper into the cushions. "I believe it. Has anyone ever fallen asleep on this couch before?"

"Plenty. Had the internet guy install my service a while back. Told him he could sit on my sofa while I got my credit card. Within a minute or two, lights out!" Mark chuckled. "When I woke him up, he was so embarrassed." Roxy let out a genuine laugh. The kind that came from deep in her chest, unguarded and real. Her family had always been distant, scattered. This grandfatherly figure, this kind stranger who'd welcomed them into his home, felt right. She understood now why Bruce had been so adamant about them meeting Mark.

"Now, come on," Mark tapped her knee gently. "Before the boys get all the good stuff." Roxy knew better than to ignore sound advice. Mark's backyard was humble but immaculate. A small Zen pool and garden occupied one corner. Vegetable beds lined the fence. A deck held a weathered table and chairs, and further back, a well-maintained barbecue pit sent delicious smoke into the afternoon air.

Bruce took a moment to soak it all in. This house, this neighborhood, had history. He could imagine families moving in during the late '90s or early 2000s. Back when kids could play outside unsupervised. Back when neighborhoods were communities.

The love held in these walls was almost tangible. Nothing bad could happen in a place like this. Everybody ate. Everybody laughed. Everyone drank. Mark hustled back and forth, playing the perfect host, refusing all offers of help from Bruce and Roxy. Jake lived up to his reputation, putting away food like he hadn't eaten in days. Chris felt a little embarrassed by his friend's appetite, but Mark's soft, commanding voice kept coming: "Eat, eat! I can't handle all this food by myself."

Afternoon became evening. Time flew. As the sun began its descent, Mark went inside the kitchen and flipped a switch. The backyard transformed. String lights came to life. Soft, warm, like fireflies dancing in the growing darkness. "I could move in here," Roxy breathed.

"Me too," Bruce agreed.

Chris excused himself so he could use the bathroom. Jake stood near the edge of the deck, his smile fading as he noticed something in the yard. "What are those things?" He pointed to small piles of stones arranged in deliberate patterns throughout the garden. Roxy elbowed him lightly. "Oh, that?" Mark followed his gaze. "It's for luck and protection."

"Are you serious?" Jake asked.

"Yes. In ancient times, people believed evil spirits wandered at night, so they lit up their homes to scare them away. When that didn't work, they made these little totems, or cairns, to channel good energy and ward off the bad." Bruce walked around the yard, studying the arrangements. They were subtle, blending naturally into the landscape. You'd never notice them unless you were looking. "You never cease to amaze me," Bruce said.

Jake stirred his leftover potato salad absently. "I can see that. People are quick to dismiss stories about spirits and magic. Keeping it just for children. But it's not just for children." His voice took on an odd quality. "Magic is real." Roxy shot him a look. *What are you doing?* "You're right," Mark said while pouring soda into a glass of ice. "Magic is real. When we're young, the world is full of wonder. We can sense the magic, and at times, use it."

He gestured toward Roxy and Jake. "As we get older, we lose that magic. Because of family pressures, peer pressure, society telling us to grow up and be realistic. But the magic is still there. We find it in other places." Jake pulled Roxy close, his arms around her waist. She relaxed into him for a moment, setting aside her earlier annoyance.

"But as we get older," Mark continued, "hopefully we get wiser. You start a family, raise children, and you see the magic come back. You see it in their eyes. In many ways, you experience it again. Through your children's eyes and as yourself. So, as you get older and life starts taking things away from you, magic comes back. Not to cure all your woes, but to remind you, to comfort you, that good things are still to come."

Bruce set down his drink. The words hit him hard. Mark, Roxy, and Bruce all had tears in their eyes. Jake nodded with respect, though his expression remained distant.

Chris walked back out, adjusting his belt. "What did I miss?"

As all good things must end, the party began to wind down. Mark started wrapping leftovers into to-go containers. Bruce and his friends insisted on helping clean up. That part was non-negotiable. Once the house was in order, dishes washed, and trash taken out, Mark smiled at his guests. "Now, please, humor an old man. Everyone gets a treat in my house."

He walked up to Chris first, handing him a wrapped package. Chris unwrapped it carefully and froze. "I don't believe this." In his hands: an autographed copy of the 1992 classic film *My Cousin Vinny*. Signed by Joe Pesci himself. "Bruce told me a little about everyone,"

Mark said. "I hope you don't mind. I wanted to be prepared."

"Mark, I..." Chris's voice cracked. "This movie is one of the most influential films about law, second only to *To Kill a Mockingbird*. I love Vinny. He's... he's..." The lessons sank in. From both Mark and Vinny. An underdog lawyer who fought for his clients with everything he had. Who used his mind and his courage when others dismissed him. Chris looked at Mark, eyes shining. "If you ever need anything, anything, call me." Mark patted his arm. "I know I can count on you."

Next, Mark turned to Roxy. "For my aspiring detective." He handed her a small crystal prism. "May you crack the case and bring evil to justice." Roxy turned it over in her hands, confused. Mark nodded toward the bookcase. "Bruce, bring me that book there."

He placed the book on the coffee table and showed Roxy how to use the prism. He held it like a magnifying glass over the book's cover, angling it toward the light. "Wow!" Roxy and Chris said together. Under the prism, fingerprints appeared on the book's surface. Invisible to the naked eye but revealed through the special crystal. "How did you do that?" Roxy asked, delighted.

"The prism refracts light in a specific way. Reveals what's hidden. Just like you'll do in your work. Uncovering the truth others can't see." Roxy clutched the prism, feeling its weight. A real tool. Something she could use. Mark handed Jake a small box. "I know you explore new areas, mostly underground, I hope you like it". Jake opened the box and inside was a little vial of semi-clear liquid. "What is it?" he asked.

"Noctilium" Mark answered "It's used to mark trails or other places with little or no natural light. My brother and I used to believe it was made from real glowworms and fireflies but nowadays is mostly synthetic but I hope it helps you out".

Jake stared at it "Actually, this will come in handy. Very handy." Jake smiled and patted Mark on the shoulder and gave him a firm handshake. Finally, Mark turned to Bruce. "For you, my friend." He handed Bruce a worn leather-bound book. The cover read: *A Field Guide to Supernatural Creatures and Unusual Phenomena.*

Bruce opened it carefully. Maps, glossaries, detailed illustrations of creatures from around the world. Diagrams showing how to protect a home. Where to place cairns, how to identify entry points for malevolent spirits, protective herbs and rituals. "I used to teach," Mark said quietly. "I used to share stories with my children and grandchildren. One of them really took these lessons to heart." His voice grew distant. "Knowledge lost is lost forever. That power fades. So, it's important that people like us keep the flame going and pass it on."

Mark's eyes met Bruce's. "Naturally, we try to pass it to our children. But sometimes things don't work out that way. I believe it's important to recognize opportunities when life presents them."

Bruce held the book to his chest, emotions welling up. "I'll read it. I promise. I want to…" Mark shook him gently. "It's okay. Take your time. I know you all have your studies, your priorities. Thank you for giving an old man a good time tonight." Without hesitation, Roxy asked, "When can we see you again?" Mark smiled as the group prepared to leave. He looked at Roxy with genuine warmth. "I'll leave the lights on for you. Come by any time."

Darkness Awakens

Sunday Night

Bruce's mind was still at Mark's house even as he drove home. The soft sofa, the string lights, the magic speech about wonder returning. All of it felt more real than his own apartment. He pulled into his parking spot and carried Mark's book inside like it was made of glass. The leather binding was worn smooth from decades of handling. Bruce settled onto his couch and opened to the first page.

A Field Guide to Supernatural Creatures and Unusual Phenomena Compiled by various scholars, 1847-1923

Maps. Glossaries. Detailed illustrations of creatures from around the world: some beautiful, some nightmarish. Bruce turned pages slowly, absorbing everything. A diagram caught his eye: entry points for malevolent entities. Open windows, chimneys, closet spaces, the darkness beneath beds. He was surprised to see modern additions, notes in different handwriting showing how creatures had adapted to enter through HVAC systems and electrical conduits.

The book had been updated over generations. Bruce found the section on home protection. There! The cairns from Mark's yard, illustrated in careful detail. Cairns: In various cultures (Native American, Scottish, Celtic), these stone arrangements serve multiple purposes: navigation markers, trail guides, and spiritual anchors. Cairns can help ancestral spirits find their way to familiar locations, bringing peace or protection in times of need. In distress or danger, properly constructed cairns summon guardian spirits to defend a dwelling from malevolent entities such as Morgrins or Soul

Jackals. Bruce flipped to the glossary, his heart beating faster.

Soul Jackal: A demonic entity that visits the homes of children and the elderly to steal their souls. Humans falsely attribute mysterious deaths to natural causes or, in superstitious times, to cats (in truth, cats ward off Soul Jackals and other supernatural pests such as snogs). These creatures collect souls for social status or trade with higher powers in infernal hierarchies. In ancient times, when a loved one died, families stood watch to ensure safe passage to the next world. If a Soul Jackal appeared, families could exile it using an expulsion spell or repel it with the Light of Creation: the greatest of all magical defenses.

Light of Creation. Bruce had to know more. He found the entry:

Light of Creation: A spell or manifestation of pure magical force, created through innocence and absolute faith. Said to contain remnants of the first dawn created by the ancient goddess Atheniferr; deity of family and protection, whose tears formed the first stars. The Light can banish entities that exist in darkness or between dimensions.

Bruce set the book down.

This couldn't be real. It was just folklore. A collection of stories passed down, embellished, mythologized. But Mark believed it. And Dr. Shelley had confirmed the Nogwyn wing was real. Bruce stared at his ceiling. His full belly and exhausted mind pulled him toward sleep, but something kept him awake. A feeling. Like the air pressure had changed.

He turned on the TV for background noise. Something mindless to quiet his thoughts. Within minutes, he was asleep on the couch, Mark's book resting on his chest.

Coralyn Bay Port Authority Office Sunday Night, 11:47 PM

The Tijuana Moving and Cleaning Company van pulled into the lot. Their slogan, painted on the side in cheerful letters: You Move, We Clean! Three men got out, hauling mops, industrial cleaners, and equipment cases. The security guard at the front desk barely glanced up. Sunday night cleaning crew. Routine.

The men worked methodically: mopping floors, washing windows, emptying trash. Normal sounds and routine. Around 1:15 AM, the guard's head began to nod. He jerked awake twice, shook himself, rubbed his eyes. But the third time, sleep took him. One of the janitors took notice and spoke into a device inside his left sleeve "Rent-a-cop's asleep, let's move".

Three men; Johnny, Vito and Rico, quickly disposed of their cleaning equipment and made their way outside. They took off their jumpsuits to reveal all black outfits with special texturized padding that disrupted RFID scanners and delayed wireless security alarms. They put on some masks that conceal their heads but allow them to see. If someone tried to take a picture or video of them, the image would be distorted. These men were experienced professionals.

Scaling the building took no effort and drugging the only security guard at the museum was no problem. Rico shot a small dart the size of a mosquito at the guard's neck which delivered a powerful sleeping agent. The security system was basic, video cameras, RFID trackers and scanners on most of the expensive items. However, their prize was not on exhibit. It was recently brought in by the treacherous Dr. Chalmers.

Vito had a blueprint of the entire museum (thanks to open records at the City Library) and he figured out the most likely location the stone would be: Central Archive and Collections. Johnny was up with the locks, he had a special scanner, disguised as a sliding cell phone that can disrupt any lock or read any combination, digital or physical. Johnny opened the door as if he owned the place. The men made no noise and communicated only with hand signals.

They walked in and used special glasses to see in the dark. Mr. Suit told them the stone had a special energy signature, but nothing was out of the ordinary. They checked the various rooms and found no traces of any recent packages, no residual heat signatures, nothing. The three specialists searched the entire archive and found nothing. Time flew by and they had to move fast, worst of all, they had to find the stone. If they came back empty-handed, Mr. Suit would have their heads, literally.

Finally, Vito broke silence. "Where the fuck is it!" Rico started to check various offices, and Johnny did a quick pattern search. He opened one office, belonging to the Assistant Director, and picked up a faint trace. "There!" The men converged to the office and searched, less methodically and crasser like a pack of amateurs in a convenience store robbery. "GOD FUCKING DAMMIT!" Vito shouted, losing his cool. Johnny, ever the calm one, ordered his men to split up and begin searching upstairs along with the main viewing areas.

"It's got to be here, our intel is tight and verified, it's got to be here," Rico said. Vito started checking all the offices. First, the Director's office. Vito started pulling out drawers, tossing books and papers, he saw a container underneath the desk and immediately opened it and dumped the contents. "What the fuck is this?" he picked up a crummy looking geode, like the ones they sell in the gift shop. This can't be the stone, the way Mr. Suit describes it will be one of a kind. "Piece of shit!" Vito tossed to the ground and some of the gray crud broke off, and it rolled underneath a coffee table. The geode sat quietly while Vito trashed the office and moved to the next one.

As soon as Vito left the office, the geode split to reveal a purple obsidian crystal with a bright orange center, magma was swirling around, and a slight hiss came from the cracks. The geode resembled an eye, and it looked pissed off. *Piece of shit?*

The specialist swept the lower levels and moved on to the main gallery and viewing area. Nothing, they found nothing. "Fucking great, we wasted all this time, and we can't find the goddamn thing!" Vito said. "What about your fancy toys, huh? What a crock of shit, you know, you're full of shit Johnny, anybody ever tell you that?".

Johnny checked his equipment. "It's here, I know it. Let me check again. Maybe if I change the wavelength, maybe this thing is radioactive". Johnny took off his gloves so he could change the settings on his tracking device. He was getting a faint signal from below. "Guys, I think its beneath us".

Vito pulled up his mask. "Hey, Einstein, we checked it out, there's nothing there! Unless you didn't check everything out like you're supposed to" Vito was losing his temper. Rico walked up behind him. "Put your mask back on dammit! Use your gloves! You drop that thing or get a smudge somewhere and it won't take the police long to track us".

"Who put you in charge, muthafucka" Vito said and he took a step towards Rico. "You know damn well I am in charge of this operation. We still have two hours before we need to be at the airport. Plenty of time to do one more sweep. Johnny, you got to be sure this time, no more fuck ups".

Johnny checked his scanners "It's got to be here, beneath us, follow me" He used his scanner to track the possible signature. Meanwhile, a strange glow emitted from Dr. Shelley's office. Johnny traced the signal to the supernatural wing; Rico was a few steps behind with Vito trailing in the back. "I lost it" Johnny said as sweat built up inside his mask. Rico turned around and saw Vito standing behind them with a gun pointed at them.

"I'm not going back to prison, you hear me! This is a setup, isn't it?" Vito pointed the gun at Rico and Johnny; He was switching targets. His face was a nervous wreck. "Put the gun down, right now" Rico ordered. Rico stood in front of Johnny, raised his left hand as if to slowly push down the barrel. Vito hesitated, this was not him, he didn't sweat things out, he didn't panic. Yet he can feel something, hear something….it was calling him.

They're setting you up. You'll take the fall; they'll keep the prize. They'll take everything from you, they've been taking anything they want from you because you're weak, you are nothing...

"Vito, man put the gun down. Let's just get out of here, huh?" Johnny said while trying to hold on to the device, it was picking up a stronger signal, right beneath them. Rico continued to slowly approach Vito, only a few more inches and he could swipe the gun away from him. Vito watched, he wanted to let Rico take the gun, take it away so he could control himself. So, he could regain his composure but the voice, smooth, persuasive yet commanding.

Everything…Anything…Nothing….

Nothing….

Nothing……...

"NO!" Vito pulled the trigger and shot Rico in the chest. Rico stopped just a hair away from putting his hand on the barrel. Committed to his decision, Vito emptied half the clip into Rico who flew backwards and crashed into the glass display with the small skeleton of a weird creature inside. Johnny dropped his device and held his hands up. "Easy Vito, easy man…let's just go, huh? Let the cops find Rico, pin it all on him, let's just go".

Blood was splattered over the broken skeleton. Vito held the gun towards Johnny, sweating, running down their faces. A strange glow was seeping from the floor and onto the skeleton. The sign on the base of the display read: North American Snow Goblin: SNOG. Vito opened his mouth to say something, but a hiss of air came out of his lungs. Johnny knew something bad was about to happen.

The skeleton started to rattle and while Johnny and Vito were busy with each other, the skeleton used some kind of dark power to drain all the blood from the floor and from the body of Rico. The skeleton began to reassemble itself; veins, muscles, ligaments and tendons began to grow back but looking more diseased and corrosive. Its skin, covered in welts and acid burns, its eyes, yellowed and burning, it watched as Vito emptied the rest of the clip into Johnny.

"Nobody takes from me and gets away with it, nobody!" Vito struggled for breath and then suddenly all the anxiety was gone and reality set in. Vito looked at his dead accomplices. "Oh shit, what have I done?". He took a step back, but something was waiting and the last thing he felt was four sharp talons slicing up open his throat.
Monday Morning

Bruce woke up to puppets on his TV screen teaching children about the letter F. His neck ached from sleeping on the couch. His mouth tasted like something had died in it. He stumbled to the bathroom, took the longest piss of his life, then splashed water on his face. His phone showed multiple missed messages.

Chris: Guys, I had the strangest dream. Can we meet at Pancake Hut?

Roxy: Sure, I can always go for a good short stack

Jake: No can do. Got to get to Crystal Valley. Lots of things to do

Dr. Shelley: Get down here or give me a call ASAP

Bruce stared at his boss' message. That wasn't good. But Chris's text bothered him more. Chris had weird dreams sometimes, but he didn't usually need emergency breakfast meetings about them. Bruce typed back to the group: On my way to Pancake Hut. Then work. He'd stop by the restaurant quickly, then head to the museum. What could go wrong?

Coralyn Bay Museum of Natural History 7:23 AM

Dr. Gloria Shelley pulled into the parking lot and immediately saw the police cars. Yellow tape blocked the front and side entrances. "What the hell?" Her hand instinctively went to her backpack. Today she was planning on getting the strange geode analyzed. *Oh no! What if it really was radioactive?* Gloria calmed herself. *No, if it was radioactive then people with hazmat suits would be here.* Something else went down over the weekend.

An officer approached her car as she parked. "Ma'am, this is an active crime scene."

"I'm Dr. Shelley. I run this museum." The officer's expression shifted. "Wait here, please."

A man in an overcoat and carrying a memo pad walked over. Late forties, tired eyes. "Dr. Shelley, I presume? I'm Detective Meadows. I need to ask you some questions."

"What happened? Is anyone hurt?"

"Please come with me."

Pancake Hut, Airport Boulevard 7:45 AM

Bruce walked into a wall of breakfast smells. Pancakes, bacon, maple syrup, coffee. His stomach growled despite his anxiety. Chris sat in a booth near the back, talking intensely to Roxy. Bruce had never seen his friend look so pale. "What's the dealio?" Bruce slid into the booth. A server immediately poured him black coffee. "You're out of your mind," Roxy said to Chris, but her voice was gentle.

"What's going on?" Bruce opened his menu. "Look, we just saw each other yesterday. I've got to get to work; my boss is freaking out about something. So, if there's an issue, tell me now or it'll have to wait."

Chris was silent, chewing his thoughts. His plate sat untouched; bacon and eggs going cold. "I had a dream," Chris finally said. "But it wasn't just a dream. I think... I think I had an out-of-body experience." Bruce set down his menu. "Chris…"

"I'm serious!" Chris's voice cracked. "Just listen."

Roxy stopped eating, her fork halfway to her mouth. "Alright." Bruce straightened. "Spill it."

Chris took a deep breath. "I went to bed like I normally do last night. I got my stuff ready for school, and organized my papers. Same routine. I felt good, so I did some light reading for class. And then..." He struggled for words. "I got lost in the book."

"What do you mean, lost?" Bruce asked while burning his tongue on the hot coffee.

"Like my mind was sucked into it. I was traveling through a forest of words. All the knowledge in the book came to me at once. But the deeper I went, the bigger the words got. Then I got swallowed by a huge letter. T or F, I couldn't tell." Bruce wanted to interrupt, to tell Chris he'd just fallen asleep reading. But something in his friend's expression stopped him.

"I fell through darkness," Chris continued. "Hit the ground hard. It was all wet, covered in jagged rocks or glass that cut through my clothes. I looked up and saw Roxy." Roxy set down her fork. "She was tied up. But not just tied; she was turning into a tree. Her arms were branches, and something kept stealing her fruit. She was screaming."

Roxy made a face. She was not comfortable with any of her friends having strange dreams about her. Wet or otherwise. Chris's hands shook. "Then I saw you, Bruce. Face-down in a dark ocean. Dead. And I heard Jake calling for help, but I couldn't find him no matter where I looked. His voice just kept calling out."

"Chris…"Bruce took another sip of the coffee.

"Then something came out of the water." Chris's voice dropped to a whisper. "It grabbed your body and tore it into three pieces. It had this strange head, like three separate creatures merged into one. Its body was made of tar and... and it ate you. It grew arms and started picking Roxy's fruit. She was screaming, so I yelled LEAVE HER ALONE!" Chris stopped, his jaw clenched.

"And then?" Bruce asked quietly.

"It came after me and then I woke up." Chris said, almost looking away. Bruce exhaled. "Look, I don't want to sound insensitive, but nightmares…" Chris stood up and pulled up his shirt. Bruce's coffee cup clattered against the saucer.

Chris's torso was covered in marks. Jagged, bloody bite patterns. Fresh wounds already beginning to scab over, as if they'd happened days ago instead of hours. "Dear God," Roxy whispered. Bruce reached out, touched one of the marks. Real. Warm. The skin around them was inflamed. "Then explain this, smart guy," Chris said, his voice hollow. Bruce's phone rang. That annoying pop song ringtone. "Yes?" He barely recognized his own voice. Dr. Shelley sounded frantic. "Bruce, where are you? I need you here now."

"I'm on my way." Bruce stood up and pulled out his wallet. He dropped some money on the table. "Chris, you need to see a doctor. Like, right now."

"Bruce…"

"I have to go. Call me if anything else happens. Anything." Bruce practically ran to his car.

Coralyn Bay Museum of Natural History 8:15 AM

Police vehicles filled the parking lot. Bruce spotted a Tijuana Moving and Cleaning van cordoned off with crime scene tape. An officer escorted him to an interview room; actually, just the employee break room with the door closed. A uniformed cop asked questions: Did the museum have valuable jewels? Works of art that could be fenced quickly?

"Nothing comes to mind," Bruce said. "The most valuable thing is the mosasaurus skeleton in the lobby, but that's not exactly portable. Most thieves want dinosaurs like a T-Rex not marine reptiles." The officer made notes and left. Bruce found Gilbert and Lester in the employee lounge. Dr. Shelley was still being interviewed somewhere. "What's going on?" Bruce asked.

Gilbert looked at Lester, then back to Bruce. "Something happened last night."

"Sometime after midnight," Gilbert continued, "thieves broke into the museum. They tried to access the underground lab, damaged a lot of equipment. We don't know what they were looking for, but they were upset. Either they found it and tried to cover their tracks, or..." He trailed off. "Or what?" Bruce asked.

"Or something else found them." Gilbert's voice was flat. "There are body parts everywhere." Bruce felt the blood drain from his face. "Yeah." Gilbert nodded. "Police are still processing the scene. Museum's closed indefinitely. Days, maybe weeks. Dr. Shelley wants a full inventory for insurance and the investigation."

"Where were the bodies found?" Gilbert met his eyes. "The supernatural wing."
Dr. Shelley's Office 9:00 AM

Detective Meadows sat across from Gloria, his patience clearly wearing thin. "Dr. Shelley, I need you to be straight with me. Someone, or something, killed three men in your museum last night. Forensics is suggesting a wild animal, but that doesn't explain why anyone would break in here in the first place. Now, is there anything you're not telling me? Disgruntled employees? Guests with grudges?" Gloria's hand tightened into a balled fist, and she glanced at something underneath her coffee table.
Help me. I will give you everything. Anything. Or nothing.

As soon as she entered the museum, that strange voice had been whispering to her. *Give him nothing. Or shower in his blood.* "Like I said," Gloria heard herself say, "nothing comes to mind." Meadows studied her for a long moment, then stood. "If something does, call me." He handed her a card. "I'll try to have my people out of here quickly, but this is a crime scene. The press already knows. We're keeping them at bay for now, but they're screaming about First Amendment rights."

He paused at the door. "One more thing. Is there a security system here? Cameras?" Gloria nodded slowly. "In some areas. The main exhibits, the lobby."

"I'll need access to those recordings." Gloria nodded and he left to grab the security footage and allowed Gloria to sit alone in her office. He said, "Don't disturb anything." Once the coast was clear, Gloria went underneath her coffee table and picked up the strange geode that Veronica left the other day. Now it was cracked open and Gloria could see the crystal and the swirling magma.

She could feel the heat, warm like a sauna, alluring like a drug. She put the stone inside her purse. She could hear it now. Not with her ears, but in her mind. The Atrox Stone was calling her. And part of her wanted to answer.

Hard Truths

Detective Meadows uploaded the museum's security footage to his desktop and started the playback, coffee going cold beside his keyboard. The timestamps told the story: 11:47 PM Sunday night, three men entered the museum through the loading dock. Professional. They knew where the cameras were, kept their faces down.

But something earlier caught his eye. He rewound to 6:42 AM Saturday morning. Dr. Shelley's car in the parking lot. She enters with another woman. Older, professional-looking. They enter through the side entrance. Dr. Shelley swipes her badge. "Computer, track subject's movement." The footage jumped between cameras. The two women went directly to the underground lab. The exact location the thieves had targeted. They remained there for forty-three minutes. No audio.

Meadows made notes. Dr. Shelley knew more than she'd admitted. He'd need to bring her back in for follow-up questions, but carefully. She'd lawyer up if he pushed too hard. He returned to the break-in footage. The three men moved through the museum efficiently at first. They accessed the lab, searched for something, grew increasingly agitated. Equipment was damaged. Drawers torn open.

Then the violence started. "What the hell?" Meadows leaned closer. The men turned on each other. One pulled a gun, shot another in the chest. The victim stumbled backward, clutching his wound, and disappeared into the supernatural wing. The two remaining men pointed weapons at each other. Their mouths moved. Arguing, screaming. But the audio was corrupted, just static. Then something emerged from the supernatural wing.

Meadows paused the video. "No fucking way."

The creature was roughly humanoid but wrong in every proportion. Too tall, too thin, joints bending at impossible angles. Its skin had a grayish-green tint even in the poor lighting. He'd seen drawings of creatures like this before. Years ago, when he was a rookie. An old case file from 1990. "Computer, analyze this frame. Cross-reference known databases." The AI processed for thirty seconds.

MATCH FOUND: Snog (Scandinavian cryptid, hostile classification)

Meadows played the rest of the footage. The shooter opened fire on the other suspect then that creature ambushed the shooter. The snog moved with horrifying speed.

The footage cut to black. System malfunction or deliberate sabotage, he couldn't tell. When it resumed three minutes later, the supernatural wing was empty except for blood and scattered body parts. Meadows sat back, rubbing his face. How the hell was he supposed to explain this to a judge? To his captain? He called his direct supervisor, Lt. Davis.

Twenty Minutes Later

Lieutenant Davis watched the footage twice without speaking. "The system confirms no digital alteration," Meadows said. "Whatever this is, it was there." Davis was in his fifties, old enough to remember things the department didn't talk about anymore. Miller's Quarry. The Coralyn Bay incidents of the '90s. The quiet policy changes that followed.

"We need to question Dr. Shelley again," Davis finally said. "But she's not a suspect yet. We play this carefully or she lawyers up and we get nothing." He stood. "Take me to the crime scene. And find someone else at the museum we can talk to. Someone who might be more forthcoming."

Bruce's Apartment 11:30 AM

Bruce's phone rang as he was trying to decide between screaming into a pillow or drinking before noon. "Mr. Brixby? This is Lieutenant Davis with Coralyn Bay PD. We'd like to ask you some questions about the museum. Would you be available this afternoon?" "Yeah. Sure. Whatever you need." After hanging up, Bruce immediately called Mark. "Mark, don't come to the museum this week."

"What's wrong?"

"I can't explain right now, but... just watch the news, okay? And stay home. Please." There was a long pause. "Alright, Bruce. But if you need me..." "I know. I'll call you."

The Devil's Maw Site Office 11:45 AM

Dr. Chalmers stared at her phone, hands shaking. "My God, Gloria, I didn't mean to... yes, yes, right away. No, no! I'll come over and pick it up myself." She grabbed her purse and car keys, nearly knocking over a coffee cup. "Dr. Chalmers, we need to talk." Jake stood in her doorway, backlit by harsh fluorescent lights. His expression was strange, almost serene. "Not now, Jake. Emergency."

"The stone," Jake said. "You took it to the museum." Veronica froze then asked "How did you..." "You shouldn't have done that." Jake stepped into the office. "It doesn't belong there."

"Jake, I need to go." Dr. Chalmers started to quickly gather some of her things. "The stone belongs here. In the cave. Where I found it." His voice was flat, emotionless. "You need to bring it back." Veronica pushed past him, nearly running to her car. Behind her, Jake smiled. Out in the distance, someone was watching them, wondering if they should get closer but something powerful was keeping them at bay.

Mark's House 2:15 PM

Roxy sat on the soft sofa; coffee cup cradled in both hands. She looked exhausted. Mark poured his own coffee and settled into his recliner, positioning it upright so he could give her his full attention. "It's okay, my dear. You can tell me anything."

"I don't know who else to go to." Roxy's voice was small. "Bruce is dealing with a crisis at work, and Chris... Chris is falling apart. I'm worried about him."

"What about Jake?"

Roxy stiffened. "What do you mean?"

"Yesterday at the barbecue, he seemed distant. Like he wanted to be there and somewhere else at the same time."

Roxy immediately defended her beau, "He's under a lot of pressure. He's working on this exciting project. He's mapping a new cave system in Crystal Valley." Mark nodded, taking a sip.

"Out by Miller's Quarry." Roxy casually mentioned while taking a sip of her own. Mark was motionless. The color drained from his face. He set down his cup carefully. "By where?"

"Miller's Quarry. Well, not in it exactly. A few miles away. Why? Do you know it?" Mark's expression changed. Sadness. Regret. Old grief rising to the surface.

"Yes. Too well." His voice was distant. "I don't know about any caves in Crystal Valley, but the locals always mentioned a place they avoided. Called it the Devil's Maw." Roxy realized she'd touched something painful. "I'm sorry, but... what happened at Miller's Quarry? I heard some kids were playing in the area and got killed. An accident?"

"No. Nothing like that." Mark was silent for a long moment, gathering himself. "There's a story to tell. I guess there's no time like the present." He took a breath. "I was young. Seven or eight. My brother and his friends always used to go out on their bikes. To the arcade, the gas station, just to have fun. It was a simpler time. I had a hard curfew, but Frankie was older. He had more freedom."

"I didn't know you had a brother," Roxy said softly.

"I don't talk about him much." Mark's hands tightened on his coffee cup. "Something happened that fall. Frankie and his friends got into trouble. Nothing simple like stealing a mascot or pulling pranks. Something serious." The front door opened. Bruce stepped in, saw Roxy's car in the driveway. "Hey Rox, I saw your car and wanted to…" He stopped and read the room. Mark gestured for him to sit.

Bruce settled onto the couch beside Roxy, and he was suddenly pulled into whatever was happening. "My brother and I liked monster movies," Mark continued. "Sci-fi, horror. If it had a monster or alien, we couldn't get enough. But that fall, Frankie found something. He changed. Became distant. Kept saying he was going to save the world one day."

Mark's voice grew quieter. "It was October 1990. Halloween was approaching. The old stories say that's when the gateways between the dead and living open. The wind picked up. This menacing howl. I saw the trees moving closer to the house. Their branches changed shape, like fingers reaching. My parents didn't believe me. But Frankie did. He went out and broke off branches to keep them away from our windows."

"Then one night, he tried to leave after 10 PM. I knew something was wrong. I was scared. What if the tree monsters came back? What if a morgrin got into the house? He promised me he'd take care of it. He told me to go back to bed, to keep my mouth shut. Said he was going to save the world."

Mark reached into his wallet and pulled out an old photograph. A young boy with a homemade slingshot. "I gave him this. My Bully Stopper. Just a slingshot I'd made, but it protected me when Frankie couldn't. I gave him all my marbles too. I knew if Frankie took it with him, it would protect him. That he'd come home."

Roxy's eyes filled with tears. "Oh, Markie. I'm so sorry." Mark smiled sadly. "Markie. That's what my brother used to call me." Mark fought back some hard tears. "Days went by. He never came home. People suspected the old couple down the street. East European immigrants with no children of their own. But their tragedy is for another day."

He stood, walked to the window. "It was November 11th when the police came. Said they'd found Frankie. I was too young to understand. They found his body and the bodies of his friends. The elderly couple too. And I tell you, they didn't do anything to my brother. Something else did." Bruce felt ice in his stomach.

"I heard Frankie talking in his sleep one night before it happened," Mark said. "He'd found something.

A cursed treasure. I don't remember if he said he had to break a spell or cast one, but it had something to do with that strange crystal he found. He said he had to take it somewhere safe to cast the spell. The only place any of us knew that was quiet and safe was Miller's Quarry."

Mark turned to face them. "Whatever he found, he felt it was necessary to destroy or at the very least hide it from whatever was looking for it. But something is after it, perhaps it's the keystone to unlocking some unholy power. My brother tried to stop it, almost did, now, I fear that thing is awakening, searching for it again." Mark stared out the window, lost in memory. "Mark..." Bruce started. Mark looked at the two young faces before him. "You know what the worst part is? Aside from losing my brother, people forgot."

"What do you mean?" Bruce asked.
"The police called it a gas explosion. The papers ran with it. Within a year, people stopped talking about it. Within five, it was just another tragedy. Within ten..." Mark shook his head. "Most people in Coralyn Bay don't even remember it happened." He leaned forward, his voice dropping. "And when people forget the magic, especially the dangerous kind, they stop knowing what to do when it comes back. They stop recognizing the signs. Stop taking precautions. Stop listening to the old warnings."

"My grandmother used to twist my ears," Mark said, touching the side of his head. "Change the channel, she'd say. When the nightmares came. When the shadows got too close. Simple magic. Protection magic. But who teaches that anymore? Who remembers?" Mark took a few steps away from the window. "They forgot what killed those children. Forgot what's buried in those caves. And now..." He looked back towards the window, towards the distant lights of Devil's Maw. "Now it's waking up again. And nobody knows what it is. Nobody knows what to do. I have a feeling that whatever killed my brother is back to finish the job."

Roxy felt a chill run down her spine. "So, what do we do?" Mark smiled sadly. "We remember. We stay vigilant. We don't let the world convince us that monsters are just stories." Mark took a second to gain his composure. He looked at his younger friends. "I meant what I said. You can come to my house anytime." His expression was kind but firm. "I'm glad you're here. But I can't help you unless you tell me what's going on."

Suddenly the TV turned on.

"*— breaking news from the Coralyn Bay Museum of Natural History. Police report that the bodies of three unidentified men were recovered from the scene. Authorities are investigating what they're calling a possible animal attack, though details remain scarce. More on this story as it develops.*"

The three of them sat in heavy silence. Finally, Bruce spoke. "I need to tell you about what happened at the museum."

Through the Fog

The Devil's Maw Site Office Monday Afternoon
Jake pulled into the campsite and noticed immediately that Dr. Chalmers's SUV was gone. The volunteers were setting up equipment for the next survey. Students checked their CaveScan drones, prepping for deployment. Something was off. Jake knocked on Dr. Chalmers's office door. It swung open at his touch; already ajar. The desk lamp was on low, casting long shadows. A coffee cup sat on the desk, still half-full, leaving a dark ring on some papers. Signs of a hasty departure. "Dr. Chalmers?" Jake stepped in and towards the back of the office.

"Dr. Chalmers will not be joining us today." said a voice in the darkness. Jake spun around. Mr. Suit stood in the doorway, blocking the exit. Jake hadn't heard him approach. He didn't hear footsteps, a door opening, anything. The man just appeared. "She called this morning," Mr. Suit continued smoothly. "Not feeling well. But she and I had a brief conversation about the project before she left. We have a proposition for you."

Jake looked at Mr. Suit and with a confident tone said, "I'm listening."

"Dr. Chalmers has to seek medical treatment that could take days or weeks. The project must continue, it is a major stipulation in the grant." Mr. Suit smiled; thin, professional, empty. "How would you like to assume leadership of the entire operation?"
"Why didn't she tell me herself?" Jake folded his arms and raised an eyebrow. Not missing a beat, Mr. Suit quickly retorted "Did you check your messages?"

Jake pulled out his phone. One missed call. One voicemail. He played the preview: "Jake, sorry to do this but something's come up that I need to handle. Can you take care of things while I'm gone? The Kingsmen rep will fill you in." Dr. Chalmers's voice. Her tone. Her cadence. "Okay," Jake said, sliding his phone back into his pocket. "I think your story checks out."

"Good." Mr. Suit pulled out a tablet and projected a holographic display. A combined 3D map of the cave system. Far more detailed than anything Jake's team had produced. "Then you'll complete the mapping. I want to know: is it possible for a person to access this chamber?" The antechamber. Starwound. "Our analysts believe it may contain rare minerals. Possibly artifacts of geological significance."

Jake studied the projection. The data was extensive; far beyond what his team had collected. Kingsmen must have been running their own surveys overnight. The topology suggested possible alternative access routes, but they'd be tight. Dangerous. "My team and I made it there last week, it is dark, but we didn't pick up any minerals or precious materials," Jake said. Mr. Suit used two fingers to rub his chin. Jake didn't trust him at all.

"That's because you don't have access to better equipment or personnel, we can provide that of course, think of it, as an addendum to the original grant. All that we require is for you and your team to use our equipment and allow some of our experienced spelunkers to join in any future explorations." Mr. Suit had casually closed the gap between them. "Just tell me whatever you need to make this happen; money is no object. But we get first claim on anything down there, no matter how trivial. Nothing leaves unless I say so." Mr. Suit's eyes never left Jake's face.

"You'll receive full academic credit, of course. This could fast-track you to a PhD program. I'm certain Dr. Chalmers and Dr. Chang would vouch for your work. And Kingsmen has... connections on various admissions boards. We could adjust your status accordingly." The forbidden fruit, offered on a silver platter. "In fact, we could take care of you and your team so that each of you graduates, debt-free and jobs in any of our companies. What do you say?" Mr. Suit extended a hand. Jake smirked and shook it. "When do we start?"

Mr. Suit noticed immediately that Jake's palm was rough. Not the normal calluses of manual labor, but something else. Like sandpaper mixed with broken glass. The texture made his skin crawl. He released Jake's hand "Immediately. I have my people bring in some new equipment. We will give you and your team some brief training today and tomorrow, let's go back to the antechamber."

"To the Starwound?" Jake asked.

"Yes, to Starwound" Mr. Suit confirmed.

"I wonder why it's called Starwound?" Jake asked as he looked at the holographic map. Mr. Suit turned it off "That's what we are going to find out". Jake walked out to talk to his team and give them an update. People in white jumpsuits started hauling in large boxes with expensive equipment. The volunteers looked confused at first. *Where was Dr. Chalmers?* They would ask. However, Jake's confidence won them over. Within minutes, he'd issued instructions to begin more human exploration of the deeper cave system. Mr. Suit returned to his private office and closed the door.

Kingsmen employed an army of specialists. Crypto-geologists. Voice artists who could imitate anyone after hearing a five-minute recording. Cleanup crews for situations that require... discretion. A cleanup crew would be needed soon. Dr. Chalmers's office would have to be sanitized. His phone buzzed. A message from his superior requesting an update. Mr. Suit typed one word: Done

He glanced out the window at Jake, now leading the team with the kind of intensity that came from corruption masquerading as ambition. The project was proceeding exactly as planned.

Two Weeks Later, sometime in October

Bruce's phone rang as he was getting dressed for work. "Bruce, it's Gilbert. Dr. Shelley wants to see us in her office this morning. Police finally cleared the scene. We're reopening in a few days."

"That's great! Wait, how's the foot traffic looking?" Bruce was busy washing his face.

"You'd be surprised. All the online chatter about the 'mysterious deaths' has attracted a new crowd. True crime enthusiasts. They're already taking photos outside, retracing the thieves' route from the Port Authority." Bruce felt conflicted. Good for business, morbid as hell. His phone buzzed again immediately after hanging up. It was Mark. "Hey Mark, how are you?" Bruce asked then he immediately smiled as he heard Mark's voice. Mark sounded warm and energized. "Much better now that we're allowed back at work. So, it's true, the museum's reopening soon?"

"Yeah, few days. I'm heading there now for a staff meeting."

"Good, good. Listen, the underground lab is still off-limits, right? But you have offsite storage?" Mark asked with increasing enthusiasm.

"We do. Why?"
"I'd like to examine some of the specimens you mentioned. The ones from Miller's Quarry. If that's possible."

"I'll find out and let you know." Bruce sprayed on some deodorant. "Perfect." Mark said. Bruce was about to hang up when he remembered something important. "Oh, and Mark, keep Wednesday night free. I'm taking you somewhere special. You'll love it." Mark smiled despite everything.

"Sounds good, Wednesday night is free. Call me later with the details." Mark replied, sounding much like a new kid who just made some friends. Bruce could feel this warm presence whenever he talked to him. "You got it, take care, bye!" Bruce ended the call and grabbed his jacket. October weather in Texas was unpredictable. At the last second, he pulled on his "Power Vest," a multi-pocketed utility vest with a breast pocket big enough for his phone and possibly a lighter or a vape.

Coralyn Bay Museum of Natural History 10:30 AM

The parking lot had a surreal quality. A few staff vehicles, some volunteers, and just as Gilbert had warned, true crime buffs wandering around with cameras and notebooks. Some of them were mapping the thieves' probable approach route. Everyone's a detective. Everyone's Sherlock Holmes. Bruce went through the new security checkpoint (metal detectors now, after the incident) and headed upstairs. As he passed Gilbert's office, a voice called out. "Over here."

Bruce poked his head in. Dr. Shelley sat in a chair looking frazzled. Gilbert stood at his workstation with a spectroscope, his back to the door. "Remarkable," Gilbert muttered. "Gosh-darn remarkable." He noticed Bruce and waved him in. "Close the door. Look at this. Tell me what you see." Bruce peered through the spectroscope.

A dark purple crystal, cut and polished. Inside, something that looked like glowing magma pulsed and moved. But at the center, a darkness that seemed to pull the light inward, swallowing it. "Boss, this is amazing! How did you make this?" Dr. Shelley's voice was tight. "Bruce, sit down. There's something I need to tell you." Bruce pulled up a chair, positioning it to face her. She looked exhausted. Eyes red-rimmed, hands clasped tightly in her lap. She kept glancing at the wall behind Gilbert, then at the door behind Bruce. Never meeting anyone's eyes.

"A few days ago, right before the break-in, a friend of mine from the university came to see me. She asked me to analyze this object." She gestured toward the spectroscope. "If you study it long enough, you'll notice it has an unusual energy variance. Not radioactive. Something else. And if you watch it carefully, it seems to change shape. But the crystal itself, the magma inside... they stay the same."
Bruce and Gilbert exchanged glances.

"I know it sounds impossible," Dr. Shelley continued, "but I've never seen anything like this. No one has. And I think..." Her voice dropped. "I think someone is trying to get it. The break-in. I don't think those men were after anything in our exhibits. I think they were after this." Gilbert examined the crystal again through the spectroscope. "There's nothing in any catalog to suggest an object like this has been documented before. Where did your colleague find it?"

"It was found in the Devil's Maw." Dr. Shelley immediately answered.

Bruce's stomach dropped. Jake's site.

"I think I know why you're sensing that variance," Gilbert continued. "There are cracks in the crystal. There is a major fracture here, and smaller ones radiating out. Someone tried to break it, probably thinking the magma inside was real. But it could be something else. A sealed container, maybe, or a prison for some evil spirit." Gilbert made a slight laugh at his bad joke. "Why would anyone try to break it?" Bruce asked. "If it's one of a kind, wouldn't it be more valuable intact?"

"Unless," Gilbert said thoughtfully, "there are more of them. If it came from the Devil's Maw, maybe there's a whole deposit." Dr. Shelley's expression shifted. Something flickered in her eyes. Yes. There must be more of them. The thought felt intrusive. Not quite her own. "Gilbert, could I have a moment with Bruce?" "Certainly." Gilbert excused himself, taking the spectroscope with him.

After the door closed, Dr. Shelley leaned forward. "Do you have any friends in the geology department? Anyone working at the Devil's Maw site?" "As a matter of fact, I do. Jake Dawson." Bruce was trying to read Dr. Shelley, but she was playing her cards close to the chest. "Good. I need a huge favor. But only if you're comfortable with it." Bruce could see the desperation in her eyes. Whatever was happening, Dr. Shelley was in trouble. And she needed help.

"I need you to take this back to the Devil's Maw." Her words came out in a rush. "You can put it anywhere. You can bury it, hide it, I don't care. But it needs to go back. And nobody can know you have it. Nobody can see you returning it." Bruce studied her face. The fear there was real. She hadn't stolen this thing. She was trying to get rid of it. Like it was cursed. He walked to the desk and picked up the wrapped crystal. It felt warm in his hands. Natural, almost comfortable. Like putting on a familiar glove. "Sure thing" Bruce said while holding on it. Its glow felt invasive for a second.

"Thank you." Dr. Shelley's shoulders sagged with relief. "Don't worry about Gilbert. I'll handle everything on this end. Just... do whatever you have to do."
"I've got this." Bruce tucked the wrapped stone into his vest pocket and left. Dr. Shelley followed him out moments later, locking Gilbert's office behind her. Neither of them noticed the painting on Gilbert's wall. It hadn't been there before. A dark oil painting in an ornate frame: an exaggerated face with small, beady eyes set in huge dark sockets. A forced grin showing jagged, uneven teeth. And if anyone had been watching carefully, they might have noticed that the painted eyes followed Bruce as he walked away.

Wednesday Night, downtown Coralyn Bay

Bruce pulled into the parking lot near Julie's with Mark in the passenger seat. "This is something we should've done earlier" Bruce said, killing the engine. Mark stepped out and looked at the neon signs, the crowd spilling onto the patio. "Wow. I remember when this place used to be Raul's. Must've been twenty years plus ago." Mark felt like he was stepping out of a time machine while Bruce grinned. "Before my time, old man."

Inside, the place was packed. Music pounded from speakers; modern stuff mixed with classic rock. The center area was well-lit and lively, but it got darker toward the back booths. Laughter, conversations, the smell of fried food and beer. Mark felt a little out of place among so many young people, but the energy was infectious. A random college girl walked past and asked him, "What's your major?"

Mark chuckled. "Retirement."
"Over here!" Bruce called, leading the way through the crowd.

Roxy and Chris had already claimed their usual booth. The moment Roxy saw Mark, her face lit up. She bounced to her feet, waving her hands like an excited puppy. Mark walked over and gave her a hug. She squeezed him tight. Roxy wanted to make sure that Mark knew that he was part of their tribe. Chris had a mouthful of onion rings and tried to swallow them quickly to give Mark a proper greeting.

Mark raised his hand. "Don't you dare rush good onion rings on my account."
Chris grinned, still chewing, and he shook Mark's hand. "So, this is where you blow off steam after a hard day?"
Mark settled into the booth, Bruce on one side, Roxy sliding in on the other. "You've got to try the Jalapeño Bombers," Chris said. "They're to die for."

Mark picked up the menu and pulled out his reading glasses. Then, with a theatrical flourish, he produced a fake pipe and pretended to smoke it while reading. "Wow, Professor Martinez over here," Roxy teased. "You know Mark, if I was a few years older..."
Mark looked up over his glasses. "If my hips were a little bit stronger..."

"Ahhh!" Roxy dissolved into giggles. Bruce put his arm around Mark's shoulders and squeezed. "Get whatever you want tonight. We're taking care of you."
Mark smiled and signaled for the server. "Hey, what about Jake?" he asked Roxy. Her expression shifted. Something between disappointment and relief. "Working late. He might join us later, but no promises."

"He's working on a once-in-a-lifetime discovery," Mark said gently. "These things take time, patience, and a good support network." Roxy nodded. "But at least I have you" and she put her arm around Mark. "My dear," Mark said, his voice warm, "I will always be your silver medal." Roxy squeezed his arm, surprised by how solid it still was, and smiled. Mark excused himself briefly to speak with the server, adding something to their already impressive order.

"Now Chris," Mark said, returning with a massive beer stein, "tell me the latest."
"Well, Dr. Cox gave us our assignments. Should keep me busy for the rest of the year, but it's all building toward next semester's final. It's all rhetoric and presentation. A good lawyer has to control the narrative."

"And tell a good story," Mark added. "It's not all about memorizing the law. It's about application. Weaving it together in a way people can understand, especially if you're facing a jury pulled from the street."

"Exactly!" Chris leaned in so Mark could hear him over the noise. "I'm hoping to clerk for the Supreme Court someday. Or maybe work at the Library of Congress."

"You can do anything you want," Mark said. "You have a sharp mind and a brave soul. If research makes you happy, go for it. But if you want to fight for truth and justice..." He tapped Chris's chest. "Listen to yourself. You have that inner strength. But you must give yourself permission to use it. Not me, not your teachers, not your parents. It has to be you."
Chris nodded slowly, feeling something shift inside him. Like chains he didn't know he was wearing had just loosened. The server arrived with appetizers: loaded potato wedges with cheese and bacon, extra-large

Jalapeño Bombers, a bowl of chili gravy, and burger sliders.

Mark picked up a potato wedge, mashed it slightly with his fingers, placed a Bomber on top, and dunked the whole thing in chili gravy. "Watch this." He swallowed it in one gulp.

"No way!" Chris was genuinely impressed.

"Try it, Roxy. Bruce. Come on, Chris. I know you're down." Mark was already assembling another potato-peno creation or a Martinez Slammer as he calls it. "Take it easy, Markie," Bruce cautioned. "You don't want to die of cholesterol poisoning." Mark slammed down another potato-peno with satisfaction. "Bruce, I want to die happy. To die full. And in good spirits." He raised his beer stein. "We only live once. Make the ride count!"

The server brought over a small soda and placed it by Mark.

"You're drinking beer and a soda?" Chris asked. "No. The beer's for dipping my potatoes in." Mark raised his soda glass. "Us cokies gotta stick together." He and Chris tapped glasses in a small toast. Bruce smiled, taking a swig of his own beer. A Beach Boys' song was playing in the background, either "Kokomo" or "Chasin' The Sky." That's why he loved this place. A little modern, a little retro, all fun.

The Devil's Maw, Crystal Valley Same Evening

Jake finished accounting for all personnel and equipment. Today had been productive: mounds of new data, mapped new pipelines to the antechamber, however, no precious stones, gems, or minerals were found, yet. Jake scanned some of the pictures taken inside the antechamber. He knew just the person to share them with. Mr. Suit approached from the administrative trailer. "Sending the daily reports now,"

Jake said, tapping on his tablet. "I think you'll find them most satisfying."

Mr. Suit pulled out his mobile device and unfolded it to reveal three screens. "Puzzling. Three paths converging to the antechamber. Is that water?" Jake pulled up the latest map. "Yes. We noted the best three possible routes. One's a tight squeeze, even for the CaveScan Drones. I'm hoping to lead another expedition into the antechamber in a couple of days, but I'll need additional equipment."

"Can you mark the paths? Lights, rope, something for navigation?" Mr. Suit asked while studying the latest batch of data.

"I don't recommend going in at night. Temperature drops significantly. It's steep, jagged. Someone could twist an ankle or fall into an unmapped crevice. No way to extract an injured person yet." Jake scrolled to a specific item on his requisition list. "But there's an alternative. Here." Mr. Suit's eyes widened slightly. "Noctilium? That's a tall order."
Noctilium: bioluminescent material harvested from glowworms and fireflies, both natural and lab grown. It created sustainable light sources for extended cave exploration. Extremely expensive.

"Yes," Jake said with absolute confidence. "But I'm sure Mr. Kingsley will approve. After all, we're about to make the greatest discovery since Columbus." Mr. Suit was about to dismiss him when something on the sonograph caught his attention. "Is that a lake? And what's this massive obstruction?" Jake met his eyes directly. There was something in his gaze. An intensity that made Mr. Suit uncomfortable. "Whatever's down there," Jake said, "it will be the gateway to riches beyond imagination. An entire universe. Everything we could ever want. But first, we need to open the door."

The sonograph image was blurry but unmistakable: the antechamber held constructed columns adorned with strange carvings. A vast underground lake. And rising from its center, a mountain. But wrong. Crooked. Bent at impossible angles. Mr. Suit stared at the image, feeling something cold settle in his stomach. This wasn't just a geological formation. Someone, or something, had built this place. And somewhere was the prize he was looking for, the rarest of all gemstones, The Sovereign Cut. "I'll forward this to Mr. Kingsley immediately," he said. "He'll want to lay claim before anyone else discovers it. Or names it." Jake smiled and for a second, didn't feel like himself.
Julie's Bar & Grill 11:15 PM

"Damn, I'm stuffed." Chris unbuttoned his shirt and loosened his belt. "Good food, good fun, good company." Mark raised another cherry soda in a toast. "Here, here!" Roxy held up her fifth margarita, slightly unsteady. Bruce nursed his last beer, glancing at Mark. He wanted to ask him about the stone. He needed Mark's expertise. But tonight, had been so perfect. He didn't want Mark to think he only came around when he needed something.

Tonight, he'd just wanted to give something back. To create a good memory. He remembered something Mark had said at the barbecue: "One day, you'll do something, say something, see someone for the last time and not know it."

Well, tonight he was making memories. And it wouldn't be the last time he saw his friends. The door opened as an old song from the 1980's called *"Burnin' in the Third Degree"* played when Jake walked in. He's always the last to arrive. He kissed Roxy and fist-bumped Mark. Chris had begun sliding into a food coma, his eyes half-closed. "Time to go, buddy." Jake helped Chris to his feet. "No, no. I'm not tired. Not tired at all," Chris slurred. "Dude, your pants are falling down and you're slurring your words."

"Did I?" Chris held up his empty glass. "I asked the server for the Tom Petty Special." Roxy's eyes went wide. "The Tom Petty Special?!"
"Yeah. Why?" Chris said with the dopiest face he ever made, so far. "Dude," Bruce said, "that has whiskey in it."

"No. No, no, no. I don't think... drink. Drinking is bad for the blood and the brains!" Chris stood up. His pants immediately slipped down several inches. "Yeah, it's time for that boy to go home." Mark tried to hold back laughter. "Boy's over here showing everyone the Moon over Miami." Bruce and Jake looked at each other, then both realized Chris was showing his butt crack. "Alright, party's over." Jake scooped Chris up with one arm. "I'll take him home. Come on Roxy."

"How did you get here?" Mark asked Jake. "Caught a ride. Don't worry about it, Pops. We got this." Jake smiled. That familiar, easy grin. "I'll see you later."

"Hey, Jake, wait up." Bruce stood.
Jake turned around almost unnaturally "What's up?"

"I've got something to talk about, super important and I need a huge favor." Bruce was always bashful when it came to asking for help.

"Come by my new office." Jake's grin widened. "I'm project manager now. Swing by tomorrow or the day after and we'll get you settled. But right now, I've got laundry to deliver. Later." Jake carried Chris toward the exit, Roxy following behind, laughing. Bruce looked for the server to pay for the tab. When he finally flagged her down, she smiled. "Your bill's been taken care of. The gentleman with the glasses paid before he left." Bruce turned. Mark was already at the door, waving goodbye to Roxy as she followed Jake out. Bruce shook his head with a half-smile. He owed Mark big time.

Obsidian Ember

Late Wednesday Night, Jake's Apartment.

One of life's greatest pleasures is being at home in comfortable clothes, relaxing in your own bed. Roxy was enjoying exactly that, wearing one of Jake's old T-shirts. It made her feel comfortable and safe. Jake was in the bathroom washing up after a long day in the caves. They'd just dropped Chris at his parents' house after his drunken Moon over Miami incident at Julie's. Roxy smiled to herself. "Project Manager," she said quietly, feeling proud. Jake was really doing it. Following his dreams. Making something of himself. She picked up the prism Mark had given her and began playing with it, fumbling it through her fingers, holding it up to the light. "Whoa!"

Through the prism, she could see things invisible to the naked eye. Dust motes in the air catching light like glitter. Traces of energy, maybe. Or it was just her imagination. She held it up to a book on her nightstand. Her own fingerprints appeared on the cover. An eyelash or two. And small track marks. Oh no, something with multiple legs had crawled across it. Sitting in your comfortable bed is priceless. Having something with fuzzy legs scurry across your feet in the middle of the night is terrifying.

Roxy peeked around, opened a few drawers. Nothing. She put the prism away, but a thought occurred to her: What would happen if she looked at Jake through it? "Everything alright in there?" Jake called from the bathroom. "Yeah, just looking for my book," Roxy lied, her face crinkling. Good thing about having a big strong man around: he could deal with the creepy crawlies.

Jake emerged from the bathroom. Freshly brushed teeth, tight tank top, basketball shorts. Roxy half-expected him to want sex immediately. He'd been ravenous lately, demanding her attention in ways that felt less like affection and more like... hunger. But tonight, he just wanted to talk. He sat down next to her and just started talking as if he wanted to tell someone, anyone about his day. Roxy sat with her legs folded.

He went on about his day, his promotion, his dreams for the future. As the story went on, they lay down next to each other. Roxy curled up next to him, looking up at his face, hanging on every word. She had her own hopes and dreams. But at this moment, if he'd asked her to give them all up, to dedicate herself entirely to building his future...
She would have said yes.
"Enough about me." Jake turned to her and looked into her eyes. "Tell me about your day."

Roxy began talking. Really talking. And to her surprise, Jake listened. Really listened. Hanging on every word like she did for him. Maybe that's all he'd needed. A little release. A little normalcy. Because until tonight, Roxy had been worried she was becoming less of a partner and more of an object. A possession. She didn't like her new pet name, "Ornament," but after everything that's happening right now, she could let it slide. For now.

Bruce's Apartment

Bruce got home after dropping Mark off. He'd promised to treat him to breakfast on Friday at the Pancake Hut. Nothing fancy. He just wanted to spend time together. He turned on the TV. *Great.* He'd left it on a news channel.

"…Police are investigating another wild animal attack. Fourteen-year-old Jackson Bullock, a Kingston High School student, was walking home near the 5200 block of Old San Jacinto Road when police believe the attack occurred. The boy is in critical condition at Lady of Whispering Hope Hospital. Authorities urge anyone with information to…"

Bruce turned it off. Too much gravity to end a good night. He went to his bedroom and opened the top drawer of his dresser. There it was. The stone. The Atrox. Bruce stared at it. The strange crystal with magma flowing inside. Heat escaped from the cracks in its surface, warming his hand even through the cloth wrapping. The glow…the longer he held it, the longer he stared at it…the glow felt like it was seeping into his very soul.

Why would anyone want this?
Why did he still have it?

He should throw it away. Toss it in the bay. Let it sink to the bottom and be forgotten. But he couldn't let it go. In fact, the more he thought about getting rid of it, the stronger another thought became: Break it. Shatter it into a thousand pieces. Sell the fragments. Purple obsidian crystal with magma. Make rings, necklaces, jewelry. Unique. Priceless. It would make you rich. Give you anything. Everything you ever wanted.

"No."

Bruce shoved the stone into an old sock and pushed it to the back of the drawer. The glow began to fade and for a moment, Bruce felt regret that the glow couldn't stay. He lay down on his couch. He didn't want to sleep in his bed tonight. Not with that thing in his room.

Jake's Apartment, later that night.

Roxy fell into a deep sleep, her lips moving as if tasting something or speaking words she couldn't remember. Jake held her in his arms at first, but as the night wore on, they turned away from each other. A lump of old pillows and comforters built up between them. Jake hogged the blankets. Roxy was exposed. Cold. And then...

She found herself at a tropical resort.

The architecture was strange. Tropical and Mediterranean influences that should have clashed but somehow blended beautifully. Palm trees and white stone columns. Warm ocean breeze carrying the scent of jasmine. She stood at a bar, looking at herself in the mirror behind the bottles. Her hair was done up elaborately. She wore a red dress, elegant, flowing, like a traditional Spanish flamenco dancer's gown. She looked stunning.

She was alone.

She looked around for Jake but didn't see him. The strange thing was... it didn't bother her. Tonight, she felt different. Confident. Powerful. Like she was the one hunting.

Time passed. People came and went from the bar. She sat at a table, nursing a delicious drink. When she raised her glass to order another, the server simply brought her something new. "What's this?"

"Obsidian Ember," the server said, setting down a glass filled with a dark purple liquid that it was almost black. "Compliments of the gentleman."

Roxy turned around, expecting Jake.

It wasn't Jake.

The man looked to be in his forties, but he carried himself younger. Strong build, broad shoulders. More pepper than salt in his hair. He looked powerful. Distinguished and commanding, with a mischievous smile that would make a fox proud. His eyes.

Those were his lure.

Roxy's first instinct was to refuse the drink, to turn him away. But she'd already taken a sip, and the taste...Warm. Spicy. Intoxicating.
The man took that sip as a green light. He approached with earned confidence. A man who got what he wanted. And he wanted her.

Don't look at his eyes. Avoid them. Be firm but polite. "Hello." His voice was strong, calm, and seductive. "So, how's the drink? It's a local recipe. Not made anywhere else in the world."
Oh no. His voice.
"Can I join you?" the stranger insisted.

"Actually, I'm waiting for someone. My boyfriend." Roxy turned her head, but she could see him in her peripheral vision. He was older but attractive. One of those men who got better with age. "I understand." He didn't move away. "Hopefully he won't keep you waiting too long. If you change your mind, I'll be outside. There's a magnificent view. You can see the sparkling sea, listen to the music, soak in the day or night. Whichever pleases you."

Roxy wanted to get up and leave. But she wanted more of that drink. It wasn't just intoxicating. It was addictive. The more she drank, the sweeter it became. "What's the name of this drink again?" She held up her glass, almost like offering a toast. The gentleman said smoothly. "Obsidian Ember."

He smiled. "I normally don't impose. If your boyfriend arrives, I'll excuse myself. I'm sure he won't be jealous of someone like me. It takes a special kind of woman to appreciate a fine vintage bottle of wine like myself. Besides, perhaps my company will draw him closer."

Damn, he's good.

Against her better judgment, Roxy motioned to the empty seat.

"Marlowe." He extended his hand.

"Roxy." She shook it, careful not to turn her hand so he could kiss the top of it. Marlowe's smile widened. *Game on.* He sat and the server brought him a glass of wine. Dark red, almost black, like he was drinking wine from Hades' personal cellar. Strange spices came off it in waves.

"So." Marlowe maintained eye contact. "What brings you out here?" Roxy had no idea where she was. "Vacation. Checking out the hot spots."

"Ah." Marlowe could tell she was lying. "Nyxara has its share of tourists. A little hideaway from the rest of the world."

Nyxara. Where am I?

"Drink," Marlowe said, raising his glass. "Obsidian Ember is best when it's served fresh." His words seemed to echo, giving off a seductive vibration that made a woman's skin tingle. Roxy looked down at her glass. No matter how much she drank, it remained full. Something called to her. The drink tasted sweeter with every sip. It made her blood feel like it was glowing. But she shouldn't. She should get up and leave. *Dammit, Jake, where are you?*

"You can do whatever you please," Marlowe said. His voice was soothing. Hypnotic. Comforting. Roxy's fingers traced the rim of her glass. Even her fingertips wanted another sip.

She looked at Marlowe. He took a drink of his wine; eyes fixed on her. Making her uncomfortable. Not in a threatening way, but in a way that made her want to stay. To listen. To lean closer. For a moment, Roxy was glad Jake wasn't here. For some strange reason, his absence made her feel free. More alive.

Music started playing. Softly at first. A haunting melody, like a siren luring sailors to their doom. But this song was meant for her. It made the hairs on the back of her neck stand up. The tingle traveled down her spine to her fingertips, still tracing the rim of the glass. Her lips were parched. Her tongue ached for another taste. The colors in the Obsidian Ember pulled at her gaze. The warm, glowing feeling in her body was fading.

She wanted it back.

The music grew louder, maintaining its slow tempo. Hypnotic. Seductive.

What's the harm? Just one more drink.

She raised the glass to her lips and tasted the sweet Obsidian Ember. She felt excited. Like she was committing a forbidden act. But forbidden by whom? She was having a drink. One drink with a stranger. With Marlowe. The glow returned. The excitement. The tingle spreading through her entire body. She felt alive. Truly alive. She could do anything. Anything she wanted. She didn't answer to anyone. She was her own person. Marlowe showed his teeth when he smiled.

Oh God, he's handsome.

Marlowe stood up and, without a word, extended his hand. The music shifted. The sirens were calling out to her. At this moment, Roxy had the choice either to listen to the sirens' call or ignore it. It's time. Roxy took his hand. He pulled her close, and they danced. At least, Roxy thought they were dancing. Every move he made was deliberate, drawing her away from her table into another room with an open ceiling.

Stars blazed overhead.

He had one hand at the base of her back, the other holding her hand. His grip was firm but not overpowering. His eyes worked some kind of magic, trying to place her under a spell. She resisted. What she was doing felt wrong. But it also felt right. The song continued to play, the melody weaving temptation into the air, each note was haunting yet soothing.
Marlowe held Roxy at arm's length, but Roxy could feel the attraction, the chemistry. Marlowe looked into her eyes. His eyes, strong and mysterious, she could see a deep abyss, yet it was filled with starlight. Roxy's will was weakening. All he had to do was speak, ask her anything, and her inhibitions would cease.

She felt warmth and the darkness in his eyes; something was calling to her…
"I can give you everything," he said.
"Everything..." she repeated.
"I can give you anything," he said.
"Anything," she repeated.
"Or nothing," he said.

She didn't repeat those last words. The glowing, tingling feeling ran through her entire body. Was it the drink? The power in his voice? The magic in his eyes? The more they danced, the more time slowed. They were alone now. The stars their only witnesses.
No more excuses. It wasn't the drink. It wasn't him. It was her choice. Her decision.

The music continued, notes seeming to emerge from the walls themselves. Roxy had a choice to make. She looked down at the floor, then up at the stars. Marlowe waited. Patient. As if he had all the time in the world and more. "Anything," she whispered.
Marlowe looked into her eyes. His body felt warm. Warmer than hers. A strong desire came over her. She

wanted his warmth around her. Inside her. He leaned in for the kiss. In that moment, all resistance vanished. All doubt. All hesitation.
Gone.

The room emptied. Everyone was gone. The music faded into darkness. His hand slid lower down her back. His other hand moved to her dress. She felt a sudden chill as her dress slid down her body and pooled at her ankles. Only the stars witnessed what happened next.

Roxy gave herself to the dark. It felt good, it felt right.

The Exchange

Jake woke up in the middle of the night to use the bathroom. He was on autopilot but had enough sense to lift up the seat. *Oh shit!* He told himself that he better close the seat after he's done. Roxy doesn't like it when he leaves it up. She stumbles in the bathroom half asleep sometimes and if she falls in, he will never hear the end of it.

He stumbled back to bed but noticed Roxy twisting and turning on her side. She was murmuring and twitching. Jake was half asleep. He needed his rest, but he swore she was curling her lips as if she wanted to be kissed. *What kind of dreams are you having?* Roxy seemed really into whatever she was dreaming. He tried to run his fingers on her side, but she wasn't having it and swatted him away. *Huh, she must have painted her nails.* Roxy was too preoccupied with her dream. Jake had no energy to try to have sex with or fondle his girlfriend, so he tried to go back to sleep.

Jake laid down and stared at the ceiling. His mind racing with thoughts, both academic and impure. The more he worked, the better he felt. The more distracted he was, the more in control he felt. But at the same time, the more he worked, the more he felt something was taking over him. *What did Bruce wanna talk about?*

The cold air kept his impulses at bay. He was losing his strength, and he could feel a pair of soft hands, like tissue paper, rubbing his temples. "Go back to sleep, there's nothing to worry about." *That voice!*

It was his grandma, five years passed on. She would rub his temples whenever he had nightmares and then gently twist his ears to "change the channel" if he was having a bad dream. Like a shadow, she hovered over him. "Go back to sleep, do not let your mind bother you. I'll take care of everything."

Something inside Jake told him not to go to sleep. The more he slept, the more he felt like something was trying to take control of him. There was something around him, a strange force or spirit. It felt like it was trying to get inside him like a thief breaking into a building. It was getting stronger and Jake did not know if he had the strength to repel it.

Jake, as a boy, heard stories of evil spirits that would look for victims at night. They would feed on your impulses, your desires and in time, take control of your mind and body. He remembered a dream he had when he was a little kid. He was lost and everywhere he turned, dark tunnels would appear that tried to pull him into the darkness. He would try to run away but the darkness would follow him.

"Look at me now" Jake thought as he tossed and turned. "Afraid of the dark yet I work exploring caves, deep underground, away from the light". The strange irony in his life choices. Many thoughts raced through his mind, and he felt as if something was stealing his energy. He tried to quiet his mind and suddenly, a dark tunnel appeared before him with a faint light at the end of it. The tunnel was quiet. Jake decided to go down the tunnel. He walked slowly and as he walked deeper into the tunnel, all the noise and his anxieties were pushed away until it was far behind him.

He reached the end of the tunnel and arrived at the edge of a dark forest, a stone path ahead of him. "Don't be afraid, the path less traveled yields the greater reward."

He walked down the path until it became lost to him. He was confused but compelled to keep walking.

He could hear something moving, getting closer. There was no turning back. "Over here, quick!" A voice. He couldn't tell if that was his grandma, Roxy, or someone else.

He moved quickly. The tree branches seemed to lower themselves, trying to stop him. He pushed through, breaking as many branches as he could. He was tired of people getting in his way, tired of self-doubt, objection, always having to prove himself. These are secrets he never told anyone. He was more than an athlete, more than a face. He had a mind and feelings.

"I am the master of my destiny, the hero of my story. I will marry my queen, and I will treat her with more respect. You hear me! YOU HEAR ME OUT THERE!" He shouted. "Yes, it has to be temptation, a bad spirit," he told himself. "I will beat you! Hear me demon! I will beat you!"

Jake thought about his behavior lately: ditching a mentor and taking her spot, treating his girlfriend like a sex object, like an ornament to be displayed and used. No longer. The dark forest cleared and he could see a lake, dark and mysterious. A canoe was on the shore. He took it and rowed towards the other side, to the Crooked Mountain. There, he knew, his unseen enemy awaited. Something was trying to invade his mind and spirit, a dark force. Jake decided to take it head on. Fight it on its own turf if he had to.

The distance was greater than he could imagine but he made it, his muscles burning from all the effort. He took the oar and walked up the path. He saw columns and pillars with a strange language written on them. He could see a light up ahead, in some deranged temple. "Come to me," a voice said.

"Oh my God!"

Jake saw a strange 'man' on top of Roxy. She was bound by her wrists and ankles. She gasped as she struggled. Immediately, Jake attacked her assailant. He struck him as hard as he could, breaking the oar. Jake took the broken oar and got on top of the 'man' and stabbed him repeatedly in his chest. He felt the 'man's' blood splash on him. "Never! You will never touch her again! NEVER!" Jake was surprised at himself. How quickly he came to anger, how easy it was for him to kill another person. It felt natural. It felt good.

The deed was done. He ran to Roxy, but she was not there, just her restraints. He felt the 'blood' stains on his face and chest, but it was more like sludge or a tarlike substance. He heard a scream coming from the other side of the temple, leading towards a descending staircase.

"ROXY!" he shouted.

He ran as fast as he could, gliding down the stairs, past spider webs that tried to stop him. He found a torch and burned them. A nest of spiders approached and many of them tried to repair the webs, not to catch Jake, but to stop him. Jake paused for a moment; he looked at the spiders. They had this innocence to them, and he had a weird feeling as if they were trying to help not hinder him.

"No, it's a trick." Jake started to light the webs, and they easily caught on fire. Some of the spiders went towards him and without hesitation, he burnt them as well. They screamed as they fled, but their scream sounded like children. *This isn't right, what have I done?* He saw a purple mist approach him. He ran further downstairs into a dark hallway. Jake knew he was inside some strange building. He could see broken windows and the building was surrounded by magma or some other infernal fire. He flew down the hallway, ignoring his pain, his fatigue, his shame of his Earthly actions.

He reached another section of some underground dungeon and saw many rooms. Jake kicked down as many doors as he could until he found one that he heard Roxy's voice. With all his might, he kicked down that door and saw his Roxy. Her feet and arms were chained up. "I will get you out of here!" He promised. "I am so sorry about how I've been acting lately. I promise never to be like that again. Please forgive me." He used his bare hands to break open her restraints.

She was free and she threw her arms and legs around him to embrace him. "We got to go," Jake said, but Roxy would not let him go. "Look, I love you and all, but we really got to go!" Roxy pulled back. Her eyes were gone. In their place, starlight pearls in sunken, rotting eye sockets. "You are not going anywhere my darling, welcome home."

Roxy's skin peeled off her face, her body became a blob of organs, and her bones molded themselves into restraints. This Dark Roxy pinned him down to the ground.

Jake's own body betrayed him, and he saw his flesh and muscle pulling themselves away from his skeleton. His mind was intact. Someone stood over him; it was that man who attacked Roxy. He took his flesh and muscles like a suit, draped it over his right arm. "I shall take everything and you shall have nothing but pain."

Its eyes, bright like lava. Its skin like the void between spaces. It stretched out his new suit and Jake could see his own face covering this mysterious entity. It was not a mere demon. It was something more ancient, more powerful. And it was trapped here like he was, but this evil being is using him to carry out its perverse will.

Jake saw this thing wearing his face, it looked just like him! His friends, his family, Roxy! *Oh God! NO! NO!* 'Jake' smiled back at himself.

Jake tried to scream but he had no voice. Darkness crept over him as this cosmodial entity poured dirt over him. Jake tried to scream, he tried to move, but he had no strength, no way to warn Roxy. His muscles were gone, his throat, and then his eyes followed.
Dear God, what is happening?

He was already dead and sealed in this sinister land. Darkness took him and pulled him deep into a void where the remains of his soul was exiled. The last thing Jake heard were the cries of this horrific entity's previous victims howling like a chorus of endless suffering.
Roxy woke up from her dream.

It felt so real. She remembered the taste of Obsidian Ember on her lips. The warmth of her forbidden lover's hands on her body. The stars overhead. And something else, a feeling she couldn't name. Like being claimed.

Roxy went to the bathroom and splashed water on her face. It felt so real, so... good. Her nails! Both her finger and toenails had this dark purple color on them. She took a nail clipper and trimmed them. The color looked permanent. She grabbed some nail polish remover, but nothing worked.

Roxy looked at her reflection in the mirror. Her eyes, her lips, and even her hair had this slight purplish hue. She decided to take a shower and while she felt refreshed, the slight coloration remained but looked natural. Yet somehow, as Roxy stared at her own reflection, she kind of liked it.

She turned off the lights and went back to the bedroom. She stopped for a moment.

Jake lay in bed, fully clothed with socks on. For a split second, he looked different. Gray, sunken, desiccated. Like a mummy.

She blinked.

Jake was fine, sleeping peacefully, his chest gently rising up and down. Normal, alive. *I'm losing it*, she whispered to herself. She tried to sleep but she couldn't stop looking at her nails. Purple obsidian with faint glitter that sparkled like starlight. The nails that were trimmed grew back almost instantly.

The Bargain

Late Thursday Night, Crystal Valley by the Maw
The worksite was quiet and the only sound was the rustling of the trees in the wind. Kingsmen Security guards patrolled the worksite, armed and ready for anything. These were not normal security guards. Each of them had prior law enforcement or military training, each of them had seen action. Each of them secretly wished someone would try something.

The guards moved in groups of three with a fourth watching from a remote area. Someone was always scanning the area. Ever since Dr. Chalmers removed an item, Mr. Suit wanted to know if anything moved or left the location. Whether there was a food delivery or a student hauling their gear from the muster location. Mr. Suit wanted to know everything.

Eyes in the dark, far away. This mysterious figure had to move slowly. The security guards moved in a pattern but to the untrained eye, it appeared random. A mysterious figure moved quietly in the dark. Something had caught its attention. The figure, wearing a special cloak to cover their bright orange vest, blended in with the trees and the very fabric of nature itself.

Tonight, something had happened to some of the trees. The figure moved slowly and reached their destination. The trees had wounds, several in fact from different sources. The figure reached out and traced some of the circular holes: bullet holes. Sap poured out like blood. The trees were wounded and needed attention. The figure watched as the security guards left their assigned area. This was their chance.

The figure removed her hood of her cloak to get a better look at the tree's wounds. It was more than just sap pouring out. Her eyes glittered like starlight as she traced the wider, open wounds. Something bit the trees but why? The figure moved to another wounded tree. She felt it still breathing. The tree was struggling but it couldn't tell her anything, not without making any noise.

"Hush. Open your mind and let me in" she said. The tree obeyed. There, she saw…a family of gnomes and their squirrel companions. They were living in harmony with the forest. One of the security guards spotted one of them and took some pot shots. One of the older squirrels did not make it home. But then, something else came after them, in the darkness.

A strange presence, obscene and unnatural. It came after the gnomes. The tree tried to hide them and its squirrels. But this foul presence took them and infected the tree and its companions with a strange poison, a curse. The figure pulled her hand away. She looked out into the forest and towards the camp.

Friday Morning

Bruce woke up to someone screaming on his TV. *"Y'argh! Y'argh! Let go of me!"* He blinked at the screen. An old Arnold Schwarzenegger movie he'd left on before passing out on the couch. Bruce stretched, freshened up, and checked his phone. Missed call and text from Mark.

"Sorry bud, I need to reschedule breakfast. Granddaughter is taking me out to eat at Sandy's. Can we meet up later or push the B-fast to mañana?" Bruce smiled. Mark trying to use slang was adorable. *"No problemo, enjoy your B-fast. I'll call you later. Don't forget, next meal's on me...BB"*

Bruce walked to his kitchen and surveyed the cereal boxes on top of his fridge. All nearly empty. In a stroke of genius, he combined every remaining box into one massive bowl of hobo-cereal. He ate it watching Arnold kick ass, feeling like a kid again. After getting dressed, Bruce grabbed the old sock containing the crystal from his dresser drawer.

He froze.

The Atrox looked different. Some kind of contamination had affected it. Maybe from being wrapped in an old gym sock. A calcification had grown along the edges of the crystal, spreading like diseased skin. But the center still had its sheen. It still glowed with that internal magma. The cracks looked bigger than before. Bruce shoved it in his jacket pocket and headed out. The sooner he got rid of this thing, the better.

The Devil's Maw, Crystal Valley 10:45 AM

Bruce pulled into the site parking lot, trying to act naturally. Students and volunteers moved equipment around. He scanned for a good spot to discretely toss the crystal when a man in an expensive suit noticed him. The man spoke into his lapel. Two massive security guards started walking toward Bruce.

Oh Shit.

Bruce quickly formulated a cover story: lost tourist, environmental researcher, something… "This area is not open to the public," one guard said. His voice was flat, professional. "We have no trespassing signs throughout the lot. We need to search you."

"Why? I haven't done anything wrong. I just got here. You have no right to…" Bruce protested as he tried to palm the crystal in his hand. The other guard poked Bruce's chest with a meaty finger. "Sir, you waived your rights the moment you stepped on private property. We can do this the easy way or the hard way."

"One more finger on him and I'll personally rip it off and shove it up your ass."
All three turned. Jake stood behind them. He looked different. Bigger. Like he'd put on twenty pounds of muscle overnight. His eyes had a strange intensity. Predatory.

"You don't get to talk to us like that, college boy," the first guard said. "We answer to Mr. Suit and…"Jake grabbed the guard's wrist, threw him over his shoulder with shocking ease, and twisted the arm into a wrist lock. The guard screamed.

Jake stared at the second guard. Without hesitation, without remorse, he snapped the first guard's elbow. The bones cracking echoed across the parking lot. "Stop crying, you pussy." Jake's voice was cold. "It's only a little boo-boo. Now, if you or Mr. Suit ever get in my way again, I'll send Mr. Kingsley both his prize and your balls in a tiny little box. Disappear. NOW!"

Jake's head turned. Unnaturally smooth, like a camera on a swivel. He looked at Mr. Suit standing by the administrative trailer. "Problem?" Mr. Suit shook his head and motioned for his guards to retreat. The injured one clutched his arm, whimpering. "Sorry you had to see that." Jake's voice shifted. Became warmer, friendlier. Jake turned to Bruce "Come to my office. Let's talk." Bruce followed, his heart pounding. *WHOLE-E SHIT THAT INTENSE!* He thought to himself.

Jake's office was practical but sparse. A desk, filing cabinets, charts on the walls showing the cave system. "Coffee? Or something stronger?" Jake smiled. Bruce thought about what Roxy had said at Mark's house. Jake had changed. Become more aggressive. Something out here had influenced him. *Don't let on. Play it cool.*

"I've got a problem," Bruce started. "Well, I don't know if it's a problem." Jake poured himself a cup of coffee. Still boiling, steam rising. He drank it in one gulp. Like it was cold water. "Nonsense. You're my friend. There's nothing I wouldn't do for you." Jake's voice dropped lower and became almost hypnotic. "Tell me. I can't help you if you don't tell me."
Bruce looked down. "If I tell you, you promise to listen first?"

"Yesssss" Jake said while steam came out of his nostrils and teeth. Bruce had to process that for a second. Jake pressed forward "You can tell me anything." Jake's eyes looked more sinister yet seductive for a second. *Damn. Jake's voice could seduce the scales off a mermaid.* Bruce said to himself then he reached into his pocket, pulled out the old gym sock, and revealed the crystal.

Jake's eyes flashed orange for a split second. "Oh, nice crystal. Where'd you find it?"
"I... wait, what?" Bruce was confused. Jake moved around his desk. Less threatening now, more reassuring. "That, my friend, is called an Atrox stone. Not quite a crystal. See the calcification on the edges? Contamination from the environment. Practically worthless. You can keep it, no biggie." He tilted his head. "Is that why you came here?"

"I've never seen anything like it before. Nobody has. Are you sure?" Bruce had to be sure. Jake leaned back into his chair "You know, maybe take it back to the museum. Doesn't your boss have all that equipment? You could smash it up, make little souvenirs." Jake smiled. "If you do, strike it hard at the center first. That'll give you a nice clean break."

"I don't know. I think it should stay here. Maybe you should take another look. Maybe it belongs in a museum or somewhere safe…" Bruce took the crystal and was about to put it on Jake's desk. "NO!" Jake's voice cracked like a whip. "Do NOT tell me what I know or don't know!" Bruce snapped to attention but stayed quiet.

Jake's expression softened. "Listen to me. What do you think will happen if you leave this stone here? Those guys in the suits, the ones who wanted to kick your ass? They'll take it to their boss, who will keep it in some trophy case." Jake walked around Bruce slowly. Circling. Like a tiger sizing up prey. "But you said it was worthless" Bruce said while looking at Jake. "Worthless as it is, but priceless to others." Jake said as he stood up.

"Take it with you. Break it up. Sell the fragments. Such beauty should be shared with others. People will pay any amount you ask. You could fund the museum for centuries. Hell, you could buy your own museum. Put it anywhere in the world." His voice dropped to a whisper. "You can have everything you want."
"Everything," Bruce repeated.
"Anything you ever desired."
"Anything," Bruce echoed.
"Or nothing," Jake added. "Just take it."

His eyes drilled into the back of Bruce's head. Bruce had to think about Jake's offer, but his first instinct was to leave it behind. He didn't come here to make a deal. He came here to return some property. He didn't want anything. "I don't know."

Jake took a deep breath and walked to a cabinet. He pulled out two glasses, added ice, and poured whiskey into both. "Just, take it with you. Think about it. If you still feel uncomfortable then bring it back. But first, let me sweeten the deal." Jake walked to his desk and tossed some photographs onto Bruce's lap. Bruce picked them up. His eyes widened. "Amazing! Where did you take these pictures!"

"In a few days, my crew will map out and clear a direct passage to the antechamber. We'll see its secrets. But these photographs are just a preview. I'll have a team down there soon to decipher the hieroglyphs on the wall, but we believe its creators called it Starwound for some reason" Jake leaned closer. "Take them. Show them to your colleagues at work. Talk to that kooky old man."

"You mean Mark?" Bruce immediately lit up and felt safe when he said Mark's name. Jake's eyes narrowed to slits. His lips curled. "Yes. Mark."
"Look at them, imagine what discoveries we will find together. Consider it an early gift for our new futures. Imagine: Your own museum. You can help me. I'll take you down there. Hell, we'll bring Roxy and Chris. Have a good time. First to see this new wonder in full. Together. Just us."

"Just us?" Bruce was unsure but Jake is his friend after all. "Yes. And if you decide to bring back the stone, we'll place it there. We'll fake its discovery. No one will ever know." Jake extended his hand. Bruce shook it. The hand was cold. Rough like sandpaper mixed with broken glass and nails. Bruce tried not to wince. "Super." Jake's smile seemed forced. "I still think you should keep it. Look at the center. Someone tried to break it before. Half the work's already done." He released Bruce's hand.

"Sorry if I seemed a little intense today. The work environment here is toxic." Bruce caught himself recoiling from Jake's grip. Bruce looked at his friend who seemed to be savoring his uneasiness. "It's okay, Jake. Just remember we're friends. And don't take anything out on Roxy, okay?" Jake's expression went dark. "What I do with my own things is my own business. Don't think I haven't noticed you and that lecherous old man glaring at my ornament. She's mine."

"Jake, calm down…" Bruce put up his hands to motion for his friend to simmer down. Bruce forgot one of life's cardinal rules: if you tell an angry person to calm down, it usually makes things worse. "Sorry." Jake shook his head like clearing cobwebs. "Like I said. Toxic over here. Thanks for stopping by. I'll see you later."

Bruce left the office. WHEW! He was more afraid than relieved.

The Morgrin

Friday Afternoon, Coralyn Bay University Common Area

The campus was almost empty as a few students walked around the common area. Many were picking up last minute supplies or testing materials. The rest were employees waiting for their workday to end. Chris sat alone in the campus cafeteria, nursing a PB&J sandwich. He looked rough. Hadn't slept well, pretty sure he'd forgotten deodorant on his left armpit.

Great. Gonna have to keep my left arm down all day. What about my date with Jessica tonight?

Before he could escape to the campus convenience store, Roxy sat down with her tray. "Hi Chris. Wow, rough night?" Chris looked up and waved his eyebrow in acknowledgement. "You wouldn't believe what happened." Chris threw down the last bit of crust. Roxy settled in, placing her backpack on an empty chair next to her. "What happened? Nightmare?"

"Yeah."

"Me too." Roxy unpacked her salad and took a sip of her bottled tea.

"Oh shit, is it going around?" Chris asked.

"What's going around?" Roxy poked at her salad.

"Midterm blues" Chris lamented.

"Maybe. So, you gonna tell me about your nightmare, or do I have to beat it out of you?"

"If you insist." Chris leaned in and beckoned with his finger. "Come closer." Roxy scooted her chair in.

"Okay, so I was in a debate with Scott Jetsky, and I'm totally destroying him. Then the lights got brighter, so bright I couldn't see. Next thing I know, I'm not in class but in some huge auditorium. I've got a dark blue power suit, velvet tie and I'm hammering my opponent. Like, I was running for some political office."

"Probably presidential," Roxy said, preparing another bite. "Maybe." Chris smiled. "Anyway, I'm cooking. Saying all the right things. My opponent is shrinking and shrinking. So, I get to the end of my speech, walk around the podium toward the center of the room, all the cameras are on me then I realize: I'm naked."

Roxy stopped chewing. "Naked?"
"Naked. And my... rod was at full attention. I froze, but then all the people clapped. Cheered. Hollered."

"I bet they did." Roxy tried not to laugh as she carefully chewed her food.
"But I wasn't embarrassed. I felt... proud, actually." Chris had this confident smirk. Roxy smiled, recalling a past memory. "You should."

"But then it gets weird. Two Secret Service agents grabbed me, threw me on top of this large table and tied me down my wrists and ankles. Everything went dark for a second and then a blinding light. Next, I was covered head to toe in sushi. Then people started coming in and eating it off my body. A harp was playing in the background. The whole time I didn't know if I should enjoy it or be afraid." Chris planted his face into his hands.

Roxy was nibbling on her salad and could not find the right words. She was torn between making a joke or offering support. Chris continued " As soon as the sushi was gone, those same people began to stab me with olive forks, tearing off chunks of my flesh. They were drinking my blood, I struggled and I swore a few of them combined to make this huge mass, like a giant tapeworm or something, it had this huge mouth filled with slimy teeth. It felt so real, I screamed!" Roxy looked up, tomato chunk on her fork. "No way."

"Yes way. I screamed so loud that my mom barges in, breaking the door off its hinges, and shoots a hole in my ceiling. My dad barges in behind her then yells at my mom, then yells at me for pitching a tent and screaming." Chris grinned. "So, I called Jessica Harper. We have a 'study date' at her place tonight. My dad told me to take care of my 'thing.' Jessica was down. So, I'll be busy tonight. Probably all weekend."

Roxy put down her fork. "I get it. Everybody's got needs. You were looking for an excuse to call Jessica and get your rocks off. That's normal, I guess. But remember, Romeo. Jessica is a person with feelings."

Chris pulled out his phone and handed it to Roxy. She listened to a very suggestive voicemail from Jessica and handed it back, eyebrows raised. "Word of advice: don't let her go. She's marriage material. You won't find another woman like that." Chris nodded. "Did you do something to your hair?"

Roxy's eyes drooped and she made a slight frown. "Don't ask." Taking the hint, Chris got up. "See you later. Love the new nail polish by the way" Roxy reflexively looked at her nails. The strange nail polish she had on wouldn't come off, no matter what she did. After Chris left, Roxy finished her lunch alone. Her phone lit up. Several missed calls. None from Jake. Jake left that morning without saying a word. She knew he was busy, but something felt off. Her mind told her to trust him. But her instincts said otherwise.

Chris's House Same Time

Joe sat at the kitchen table, grumpy faced, while Carol cooked burgers on the stove.

"Carol, do you think I'm too hard on the boy?" Carol pressed a burger firmly on the pan. "A little." Joe sat back on his chair. "I don't mean to be. Sometimes, I just don't understand him. He had a good job working at that electronics factory then suddenly it wasn't good enough, or fulfilling as he says it. Now, he wants to become a lawyer, piling on more student loans. I tell ya; the boy is never moving out of the house."

Carol continued to cook the burgers, flipping them with precision. She planned on setting a few aside for Chris so he could eat something when he got back from school. "Joe, relax, Chris knows what's he doing. He's a smart boy."

Joe chomped on a pickle spear. "Smart huh?" He looked away for a moment. "I wished he got his act together. He had a stable job, he could have gotten his own apartment, a house even, maybe a new truck, settle down. I mean, what happened between him and the pretty Latina that used to come around here, you know, curly hair and big..." Carol immediately turned around and pointed her spatula at Joe, flinging some greasy his way. "Don't talk about Roxy that way. They've been friends since they were little".

Joe waved a dismissive hand. "Point is, Chris should focus on himself. His future." Carol put the cooked burgers on a plate and put some fresh one on the pan. "He is. That's why he keeps his nose in his books. He's got plenty of time." Joe folded his arms across his chest. "Did he say where he's going today?" Carol kept her eyes on the pan, cooking a burger is not just flipping them at random. It takes skill, almost like a lost art form. "School. Midterms or something. Said he's spending the night at a classmate's house." Joe sneered "Who? Not that troublemaker Bruce?"

"No, he's over at Jessica Harper's house, I think." Carol watched as the burgers sizzled. Joe's eyebrows relaxed. "Good. Good." He paused. "You know, I may not be the best dad, but I love my boy. I just want him to be happy." Carol timed it right and was able to use the pan to flip the burgers. Nice! "He is happy. He's living his best life. No matter what anyone tells him, he keeps being himself. Remember when people bullied him for wearing that Bigfoot costume when he was eight or nine?"

Joe remembered but he honestly thought Chris still wore it. "Every day for six weeks, Carol. That's not the same..."

"It is the same. He was just Chris. All his life, people tried to push him down, but he didn't let it bother him. He keeps showing up, hitting the books, going out whenever he wants. He has friends, his own life. He's gonna be a successful lawyer one day. A real success. So do you want to be part of that or not?"

Joe lowered his head. "I want to tell him. I need to tell him. I'm... proud of him. You're right. All this time, he was fighting his battles. He doesn't need his old man fighting against him. I should be fighting with him." Joe felt ashamed. Carol looked away from the stove for a second. "Chris is gonna blow off steam this weekend. When he comes home, you can talk to him." Joe sighed. "Yes. Let the boy enjoy himself. When he gets back, I'll talk to him."

Joe closed his hands together, making a little steeple with his fingers. Chris used to like that when he was little.

Vespucci Park Two Miles from the Museum 3:45 PM

Bruce walked in nervous circles. He needed help but didn't know where to turn. Dr. Shelley thought he'd got rid of the stone. Mark wasn't picking up. Jake was acting... wrong.

Bruce needed a moment to think.

The Bay.

It was right there. He could throw the stone in the water. Let it sink. Be done with it.

Bruce held the Atrox in his hand and pulled his arm back like a quarterback. *Extend and release. Simple.* He froze. He couldn't do it. No matter how hard he tried, Bruce couldn't throw the stone away. It would be wrong. He had to know what it was. What if it had historical value? What if Jake was right about it being worth a fortune?

A good curator would want to know more about an artifact before deciding to display or store it. Bruce decided to go home. Away from temptation. Somewhere he could feel safe.

Gino's Grill 4:15 PM

Mark stood by an old-fashioned phone booth, but it was anything but old-fashioned. He had to get his granddaughter to help him dial Bruce's phone number but after all that effort, he only got Bruce's voicemail. Mark returned to his table where his granddaughter waited for him. Mark's granddaughter is a young woman in her mid-twenties. She stirred in some sugar substitute in her tea. "Anything?" she asked.

"No, mi hijita. I'll try again after dinner. But I'd like you to meet my friend. I think you'll really like him." The young woman's eyes bulged with embarrassment. "You're just as bad as Grandma!" Mark sat back on this chair before taking a sip of his tea. "Hey, your Abuelita and I want the same thing for you; for you to be happy." She picked up a ketchup-covered fry. "I am…. happy not lonely grandpa." Mark nodded "Okay, okay. But you know I want to see some great grandkids before I go to heaven."

The young woman threw up her hands, shaking her head. "Grandpa, please." She looked at him with all the love and admiration a person could give their grandfather. "You know, I hate when you talk like that." Mark looked around for their server and then back to his granddaughter "Talk like what?"

The young woman said "Talk about leaving, going to heaven, things like that, please. I don't want to think about that". Mark looked at her and held her hand. "Sorry, I didn't mean to upset you. I just..." he got lost in a train of sorrow filled thoughts. The young woman squeezed back "Grandpa, if you say you will live long enough to see me become a mom, then I believe it and will hold you to it". Mark nodded while fighting back a tear.

The server returned with two massive double-decker Philly cheesesteak sandwiches. Mark smiled. "I don't know how much time I have left, but I'm gonna enjoy them along with this monster sandwich." They dug into their meals and Mark realized his eyes were bigger than his stomach. It didn't matter to him; leftovers are always good. Mark talked about his recent adventures with his new friends. His granddaughter listened as she always does, soaking in every word.

Bruce's Apartment 6:30 PM

The evening went by fast. The night sky was wrestling with some clouds that seemed to linger longer than they should, as if they wanted to witness the night's events. Bruce unlocked his door and saw it immediately: that ugly painting leaning against the wall.

What the hell? He'd thrown that thing in the dumpster weeks ago.

Bruce picked it up, carried it outside, and tossed it in the broom closet. Good riddance. He took off his shoes and checked the fridge. Leftovers again. He opened the cabinets. Maybe some popcorn or ramen. Something light. A few cans of beer and soda. Couple of hot dogs but no bread or mustard. Maybe he'd walk down the street to a food truck. *I really need to pick up groceries on the way home more often* Bruce said to himself then looked up.

His TV had been taken off its mount. The ugly painting hung in its place. "Okay, what the fuck?" He walked to the painting, yanked it down, open the door to his balcony and threw the ugly fucker outside. Harder this time. He heard a thud and hoped he didn't throw it on top of somebody's car. Bruce quickly went back inside. Then he noticed a faint orange glow came from his bedroom. *Oh no. The stone.*

Bruce walked to his bedroom. The Atrox sat on his dresser, glowing brighter than before. The cracks looked bigger. Heat radiated from it. *I'm not sleeping here tonight.* He smelled something burning. Bruce rushed to the kitchen. The microwave was running on high. Inside: his hot dogs and ramen, mashed together into a disgusting mess. Smoke poured from the vents. Place is going to stink for a while.

Bruce looked up, wondering if the smoke alarm would go off. His phone rang. "Smooth Operator" by Sade. Mark's ringtone. *About time.* Bruce reached for his phone. It wasn't on him. He checked his kitchen countertop and living room. He must have left it in his bedroom. Bruce went back and found his phone on top of his slept-in mattress with all the blankets crumpled up in neat, yet dirty pile.

In the hallway, right outside his bedroom, the painting was back. This time, the picture looked more grotesque than before as if someone threw acid on the subject before painting it. The orange glow from the Atrox made the subject's grin look alive. The phone rang again so Bruce answered it "One second" he said to Mark.

Bruce stared at the image. The 'thing' with a hairy face and beady eyes. It looked bad before but now, something about it made it looked worse. Bruce had enough, he tried throwing it away, not once but twice. He put his phone in his pocket and pulled down the painting. "Get the fuck out of here, dammit!" Bruce took the painting and slammed it hard on one of his dining chairs. Then for good measure, he put a foot in the back of it and pulled until the wooden frame snapped.

"Sorry Mark, I had to do some emergency redecorating". Bruce walked to his living room when suddenly a pair of rough hands grabbed him behind and threw him against the wall, breaking some of the sheetrock. Bruce hit the floor hard, rolled, and tried to get up. Something swept his legs out from under him. Then it grabbed him and threw him into his kitchen table. Glass shattered and a shard sliced Bruce's forearm. Blood was gushing. Bruce's phone was on the floor, the call still connected. "Bruce! Bruce! Are you okay?"

Bruce held on to his forearm. He tried to regain his bearing and see what attacked him. Bruce heard the intruder go back in the hallway towards his bedroom. The Atrox! Bruce grabbed a towel and tied it around his forearm. He got a large butcher knife from his kitchen drawer. Against his better judgement, he slowly walked towards his bedroom.

Sweat ran down his face. He took small steps and held the knife in front of him. He could hear something and see a strange shadow against the hallway. The intruder grabbed the Atrox and suddenly yelped "AIYYYYEEE!" as it dropped the stone and barged out the door where it stood face to face with Bruce. The creature looked warped as if something wounded it, its skin was bubbling and it looked to be in pain.

Suddenly, the creature leaped forward impossibly fast, knocked Bruce down and sat on his chest. The knife flew away far from Bruce's reach. The creature's arms stretched out and its hands closing around Bruce's throat. Bruce's phone was very close so that he could feel it with his fingertips. He could hear Mark's voice, tiny and distant, asking if he was alright. Bruce looked up at his attacker.

It was four, maybe five feet tall at most. Dirty overalls, ruffled hair, bushy beard, smooth yet scaly skin but covered with warts and acid burns. It had beady eyes with no eyelids that looked recently ripped off. Its ears were long like bat wings that could fold itself to look like horns. It had a massive grin showing rows of sharp, uneven teeth. Its arms were long and powerful, ending in retractable talons. Stubby legs but strong. It looked like it weighed less than a hundred pounds but felt like three hundred. That face. The same as the painting.
Oh shit.

Bruce struggled, but couldn't muster the strength. His vision blurred. His breath weakened. He kicked his legs, searching for leverage. The creature made itself heavier and its grip grew stronger. Bruce could hear it laugh but the sound did not come from the creature itself but rather, it came from around it. Then he heard something. A chant. A song. A spell.

It came from his phone; Mark's voice, speaking words Bruce didn't recognize. But as his life began to slip away and Bruce accepted that this thing was real, supernatural but real enough to kill him, the words became clearer. "Sleep, Charkoth! Go back to sleep and dream!"

The creature winced. It loosened its grip slightly. Not enough for Bruce to escape, but enough for him to breathe. Bruce struggled with all his might, not to fend off the creature but to breathe. Mark's words began to echo in the room, bouncing off the walls. The creature leaned back and uttered something to itself; it sounded like "Protect me Charkoth". Then suddenly someone burst in and immediately went to the hallway.
POP! POP! POP!

The creature was hit twice in the chest then once in the head.
POP! POP! POP!
It was knocked clear off Bruce.

He couldn't speak, but he heard someone walking in. Shoes crunching over broken glass. Roxy stood over the creature, smoking Glock in her hand. She looked down at it. "Nothing messes with my tribe." She fired three more rounds to confirm the kill. Roxy grabbed her phone. "I'm here. Get an ambulance!" Bruce reached up instinctively and pulled down her hand. His throat was too damaged to speak, but his eyes said it all:
No. What will we tell them? Who will believe us?

Revelations

Roxy holstered her weapon and helped Bruce to his feet. His throat was already bruising, and he was struggling to breathe. The front door burst open. Chris ran in wielding a baseball bat. "I called an ambulance and I…what the fuck is that thing?" He pointed at the dead creature. Half of its head was splattered against the wall in a dark, viscous mess that didn't look quite like blood.

Bruce rubbed his throat, struggling to speak. "Don't know. But we can't let anyone see it. Not yet." He looked at the creature's corpse, its beady eyes still open, its grin frozen in place. "How did you know I was in trouble?"

"Mark called me," Roxy said. "Told me you needed help." Bruce hugged her tightly. Chris looked around and waited downstairs for the EMTs. First responders arrived within minutes. An EMT examined Bruce's throat. Severe bruising, possible damage to the larynx, but he'd live. They recommended a hospital visit. Bruce declined.

Roxy and Chris gave statements to the police. Both felt wrong lying to the cops, but they agreed: for now, it was necessary. The official story: Bruce interrupted a robbery. The intruder assaulted him and fled empty-handed. Description? Medium height, wearing a mask, dark clothes. Gone before they arrived.

Mark showed up as the police were finishing their report. Bruce vouched for him, and the officers let him through. Mark gave Bruce a hug. Bruce held on tight. "Are you alright? We should take you to a doctor." Mark took Bruce's hand and tried to lead him to the ambulance, but Bruce waved it off. "I will be fine, just a little shaken up" Chris brought Bruce a glass of water, his throat was sore, but the water helped calm his nerves.

"Would you mind if I crashed at your house for a couple days?" Bruce's voice was barely a whisper. He was wavering but did his best to stand tall. Mark held him up. "Of course, let's grab some of your things. No way I'm letting you stay here". Mark noticed broken wood on the floor, pieces of a picture frame. He kicked some aside, his expression thoughtful. As the police began clearing out, Roxy took out her prism from her one of her pockets and examined the room.

"Dear God. It followed you home. There!" She pointed to a spot on Bruce's living room wall. "It manifested itself there as a picture or a painting. It was watching you, learning your habits. But there is something else, I can't make it out, but I think there was two of them." Roxy examined Bruce's apartment and could see all kinds of trails: insects, a few rats that were passing by and something with large, heavy feet.

Roxy handed Mark the prism and he looked around. "I know what this is" he looked at Roxy and Chris. Mark looked around the apartment. "Chris, Roxy. Get some towels or a blanket. Wrap it up tight and load it in the back of my truck. Here's the keys". Chris hesitated for a second until Roxy got behind him and shoved him to the hallway.

Chris grabbed a few towels and an old blanket so he and Roxy could wrap up the dead body of this strange creature with no eye lids. "It's looking at me" Chris said while making the ewww this is gross face. Roxy shot a "Shut up" look at Chris and they wrapped up the dead monster and tossed it in the back of Mark's truck.

Bruce packed a gym bag and grabbed his backpack. Mark handed him a "cough drop" and Bruce immediately swallowed it. "Good, in a few minutes, you will feel a lot better" Mark slapped Bruce on the shoulder and steadied him out the front door. The group drove back to Mark's house.

Mark's House 9:47 PM

Chris and Roxy unloaded the creature from Mark's truck and placed it on top of a work bench. Mark took out a wooden quill and wrote down a few words. "Who is this Charkoth?" Chris asked. Roxy elbowed him while Mark finished his little ritual. Mark took out a shopping bag with pieces of a broken wooden frame. He placed it in his charcoal grill and lit it on fire. A strange hiss came out of the smoke. "It will bother us no more" he said while Chris and Roxy watched. Bruce was inside drinking another glass of water.

"How you feeling?" Chris asked.

"Much better, what was that you gave me?" Bruce asked.

Mark smiled. "An old recipe to help with aches and pains given by supernatural pests. Let's go inside. We have a lot to talk about." Normally, Mark would make coffee but considering Bruce's condition and Roxy's recent fight with the morgrin. Mark made a special green tea. Chris sat down with Bruce to keep him company while Roxy watched as Mark made the tea. Mark used a green powder and mixed in some spices, herbs, skin peel from some pink guava and sprinkled some sweetener but it looked natural and not refined.

Roxy felt so relaxed, comfortable and reassured whenever Mark was around. Mark poured the mixture into a tea pot with boiling water. Roxy helped set up the tray, but Mark wanted to carry it out and serve his friends. Once everyone had a cup and took a few sips, Mark waited until the tea worked its magic. "That thing that followed you, that attacked you, is called a morgrin. A pesky creature from Norsica or what we call Scandinavia now. When a morgrin imprints on a person, they usually follow them home and later manifest itself as an ordinary object like a cup, a chair or even a painting. They like to watch the people in the homes they are pestering and single out a person."

Bruce felt his throat and if he didn't know any better, it was healing fast. He could taste the strong flavor of the tea and swallow without wincing. Mark continued "Once a morgrin commits to its victim, it will usually be disruptive like breaking dishes or causing havoc within the household, but they never attacked a person like that. They cause mischief, break things but never kill, not even the pets. Most unusual". Mark took a big sip so he could hide his face for a second.

"I don't get it, why Bruce?" Roxy said. Chris looked nervous "Do you think there are many more of them out of there?". Mark put his cup down. "If there are any more of them out there, they would be searching for new hosts to pester but since this one tried to harm Bruce, I think there is something else at play. Something fouler that can corrupt nature or supernature itself". Mark took a deep breath. It was starting again.

Bruce could feel his strength and courage restoring as if he had been resting for a few days instead of a few moments. He took a deep breath. "I think I know why that thing followed me, why it attacked me" and he looked up at his friends while taking out a brown bag from his coat pocket. He unraveled a strange object from a motley crew of sweat socks.

A dark purple geode with streaks of obsidian ash and inside the geode was an orange crystal with swirling magma trapped inside. Roxy put down her cup and clasped her mouth while muttering "Oh my God!". Chris gently put down his cup and his eyes bulged. Mark looked at it and the hairs on his neck stood up. "Where did you get that?"

Bruce looked at Roxy. He hesitated for a moment. "A friend of mine brought it in for testing and classification. I don't know what it is, nobody at the museum knows what it is but I think whatever attacked me, wanted this stone, for some unholy reason". Bruce looked at Mark. "I was hoping you could tell me." Mark stood still while his mind raced. Roxy looked at it and said to herself "Oh Jake".

Mark's face went pale. His cup slipped from his hand and shattered on the floor. Tea and ceramic fragments spread across the hardwood. "Dear God." His voice cracked. "Not that thing. Not that thing." Roxy went to him, holding his arm. "Are you okay?" Mark was quiet and he tried his best not to shake but Roxy could tell, and she held on to him to reassure him.

"I know what that is." Mark stared at the stone like it was a snake about to strike. "My brother found it. All those years ago. I thought it was buried. Where did you get it?" Bruce hesitated and then asked, "Do you know what it is?" Mark nodded slowly. "The Atrox Stone. A relic of great evil from beyond our time, beyond our history, something I hoped was lost long ago."

Mark looked at Roxy and reassured her that he was okay. She stayed close to him while he stood up. "It makes sense now, all these sightings, all these creatures coming back after so many years. I thought maybe they were at rest or transitioned into another plane, but perhaps, they were hiding from a greater evil. Something that can kill them as easily if not easier than one of us."

Bruce held it and watched the magma swirl. He could hear a voice, calling out to him. *Everything, Anything, Nothing…you can be the hero, the one who saves* *the world, return me to my home, help me…*Bruce looked at it, feeling the warm glow covering his face until it was gone. Mark placed a handkerchief over it.

"It can't stay here," Roxy said as Mark took the stone from Bruce and put it inside a drawer. "There's got to be someplace to put it. Somewhere far away." Roxy's gut feelings told her that thing will get them all killed. "What are we even talking about?" Chris waved his hands dismissively. "How do we know any of this is true? I mean, I heard stories as a kid, but I never saw any Easter Bunnies or gremlins in my house. Come on."

Mark's eyes flashed with passion. "My brother died because of it. People are getting hurt. Have any of you watched the news lately? Hold on" Mark went to his living room and turned on the news. Bruce, Roxy and Chris heard the various news stories. A man was attacked by a wild animal while on a nature trail in South Coralyn Bay. An abandoned car was found outside Crystal Valley. The driver was killed by a passenger who used multiple serrated knives. A kid in North Coralyn Bay had to be taken to the emergency room when their parents shot at an intruder who broke the child's jaw while extracting all their permanent teeth.

Everyone was silent. After a few minutes, Mark turned it off. "What do you think is causing this? Do you think we own this world? That magic doesn't exist?" Mark looked at the drawer where the Atrox Stone rested. "My brother and his friends died trying to save us, all of us. I can't ask any of you to help. This is my fight, my burden. I will take it back to Miller's Quarry. I will finish what my brother tried to do. I will finish it…. I will finish it…" Mark couldn't fight it anymore. He broke down, shivering, the memories coming back, old wounds reopening. Bruce and Roxy caught Mark before he could fall. Chris hovered a step behind them, wide-eyed, breathing hard. "No," Bruce said, steadying him. "You're not alone."

Roxy's voice trembled, but her grip didn't. "I'm not letting you face this thing by yourself. Whatever it is, we fight it together." Chris walked up to Mark and placed a hand on his shoulder. They nodded at each other. The four of them stood silently. "What do we do now?" Bruce asked. Mark looked at his friends "I don't know but I'm sure we'll think of something".
The Devil's Maw, later that night.

Kingsmen security finished their sweep. Mr. Suit read Jake's report. Nothing out of the ordinary but Mr. Suit could sense that something or someone was watching them. He doubled the guards. The second guard unit began patrolling the outer area, they wore black tactical gear and carried rifles. Up in the trees, someone was watching them, learning their pattern.

Out in the darkness, in the very air itself, another being was watching everything. A strong howling wind rushed through the forest, knocking down the security detail with such force, they felt as if they were hit by a large truck. The wind gust slammed the door to Mr. Suit's office. The wind flowed into the antechamber called Starwound. The faint echo of a suffering morgrin was heard before it was pulled into the darkness.
Mark's house, after midnight.

The house was quiet. Mark set up Bruce in one of the upstairs bedroom currently not occupied. It had the essentials and Bruce slept like a rock. Mark got up to use the bathroom and then walked down the hallway to check on Bruce. All is well. Mark returned to bed, kicked off his slippers and slept in the middle again. He grabbed as many pillows as he could and made a little fort for himself.

He remembered a time when he and his brother had to share bunk beds. Frankie would take the top bunk bed because Mark was afraid of climbing up the ladder. Frankie would hang upside down to tease him. "Look at me! I'm Luke Skywalker trapped in the ice cave" and Frankie would pretend to reach out for his lightsaber. "Ahhh!" Frankie slipped and fell down face first. They would laugh; their mom would burst in and tell them to go to bed.

Mark turned and grabbed a pillow. He remembered when he shared the bed with his wife. How warm she was, sometimes her hair would get in his face, or they would elbow each other if one of them snored too loud. The dog, Frito, would sleep across their feet. Mark was in heaven and didn't know it until much later, until it was all gone. The night crept in and whispered a sleeping spell on Mark, like it does all others, and soon, Mark could feel himself dreaming and all his cares, his worries faded away.

Wait a minute!
Something's not right.

Mark got up and had an urge to see the Atrox Stone. It was calling out to him. "Help me Marky, help me!". Mark raced downstairs and opened the drawer. There it was, glowing and billowing heat, the handkerchief was burnt away. The magma swirled, the purple obsidian around it felt cold. Mark stared into it and he heard voices, strange voices. He could feel agony, fear and unbearable pain. He held the stone and looked into it. "No, it can't be, it CAN'T BE!".
Halloween 1990.

Frankie was with his friends. The Atrox was placed on a top of a pile of cement blocks. Each of them had mallets in their hands. The old Eastern European couple were in the back, holding books, reading a spell. "Hurry, we haven't much time" somebody said. The five boys took turns smacking the Atrox. Some powerful spell protected it. "Hurry boys, we must break the stone!" said the old man.

Mark was there, not as a child but as he is now. He saw his brother. Frankie. It was Frankie's turn again. He swung the mallet and hit the Atrox in the center. SMACK! Mark could see it. A crack, a hairline crack. The Atrox started to hiss, the ground started to shake. "Hurry, before he gets here," said the old woman. The boys tried their best, but the protection spell was too strong. The old couple were talking, preparing another spell to weaken the evil magic that was protecting the Atrox.

Mark heard something behind him, a scurrying of feet. Something was approaching. "Hurry Frankie, hurry!" Mark shouted but nobody could see much less hear him. The old couple resumed their anti-spell chant. The boys were arguing amongst themselves. Frankie kept hitting the stone. Each hit was stronger than the last. The old couple chanted as fast as they could until something stabbed the old woman with a large spear. Blood and guts gushing through her chest, her voice gargled with blood.

"NO!" one of the boys shouted. The old man dropped his book and as he turned around something with long arms and serrated claws reached out from up on the ceiling and pulled the old man up. Mark could hear the old man's screams and saw something spit out a chunk of the old man's face. The boys panicked, dropped their mallets and started to run away but towards the wrong direction, away from the light. Frankie kept hitting the stone. SMACK!

"AAARRGHHH!"

Frankie kept hitting the stone. He ignored the cries and screams of his friends. He could save all of them if he just broke the stone. The darkness gathered around him, but Frankie ignored it. He kept hitting the stone. Mark was frozen in fear. He saw something, a strange pair of feet, it had no skin, just exposed muscles, ligaments and bones. Tar covered it, something sinister and sticky like webbing. A hand with two thumbs on each side, one on each end of the hand, out of place, unnatural.

The darkness took over until the only light came from the sole crack that Frankie made as he tried his best to break the stone. Mark tried to close his eyes, but some unseen force kept them open. He saw what this thing was, as it approached his brother. Mark wanted to scream but he had no voice. He wanted to move but his feet were welded to the ground as if something held him in place. A series of spiked vines reached out and held Mark's arms apart. Something wanted him to stay; some evil wanted him to watch.

The sinister hand with two thumbs reached down and pulled Frankie by the neck. Mark's heart was beating so fast he felt it was about to burst from his chest. He saw it, an unnatural hand on Frankie's neck, he heard the sound, cracking of bones and gushing of wind and blood. Mark tried to scream but he had no voice, no breath. He was alone in the darkness.

Suddenly, Mark was alone in a dark cave, and the only sound was something dripping in the darkness. A single light came from an unknown source and there on an altar made of obsidian stone was a single crystal.

Mark looked at it and could see the swirling magma. He looked deeper into the magma and suddenly it was pulled away towards some deep abyss. He could hear voices; all of them moaning and crying in pain.

In his hand, he held a mallet. He walked up to the crystal and could see faces. Faces that were stretching and pulled in towards the abyss. Hands were reaching out and touching the inside of the crystal. "This can't be" Mark whispered to himself and he heard a familiar voice. He tightens his grip on the mallet and raised it. Just as he began to swing it down something grabbed him by the wrist. He turned around to see who or what stopped him.

"NOOOO!"

Bruce ran in as fast as he could and with a quick fluid motion, turned on the lights. "Mark, are you okay?" Mark sat up, covered in sweat. "I know what to do".

The Tragedy of Spiders

Saturday Morning

The night flew by, and dawn arrived like a reprieve. Mark couldn't go back to sleep. The dream was much too real. He inspected his house and felt like something was off. He checked his garage and the body of the morgrin was still there. Bruce was asleep but he looked like he was struggling all night as well.

Mark couldn't figure out what was out of alignment but figured it must be the presence of the dead morgrin and bad energy from the previous night. Mark knew that while Bruce was on the mend, everyone would need their strength for the challenges ahead. Sunlight streamed through Mark's windows, making the shadows of fear retreat.

Mark made omelets for breakfast. Bruce emerged from the guest room looking haggard but alive.

A car pulled up and Bruce saw that Roxy had returned. She looked worried and it was obvious she lost some sleep last night as well. Mark had the table set up with plates, orange juice and a pot of coffee brewing. "Morning everybody, please sit down. Breakfast is almost ready." Roxy looked at Bruce and with her hand, turned his head side to side, to inspect his neck.

"Whatever Mark gave you, it really worked. How do you feel?" she said. Bruce rubbed his throat. "I feel better, but it will take a while before my nerves settle down". Roxy rubbed his shoulders and then poured herself a cup of coffee. She was so relaxed and felt like she was at her own house. She knew where Mark kept the cups and silverware. Everyone ate and could feel the warmth from the kitchen and from each other. Bruce helped washed the dishes afterwards.

"So, what happened last night guys?" Roxy asked while pouring herself another cup of coffee. Bruce and Mark looked at each other, trying to figure out what to tell her. "Where's Jake?" Bruce asked. Roxy sat down, holding the cup in both of her hands and with a sullen breath, blew the steam off the top of her coffee. "He worked late last night. I explained what happened, but he is preoccupied with the cave project. Hard deadlines, high expectations. Plus, I think he felt weird because he didn't know what to say".

"I know the feeling. Yesterday, I thought fairies and goblins were all fake, until one of them tried to…" Bruce couldn't finish his thought. He felt the strong yet gentle hand of Mark behind his back. "It's okay. I wished none of this would've happened. I wished this was all buried in the past. Perhaps I have some fault in this, I was so worried about certain events, certain things, certain people would be lost, forgotten forever. Perhaps my grief and my vanity did this" Mark said as he fought back his pain, his grief, and his worry.

He looked at Bruce and wished he could take all this way. Bruce turned around "No, don't ever say that. It's not your fault. It's not anybody's fault. People tried to forget, the world moved on, some things just got buried with time. If it was not now, then it would've been sometime later. I spent my life trying to preserve the past. Well, its back alright but now, we need to figure out what to do."

Mark felt a weight coming off him as Bruce put his hands on Mark's shoulders and with a gentle, yet firm squeeze, reminded him that he was not alone anymore. Roxy got up and the three of them hugged. Mark pulled

back to look at his new friends, his new family. "I know what we have to do but there are things that I don't know, and I could use some help."
Crystal Valley, The Devil's Maw Expedition Site. Mr. Suit's Office.

Mr. Suit was reading a dossier and preparing an update for Mr. Kingsley. Most background checks can take a few days but with Mr. Kingsley's resources, it only took a few minutes. Mr. Suit reviewed the summaries:

Jake Dawson. 27. Unmarried. No Children. Father: Gerald Dawson. Mother: Erica Lynn Tyler- Dawson. Parents divorced. Father current location Astoria, Oregon. Mother located in Victoria, Texas. Social Media sweep indicates no relationship with father. No siblings.

Veronica Chalmers, PhD. Unmarried. No Children. Parents deceased. No siblings. Social Media sweep indicates no active profile. An older social website has friends list. Gloria Shelley, PhD, lives in Coralyn Bay, Director of Museum of Natural History.

Mr. Suit likes to understand who he is working with and to understand what levers to pull or what buttons to press. He continued to read Dr. Chalmers' dossier and found an old blog entry of interest. He saw a red blinking light on the bottom of his toolbar. He minimized the dossiers and pulled up the chat feature. Immediately, he pressed his right earpiece. "Talk".

A Security Captain spoke "Sir, we intercepted an interloper last night. I think you could and look at this". Mr. Suit smiled like a snake who just cornered its prey. "On my way".
Mark's House

Roxy and Bruce sat on the soft sofa while Mark shared the details of his story. Like some people of his generation, Mark uses his hands in his storytelling. A few hours felt like minutes. The reality of the situation set in and Roxy looked up at Mark. "I think we should just get rid of it. Find a deep hole and toss it in."

"No, we can't do that. That's exactly what it wants, to hide. Whatever this thing is, it corrupts, it kills, and it collects trophies. Lord knows how many trophies it has collected over the years. If Frankie tried to destroy it then that must be the solution. Question is, an artifact like this must have some safeguards, protection. How do we get around it?" Bruce said.

Mark was quiet but processing everything. "Whatever made this crystal, this stone. It was mighty powerful. Aside from the physical, we are dealing with magic. Some kind of spell protects it but look" Mark brought out the stone. He held it up so Bruce and Roxy could see it. "Cracks. Others have tried before to destroy it, to save the world. We need to understand what magic protects it and how to destroy this thing so that not a piece of it remains."

Bruce held the Atrox Stone in his hands. It has some weight to it but also felt light. "I wonder if Jake could help us. I mean, after all, he found it, he studies geology, surely, he can figure something out" Bruce looked at Roxy. Roxy didn't make eye contact "I can talk to him about it but he's super busy lately and when he comes home, he just wants to…relax". Roxy instinctually rubbed the back of her neck. Mark saw some light bruises on her neck and below her armpit.

Mark wanted to say something but his own experiences with his daughter and granddaughters told him that it would be best for him to wait for a while. "Is there anyone else that can take a look at the stone in the meantime?" Mark looked at Bruce. Taking a deep breath, Bruce mentioned a few people he knew including a few undergraduates that he works with at the museum. "I can't take it back there, my boss thinks I got rid of it. If she saw it there, she would have a massive nuclear attack".

Roxy looked at the Atrox. Its glow was pulling her in and for a moment, she remembered the exotic locale of Nyxara. Suddenly she felt a cool wind blowing through her hair, something was pressing on her lips as if some spirit planted a kiss. It had a sweet yet forbidden taste: Obsidian Ember. "I think we should do some research first. Get to know what we are up against" Roxy said while she subtly licked her lips for any hint of the Obsidian Ember.

Mark's suspicion that something was off in his house was confirmed. While it looked like Roxy stared into the stone for a second. Mark noticed the drop in temperature and stepped away to see if he left any of the windows open. Bruce noticed that Roxy had turned on her headlights. Roxy snapped out of her little trance, noticed where Bruce's eyes were for a second and excused herself to freshen up in the bathroom.

"Sorry, I was just checking something out" Mark noticed Roxy walking down the hallway with her arms crossed over her chest. Bruce was wiping off a wolfy smile off his face. Mark looked at Bruce, "Did I miss something?"

Emerald Tower, Neon City

Grant Kingsley walked in with a strong swagger. While most businesses would give their employees the weekend off, not Grant Kingsley. He demands dedication, results, victory and will settle for nothing less. Success, like money, doesn't sleep or take vacations. So, Grant has an army of employees working all day, every day. No holidays. *Holidays are for children and retired people.* That's his motto.

A young woman in her early twenties sat at the receptionist desk. Her eyes were alert and her body perky. "Good Morning, Mr. Kingsley". Grant walked by with such force that the receptionist could feel a stiff breeze behind him "Hold all my calls. I don't wish to be disturbed!". The receptionist smiled and blinked in acknowledgement of her orders. As soon as Mr. Kingsley entered his office, she pressed a single black button on her security console: Stealth Mode activated.

Grant walked to back of his office and grabbed his already prepared drink: Bourbon on the rocks. He looked over the vast city. Streams of cars going up and down streets and freeways. Billboards with all kinds of advertisements. People carrying on with the day like if they were ants. Grant took a swig of bourbon and got to business. He wore a wristband and it pressed with twice so that an LED light blinked and he was patched through to his field office in Coralyn Bay.
"Report".

Mr. Suit and his assistant, Ms. Reyes, stood behind him. Ms. Reyes was a career woman. No kids, no husband but she took excellent care of herself. She wore a tight, white blouse with the buttons hanging on to the shirt for dear life. Grant couldn't help but admire her but he had younger options available. Mr. Suit pulled up a manila folder. "I have this year's hunting report."
"Go on"

"We have an upstart coyote that is causing trouble in the area. I recommend that we let the coyote thin the herd before capture". Mr. Suit looked up at the camera. "Sometimes, even an upstart can have their usefulness". "Agreed. Anything else?"

Mr. Suit nodded to Ms. Reyes, who lowered her head and stepped away. "My men and I have been tracking a new item for your collection". Grant took another swig from his glass. "What kind of item? Did you find it? The Sovereign Cut?"

Mr. Suit lowered his head in submission. "We are currently in progress of acquiring your prize. It is still in the area. We are confident that it will be brought back to us, but I am working on expediting the order. Sir, if I may. Let me show you something." Mr. Suit held up a photograph so only Mr. Kingsley could see it.

"Beautiful, simply beautiful. Where did you find it?"

"That's the thing, sir. It found us" Mr. Suit kept his head lowered.

"Take no action with that until I arrive".
Outside the Devil's Maw, in Jake's Office.

Jake was alone. Later, some students and volunteers will come in to continue mapping out the cave and take photographs of Starwound and another antechamber they recently found. Jake liked having this time alone. He closed the door to his office and took off 'his suit'. The mound of skin and muscle slumped to the floor as the fragment of the cosmodial entity soaked in the darkness. It heard plans on top of plans. Schemes working against him. Its eyes glowed and heard voices from far away. Ammuzol let out a crooked smile while it stretched out his suit. *Another dish preparing itself for my pleasure.*
Coralyn Bay-Mark's Driveway

Bruce and Roxy left Mark's house, each going in a different direction. Roxy will meet up with Chris to do some research, and Bruce had a full day ahead. He planned to take the Atrox to the museum's GIS department to use their equipment. If someone or something had reinforced the stone, maybe, the museum staff could figure out what materials were used. He hoped to find a counteragent to shatter it.

Mark will do some research as well, but he will comb the main library downtown. It was a good thing everyone got up early as there is much to do with who knows how much time left. Red lights are often a curse but today they are a blessing. Bruce does some of his best thinking when he's stuck on a red light. In his mind, Bruce knew it had to be shattered. That's what Frankie tried to do. That's what Frankie died for. By the grace of all that was holy and right in the universe, Bruce would see this task done.

Mark took the photographs Bruce had received from Jake down to his private library. He began to read, research, and investigate. The markings were unfamiliar, yet they told a story he felt he'd heard before, possibly in a dream. Roxy got a hold of Chris, but he was busy studying. She swore she heard Jessica's voice in the background. No matter, everybody has their mission, their urgency and their lives to live. In many great stories, the heroes focused on their quest without delay. But, in Coralyn Bay, just like anywhere else, life goes on.

Roxy did see Jake later that evening, but he was in no mood to talk. He was hungry as soon as he saw her. He pulled her close and kissed her. No foreplay, no conversation, just demand. He read her intentions immediately and took pleasure from her. Considering the sensitive subject she wanted to discuss, Roxy figured she would make him happy first. Tonight, it felt routine, but when she opened her eyes, she didn't see Jake but Marlowe. She knew it wasn't him, but she allowed her imagination to take over. Everything felt right, felt pleasurable. Back in her mind, she wanted to taste the drink again, Obsidian Ember, and she slowly forgot her urgency.

Later, as Jake spooned with her. He held her tight, cupping her. She began to feel weak and forgot what she wanted to ask him. She wanted to ask him so many questions, aside from the Atrox. She noticed that Jake doesn't eat or drink anymore. He doesn't use the bathroom unless to shower. Is he taking care of himself? Is he seeing somebody else? Did she become "the other woman"?

The Next Few Days

Time passed quickly, yet no answers were found. Bruce and his friends went about their business: attending lectures, studying for exams, writing papers, going to work. But all of them were distracted. Jake was detached. He'd show up to class, complete his work efficiently, and leave immediately for the caves. No small talk. No hanging out. Dr. Chalmers hadn't been seen in days. Rumors spread she'd run off with a younger student, gotten involved with sketchy people, had a mental breakdown. Eventually, someone filed a missing person's report.

Bruce knew something was in the air. Something foul. The red tide had come in unusually late this year, and the smell of dead fish permeated Coralyn Bay. Dr. Shelley seemed nervous, often upset, but she wouldn't tell anyone what was bothering her. Gilbert just said, "She's having family issues. Leave it alone and respect her privacy." Bruce had gotten the results from the GIS

Department from the university and from his friends at the museum.

It wasn't what he wanted to hear. One report read:
Specimen Analysis — GIS Department, Coralyn Bay University Submitted by: B. Brixby
The submitted specimen presents as a standard geode formation, exterior consistent with sedimentary calcification common to limestone cave systems in the Crystal Valley region. Interior crystalline structure suggests natural formation over an estimated 10,000-50,000-year period. The purple coloration is consistent with amethyst or fluorite deposits. The luminescent quality noted by the submitter could not be replicated under laboratory conditions and may indicate prior exposure to phosphorescent materials or submitter error in observation. No unusual radioactive or chemical properties detected. Classification: Natural geological specimen of moderate interest. Estimated value: $200-400 as decorative mineral.
Recommendation: No further analysis warranted.

Bruce read the other report from the museum lab.

Artifact Assessment — Coralyn Bay Museum of Natural History Materials Analysis Division Re: Decorative Mineral Specimen
The submitted object appears to be a commercially produced decorative piece, likely manufactured in Southeast Asia or Mexico where similar items are widely available in tourist markets. The exterior coating simulates natural calcification but shows evidence of artificial weathering techniques commonly used in novelty production. The interior "crystal" displays coloration inconsistent with natural mineral formation and is consistent with resin casting with embedded LED or phosphorescent powder to simulate luminescence. The apparent "movement" of interior material noted by the

submitter is likely an optical illusion created by the resin's refractive properties.
Similar items retail for $15-40 in gift shops and online marketplaces.
Recommendation: Not suitable for museum collection or academic study. Suggest returning to original owner or disposal.

Bruce twisted the print outs like an old breadstick from a bad restaurant. This can't be right. This thing is not a fake. It's real. How can they not see or feel the heat coming off it? How the stone seems to change shape depending on who's…. oh no. Suddenly, Bruce realized that the stone is very real, and the reports confirm the physical properties of it. Magic. The stone is of supernatural origin, maybe, something older. He had to take it back to Mark.

Thursday Evening, Mama Rona's Italian Restaurant

Mark called everyone for a meeting at his house, but Jake declined to attend. Instead, he offered to pay for dinner at the best Italian restaurant in town. Not wanting to appear rude, the group accepted. They'd skip their usual Julie's visit and make this week's gathering special. Mark arrived first, claiming a table in the back. Bruce, Roxy, and Chris joined him shortly after.

"Are you sure he's okay?" Mark asked Roxy as she studied the menu. "He's fine. He's been super busy lately. He keeps going on and on with the mapping project. Apparently, he found another antechamber with even more hieroglyphs that pre-date the Egyptians. It's a really, big deal." Roxy mentioned while thumbing through the drink specials.

"Pretty pricey place," Chris said, eyeing the menu. "Are you sure Jake's got it covered? Did he win the lotto or something?" Then a server with a distinguished scar on their cheek approached. "Good evening. Mr. Dawson came personally to arrange payment. All you need to do is order. He specifically stated that price was no option." Chris' eyebrows went up like two fuzzy worms. "Damn," Bruce muttered. "He's got that Kingsmen money now." Roxy elbowed him sharply.

The group ordered. Hot, chef-prepared food and wine flowed freely. For a while, they forgot the purpose of their gathering, forgot about morgrins and cursed stones and missing people. Mark waited until everyone had a few bites out of their food. "So, did anyone learn anything new, about our stone?". Bruce was waiting for the right moment to bring it up. He didn't want to be the one to sour the mood. Once again, Mark comes to the rescue.

"Yes. I had the stone analyzed by two different labs and got two different results. It's real in a physical sense but if I didn't know any better. You would think I sent two different specimens. I think it is reactive". Bruce took a bite out of his Chicken Carbonara. Mark was cutting a piece of steak he ordered with his Penne alla Vodka. "Mmmhmm. Right, so that confirms its supernatural origin. I was hoping for a more flat or rational explanation. But I fear the worse now".

"What do you mean? Fear the worse, supernatural origin? I mean, what is this thing anyways?" Chris reacted as he played with his spaghetti. Roxy was tearing up her own Shrimp Fra Diavolo but as soon as she heard Chris, she immediately gave him a *"you can't be serious?"* look. Mark took a few bites out of his meal, chewed with purpose and then took a big gulp of the house wine. "My friends, let's not pretend that we don't know what is going on here".

Chris looked irritated. He was having such a good dinner, his life was back on track, and he successfully put away the thought of supernatural horrors coming back to life. He convinced himself that Bruce was really attacked by a prowler, not some horrible creature. "I'm not doing this" he started to get up when Roxy reached up and pulled him down. With one look, she scolded him. Chris looked at her and then his friends and said "Sorry. Please continue". Chris exhaled and knew that whatever Mark had to say deserved his full attention.

Mark had finished most of his meal. He knew what he had to say wasn't going to be easy. "I know none of this makes sense. None of it. How do you think I felt when I was a little boy? People back then acted the same way. A werewolf could go on a rampage downtown, leave a ton of evidence and the next day, newspapers would call it a hoax." Roxy put down her plate and took a big sip of her wine. She licked her lips quickly, but it was much slower in her mind. Her dark purple fingernails in full view. The wine was good, but she had better…Obsidian Ember. Roxy snapped back to reality and said "I took a sample of the creature down to a friend of mine who works in forensics in CBPD. She thinks it belongs to an animal of some sort. Said she was going to talk to a friend of a friend who used to work there in the 1970s. We chatted for a while. There are some things I can't share but I will say this: there are plenty of cold cases in which I think the police had solved but either were not ready to share the evidence due to public skepticism or were leaned on by public officials to keep it quiet."

"Now you're sounding a like a conspiracy theorist" Chris retorted. Roxy looked at him, losing her patience. "This not about conspiracies but cover ups".

Bruce folded his hands. He kept thinking of the lab reports. *They were wrong.* He knows what he knows and after his near-death experience with the morgrin. Nobody was going to tell him differently. "Magic is real. Always has been. People don't like the unexplained. So, they compartmentalize it, but in a neat box, and put it away. All the stories, the myths and legends, what if they were true? Or had some truth behind them?" Bruce wondered.

Mark was drinking his wine, not to catch a buzz but to calm his nerves. "I did some digging around as well. I may not be as tech-savvy like the rest of you, but I did have some young lady at the library help me find some information. I talked to the computer, and it helped me find something that makes total sense to me." Chris looked at his friends with a raised eyebrow, Roxy's eyes lowered with a *Don't you dare!* look and Chris kept his mouth shut.

Bruce continued "What did the computer tell you?" Mark swirled the wine in his glass. "The computer or Arica as she calls herself, ha, I know. It's cute and so helpful. Well, it turns out there is a book that could help but it will take six to thirteen weeks to get here. So, Arica was able to provide a summary and helped me install an app on my phone, give me a sec". Mark pulled out his reading glasses and looked at his phone. He kept it away from himself at arm's length while he used his index finger to push the various buttons.

"Ah, here we go. Hi Arica, its Mark, do you remember me?". Chris nodded his head in disparagement and was about to offer Mark some help with his phone. "Mark! Hello. Yes, I remember you from this morning. I have finished my summary and it's ready to share. Would you like for me to do so now?" Chris was confused as he could see Mark's screen and it was on the home page, yet no apps were opened. Mark looked at Chris "Seniors get the special edition." Chris swore he saw Mark's phone wink at them.

"Would you like me to read it to you? I can prepare a text version if you prefer but I would prefer to tell you so you can ask me questions at any time?" Arica chimed in as Mark smiled at his phone. "Yes, please but I am having dinner with friends at a restaurant so keep your voice down" and he winked at the phone. "Certainly" Arica said in a chipper voice.

Bruce, Roxy and Chris nudged their chairs closer to the table as Mark placed his phone on top of it. "The images you shared this morning do not match any known cave drawing or item in my database. A web search shows a few possible matches involving several non-connected pre-industrial societies". Chris looked up with a confused face. Roxy translated "Arica found possible matches across various cultures in history, but they had no natural connection."

"Until now" Bruce concluded. Arica continued "The images were created by a single user. It retraces several stories, but the most dominant thread comes from the Dawnweaver myth." Bruce tried to recall where he heard that word before and the only thing that came to mind was a lecture he attended years ago that prehistoric man worshipped nature and there was a rumor of a forbidden tribe that worshipped spiders. Mark leaned in "Tell us about the Dawnweavers, please"
"Certainly Mark"

Roxy and Bruce looked at each other, and they both thought of the same thing: "Did that machine just used a flirtatious tone with Mark?" Arica began her summary:

"Long ago, evidence points out there were pre-industrial civilizations that existed as the Earth shifted its plates into the land formations we know today. Ancient humans used to cross land bridges before they were separated by the oceans. A common myth was that the universe was created by a celestial race of spiders, who weaved the world and the galaxy into existence. The spiders had a natural predator."

"Like a hunter or some monstrous demon?" Bruce asked.

"Negative. This natural predator had no ties to religious or natural phenomena. The closet distinction would be Cosmodial Entity."

Everyone's eyes got bigger and their thoughts immediately raced to the Atrox Stone. *Who created it and why?* "So, what happened to these Dawnweavers?" Chris asked.

"The cosmodial entity emerged and killed them. But this being had an enemy of its own, a cosmological counterpart."

The groups waited patiently for Arica to finish, after a few minutes. "Arica, please continue the story" Mark asked. Arica paused "Unable to complete that request at this time, sorry Mark, please don't be mad." Mark smiled and patted his phone the way he would like a dog. "You did good Arica, thank you".

"There you have it. We can keep digging but I might have some books in my personal collection. Perhaps some of you can do your own computer searches and see what you can dig up." Mark said with a small hint of defeat. Bruce was thinking the whole time. "Wait a minute, there is still something we can do. Chris, you're good at research, do you think you can dig into this a little bit?"

Chris was compacting all this new information. "I think so, winter break is coming up. I was planning on blowing off some steam with Jessica but digging up supernatural horrors seems like a better idea."

"Roxy, talk to Jake. See if we can get inside one of those antechambers. If we can get a closer look at them" Bruce pointed a finger at Roxy who was coming up with a plan on her own. "Yeah, Jake mentioned he wanted to take me down there soon, let's talk to him together, if you don't mind?" Bruce immediately answered "Yes, I think that's a good idea". Mark put away his phone. "We have a plan then. In the meantime, I will keep the Atrox safe at my house. Besides I won't be alone." Mark smiled at Bruce.

"Yeah, about that" Bruce looked uncomfortable "My landlord is almost finished with my apartment, and he won't let me out of the lease, believe me, I've tried fighting it. I was planning on going back to my place soon." Roxy looked at Chris. Chris shot back a look at Roxy "I'm a law student not a lawyer! I can't help, yet".

"No problem. I expected you would be going back to your place sooner or later. Remind me later, I have something for you so when you go back to your place, it will keep you safe. Either way, my grand-daughter visits regularly so I'm never alone.'

"How come we haven't seen her yet" Chris asked. Roxy looked up in agreement. "She's has a life of her own. Plus, she's visiting her parents in Neon City. Don't worry, you'll meet her soon enough, I tell you Bruce, you two should meet, I think you two would make a great couple!" Mark looked proud as Bruce almost spit out his wine. Roxy and Chris tried not to laugh.

Bruce has his fair share of blind dates and hookups, none of them were successful. "Thanks, I'll keep that in mind" Bruce looked with a bug-eyed stare at his friends while Mark looked away for a second. The server came by and cleared the table. The group shared a dessert and a cup of coffee. Bruce looked at his friends, and he could tell they were thinking of the same thing, it was moments like this, they wished it could last forever.

The Secret Cove

Compound 3784, a few miles away from Crystal Valley
A few guards stood by some large gates. The compound was unremarkable. Large modular buildings, parking spaces and a helipad. A luxurious, off-road vehicle rolled up, and the gate commander immediately issued the orders to let it pass without delay. Grant Kingsley is making a "surprise" inspection.

The vehicle pulled to a large hangar and two security officers stepped aside to allow the mechanized gates to open and allowed the large vehicle inside. Once the doors closed, the floor opened to reveal a downward sloping ramp that led the vehicle inside a secret facility. This was Grant's private research facility. Nobody got in or out without his personal approval. The guards knew accepting this job was a one-way ticket, hopefully if their service is impeccable then they can get a transfer to Maranoa, Mr. Kingsley's private island. There, they can hope to live out the rest of their lives in peace and comfort. The only trouble is that Mr. Kingsley only allows a set number of guards to live full-time on his island.

The only way to get a transfer is for one of the existing guards to die. Too bad the island has one of the most respectable safety records in the world, at least, on paper.

Grant's Private Office
"So, where is my prize?" he asked as all the monitors immediately turned on and Mr. Suit and Ms. Reyes walked in. Mr. Suit handed him a small tablet, and Mr. Kingsley immediately reviewed it. "It will be in our possession soon; we tracked it down to Coralyn Bay. The

individual in possession of the item must have had it appraised but made no effort to sell it to any open retailer or post it on the black market. We are monitoring the situation." While this wasn't the news that Mr. Kingsley wanted to hear, he nodded in approval. This had to be handled delicately.

"Sir, if you would please follow me?" Mr. Suit used his right hand to point in the direction that they needed to go. Ms. Reyes had no expression on her face, but she knew what was about to happen. Mr. Kingsley walked into another office with several monitors. "We have a special visitor. And she is detained exactly as you requested" Mr. Suit and Ms. Reyes bowed their heads. Grant looked at the monitor, his eyes flashing with excitement. "Excellent. I like my game, unspoiled. How soon can I meet this thing?"

Mr. Suit kept his gaze low "You can meet your guest at your leisure". Grant looked at the monitor. He was a man of expensive tastes. His competitors would stop at nothing to achieve greatness or immortality. Whether it's access or control over natural or precious resources. A few of the world elites knew of a hidden world, far beyond most human expectations. The first one to find a way into this world would be the one to lay claim over it and its riches. But first, Mr. Grant wanted to conquer another challenge.

"Has 'she' been cleaned up?" he asked.

"Yes sir. I saw to it myself" Ms. Reyes said. Mr. Suit shot her with a disapproving side eye glance. Mr. Kingsley smiled. "Mr. Suit, as for the other matter, get right back to work. I will spend some time with our guest, make her more comfortable". Mr. Suit left immediately, taking Ms. Reyes with him. Grant looked at the monitor "Such a rare treasure, so beautiful, radiant.

Sentinel AM, activate privacy protocol, I don't want to be disturbed with my guest". The AI-powered security system acknowledged the command.

Jake's Office, Devil's Maw

The Kingsley security force checked in two visitors. Routine. Roxy and Bruce drove up to the parking area in his little jeep. The rest of the students and volunteers haven't arrived yet. They were hoping for more people to be around besides some security guards who couldn't give two shits if something happened to them. Bruce parked a few spaces away from Jake's car.

"Are you nervous?" Bruce asked. Roxy seemed to have frozen in her seat for a second. "No, course not. Let's go" she said trying to convince herself that everything will be fine. They got out of the jeep and Roxy led them to Jake's office. The light was on and they could smell cheap coffee brewing. Jake was pouring himself a big cup, turned around and for a second, his face seemed wrinkled like an old t-shirt. Jake used his free hand to smoothen out his face. "Ah, what a nice surprise! Roxy, Bruce!" Jake's smile was warm, welcoming. "I hope everything's alright?"

"We need to talk," Bruce said. Jake motioned for them to come in and make themselves comfortable. "Please, sit. Would you like something to drink? Roxy, I have this special tea blend that I wanted to share with you. Amazing flavor, it will knock your top off." Roxy shot Jake an *Excuse!?!Me* look and Bruce did a double take. "Socks off, what did you think I said?" Jake grinned. He turned to Bruce. "I take it you reconsidered my offer?"

"Not exactly." Bruce sat down. Roxy stood behind him, arms crossed. "Don't worry, Roxy knows."

"Sure, no problem." Jake leaned back in his chair. "I don't keep anything from my favorite ornament." Jake winked at his "ornament". Roxy's jaw tightened. She wanted to tell him to stop calling her that, but the situation was delicate. Jake drank his steaming coffee like it was a soda then he propped his feet on top of his desk. "What's up? I've got a full day ahead. CaveScan Drones are breaking down; people are getting stuck in passageways. I told them to wait for my approval!" Jake ran a hand through his hair. "It's a mess. But we're finding amazing things. I know it's later than I promised, Bruce, but once we map a safe passage, we'll all go down there. Together."

Bruce and Roxy shot a glance at each other. *This was easier than we thought, he is inviting us in the caves, great, a win for us.* Roxy felt some stress leaving her while Jake undressed her with his eyes. Bruce felt like a third wheel for a moment, but he knew he had to refocus everyone to the next topic of the conversation. "We need to destroy this." Bruce pulled out the Atrox and placed it on Jake's desk.

Jake looked at it like a child examining an expensive dish. "Naturally. I told you that. What do you need? A rock hammer? I've got tools, but it looks like there's glue or cement on it. You might need some kind of dissolver." Roxy noticed something about Jake as he was handling the Atrox. As if he was very familiar with it. Yet there was something in his eyes or rather something missing. She took half a step forward and stopped herself from saying something, but Jake immediately noticed.

"I love what you've done with your nails and your hair, that tinge of purple, so dark and exotic. Really brings out your beauty, I wonder if you could make your eyes and your lips match the same color?" Roxy took a step back. Bruce didn't know what was going on between them, but his instincts told him it was wrong. Roxy is his friend first. Bruce knows her a lot longer than Jake and something inside him told him that they needed to leave soon. Bruce casually got up and got in between Roxy and Jake. "You're right. We are working on something but uh, yeah. If this stone is not inherently valuable, then I would like to recycle it to its base materials." Bruce cringed for a second, his nerves starting to get the better of him.

He can feel the negative energy between Jake and Roxy. Something's going on but since Roxy never said anything, Bruce assumes she got it under control. Jake got up to fetch another boiling cup of coffee. Bruce used his left hand to reach back to Roxy, as an offer of support. She reached out and squeezed his hand to reassure him, she was okay. Jake sneered. He put down his cup.

Jake turned around with a crocodile smile. "Absolutely. I'm here to help." Jake went over and shook Bruce's hand and then put his arms around Roxy, squeezing her waist then squeezed her ass. Roxy stiffened but didn't pull away immediately. "By the way, did you look at those photographs?" Jake asked. "What do you think? There's more drawings out there and my team is building quite the collection."

"Wait, you mean there's more?" Roxy asked. Jake caressed her firmly before pulling away and going back behind his desk. "Yes, quite more. So far, we have discovered two antechambers. We are using everything we must decipher the stories on the wall. I have the director of the Tri-Coastal County Historical Society himself on site. He thinks it's a lost mythology. A tragic tale of a wonderful being who's peace was disturbed and when he tried to clean house, he was punished for it". "What?" Bruce said.

Jake smiled as he leaned back into his chair. Bruce noticed Jake looks older, leaner and somehow more muscular as if he ate only protein and lifted heavy weights all day. Roxy stood behind Bruce. She shook her head as a thought entered her mind. *Jake doesn't appear to breathe anymore. No, you're losing it girl.* Bruce looked at the printouts on Jake's desk and the maps on the wall. Bruce was both awestruck and terrified. "You got people going in these narrow passageways?"

"I said that earlier, Yes. I also said when people don't listen to me, they get stuck and it's a pain in the ass to pull them out. The CaveScan drones can only do so much. The TPWD already warned us to be careful. Anyways, what do you think? I have so much more to show you?" Bruce felt as if something was pulling him in and when he tried to break away, that same force was about to push him in. "I showed the first batch to Mark. He's interested in seeing it too." Bruce said without thinking of the consequences.

FUCK. Why did you bring Mark into this? Bruce said. However, the mere mention of Mark's name gave Bruce and Roxy some courage. Jake's expression shifted, something dark flickered across his face. "You took them to Mark? What did he say?" The light above Jake began to flicker out. Bruce continued but chose his words more carefully. "He found some kind of story. Thinks it's incomplete. Can I bring him by? I'm sure he'd love to know more about the story of the Dawnweavers."

Jake snickered "Oh, you mean Ammuzol and the Dawnweavers". Jake's eyes flashed orange for a split second. "Yes, an ancient story that belonged to long forgotten world, a story that shouldn't have been forgotten and deserves its recognition. But I have somebody working on it already. Besides, Mark is old. He'll probably fall down, break a hip or something. I don't want a liability issue, know what I mean? If he gets hurt then safety regulators come in, shut everything down. It will be a huge setback for a lot of people" Jake got up, push past Bruce and wrapped his arms around Roxy. He lifted her chin up. "We wouldn't want that, would we?" Roxy started to answer but Jake kissed her. Roxy winced as Jake kissed her French style and as soon as Jake's hands started to explore her body "Hey, Hey!" Bruce interrupted "Calm down Don Juan McDawson!"

Jake gave Bruce the side eyed *"Don't cockblock me bro"* look but Bruce wasn't having it. "Oh, sorry if my little ornament and I are making you uncomfortable." Roxy seemed out of it like she was in another world. Bruce snapped his fingers around her face. She was moaning "anything" until Bruce snapped loud by her ears. "Whoa! Sorry" Roxy said then straighten out her shirt.

Bruce looked at them. Now he knows something is little off with them. Jake meanwhile turned away as if he heard something. He held up his hand as if he wanted everyone to wait a second. Jake closed his eyes and thought to himself, *so, the little tyrant wants to play rough, eh? Nobody can claim what is mine!*

"Jake are you okay?" Roxy said.

"Fine, fine. Sorry, lots of pressure on me, I am not acting like myself. Listen, there are a few things I need to take care of so don't worry if I am M.I.A. for a while. Take some of the pictures on my desk with you. Show them to Mark. I'll get back to you later." He reached over and kissed Roxy, gently this time.

The students, volunteers and Kingsmen crew were setting up in the muster area. This was Bruce and Roxy's cue to leave. They headed back to Bruce's Jeep and Bruce noticed something different about Roxy. *Was she always wearing purple lipstick?*
On the way to Mark's House, later that morning.

The ride back to Mark's house was awkward. Roxy kept looking at herself in the passenger side mirror. Bruce didn't have to say a word but Roxy's hair, nails, eyebrows and lips have a purple tint, not like makeup or dye, but natural. "I didn't tell anyone this, please don't say anything but I went to the doctor the other day. He can find no reason why this is happening to me" Roxy said.

Bruce kept his eyes on the road, but he was full of questions. "Rox, are you okay? Like for real? No bullshit. Is he hitting you?" Roxy looked at Bruce with defiance. "I can take care of myself! I don't need someone to save me, alright?". Bruce kept his cool. He knows Roxy can take care of herself. "Look, I'm sorry, I am not trying to be intrusive but..."

Roxy soften up a little bit "No, I'm sorry. I know you care; I shouldn't have..." She put her hand on his shoulder and squeezed three times. Bruce nodded. Something is wrong. Jake seems off. This Atrox has a bad effect on everything around it. He knows that Roxy must have seen a change in Jake. Perhaps it's time to bring in the big guns.

Roxy turned on the radio and kept searching for a channel with good music, then she stopped when she heard this broadcast:

Police were called into the 5200 Block of Evenhart Street outside Cataloo Park yesterday evening. Eyewitnesses report that a wild animal, possibly an escaped exotic animal from the nearby wildlife refuge attacked and maimed a 14-year-old boy on his way home. Medical and wildlife experts report the attack was consistent with a javelina attack, but the animal left strange tracks that police believed to be manmade. In other news…

Roxy kept changing the station and every once in a while, they would pick up other news stories. Wildlife seen moving away, even those that don't migrate for the winter. Strange occurrences happening away from the Tri-Coastal area with reported "Wild Man" sightings as far up as Neon City.

Finally, after what felt like forever, Bruce and Roxy made it back to Mark's house. He was outside watering his flowers. He waved at them as they pulled up. Roxy jumped out of the jeep, ran up to Mark and hugged him. "Hey, good to see you too. Are you alright? You're acting like you haven't seen me in a month, kiddo". Roxy looked at Mark and immediately he put away the water hose and took her in the house.

Bruce got out of the jeep and made his way to the kitchen to find something strong to drink. Besides, Roxy and Mark need a few minutes to themselves. Bruce went to the living room and sat on the soft sofa. Hmm? I wonder if this sofa really is under a sleeping spell…….
An hour later

"Wake up Prince Charming, it's your turn" Mark said. Bruce got up and couldn't believe how fast he fell asleep on the couch. He looked around and Mark immediately answered "Roxy's gone home. She needs to take care of something personal, but she will call you later." Mark extended a hand to Bruce and pulled him off that insidious yet comfortable sofa.

"I don't know where to begin" Bruce said. His mind was racing at a mile a second. Mark smiled. "How about from the top?" Bruce shook off the residue of sleep and stretched his arms and legs. "How much did Roxy tell you?" he asked. Mark curled his eyebrow for a second "Well, we talked about a few things. But I figured with everything on her plate that you would catch me up".

Bruce nodded. Roxy did have a full plate. So, Bruce told the story about their meeting with Jake. Bruce tried to leave out some of Jake's raunchy behavior but Mark's no fool. Whenever Bruce got to a sensitive moment, Mark would raise his hand and say, "I get the idea" and moved the story along. Bruce showed Mark the pictures. Mark studied them carefully and looked up at Bruce "We better talk somewhere more private. Follow me".

Mark escorted Bruce to the main hallway on the first floor. "What I am about to show you, only my closet relatives and trusted circle know, if you say anything to anyone. I will have to kill you" Bruce's eyes widened and Mark realized he sounded too serious "Just kidding, I'm taking you to my secret office, sorry if I was being too dramatic" and Mark posed like he was acting in a bad Shakespeare play. Bruce pretended to clutch his pearls.

"My stars!" Bruce said in his best old granny voice. Mark tapped the wall by an old picture of himself with his family and Bruce heard a small creak. Then Mark opened a hidden passageway that led to another room filled with books like from some old castle. Bruce walked in his natural voice said, "My stars!"

"Welcome to my secret cove. I used to come in here when the kids and later when the grandkids got too rowdy. Oh, Janet would come in too sometimes to get a breather or watch her soap operas in peace. Well, eventually the kids figured it out because they could come in when one of us had the tv on in here. Take a look" Mark said. Bruce looked around and he could see an old crafting table, possibly belonging to Janet. An old workbench with some tools. Custom bookcases built right into the walls. Lots of books, some older than Mark, lined the walls. "Incredible" Bruce remarked.

"I'm glad you like it. Take a seat, let's talk about this Atrox and these pictures" Mark sat down and pulled out his glasses. "Whatever made these carvings, was clever. You can see here that it wanted you to think it was made by several other people, but it wasn't. I don't know how to explain this, but it was made by several 'people' yet it was from the same entity, does that make sense?" Mark looked at Bruce with some confusion.

"You mean like in those old action serials from the 1990s where a group of robots or people in bad spandex worked together yet they can combine to make one big robot or something like that?" Bruce asked.

"Yes, exactly. I did some light digging. This thing we have here is no ordinary crystal. The Atrox is old, like really old. I don't think we have the technology to properly identify what this thing truly is so people make up whatever they can to explain away something they don't understand". Mark said while exhaling a trouble breath. "Roxy did share somethings with me, things you know or suspect. I think our pal Jake is in serious trouble".

Bruce took a deep breath himself. "What do you know about demon possession?" Mark looked at Bruce with a serious but not reassuring look "To call a good priest and pray. But that's the thing. Whatever made this stone, is not some ordinary devil, it's something worse, like a force of nature".

"How do we fight it?" Bruce asked.

"We don't. We hunker down and let this thing pass through" Mark said. Bruce shook his head. "No, I'm afraid that's unacceptable. People are dying out there, I know you hear it on the radio and see it on the news too. The thing in your garage, yeah, that's no fairy tale. It tried to kill me. Jake is not himself, I think he's in trouble because at one moment, I am talking to my friend and other, it's like I'm talking to somebody else. There's got to be something we can do."

"There is but Bruce, there is. I told Roxy the same thing but understand, magic is real but magic is not the force, okay?" Mark stood up and walked over to Bruce. He put his hands on Bruce's shoulders like a real father would. "I will do everything I can to help. We will help Jake, but we need to confirm whether it is possession, demonic or otherwise. This might sound weird, but I truly hope that those Kingsmen people just showered Jake with gifts and money and he got this big head and he's acting out this way due to bad human influences".

"I wish that was so, but I saw him, something is off, Jake's a fighter. He will fight to the bitter end, but we must do something." Bruce said. Mark stared at him in the eyes. "We will. I am working on a solution right now. A counterattack for possession. But like I told Roxy, I think if we destroy the stone then this evil being will cease to exist. Everything will go back to normal and its hold over Jake and our world will be gone." Mark smiled and hugged Bruce. Bruce hugged back and fought back tears. "It's okay son, it's okay. Family always helps family and friends are family…just don't ask me to cosign any loans, okay?" Bruce nodded and gave out a light chuckle.

Bruce and Mark went back to the kitchen. It was later that evening. Bruce was heading out to his jeep.

"Now, remember, we have time, not much but little. I am working on the counterspell as we speak but it takes time for the magic to reach its full potency. I am not a wizard just a retiree with a good imagination" Mark said. Bruce stopped and now he held Mark's shoulders "You are a wizard, and a damn good one. Mark the Light Bringer, Bane of Darkness."

"Bruce, come on now, don't make fun of an old man like that" Mark said. Bruce shook his head "I mean every word. Will you be okay? Do you want me to stay?" Mark grinned like he was thinking of inviting his best friend for a secret pizza party. "Nah, I am good. I got work to do. Now, you and Roxy, go back to your daily lives. I will call you when I am ready, then the three of us will talk to Jake when he invites us down to see this mysterious cave, what's the name again?"

"Starwound."

"Yes, Starwound. Get some rest and by the way, here, take this" Mark handed Bruce an old lighter. "I know you don't smoke but you never know when you might need a light. Good night." Bruce waved goodbye as he got into his jeep and drove away. A lighter? I knew it, Mark the Light Bringer.

Mark locked down his house for the night. If his granddaughter came by, she had the keys. Mark went back to his secret cove and began looking up anything and everything he had on Starwound. Hours passed by as he read every single word in every book about or mentioning Starwound. He slumped in his chair. This entity is no mere demon, it is something worse and in truth, Mark doesn't know if he can beat it.

The Soul Jackal

Edgar Jackson was making the final arrangements for tomorrow's funeral procession. The family of Nelda Esterhouse had just left for the evening. Edgar was sweeping up the floor and noticed a small bracelet on the floor. He picked it up and put it into his pocket. Some of the flowers were beginning to wilt, which is unusual since many of them were delivered fresh but a few days ago.

Edgar walked back to his office and took out a plastic bag and a marker. He wrote down the name and date of the funeral; in the event someone comes back to claim the missing bracelet. Most people who lose something at a funeral home rarely come back to claim it. However, in the off chance that they do, Edgar keeps all items in his middle drawer in his desk.

He opened the drawer and it was halfway full of other plastic bags. Some of the bags were dated as far back as the 1990s. He placed the bagged bracelet into the drawer when he heard a shuffle and a mischievous laugh. He sprang up "Who's out there?" Edgar went outside his office and checked around the area. Edgar always checked the main viewing area before he left because one time in the 1970s, when the business was ran by his father, a baby was left behind overnight. His father said the baby was fine but had this thousand-yard stare.

Many people have stories about funerals and end-of-life rituals. Some cultures have families stay overnight to watch the body and other people use "magic" spells and trinkets to protect their loved ones on their journey to the afterlife. Edgar was familiar with the placement of coins on the closed eyes so the dead can pay for passage over the river Styx. Either way, Edgar checked the main viewing area, the lobby, and the office areas. Nothing. One of Edgar's employees came out the back area "Did you see anybody back there?" Edgar asked.

"No sir, the preparation and in-take areas are cleared and locked down. The hearse is prepped and I made the final checks myself" the employee handed over a clipboard with a sheet of paper with a list of closing duties and check marks next to them. "Good, let's go, tomorrow is a big day" Edgar turned off the lights in the office areas. The lobby was dark and only the viewing had some of the lights on. It was quiet and moments after Edgar and his employee left for the night, there was a shimmering of soft lights.

The spirit of Nelda woke as she gently sat up and realized where she was and felt the coldness of death. "Nelly" a gentle voice said. Nelda looked around and saw from the Aether, the form of her late husband. "Charles!" Nelda got up and embraced her husband. "Is this real? Is it time?" she asked. Charles looked upon his wife "Yes, how I missed you". Nelda embraced her husband, lingering in the moment then the soul jackal arrived.

Soul Jackals. They've been around since Ancient Egypt, rumored to be the spawn of a carrion priest and a female spirit who possessed a jackal. Foul creatures who often wear tunics, belts and robes with many deep pockets. This one had a small cane that is used to harness its magical power. It crept into Edgar's office and opened the second drawer. "Ah! Fresh leads" the soul jackal collected all the loot from the lost and found drawer. Names and dates, there are no expiration dates on souls.

The soul jackal put his bounty into a burlap sack and then hurried over to the main viewing area and opened the casket. Its eyes opened with glee and dropped some drool over the body as it smiled. The soul jackal held its wand over the body and began a chant; sparkling light started to flow towards the body and the soul jackal tapped Mrs. Esterhouse's forehead. A voice, more like an echo, began to fill up the room. "Charles! What is happening, don't let me go! Charles! CHARLES!" the soul jackal cackled with glee as he pulled the spirit of the deceased away from her journey and collected it into a small gemstone.

The soul jackal inspected it. "Pure innocence, a woman who never harmed a fly. I'll fetch a good price in the Infernal Market". The soul jackal placed the gemstone in a small bag that it kept tied to its belt. Other stones and crystals were inside, other souls it had collected. It is known in many cultures that there are two spheres of influence, Angelic and Infernal. The soul jackal planned to take his bounty to Iblys Byterra, the home realm of sinister creatures and spirits. Many demonic forces and lords would pay a hefty price for a human soul, especially one with such potent innocence.

Something was watching the soul jackal at work. The soul jackal looked at his bounty and found another name. Time to visit the cemetery. As it began to leave another force was entering the area and with a dark power the soul jackal never encountered, this new presence prevented him from leaving. "Hey! Begone demon! These are my souls, get your own!" it shouted into the dark mist surrounding it. "Demon? I am no demon, no devil, neither imp nor god. I am Ammuzol and I place you in my service, Jackal".

The soul jackal shouted obscenities at the dark mist until the mist began to take form and forced itself into the jackal. "AHHHH! AHHHH!" By sunrise, Edgar and his employees returned to the funeral home to prepare for the procession. The only odd thing that Edgar noticed was someone or something had looted the lost and found drawer. No broken doors, windows, or locks. It was as if something came in and left without a trace. An employee walking through the main lobby noticed a strange claw or tooth on the carpet and picked it up. The employee looked at it for a moment then assumed it was a fake or novelty item. They toss it in the trash can.

Mark's House, in the Secret Cove.

Mark woke up from his desk. It had been many years since he fell asleep on a desk, much less in the one in his house. Mark got up and went to the kitchen. *Nah, today, I am going out for breakfast.* Mark wanted to call Bruce or Roxy, but he knew they were busy. He tried to call his granddaughter, but his call went to voicemail. *Okay, I guess I will go out solo.* The weather was quite pleasant for this time of year. All Mark needed was a light jacket. He decided to walk over to the neighborhood restaurant.

Southwest Coralyn Bay towards the CBU campus

Traffic always seems to stand still when you are in a hurry. Bruce had many things to do but in truth, schoolwork was the last thing on his mind. Recent events have shattered his worldview: monsters are real. Hell, one nearly killed him and its corpse is rotting in the garage of his friend and mentor's house. Bruce wanted to do something, anything, but the tasks ahead of him would not go away on their own. Final exams and papers are due. Life goes on. If Mark was here, he would tell Bruce to focus on his classes and do his best.

Bruce wanted to help Mark, to channel the energy of the cosmos, to do something to help deal with the threat of the Atrox Stone. It's been some time since his last visit at Mark's. Bruce hadn't seen his friends in a while either and they were not texting as much as they used to, too much happening. Maybe he will get lucky and see someone, anyone. Bruce wrestled with the thought that a lot of things are out of his hands right now.

He had to trust that Mark would call them when he was ready. The phone, like friendships, is a two-way process. *Once I am done with my paper and turn it in, I will call somebody. It's been awhile since the gang, and I hung out at Julie's.* Bruce knows that after they graduate, eventually, everyone will go their separate ways. But it is not now.

Roxy's Apartment.

Roxy stood in her underwear looking at herself in the bathroom mirror. She turned her cheeks side to side then checked herself out before putting on her bra. Her skin tone was slowly changing color from her nails to her hair color, to her lips and other private areas. She asked some of her classmates and her doctor if they could see a light velvet purple hue or tint on her but nobody else noticed.

By the countertop, Roxy had a small pink box made of some type of stone, probably sandstone and inside was a small unremarkable crystal. She took it out and waved it around her body. She looked at it and saw that it was pulling the intrusive energy away from her body. She smiled as the crystal that Mark gave her a while back was working. She put it away when Jake walked in. "How you feeling babe?" he said while wrapping his arms around her and kissing her neck.

"Good. I'm heading towards campus. To study for finals" Roxy said while putting on earrings. Jake's hands were sliding up her rib cage. "You can study right here with me, right now". Roxy pushed Jake away using her rump. Jake smiled and caressed her ass on his way out. "No problem, babe, I got things to do as well. I will see you later. Hey, what happened to your new look?"

"What new look?" Roxy's curly hair bounced as she turned around to look at Jake hanging around the doorway. "You had this exotic look, purple, your hair, nails and other delectable parts of your body. Jake reached over and started to pull down Roxy's bra straps. "Hang on Rascal, not now. I mean..." She looked at him, at Jake, at least, she hopes it was Jake and not whatever she thinks it is, "We got stuff to do, remember?"

Jake smiled, not a naughty smile but warmer. "You're right. Sorry. Hey, I got finals too, plus I am going to work, probably another all-nighter. It is almost time before I can bring you down to see the wonderful discoveries I made". Roxy looked at Jake "You mean, me and the boys, right?" Jake nodded in agreement. "See you later" and he left with making any noise except when he turned on his car. Roxy checked her phone. No calls or texts from anyone, not even Mark or Chris. *Later, I will call the boys and give them hell for ignoring me. Mark's House, in the Secret Cove.*

After a lovely breakfast and a brisk walk. Mark was back at home and mentally recharged to continue the work at hand. However, he also checked out two envelopes with Roxy and Chris's names on them on his desk. He gathered a few more items into a wooden box: sage, a silver coin, incense and a vial of salt water from the Dead Sea. He put a bookmarker into a small leather-bound book and placed it in a side drawer.

Mark continued to review his notes. He tried to get Arica, his AI assistant, to help with some research but she kept coming back empty or with some other nonsense. Mark scanned his library for books, looking for something that he hadn't read yet. Then suddenly, a book fell from overhead and plopped on the floor next to him. He picked it up; it was an older book. Handwritten in a foreign language. Mark took a picture of it and shared it with Arica AI. "No known language or script in my database or any online source. Sorry Markie, I keep letting you down".

"Nonsense Arica, you're doing just fine" Mark corrected his phone app. This must mean something he said to himself. He calmed his mind. He sat in his Imperiale style office chair and let himself drift, beyond time, let his mind travel to distant lands far away. He saw two great beings fighting over the ocean and inside a massive Earth-shattering hurricane. Mark got pulled into the hurricane and was thrown around into he reached the eye.

There he saw a sinister figure holding a dark purple crystal and dipped it into the blood of the Earth, raw magma. The crystal pulled in the magma and kept inside, forever churning. The sinister creature chanted a spell, a few words which Mark knew:

Bind

Mirror

Shield

"That's it!" Mark pulled himself back from the ether. Mark raced to several books and had Arica pull some information about spells. Spells that bind, that mirror or reflect energy and spells of protection. "Arica, find out how to cast and how to break those spells, from history or mythology, and hurry!" Mark had some spell books on hand, but now, he can complete his task.

Coralyn Bay University, Library Annex

It is quiet madness at the university. Finals are bad enough, but Chris, Roxy, and Bruce are dealing with a heavy courseload on top of their daily lives. Chris is surrounded by law books stacked in several spots on his table. He is burning through highlighters, preparing for one of the toughest finals in his law school career. Second year law students call this the workhouse year.

Stacks of legal pads are scattered around the table, and a few of them fell over by Chris' sneakers. So many classes, so much to do, so little time. Contracts are some of the worst, so many details, so many things to remember. Chris is highlighting passages in his books and cross-referencing them with a practice exam.

Steam is still coming out of his ears, he and his partner, Jessica, had survived a hell of a moot court exercise. Chris felt as if his confidence was improving as his voice didn't crack once this time. Chris looked at the clock and realized he had time to review evidence and criminal procedure. Jessica came over and dropped off some paperwork in a manila folder.

"What's this?" Chris asked. Jessica leaned over and brushed some hair out of his face. "Remember that thing, we were talking about a few weeks ago. Your friend at the museum and the heist gone bad?" Chris had to think for a minute and recalled the right memory "Yeah, it was a few weeks ago, if I remember, why?"

Jessica's face soured "You asked me if I could run a few traces to see if similar events had happened related to any precious metals or gems with a matching description of purple crystal-thingy with orange glow?"

Chris jogged his own memory "Yes, of course. Thank you!" Jessica pecked him on the cheek and gave him a friendly slap on the other "Don't forget to go outside and touch grass, bye".

Science Lab-Forensic Biology

Roxy has her plate full as well. She had to finish a lab project related to a crime scene simulation. She had to document evidence, photograph the crime scene and collect and preserve crucial information. She also had to run mock DNA samples. Once the lab was cleared, she pulled out a few DNA samples she collected from Jake, hair and tissue mostly. The equipment works but it will take time for the results to come in so she logged her lab time as practicals for next semester.

Roxy finished up her lab work and headed off to the library to finish her analytical chemistry studies and prepare for next week's forensic biology final. Along the way, she met up with some classmates, and they discussed contamination and precision collecting techniques.

Main Library, second floor study area.

Bruce carried two backpacks with him. He was stressed and tired. He had to complete a mock grant application and budget proposal. He still had to complete his review for next week's conservation fundamentals exam and shortly thereafter collections management exam. The biggest hurdle was the grant and proposal deadlines. One of the most important tasks that a curator must do is get funding. No funding = No job and No money.

Chris, Roxy and Bruce all got there as soon as the library systems opened. They worked all day and into the night. They did the same routine until the end of the semester. Long hours, gallons of coffee and energy drinks. All three of them in the same campus but none of them crossed paths. Until the last full day of school. The campus was nearly empty as many of the undergraduates had completed their exams, and many others had finished their work and were about to graduate that weekend.

"Trotter! You son of a bitch!" Chris looked over to see who called him that and walked over to the guy. Chris rolled up his sleeve and without missing a step, as if these two men rehearsed it, they slapped hands and tightened their grip as if in an arm-wrestling contest "Brixby, what's the matter, can't handle it?"

"Okay, okay" Bruce said as he relaxed his grip. "I should know better than to tussle with a 2L workhorse". Chris smiled. "Damn BB, where've you been?" Bruce rolled down his sleeve. "Busy, schoolwork, regular work and trying to figure out how to prevent the end of the world".

"Most people get a hobby or get laid" Chris said. The guys heard a loud THUD! behind them. "Now you two peckerheads have better have a good excuse for ignoring me!" Roxy said as she walked over with only one hitch in her step. She hugged the guys and Bruce felt a little embarrassed as he felt Roxy's breasts pressed up against him. It was the closest thing to having sex he had in a while.

"So, how's everyone?" Roxy said as Bruce wiped off the dirty little smile he had for a second. Bruce was full of questions, but he knew it could wait, so he said "Busy, I just turned in my mock grant and budget proposal to Dr. Addler. I finished my exams and saw my grades, not bad, not as high as I would expect but anything over a B is a win in my book" Bruce said. Chris immediately chimed in.

"I am tired as fuck but glad to have finished my exams too. I turned in my paper on constitutional analysis with a case study on that lady who burnt herself with drive-thru coffee. Interesting stuff, poor gal only wanted her medical bills paid. I am here to turn in some books before I get dinged over the holidays. And you?" Chris looked at Roxy.

"Same, I came to pick up a lab report I ran and I am almost scared to look at them" Roxy said fiddling with her phone. Bruce looked at her "How's Jake?". Roxy was about to say something when Chris interrupted "Yeah, it's a shame about Dr. Chalmers, he needed that class to finish his degree. Now he's gonna have to wait until she turns up or if the powers that be assigned another professor." Then Chris remembered something else. "I saw Jake the other day, he looks kind of disconnected, did you notice anything Rox".

Roxy looked worried. "Actually, yeah, Jake's been under a lot of pressure lately. Dr. Chalmers disappearance. He passed his finals exam with perfect grades. He spends a lot of time in Crystal Valley". Chris looked at her. He knows Roxy too well. Something is wrong. "Yeah, with all the students gone for winter break, I am sure the Kingsley people will take time off too".

"I doubt it" Bruce said. "People like Grant Kingsley don't take time off. If anything, I will bet he will have people working all through the Christmas break and then some." Bruce noticed that Roxy's purple highlights have softened yet it looks like she put a fresh coat of that cosmic purple nail polish again.

"Hey, is anyone else hungry? I'm starving" Chris said. "let's go grab dinner, Julie's? or we can go to the Shrimp Shack?"

"Anyone hear from Mark?" Roxy asked.

"No, I am worried. I haven't been able to reach him in a while and it's not like him to not call" Bruce said. Chris patted Bruce on the back, "Come on, BB. Mark is a grown man. He's probably spending time with the grandkids or maybe hooking up with some sweetie from the bingo hall. Let's give him a call when we get there, so what shall it be: Julie's or Shrimp Shack?" Chris smirked while holding up his arms like a chubby scale of justice.

The Secret Cove, Mark's House

Mark printed out all his notes and placed them in a marked folder in his filing cabinet. His assistant, Arica, had made bookmarks on several websites and saved a few of their voice chats as texts so Mark can share with his friends. Three spells. Mark will need to channel some energy and cast three spells to undue the protection spells currently on the Atrox.

Unweave.
Trueform.
Sunderlight.

The sequence and casting information are all documented. Now, all Mark needs to do is gather the resources to cast them and the Atrox will be vulnerable. Mark went out to get some fresh air and walked around the perimeter of his house. He noted which items he already had in his garden and what other things he will need to cast the counterspells. Mark tried to call Bruce but got sent to voicemail. Roxy too.

Strange. He thought. It's not like them to not answer or text back. Maybe they are busy with finals. Hopefully they are done and are blowing off steam. Mark walked into this garage and lifted the lid to the makeshift casket he made for the dead morgrin. The morgrin showed no signs of decay. Mark sealed the casket and went upstairs to prepare dinner. As he walked into his kitchen, he heard a noise. He went to investigate and didn't see or feel anything wrong. However, the door to the Secret Cove, something closed it.

Downtown Coralyn Bay

"I hate bubblegum pop" Chris said. While Julie's was their first choice, Bruce and his friends forgot to consider that it is Thursday, so everyone is downtown getting ready to blow off steam from work and school. The upcoming holidays don't seem to slow things down either. So, since Juile's was not an option, the Shrimp Shack was the winner. Bruce and Roxy fiddled with the menu. No drink specials. Just a plain family restaurant but the endless shrimp bucket looks promising.

"Yeah, well, it could be worse" Bruce said while figuring out why he can't reach Mark. His gut tells him to just go over there. "Anything?" Bruce asked his friends. "Nothing" Roxy answered.

"What do you mean nothing?" Chris said. "There's plenty and you like seafood". Roxy snapped back to reality. "No, I meant, nothing from Mark. Hey, maybe, we should go over there". Chris looked at Roxy with maximum annoyance. "Roxy, give the guy some room. He kept talking about his granddaughter, he is probably with her. Unless..."
"Unless what?" Bruce said.

Mark realized he stepped on a landmine "Unless he's in the hospital".
"NO, NO, don't you put that on him, on us!" Roxy said. Chris raised his hands in a "Calm down" motion. The perky server came up "Are you ready to order?"

"Give us a little more time" Bruce while giving out his best fake smile.

Mark's House.

Mark finished cooking his dinner: Steak marinated with Brazilian and Moroccan spices. A large baked potato and some veggies. He ate his dinner while watching an old movie from the early 2000s. Mark put away his phone, cleaned up the kitchen and went to his living room and sat on the soft sofa. Memories were coming back to him. Then he was taken back in time.

"Tommy! Put that down. Hey, hey. Alyssa don't put makeup on your little brother!" Mark smiled as he let the soft sofa work its magic. Warm vibes, good times, lost love and deep memories. Mark felt a familiar presence, and he called out a name "Janet". He felt as if he left his body and rejoined the memories locked into fabric of his house.

Janet, as lovely as he remembered, caring like the most benevolent being in all of creation. "Mark" she caressed his cheek with her right hand. "Some mysteries can't be solved. Sometimes you must walk away from a puzzle to solve it". Mark was confused. He felt his wife's embrace. "Beware the answer that comes too easily. Beware." She looked at him and kissed him. "Wait, please don't leave me" Mark asked.

"Your journey is not complete. I shall come back when you are ready to start the next beginning. In truth, I wish I could stay with you longer, but I only have a few moments" Janet got closer and sat next to Mark on the soft sofa. She held his hand and they squeezed each other's hands. Mark felt something in his chest, a sense of love and relief…. then of horror! "Go my love! Leave! Go NOW!" Janet's spirit had a look of distress and Mark said a few magic words and forced Janet to dematerialized.

Mark reached into a drawer in one of the end tables and pulled out a small handgun. He walked over to the hallway and now to the den that led to the garage. Was it the morgrin? He heard something running but not in the first floor but in the attic.

Big Ray's Bar, just a block from Julie's

"Well, that sucked" Bruce said as he nursed his only beer. Roxy was stirring her daiquiri and Chris was chugging his fifth Dr. Pepper. "Yeah, the bottomless shrimp sure had a bottom" Chris said. Roxy looked up "You ate four big buckets". Chris burped and it smelled like fried shrimp and soda. "Yeah, and got the record too!" He opened his vest to show off a t-shirt that said, "I got tossed out of the Shrimp Shack!".

Roxy looked upset and nervous "Hey Foxy Roxy, why so gloomy" said a voice from behind them. She turned around and it was Jake. He came over and hugged Roxy, high-fived Bruce and accidently smacked Chris in the forehead when Chris mistimed his fiver. "Well stranger, long time no see" Bruce said. He immediately shook off any weariness, and all his senses were intact and focused. Roxy felt uncomfortable as Jake wrapped his arm around her waist and kept her close to him. His body was warmer than usual.

"Yeah Jake, what gives? I figured you moved into the caves" Chris said as he tried unsuccessfully to crush his soda can. "How's the rest of the class handing Dr. Chalmers' absence?" Jake looked at Roxy with hungry eyes then tilted his head towards Chris "What's with all the questions?"

"He makes a good point" Bruce said while raising his bottle "after all, it's just between friends, right?" Jake smiled with an entitled expression. "Yeah right. Maybe I wanted to check up on my little ornament" Jake leaned for a kiss and Roxy instantly turned away and let Jake kiss her cheek. "I can only stay a minute, long day and I am hungry, you guys eat already?" Jake seemed normal for a second.

"Sure did" Chris showed off his shirt again. Bruce confirmed "Yeah, we just got out of the Shrimp Shack, don't go". Roxy saw a notification on her phone: Lab Results In: CBU-FB-Project 5784. She got up "I have to go, I think it's my mom, excuse me". As she got up, Jake caressed the curves of her ass "Don't go far away, my ornament, my Roxalyn". Roxy froze for a second and made a beeline through the crowd.

"Dammit Jake, we talked about this! Be respectful!" Bruce tossing the remnants of his beer at Jake. It was loud and busy; nobody noticed how the beer immediately turned to steam as it hit Jake. "What? Look at around. I'm not doing anything different than anyone else". Bruce looked and could see a man in a tuxedo with a blond woman in a revealing black dress with his hand on her ass. Across the bar, an older woman is laughing while her younger boy-toy is behind her fondling her breasts.

"I know what you need" Jake said as half of his lips curled. Bruce turned back to face his friend when a hand reached out and grabbed his arm. "Hi, you're the guy who works at the museum, are you not?" another blonde woman with short hair and a thick Eastern European accent said. Bruce knows where this is headed "If you're want to know more about the failed heist, I suggest looking it up online, Arica AI is pretty good at gathering the details"

"No, I want to talk about the wing, what is a Nogwyn?" Bruce immediately turned away and saw this woman had unnaturally icy blue eyes, the kind of eyes that would put Meg Foster, legendary actress, to shame. "Well, I…" Bruce said as he felt dizzy for a moment. His senses snapped back online, and he was at the other side of the bar, in a booth with his strange "date". He looked over and saw Jake with a sinister smile. Before Bruce can say anything, the mystery woman waved her hand over to pull him back to the conversation.

"Sorry, I am so rude. My name is Yulia" she extended her hand to shake Bruce's. Bruce shook and noticed her hand felt smooth and icy. Yulia was fondling Bruce's fingers and palm. "I would like to continue this conversation, somewhere less nosy". Bruce immediately corrected her "Noisy". Yulia giggled "Yes, we can go back to my place unless you prefer yours?" Bruce stopped for a moment. This is too good to be true. Against all his instincts, against every man rule that states: never turn down a sure thing…" I got to go".

Something about her eyes, almost hypnotic. Her voice would put a siren to shame. Yulia looked disappointed that her prey got away. No matter, the night is young. Bruce returned to his original table and Chris was there, by himself, chugging away sodas as if he had a diabetic death wish. "Dude slow down" Bruce said. "Where's Jake? Where's Roxy?" Chris unbuttoned his pants button. "Jake took off, said he was tired and hungry. Roxy is over there, on the phone with somebody".

Roxy got off the phone and looked around before heading back to her friends. She looked nervous. She saw Bruce and pulled him to side. Chris felt like a third wheel, again. "What's up?" Bruce asked. Roxy's eyes looked like she seen a ghost. She showed him her phone: DNA test is inconclusive. Error message ID41. Bruce scrolled down. ID41= unknown containment in sample.

Bruce gave Roxy her phone back. He took a deep breath. Roxy is one of the best students on campus and a hell of a cop before her injury. Roxy is steady and doesn't make mistakes.

Bruce looked at Roxy. He knows. She took a DNA sample from Jake and tested them. If it was Jake, the results would show biometric details. This has to be a hoax, which isn't. There must be a problem with the collection or the equipment, that would explain a lot. But Bruce knew that there is nothing wrong with the equipment or the sample. This confirms what he and Roxy suspected for a time. Something is wrong with Jake, if it is Jake anymore.

"Let's go see Mark right now" Bruce said as Roxy went to grab her purse from the table.

Chris noticed them taking off, "Hey guys! Where are you going?" Before he knew it, he saw Bruce and Roxy's vehicles take off. "Rats!" he said while he called his house to ask for a ride home. Luckily, tonight's bill was on Bruce's tab. It was an hour until Chris' dad showed up. Chris got in the car and they took off. Chris felt a little woozy whether it was the stress from all the exams or overdoing it with the Dr. Peppers. Chris' dad seemed a little stressed too. "What's wrong dad?"

"Chris, I am glad we had this chance to talk, you know, man to man. Listen, I know I can be hard on you sometimes. I don't exactly have the best words and it's hard for me to share my feelings. That's not the man I am but I want you to know son, that I am proud of you, and I know you will make yourself one hell of a lawyer someday" Chris' dad sighed in relief then turned to look at his son. Chris was fast asleep. "Good talk son."

5200 Sea Crest Street, much later

"Pop, pop, pop!"

Agnes Meriweather woke up to some strange noises. She turned on the lamp by her nightstand and immediately woke up her husband Bert. "Bert, get up, I think somebody is shooting a gun outside!". Bert half-opened one of his eyes and an ear and listened. "Go to bed, Aggy. There's nothing out there, probably some teenagers firing bottle rockets".

5208 Sea Crest, Mark's House

Mark emptied his clip at his foe. The soul jackal has arrived. He had probably sensed Janet's spirit and arrived to collect her. Mark was afraid this would happened, the longer a person's spirit stays on Earth, the probability of a soul jackal or something worse would appear to steal them. Mark was not about to let that happen without a fight. The soul jackal roared and lunged at him. There was a struggle and it threw Mark down the attic steps, breaking his right wrist.

Mark was in pain; his age was working against him. He felt something was wrong with his left knee as well. He limped towards the living room. The soul jackal was lumbering behind him. "You will never take her from me! YOU HEAR ME! Never!" Mark stumbled over the couch across from the soft sofa. He reached to the table and yanked out the drawer. He picked up another weapon: The Last Light.

Mark looked at The Last Light, a knife tempered in special steel and dipped with a layer of silver and blessed by seven priests. It can slay demons, repel possessors, and pierce the thickest hide of the most stubborn troll. He held it out towards the soul jackal who looked at him. "For thirty years I tried to forget, to move on, to accept but no more. A thing like you killed my brother! Now, you're after my beloved. No more! Evil begone and leave my family alone!"

The soul jackal hissed and lunged at Mark who, using his offhand, stabbed the soul jackal in the neck. The jackal held its neck to stop the bleeding but Mark, using the last of his strength, shoulder-checked it with all his might, falling on top of it. He repeatedly stabbed the soul jackal with The Last Light. Dark reddish blood was all over his hands and shirt, but Mark kept stabbing, reliving his brother's final moments and protecting the soul of his wife, who he can feel is still nearby.

"Ahhrrhh" Mark's strength was spent. The soul jackal was dead. He slumped against the soft sofa. He was out of breath, tired, wounded, and scared. Mark took a minute to catch his breath and regain his senses. "My phone!" Mark needed to call for help. He needs to call for an ambulance. He tried to crawl to the kitchen. The last place he remembered leaving his phone. The soul jackal's neck snapped behind him. Mark turned around and saw the dead, limp soul jackal floating in the air as if it was propped up by invisible strings. It spoke without moving its mouth.

"I'm not here for your wife. I'm here for you." Bruce and Roxy were tail to tail on their way to Mark's house. If it wasn't for all the red lights and dipshit drivers quickly switching lanes or making illegal U-turns without warning. They would have arrived sooner. Both tried to call Mark. Nothing. They had to get there fast! Finally! Sea Crest Street. Bruce parked his jeep on the curb while Roxy parked a few feet past Mark's house. The porch light was still on as were the back porch lights. His car is parked in the side driveway. He was home.

Both Bruce and Roxy gave each other a half hug and proceeded to the side door. Something was wrong, it was locked. Mark doesn't lock the side door. Bruce knocked on it and waited for a few minutes while Roxy went to the front door and rang the bell. After a few minutes, nothing. "Maybe he fell asleep?" Roxy guessed but her own intuition said otherwise. "No, he's here. The lights are on, he would have turned them off if he was going to bed, I know his routine." Bruce said. He knocked on the door again. "Mark, Mark, its Bruce, I am here with Roxy, can we come in?" Roxy tried the front door again and by chance tried the knob. "Bruce!"

They entered the house and immediately knew something was wrong. Roxy stepped up first and pulled out a gun from her purse, Final Verdict, a customized handgun made for dangerous first encounters of any kind. Her police training was in full effect as she cleared many rooms until they reached the living room. "Good God, No…"

Blood, overturned furniture. Signs of a struggle. Dark red blood that looked like it belonged to an animal of some sorts. Footprints, one man and another thing with big, pawed feet. Roxy led the way: checking the kitchen. Mark's phone was on the counter. Multiple missed messages with a "KayKay" calling multiple times in a very short span. They checked the rest of the first floor and Bruce noticed the Secret Cove was closed.

They went upstairs "Don't' touch anything" Roxy said. They followed the trail of blood to Mark's bedroom. Both were beyond stressed out and scared out of their minds. They were afraid of what they were going to find. Roxy had her gun lowered in a standard approach position, ready to draw her weapon at the first hint of danger. "Dear God in heaven" Roxy said.

There he was. Mark Martinez. The kind old man from the museum. The kind old man filled with stories, good cheer and warmth. There he was. The man who felt like a father figure that Bruce never had. A kind mentor and protector.

There he was, on the floor, his eyes wide, filled with terror. His hands reaching out, his right wrist looked broken, his mouth opened, the last words of his life lost in that dreadful moment. Something was trying to pull him under the bed. The floor is flat, but when Bruce and Roxy looked, it seemed as if the bottom of the bed, where its darkest, looked open, like a trapdoor. Mark's legs were ripped. Pieces of pajama bottoms, skin and blood by the floor. Claw marks on Mark's face, his back shredded.

Bruce looked under the bed and saw an arm torn off above the elbow, its talons buried in the muscles of Mark's left leg. Chunks of muscle, a rib and a skull with a corrosive acid burning away at the skin and hair still on it, it looked like a dog-like creature. Roxy put away her gun. Bruce stared in silence. He didn't know how, but he knew. Whatever did this, didn't just kill Mark. It took his soul. Mark looked empty. His corpse, a grim reminder of what evil had been unleashed. Bruce could feel it, he knew it. Bruce's eyes swelled up with tears, his heart fracturing. Mark's death could be the end of the future. All the knowledge, all the wisdom, the warmth, the love he had to give to his family and strangers such as himself, were all gone, stolen by some unknown evil.

And Bruce doesn't know how to fight it.

Roxy stepped away and she made a call to the police, her voice calm and steady. As soon as the police confirmed they were on their way with an ambulance, she put away her phone and broke down. She and Bruce wanted to reach out and hold Mark, one last time.

Fractures

It was an hour before the police arrived. Flashing red, white, and blue lights littered the front yard. Cars parked crooked. Neighbors emerged from their homes, spying on the activity. Bruce sat on the porch steps, disheveled, completely lost. Roxy maintained her composure as she spoke with police first and framed the story: They were checking on an old friend. They found him in his bedroom. The police asked them a lot of questions, but the physical evidence is obvious. At least, it should be.

EMTs arrived and confirmed what the police already knew: Mark was dead. But it wasn't a stroke. No signs of a break-in yet lots of physical evidence to suggest more than foul play was involved. The detectives on site questioned Bruce and Roxy thoroughly and, based on the physical evidence, determined they were free to leave but they strongly recommended they do not leave town.

Something big and nasty had attacked Mr. Martinez, and dragged him upstairs. Mr. Martinez died from massive heart failure in conjunction with physical trauma. Then the assailant abandoned the body. Or staged it. Detective Meadows: the same detective who'd investigated the museum massacre, had seen it all. Literally. He spoke with the officer in charge, Lieutenant Davis, and confirmed: single assailant or possibly a huge wild animal. Either way, no physical evidence that Bruce or Roxy was involved in the incident.

Detective Meadows gave Bruce his card. "In case you remember anything else." Lt. Davis examined the crime scene. Claw marks on the banister, the ceiling, and the walls. Forensics found strange hairs: possible boar or something else. The lab would confirm.

Davis had a strong hunch about what did this. He looked at Detective Meadows. They nodded and stepped aside while forensics continued their work. Davis knew his next task: contact Mr. Martinez's family with the grim news.

"You know what did this?" Davis asked quietly. "Yeah. The lab will come back and say it was a wild boar or something similar. That it attacked Mr. Martinez, tried to eat him before those college kids showed up. Probably spooked it. Ran off through a window." Meadows's jaw tightened. "You know that's not what happened."

"I can't believe it." Davis shook his head. "I heard stories. Remember things. Feelings, mostly." Meadows held his breath. "Soul Jackal." Davis's eyes went dry. He nodded slowly. "Gather the evidence. If those 'friends' had nothing to do with it, fine. If it was a wild animal, fine. But we are not putting the cause of death: 'scared to death by the boogeyman' on any report." Meadows nodded. "Yeah. But sooner or later, somebody's going to find something. A tooth. A claw. Or…"

"Until then, don't say a word. Focus on facts. Evidence. Not speculation. Clear?" Davis's eyes were like daggers. Meadows knew there was only one right answer, "Crystal."

Since they weren't family, police recommended Bruce and Roxy to clear the area. Detective Meadows knew his next task wouldn't be pleasant: notifying next of kin. Roxy fought back tears, imagining the phone calls Mark's family were receiving right now. Somehow, Bruce and Roxy thought of the same thing: They felt responsible. On the drive home, Bruce couldn't help but feel hollow. Ashamed. He should have been there sooner.

Should have listened to Mark sooner. Believed sooner. Bruce should have noticed the change in Jake, said something, did something. Now, one friend is dead and the other, who knows? Roxy was thinking the same thing. All those signs, the strange behavior, the insatiable lust, "Ornament", Jake was in trouble, still is, and whatever evil power that has a hold on Jake probably killed Mark.

Roxy couldn't fight back the tears. Tears of rage, of loss, of shame. She should have known, she should have made the time to see Mark. So many thoughts, so many ideas. Roxy drove almost clear out of town by the time she realized it. She pulled off to the side of the road and realized, out of grief or some other strange power, she was driving to Crystal Valley, heading to The Devil's Maw.

Mark's House.

The police did a sweep of the house. They were looking for any physical evidence of a break-in. Often, the victim knows their killer and allowed them in but there were no traces of footprints, aside from the gentleman and lady who found the victim. A uniformed officer checked the hallway and found a knob on the ceiling. He pulled it down and a staircase toppled down leading to the attic.

The officer climbed the ladder and turned on a flashlight. "Over here!" Other officers came in along with Lt. Davis. The assailant came in through the attic. Signs of a struggle along with bullet casings. "The victim probably surprised whoever came in here. Emptied a full clip." Said the uniformed officer. Lt. Davis wasn't satisfied. He saw footprints. Not shoe prints or animal prints. Inhuman, something that tried to resemble a canine-type foot.

Detective Meadows checked out the garage and found a strange coffin. *Oh God, what is this?* He approached the coffin. Something bad happened here, maybe a drug deal gone bad. A grudge of some sort. Despite his better judgement, Detective Meadows opened the coffin. He heard an officer behind him say "What the fuck is that?"
Meadows froze, he knows what this is, his grandparents told stories about one to these things. One of them killed his grandaunt during a drive home to the South Texas brush country. "A morgrin".

Suddenly, something bumped into the table and the coffin tilted, dropping a broken pencil and a homemade shroud. A light mist disbursed and then the morgrin's body began to dissolve, melting into black sludge." No! No! NO!" Meadows called out. The morgrin had a sinister smile on its rotting face. As if it knew: the evidence that Meadows needed to prove to his superiors, to the world was melting away.

Detective Meadows knew they couldn't keep this quiet much longer. Those two people from earlier had nothing to do with this crime. The assailants were supernatural. Their attacks were getting bolder. More open. He took a deep breath. It was only a matter of time before the world went apeshit.

Roxy made it back home. Her eyes were dried and her lips chapped as if she had been wandering in some wasteland for days. She sat on her couch. She felt alone, scared, tired, and confused. The Christmas holidays are next week. The season of giving but something made sure to take everything she held precious away. In her hand, she held Mark's Prism. She held it, letting it tumble through her fingers.

Jake could come back at any time. She hoped he didn't. She hoped he would get stuck in the caves. Maybe she will get lucky and he will go away for the holidays, find another woman to spend with, go see his mother. She couldn't face him now or anytime soon. She needed to be alone for a while. Roxy lay down on her sofa, holding one of the pillows. Her nails darkened again but had little specks of glitter that shined on their own. She can feel that purple tint coming back, reclaiming her body. She didn't have to check the soapbox, the other charm that Mark gave her, to repeal the supernatural markings, was gone. She can feel the absence of its power, of its warmth, of its security.

Bruce made it home. He opened the door, dropped his keys on the floor and sat on the couch and stared at the wall for hours. He was too numb to speak, to think. Too shaken to sleep.

Outside, the rest of the world celebrated the holidays but for a few people, their world got smaller and a lot more dangerous. Meanwhile, inside The Devil's Maw. The air was stale; the place was quiet and empty. Even the Kingsmen team were absent. A single light was on in the CBU field office. Deep in the recesses of the antechamber, there is a hidden passage that descends into another area, not on any map. Starwound. Inside, the husk of Jake Dawson floated as if it was being aired out.

Something screamed and then silenced. Deep in Starwound, at its apex, a portal of energy was pulling in the very fabric of space and time, creating a void that human knowledge can't understand. Inside the abyssal portal, a dark power rested, feeding off its recent kills. Savoring its most recent trophy. Mortals can provide fuel but supernaturals are more potent. Many of them fled but it won't matter. Ammuzol rested in the void, summoning more of his great power from an unfathomable distance away.

Three Weeks Later

Bruce and Roxy recovered as best as they could from their wounds. It was hard, Roxy had to visit family and keep up appearances. Luckily, Jake had disappeared during that time. He didn't call or text, he was just gone. Roxy needed the time away, but she knew that sooner or later, she would see him again.

Roxy was worried someone in her family would notice her new "look" but thankfully with today's fashion, nobody noticed or cared enough to make a comment. Bruce noticed but kept it to himself. The spring semester would start soon, and it was hard trying to go back to class, to go on like nothing happened. Chris was busy, often disappearing for days on end, and when he would show up, it was to eat or sulk about Jessica.

Over the holidays, Jessica decided that Chris was a distraction. "I need to focus on my studies. I don't have time for this, besides, if you get lonely, you always have options" and she waved her hand and flexed it in a certain way, so Chris got the hint. Dumped again.

Jake was seen occasionally. He made no effort to see his friends. Roxy knew it would be a matter of time before he came looking for her. She always kept Mark's Prism close by. She needed to know and her instincts told her, the Prism would reveal the truth about Jake.

No word on the missing Dr. Chalmers. The university was close to pulling the project, but Grant Kingsley stepped in and had a few words with the chancellor and the state governor. The project continued. Jake's mom called Roxy and told her that Grant Kingsley offered Jake a job to continue the project should the university pulled the plug on it. Roxy checked her phone and searched for the local obituaries. Mark's funeral is this weekend.

Bruce's Apartment Evening

Bruce sat on his couch, feet on a stool, wiggling his toes. Trying to focus. Trying to pull himself together. He flipped the top of his lighter repeatedly. Open and close. The last gift from Mark. There was work to do. Bruce couldn't concentrate on school and he was missing work. What would Mark say? What advice would he give?

Bruce closed his eyes and tried to reach out to Mark. He didn't know what he was doing but he thought if he tried hard enough, maybe Mark would reach out, give him a final message. After a minute, Bruce felt tired. He thought that if Mark could come back for one last Earthly visit, it would be to a family member and not to a guy like him. Bruce looked at his phone. A photo he'd taken of himself, Mark, Roxy, and Chris having dinner at Mama Rona's. "I will finish what you started. Your sacrifice will not be in vain."

Roxy's Apartment

Roxy knew Jake would come back. He did with hungry eyes again, but Roxy needed to get close to him. She needed to know the truth. "Hedy Lamarr" Roxy told herself as Jake began to undress her.

Hedy Lamarr is one of Roxy's idols. A strong, independent woman who was a Hollywood star and inventor. Hedy had moments like this, giving the devil his due, often times to just to survive. It's an ugly reality. Later, as Jake slept, she reached out to her nightstand for the prism. But it was gone.

Jake pulled Roxy closer to him, wrapping his arms around to squeeze her. She felt trapped. She shifted to give herself distance. He just pulled her closer. She didn't feel like a lover being held but like a possession. She felt cold. Her eyes drifted to the nightstand.

The prism Mark had given her: she swore she'd left it there. It was gone. The world felt empty, yet life went on. *Chris' House.*

Chris stared out his window. He could hear his parents watching the news downstairs.

" – another attack reported this afternoon. A Tri-Coastal County employee was found dead outside Graham, sixty-five miles from Coralyn Bay. Authorities report that the 55-year-old employee was conducting maintenance at a solar substation when he was attacked by a pack of wolves. Eyewitnesses reported that it is a pack of Wargens; large hyena-wolf hybrids. Police and wildlife officials are tracking the creatures but caution the public to avoid the area until further notice. In other news"

Chris closed his bedroom door. His world is falling apart. He neglected his friends, even the nice old man who gave him the Joe Pesci signature. He didn't mean anything bad to happen, he was just focusing on himself and law school. The finish line is in sight. But deep down, ever since Jake found that stupid rock, things slowly kept getting worse.

This is all a bad coincidence. Nothing more. Yet something was wrong. He could see it in Roxy. She was stressed out, the new color, not just in her hair and nails. The lining of her lips and other body parts that Chris didn't want to mention. Was she sick? But now, wild animal attacks, strange happenings at day and night. A foulness in the air. Chris didn't know or want to know but he knew this, Roxy needed his help.

Elsewhere…

In the Devil's Maw, a coldness filled the area. All the security equipment was offline. A maintenance technician was dispatched to find where the power break was and never returned. Mr. Suit did not want to alert the authorities as it will bring too much attention to their real work.

An hour later, the "cleaner" reported he couldn't find any evidence of the technician. Deep in the Maw, in one of the tunnels, the remains of the technician were flayed, each drop of blood was absorbed by some unseen force, then the rest of the hair, skin, muscles and finally the pulverized skeleton was pulled into a vortex. Jake felt his strength returning and he gripped Roxy tighter.

Jake crossed his arms around Roxy's chest, cupping her and squeezing as he was excited about what he was about to do next. He was going to pay Bruce a visit. Jake froze and his body was on an autopilot of some sort, and his essence left his body and into the night air. *Bruce's Apartment, much later.*

Bruce finally fell asleep. He felt as if he was out of place and time. He saw his life flash before his eyes as he visited many places in different points in his life. He saw his mom as a younger woman. He was amazed how many men were hitting on her while she held his little hand. Then, he remembered high school and all the drama, the awkward dating and learning how to deal with people, especially bullies. He remembered his love of books and history, his gift of storytelling and the occasional wrestling matches his uncle would take him to when he was a teenager.

Suddenly, he felt as if he was riding a bullet train but on the outside of it. Suddenly, he was thrown off the train and smacked into something in the darkness. "Are you okay, Bruce, are you alright?" A soft yet firm hand was nudging him awake. Bruce opened his eyes. "Mark!" Bruce woke up in Mark's house, in the spare bedroom, it had to be a dream. But Bruce can feel sweat, he can hear Mark breathing, and he can smell the fresh mist from the early morning air.

"It was a strange dream; I thought that you had..." Bruce couldn't bring himself to finish the thought. "What, you can tell me" Mark said while sitting down on the edge of the bed. Bruce can feel Mark's weight as it tipped the mattress down. Bruce sat up next to him and continued "I dreamt that you died, killed by a soul jackal or something like it." Mark smiled as he listened to Bruce's wild story.

"I am okay, it was just a bad dream. Sometimes, our dreams are just our mind telling us stories or trying to work out a complex problem or..." Mark stopped, his hands were frozen in place. Bruce shook Mark to see if he was okay. "Or sometimes, it is something from beyond our understanding, trying to talk to us." Bruce took a deep breath "You had me scared there for a moment, you froze up on me like if you were stuck or buffering." Bruce laughed as he realized the last few days were just a stress dream. "Yes! Stress dream from work, school and the lack of a sex life, for the moment" Bruce told himself.

Mark got up. "Come downstairs and I'll make you breakfast." Bruce wanted to say something but then realized, it didn't matter. He was back in Mark's house and what the hell, let the old man cook you some breakfast. "How does pancakes sound? Bacon? Sausage? What the hell, we can have both, live a little, huh?" Mark said.

"Sure" Bruce answered and Mark got up to make breakfast. Bruce went to the bathroom and washed his face. He felt the cold water splash his face, he felt the stubble on his face, and the grumbling in his stomach. Yes, it was a dream. I am here and now...it will be okay.

Bruce washed up and went downstairs. He could smell something burning in the kitchen. Bruce went to check it out and he could see some burnt bacon in a frying pan.

He immediately turned off the stove and opened the side door. "Mark, hey, did you have to go to the bathroom or something?" Bruce placed the frying pan outside so the smoke wouldn't set off the smoke detectors. Bruce looked around the kitchen, then the living room and finally down the hall. He knocked on the bathroom door. "Mark, hey, are you okay?" The door opened and nobody was there.

Bruce went down the hallway and tapped on the secret panel to access Mark's library. "Mark? Hello!" Bruce entered the library. "Are you okay? Hey, we can always go out and get something to eat, my treat….hello?" Nothing. Bruce was worried as he didn't see Mark in the Secret Cove. He checked the rest of the house and saw a mirror in the hallway that he didn't recognize so he went over to see it. Nothing but his own ragged reflection.

Bruce turned away when suddenly a hand reached out and grabbed him by the neck. This thing pulled him in the mirror. Bruce was thrown to the ground, and he instantly jumped to his feet. Whatever pulled him in was gone or hiding. Bruce looked around to get his bearings. It was dark and the only thing Bruce noticed was the cooking of some meat…a scent he didn't recognize. *Don't go…. but what happens if you stay?* His mind asked himself.

Bruce ignored his own gut feelings and decided to follow the scent. He didn't think it was possible for the strange place to get any darker, but he swore he felt something run across his feet. Fast, spiny legs. Bruce wanted to jump and yell out of fright but caught himself.

Then, he saw lights…a feast of some sort. Large rocks came into view and Bruce realized he was above some feast…strange creatures, all muscular yet flayed, sticky and gooey. There was something cooking over a fire, an animal of some kind…. until Bruce got a better look…

The roast had its arms and legs chopped off; a skewer ran up between its legs and came out of its mouth. It was a man…. that looked like Chris. On the other side, these foul creatures were doing something else that made Bruce freeze…*is that, Roxy? What they doing to her…milking her? What the fuck is going on?* Bruce saw another young woman tied up with a bloodied cowl over her face. These creatures were eating someone…. Bruce heard screams…. *Dear Lord, it was Mark!*

"Invale-dur, obvilionus nul…Welcome Bruce Brixby."

"AHHHHH!!!!" Bruce woke up in his own shabby apartment. He woke up on the floor, face down and with Mark's lighter in his hand. Bruce got up and opened the front door. It was a cool night, various cars and trucks parked, streetlights in the distance. He went back inside and to the bathroom. He turned on the lights and there was Mark on the other side of the mirror. He was trying to break in from the other side, a look of pure fear and terror on his face.

Bruce found the nearest blunt object and tried to break the mirror. Mark was trapped and Bruce tried everything to get him out. Then he felt something brush by him and then some unseen force pushed him down. Something behind Mark snatched him and pulled him into a swirling vortex.

"BLAM!" Bruce fell off his couch. He immediately turned around and…. saw Mark's lighter was lit and burning a small hole on his carpet, so he flipped the cover to put out the flame. "Fuck!". It was real. No more dreams or fake outs. He was awake. He saw his phone had a few missed calls and messages. It was Roxy and Chris, today is Mark's funeral. Bruce looked at himself in the mirror and saw that his right ear was red as if someone had been twisting it.

Saturday, a cold day, Seaside Memorial.

Mark's family held the wake at Seaside Memorial Chapel. Bruce and his friends had already made their awkward introductions to Mark's daughter, Alyssa. She'd asked how they knew her father. Bruce showed her the picture from Mama Rona's. They were allowed to attend services but requested to stay in the back and to stay quiet.

Jake was there too, on his best behavior. He didn't lay a hand on Roxy once. Chris had his protective instincts kick in. He tried to position himself between Roxy and Jake whenever possible. Given the delicate situation, he could get away with it. In truth, 'Jake' had other plans. He was summoning his own strength. His eyes lingered on another jewel, a companion piece for his ornament. This one looked feisty.

Mark had a large family. Three children and seven grandchildren, most of them grown adults with a few younger ones. Lots of tears and the sorrow was overwhelming. Bruce and his friends stayed as long as they could. They saw another woman with a black veil kneeling at Mark's coffin, holding on tight. They could feel her pain. They wished they could kneel with her and hold on too. Roxy and Jake left together. Chris left on his own. Bruce stayed until sunset. He left moments before the veiled woman and her father.

Jake's Apartment That Night

Roxy sat on the couch, sipping tea. Her mind was a hundred miles away. Jake came up behind her and held her. That's all she wanted. To be held. Comforted. She put down her cup and looked at him. Tears rolled down her face. He placed a hand under her chin and tilted her head up. For a moment, there was concern in his eyes. Then he leaned in and kissed her. At first, she let him. But then he became aggressive. His hand pushed the top of her blouse off her shoulder. Roxy shoved him off. "What is it with you?!"

Jake acted surprised. "What do you mean?"

"It's never enough, is it? I let things slide the first few times. I know the stress you're under, but this is not the right time." Roxy stood up and balled her fists. "What's with me? What's with you?" Jake's voice rose. "Hey, baby! Life goes on! He was just some guy we met. For shits and giggles. He wasn't family. I'm your family. I have needs. You're supposed to take care of my needs!" Jake stepped towards Roxy. She took a step back to reposition herself.

"I don't know you anymore. Ever since you went down to that cave, you've changed." Roxy said while surveying the room and Jake. His eyes were pale for a second. He blinked. "I don't know what you're talking about. Of course I've changed. I'm trying to build a life. Make myself a success. I make no apologies. I like what I like, and I am what I am." He grabbed her blouse and tore it open. Roxy punched him as hard as she could. His face felt like granite. Cold. Jake turned. For a moment, his eyes had an orange sheen. "I like it rough." He reached for her again.

Roxy grabbed his wrist and threw him over her shoulder. He hit the floor hard. "You need to cool off." Roxy immediately put distance between them. Jake smirked. His head tilted unnaturally. Then suddenly, he seemed distracted as if something was pulling him away. He raised a finger. "Later. I've got things to take care of. We still have the Atrox Stone to deal with. Where is it?"

"I'm not interested in talking about the Atrox or anything else!" Roxy kept her hands up. Jake seemed distracted and then turned to face her. "You're right. I'm not myself. Ever since... ever since I found that cursed stone! Yes! It must be destroyed. Otherwise, all is lost." Roxy held her guard. "I think we need some time away from each other," she said.

"I agree." Jake nodded with a half-crooked smile. "A break."
Tears ran down her face. "Yes." Jake grabbed his jacket. "I'll be back in a couple hours. That should give you enough time to get your things. Otherwise..." Roxy held firm. "Don't worry. You'll have your space." And like that, Jake was gone. Roxy gathered her things as fast as she could. There was only one place she could go.
Chris's House

Chris fell asleep in his chair facing the window. A knock on his door woke him. His dad popped in. "Hey, Chris. There's a girl here to see you." Chris rubbed his eyes. "Who is it?" Chris yawned and stretched his arms out. "Some Latina with big—" Chris knew who that was and immediately shouted at his dad. "Dad! No. So wrong." Chris pushed his father out of the way and went downstairs. There she was. Holding a bag. Strange purple nails. Curly hair. Eyes a person could fall deep in love with. "Roxy?"

"Chris, can we talk?" She was upset. "Yeah. Upstairs." Chris gave his dad a don't say anything stupid look. His dad let the young woman pass. As soon as they were out of sight, he kicked one leg in the air and made a fist pump. "That's my boy!" Chris closed the door behind them. "Are you okay?" Roxy's head was lowered, as if ashamed. "I didn't know where else to go." Chris held her by the shoulders, guided her to his chair by the window, and sat on the edge of his bed. "It's okay."

He knew. She'd broken up with Jake. For how long, he didn't know. But he recognized a breakup when he saw one, especially since he was usually on the other end. When Roxy raised her head, she noticed Chris was making eye contact. He always paid attention. He gave her tough love as needed. He always had a shoulder to cry on, ever since they were little. Not once had he ever put his hands on her without permission. He never tried to steal a glance at her cleavage. Always respectful.

Roxy told Chris everything. The fight with Jake. The assault. Chris was silent. He didn't offer commentary or advice. he just listened. "I don't know what to do," Roxy said.

"I do." Chris got up, turned off the lights, and switched on a small globe that projected the night sky, all the planets, even a hint of the Milky Way's edge. "Remember when we were little and we both wanted to be space cadets?"

"Yeah. We were supposed to join Space Force together. Get assigned to the USS Ajax." "It was simpler then. We could do anything. Dream anything." Their eyes locked. They didn't notice they were holding each other at arm's length. Chris hesitated. He wanted to cheer his friend up not take advantage. But Roxy gave him a look. A look he'd hoped for. Dreamed of. And now, there it was. They slowly started to pull apart, hands touching each other's arms gently. But neither could separate. They kept their eyes on each other, each trying to decide if they should be the first to let go. Chris could feel his heart beating a mile a second. Roxy smiled; she could feel him vibrate from his nervousness.

So, she decided to take a chance herself. She pulled him closer. Chris took a step forward. They lowered their faces. Foreheads touching. Lips just an inch apart. Roxy had always wondered why Chris never asked her out. Why he never took a chance. But then she felt his hands caressing hers. He was finding his courage. Testing boundaries. His fingers moved up her arms, then to her sides.

She gasped. He tried to pull away; thinking he'd crossed a line. She pulled him closer. They felt something. Electricity flowing between them. Magnetism. And something else. *Oh my God*, they both thought. They'd found magic together. They held each other for a moment longer. Then Chris closed the window blinds. What happened next was a secret. A secret only Chris and Roxy would keep for the rest of their lives.

The next day, at Mark's house.

Thomas Martinez, Mark's oldest son, heard the doorbell. "Who could that be?" he said to his daughter. Thomas opened the door and saw two well-dressed men. "Good morning Mr. Martinez. I am sorry for the intrusion, I am Mr. Suit and my associate is Mr. Horne. Grant Kingsley sends his deepest condolences. Mark Martinez was in possession of something that is very important to us. Can we go inside?"

Hello KayKay

Two Days After the Funeral

"This is fucked up. What are we supposed to do? Go up there and say, 'Hey, we know your dad just died, but can we have some of his books? It's for a class project'?" Chris shook his head. "I'm just saying, there's got to be a better way."

"Nobody's forcing you to come along," Roxy said.

"No, but if I'm going to get hit by a bus, I want to be the one driving it." Chris snapped back. "Sooner or later, you guys always drag me in. This time, I want to get ahead of it." Chris seemed equally determined and irritated. "Guys, listen." Bruce raised his free hand. "If we can't get the books, all I need are the titles. I'm sure there are other copies out there." Bruce pulled his jeep up to the curb. "We're here."

"Let me do the talking," Bruce said. It had been weeks since Bruce and the others were at Mark's house. They could see at least two cars with out-of-state plates in the driveway. Bruce summoned his courage and knocked. An older man: mid to late forties, opened the door. "Can I help you?"

"Yes." Bruce's voice cracked. "We're friends of Mark. I mean, Mr. Martinez. I was wondering if we could come in." The man looked at the group with barely concealed irritation. "This is not a good time. And I don't appreciate solicitors or surprise guests any more right now. This is a sensitive moment for me and my family, so I'll only say this one time: Leave us alone and get the fu…"

"Dad!"

A younger woman appeared: very attractive, in her mid-twenties. "They're with me. Friends from school. Thank you, guys, for coming. Grandpa would have loved to see you." She kissed Bruce on the cheek and pulled them inside. Bruce had no idea who she was, but she'd just saved their bacon.

"Okay, sorry, KayKay." The older man's tone softened. "Hey, guys. Sorry about that. As I'm sure you know, we had a death in the family recently. A lot of us are on edge. Please, come in. Make yourselves comfortable."

"No harm, no foul, sir. I'm Bruce." Bruce extended his hand. "Thomas. Kira's dad." They shook hands. "I'm surprised Kira has friends as busy as she is." Roxy looked at Thomas with fake confidence. "You know our KayKay. She can be absent minded about her bestie over here…I mean..ah, let's go." She pushed past Thomas. Chris followed like a sheep. "This way, guys." Kira led them toward Mark's private library.

Bruce looked at the shelves, the antiques, the careful organization. They would never have found what they needed on their own. Kira sat in her grandfather's leather chair. "This better be good. I don't know what you're doing, but I want the truth. Any bullshit, and I'll have my father throw you out."

She turned to Chris. "And press charges for trespassing and illegal solicitation." Chris' eyes went wide. He swallowed hard. "Okay." Bruce took a breath. "I'll level with you. I need a book. About supernatural confinement spells."

"Confinement spells, huh?" Kira's expression didn't change. "What, you looking to enchant some SimpMate chick or nude model you met online? Last chance. Spill it, or else."

"Shit. You're not going to believe me." Bruce trying to find the right words.

"Try me." Kira pushed back. Roxy and Chris exchanged glances. Chris lowered his gaze. Bruce summoned more courage. "Alright. We think some sinister, evil force is out there killing people. Your grandpa, Mark, he told us stories. Stories we didn't believe at first. But he was such a charming old man, we humored him. Until one night..." Bruce paused, thinking. "One night, I was attacked by this hideous creature. Dirty overalls. Red beady eyes…"
"A morgrin?" Kira asked.

"Yes. A morgrin. I thought they were legends. Stories to frighten children. NPCs for video games. But I'm telling you these things are real." Bruce rolled up his sleeve, showing a large scar on his forearm. "Nasty cut. Let me guess: body trimmer?" Kira raised an eyebrow. "No, dammit! Sorry." Bruce stopped himself. "Sorry."

"I'm still waiting for the truth. Start from the beginning." Kira said with a firm finality to it. Bruce looked at his friends. He sighed and decided the truth would set them free or be the reason Kira called the cops. Bruce noticed something about her, a powerful presence. "Okay. My name's Bruce. This is Roxy, and the sheep over there is Chris."
"Hey!" Chris protested.

"I'm a graduate student at CBU. I work at Coralyn Bay Museum. That's where I met your grandfather during Free Seniors Wednesday. He told us about the Snog and the Night of Tears. Halloween 1990."
"Go on." Kira leaned in, listening carefully.

"Then the break-in happened. Some guys tried to rob the museum, but something went wrong and they killed each other. You might have heard it on the news.

One of the thieves was killed in the Supernatural wing and we're not sure but we think he might've bled on the skeleton of the Snog. And we think that's what woke it up." Bruce slammed an open palm on Mark's desk.

"Don't do that." Kira pointed at Bruce's hand on the desk. He pulled it away immediately. "A Snog? In Coralyn Bay?" She crossed her arms. "You know Snogs are native to northern climates. It's too warm here. If a Snog came back, it would immediately head north." Kira stood and walked closer to Bruce, making eye contact. A small shiver ran down his spine. "Keep going."

"I had to take inventory. See what was missing, lost, or broken. Then my boss told me about an artifact that her old college buddy brought in for examination. An ugly thing, really." Bruce looked at his friends. They nodded. "What thing?" Kira folded her hands just like Mark when he was telling a good story. "An ugly gem. Sometimes it looks like magma stuck in some kind of dark purple crystal. Other times, it looks like a calcified tumor. Or a large eyeball like those toys from the '80s. Other times, people claim to see a hideous face leering at them." Bruce could tell he was losing her.

"The Atrox Stone." Kira's expression changed instantly. "You're telling me your museum had the Atrox Stone. THE ATROX STONE. How in the hell did you find it in the first place?!"

"I didn't find it! The Chief Curator did or rather, a friend of ours who works for the curator's friend." Bruce was getting desperate. It was a hard story to tell much less believe. "Oh shit! You have no idea what's at stake, do you?" Kira's voice rose. "Aw, fuck!"

Chris had enough and he decided to find and test his courage. "Hey, lady. It's not our fault. Besides, who are you? Next, you're gonna tell us your family's been fighting monsters and demons for centuries, right?" Chris got up in Kira's face. Kira moved her head back as if he had bad breath.

"Listen. It's not about legacies or bloodlines. It's about knowledge. The passing down of knowledge. Over the years, many things were lost because people chose to forget or didn't protect. How the Romans made concrete. What happened to Atlantis. Early quantum computing from the Enlightenment. One more thing..." Kira grabbed Chris by his collar.

"If you ever step up to me like that again, I will rip your balls off and put them right here." She patted his left chest pocket. "Okay?!" Chris felt his balls climb inside him for safety. He sat down. Roxy and Bruce stood silent, afraid to draw Kira's attention.

"Okay. Well, now that's out there, let me introduce myself properly. My name is Shakira Karae, my family calls me KayKay, but you can call me Kira. The angry grump upstairs is my dad, Thomas."

"Mark mentioned he had three kids," Bruce said. "Where are your uncle and aunt?"

"They've gone home. The funeral was hard on everyone. Truth be told, I'm still unpacking things myself." Kira's guard lowered slightly. "My dad's here for a few days. I'll be moving in for a while at least until I finish school. I'm an undergrad at CBU too."

"What's your major?" Bruce asked.

"It was history, but my dad said there's no future in history. Probably right. I'm transitioning to business, but I have to take more foundational classes." Kira folded her arms across her body.

"Management," Chris said quietly.

"What?" Kira turned.

"Management. You should look into management. While I'll keep my opinion to myself... I see leadership potential." Chris crossed his legs, shielding his crotch with his hands. Kira smiled. "Look, I'm sorry, alright? I deal with a lot of guys always trying to get fresh or coping an attitude. Plus, you guys kind of just invited yourselves to my house. I have no idea who or what you are." She looked at Bruce. "But I believe you."

"Let's go upstairs for some fresh air. Does anyone want anything to drink? We've got coffee, tea, coffee, soda, coffee, and water. No alcohol. My grandfather had some issues with alcohol when he was younger. Can't say I blame him, but he never took it out on anyone. I think he drank to sink something deep down." Kira said while leading the way.

"Coffee's fine," they all said.

"Can I help?" Roxy asked. Kira smiled and led the group upstairs. "Your mom and I are stepping out," Thomas called from the living room. "Do you need or want anything?"

"We're good. Probably hang out for a bit before stepping out ourselves." Kira winked at her new friends. "Totally," Chris said, making a hand gesture with his pinky and thumb.

"Alright. Have a good time." Thomas hugged his daughter. Kira watched as her parents left.

She got her new "friends" settled in with coffee. Many thoughts raced through her head. Chris and Roxy. Those names were on the envelopes on Grandpa's desk. She knew where the book Bruce was looking for was and knew she had to give it to him.

"I have you at a disadvantage, and for good reason." Kira's voice was steady. "For all I know, you're the reason my grandpa is dead." Kira looked at Bruce then exhaled a deep breath full of frustration. "I want to make sure everyone understands what's at stake here." Bruce, Roxy, and Chris looked at each other, then back at Kira. "Hey, we didn't ask for this," Bruce said, speaking for all three. "But we'll see it through to the end." Kira stood and turned suddenly, as if something had brushed past her. "You alright?" Roxy asked. The hairs on the back of Kira's neck were standing up, and not in a good way.

"Yeah. Let me get the coffee." Kira headed to the kitchen. Roxy followed. Bruce rubbed his temples. Chris winced, his brain working overtime. Bruce noticed Chris looked different. Older. More mature. Bruce had to ask "Hey, so what's the deal with you and Roxy?" Chris brushed off the question, watching the two women in the kitchen pouring coffee into cups. Things were a mess. Life was complicated and hard. But sometimes, if you knew how to quiet the noise, things became clear. "I'll tell you later," Chris said.

Bruce leaned in. "Listen, you and Roxy are my friends first. Jake's okay, but we have history. No offense to the J-man, but…"Chris turned. One look told Bruce everything: the weight of his world had gotten heavier, and he didn't know if he was strong enough to carry it. Bruce gave him a nod. You are. Chris smiled and nodded back. Men had their own way to communicate. Sometimes it only took a nod.

"Let me know if you want cream, sugar, milk…" Kira produced a small flask. "Or whiskey." She poured some into her own coffee. Chris moved his cup toward her. He could use a stiff drink. The coffee flowed. The gravity of their situation settled over them like a weight. There was no going back. Evil knew them. Knew what they looked like. Where to find them. Running was useless. They'd have to take this thing head-on. Kira waited until her guests finished their coffee. "Last chance to back out."

Bruce held his cup with of his hands. He thought for a second. He put the cup down and took out his lighter. "I think, even if we wanted to, there is no backing out. I'm in" Chris finished his cup, looked at Roxy, then Bruce. "I'm in." Roxy nodded. She felt like she had a score to settle for many personal reasons. Besides, Roxy is never afraid of a good fight.

"So, what's the plan?" Bruce asked. Kira stood up. "Stay here." She disappeared into the Secret Cove and returned moments later with a book with a dangling bookmark and two envelopes. "My grandpa wrote your names on these." She handed one envelope to Roxy, one to Chris. "So, I know he meant for you to have them." She gave the book to Bruce. "Same with this. As I said, I have you at a disadvantage." Kira smirked at Bruce. *"She's got a cute smile"* Bruce thought to himself as he reached for the book.

"Why do you keep saying that?" Chris asked. Kira turned around snapping out of the connection she and Bruce were trying to make. "My grandpa's a chatterbox. He told me everything." Kira sat and produced another book; one with worn reddish leather that looked almost like a slab of meat. "I'm not sure Grandpa was right. I don't think the Atrox needs to be destroyed. It needs to be protected." The group gathered behind her as she thumbed through pages. Roxy instinctively turned on a nearby lamp.

"Years ago, I was on a trip to Paris and saw the Catacombs. Well, it turns out there is another secret passage but only if you know the right people." Kira said. "Or look cute?" Roxy looked at Kira. They exchanged glances and understood the power of persuasion that a nice body and a cute smile can do.

"Anyways. I went down this tunnel into a room, I was with some friends, no way would I go to some scary underground cave by myself" She looked at Roxy then at Bruce. "There were these strange carvings that looked like it was made by some older creature."

Chris teased his hair, so it stood up straight and made a goofy face then said, "you mean, aliens? You're saying this thing is an alien artifact?"
"No, dipshit. I'm saying it was made by something older than man." Kira looked at Chris with the classic *Fuck around and Find out* look. Chris made the zip the lips motion with his right hand. Kira turned to her book and pointed at a passage.

"The Atrox is probably a piece of this cosmodial entity, but I believe the entity was exiled into a pocket dimension. Kind of like a prison. Think about it; if the stone needed to be destroyed, why hasn't anything evil done it already?"
"Simple," Chris said. "Evil begets evil. Destroying it would be like the U.S. suddenly dismantling its Navy. You don't do that. You keep your best card."

"Or maybe other evil creatures realize that destroying the stone would unleash something more sinister." Kira's eyes were intense. "Not just competition. The apex predator of all apex predators."

"It doesn't make sense." Roxy frowned. "All of this happened when the stone was found. It had a large fracture. Was chipping on its own." She hesitated. "My boyfriend…" She glanced at Chris. "My ex-boyfriend. He changed. His behavior. Something happened to him after he found that stone."

Chris read between the lines. Roxy still had feelings for Jake. If anything, she wanted to help him. If this stone truly influenced him, Jake had never been a bad man. He deserved a chance to be saved. Deep down, Chris knew: if he was in trouble, if their places were switched, Jake would stand up for him. Fight for him. And if he had to, die for him.

"We need to be sure," Kira said. "If this thing, this Cosmodial Entity, if it is trying to get out, possession would be a useful trick. But we have another problem. The Atrox Stone is not here." Kira said. "Grandpa told me about a glowing crystal he had but I can't find it."

"No, we left it here with Mark. For safe keeping." Bruce said then Kira's phone was ringing. "Hi dad." Bruce, Roxy and Chris followed Kira as she was talking to her dad. They were trying to get her to ask him about the Atrox and Kira nodded. "Hey dad, my friends and I were looking for our science project. It was a purple geode with an orange crystal in the middle. Uh-huh, oh…okay…I'll tell them. Okay, no, I'm fine. Yeah, I'm good. Okay, bye". Kira hung up the phone. "My dad gave it away".
"He what!" the three of them said simultaneously.

"My dad said a few guys from Kingsmen International came by and picked it up. They said Grandpa found it and called them to return it. It was reported as stolen. They had a police report and everything. Cheap bastards only gave my dad a few bucks." Kira said.
"Fuck, now what are we gonna do?" Bruce said.

"I know, let's forget about it and go on with our lives" Chris said. It was at that point a strong wind gushed in and pushed down Chris. Bruce stood up and the wind pushed him against the wall; it brushed by

Kira's breasts and grabbed Roxy's ass. Kira immediately went to her room and brought out a silver scarf. "Everyone, gather round, quick!"

Kira wrapped the scarf around them as best as she could. The strange wind left the house and slammed the doors. A few pictures fell off the wall. "You all felt that, right?" Kira said. Everyone nodded. "It knows our names, our faces. We have no choice, but the question is, do we seal or destroy this thing?" Bruce said.

Chris chimed in "It's a moot point until we get the Atrox back, this Cosmodial creature will only get stronger. It won't be long until it kills one of us.". Kira looked down. "It already has." Time seemed to stand still until they heard a truck pull up. Thomas and his wife Connie stepped in the house and saw Kira and her friends in a semi-circle with a silver scarf wrapped around them. "What are you guys doing?" Thomas asked.

"Prayer circle. The latest trend, it's a generational thing" Kira said. They pretended to finish a prayer, and Kira started to escort them out. "I will find out what I can from my dad." Kira said. Roxy looked worried. "I think I know someone I could ask about it". Kira sensed something was awfully wrong. "Do you want stay awhile, hang out?" Bruce and Chris instantly sparked up then Kira shut it down "Not you two! My dad would have a fit."

"Actually, yeah. I would like to hang out for a while." Roxy said. It felt good to have another woman in the group. Chris remembered the envelope that Kira handed to him. He opened it up and a challenge coin fell into his palm. "What is this?"
Roxy leaned over. "A challenge coin. Often awarded by law enforcement or military for achieving certain goals."

Chris held the coin; an eagle holding a gavel and a bundle of arrows. A small note fluttered out. It read:

"To Chris, Bravery comes in all forms. Your words and your mind are your weapons. Your courage is infinite. If you need it, may this coin remind you of what I already know: you're brave and strong. — Mark"

Chris fought back tears. His chest trembled. He sucked in as much air as his lungs could hold. The last twenty-four hours had been a rollercoaster. He'd need all the strength he could get.

Roxy opened her envelope and found a note and an old arrowhead.

"To Roxy, It takes strength to do what is right. To fight for those who can't fight for themselves. Follow your instincts; whether you bear a shield to protect and defend, or use your wits and a flashlight to uncover the truth. I know you will make me proud. But most importantly, you will make yourself proud. — Love, Mark"

Roxy couldn't hold back her tears. She looked at the arrowhead and slipped it into her front pocket. She felt like nothing could stop her now. Nothing could harm her now. She would resist all evil that tried to impose itself again.

"Are you two, okay?" Kira asked gently. Bruce smiled. He knew what his friends were going through. He felt it every time he looked at his lighter.

The Angler

Javier Torres was having dinner with his family when his phone rang. His wife, Maria, caught his eye across the table: she already knew that his boss was calling. There is no such thing as an off day in the oil and gas industry. Eight-year-old Diego showed off on how far he can shove a breadstick up his nose. His little brother Marcus tried to copy him but was not too successful. Their daughter Sophia, barely three, was painting her face with mashed potatoes.

"That's enough you two!" Maria said without looking at them. She was watching as Javier got up from the table to answer his phone.
"Hey Travis" he answered.

"Yeah, just having dinner with the familia" he took a few steps away from the kitchen to avoid the chaos at the dinner table. "Okay, Marathon? Tonight?" Maria put her fork down, took a napkin to wipe some mashed potatoes from Sophia's face and tried to listen to her husband's conversation.

"Yeah, hell yeah, let me get things settled here and I will be on the road in a few, sure, I will check in when I arrive, see you out there". Javier turned around to see Maria looking at him from the kitchen doorway.

"How long?" she asked. She gave him the interrogation eyes; the kind of eyes that would make even the hardest man break down and confess to anything.
"Two weeks, its double overtime, we can use the money" he said as he took a few steps closer to her. "Hey, I know I just got back but this is a tremendous opportunity, not only will I get an entire month off, but Travis is putting

me up for a supervisor's position" Javier wrapped his arms around his wife. Maria turned her head away.

"Mira, Mira me." He said. "When I get back, I am taking everybody to Disney World. We're gonna see everything, go on all the best rides, give Sophia the whole Disney princess experience, it's gonna be great". Maria turned around, her eyes more irritated than angry. "Diego has a game Friday; he's been practicing every day for two weeks. You promised you would be there". "I know but."

"You always know but you got a commitment, you got to be there, he's only gonna be little for so long". Maria chastised her husband. Javier took a deep breath. "I'm doing the best I can, okay? It's a tremendous opportunity, if I pass it up, there will be no next time". Maria shrugged, she knew he was right.

Javier looked past her at the kids. "Let me talk to them". This was the part he always hated. Maria stepped aside to let him face the music. Javier walked back into the kitchen and knelt to talk to his boys. "Hey guys, I got some news, papa's gotta go back to work, tonight".

Diego's smile erased immediately "You promised to be at my game Friday!"
"I know, I know mi hijito but it's something I have to do, when you get older, you will understand but I'm gonna make it up to you and your brother and sister." Javier said while holding his son. "When I get back, we're all going to Disney World. All of us, you can see Spider-Man and Iron-Man, all the Mans. Marcus, you can go on all the rides you want, and Sophia, I will turn into a magical princess" he tickled his daughter's belly.
"Space Mountain?" Marcus asked.

"Sure, we can even go to Star Wars land and eat from that cantina like the one in the movies, it's gonna be great". Javier looked at Diego "Plus, I get to be home for an entire month, okay, I will go to all the games and even help you practice".

Diego sniffed back some tears and nodded his head "yes". Javier winked at his son, proud that he acted like a big boy. "Take care of your mom, your brother and your sister when I'm gone".

Maria watched as Javier went back to their bedroom to get ready to leave. Twenty minutes later, his truck was loaded and Maria brewed a large thermos of coffee for the long journey ahead.

Maria walked with him to the truck as the kids were on the porch. "A month, you promise".

Javier kissed her "I promise, everything's gonna work out. I'm gonna be a supervisor someday, less traveling, more money, it's all gonna work out". Maria nodded but didn't smile. Javier always makes promises and kept very few.

Javier climbed into his truck and pulled away. In the rearview mirror, he could see his kids with Sophia in Maria's arms. It was cold but they wanted to stay there to watch as their father left them again.

"I'll make it up to them" Javier said to himself.

The lights of West Austin faded behind him. He has a six-hour drive ahead of him in empty country. The trees would give way to scrubland, then desert, and then dark mountains around Big Bend. The temperature was already dropping, and the night has just begun. An hour on the road and West Austin was behind him. Highway 290 stretched ahead, straight and dark. Javier sipped his coffee and tried not to think about Diego's face when he turned away from the window.

"This is something I have to do" Javier told himself, "To give my family a better life".

City lights became scattered ranches and trees, with dense oak and juniper forests surrounding both sides of the road. The radio signal weakened, the music kept dropping or changing into another station, so Javier turned off the radio and listened to the hum of the engine and the noise of the road.

Around mile marker 47 or so, his headlights caught something on the side of the road. An old woman walking by herself. White hair, hunched posture, moving slowly in the cold. Javier didn't see any disabled vehicles on his way, what the hell was she doing out in the cold, at this time of night, by herself?

Javier slowed down and moved into the right lane. As the headlights swept over her, he got a better look: a dark coat, bare, wrinkly hands and pale blue eyes. She was walking with a purpose but to where? There were no houses or gas stations nearby. He slowed down and gently rolled down his window "Ma'am, do you need any help?"

The old woman stopped walking, her back looked crooked, she turned her head slightly as if she heard him but didn't make eye contact. Instead, she walked off the side of the road and into the forest. Just disappeared into the trees.

Javier stopped to look for the old lady. Nothing, it was like the forest swallowed her in the leaves and darkness. "Ma'am?".

Nothing.

"What the hell?" he muttered to himself. He waited for a minute or two before slowly heading off and back to the road.

She probably lives here, in an old house on some unmarked caliche road. She was probably taking a short cut; this was just too strange. Javier continued his way, stepping on the gas to make up for some lost time. He tried the radio but kept getting static or mixed signals so it sounded like a blend of music and somebody talking, nothing too clear.

A few minutes later, the forests began to change into scrubland now, scattered mesquite and the landscape opened itself to the night. The temperature was dropping, close to freezing now.
That's when he saw her.

A young woman, mid-twenties maybe, walking along the shoulder. Pink beanie over soft brown hair. She is wearing a white and brown fleece jacket. Black leggings that…Jesus, those leggings showed everything, every curve from her tight calves all the way up her hips. Javier eased off the gas and thought "what is she doing out here?"
Again, no houses, gas stations or disabled vehicles. Maybe her car broke down up ahead and she's walking back?

It's 34 degrees, she's gonna freeze out there. Javier slowed to a crawl, watching her in his headlights. She had her hands in her pockets, her breath visible in the night air. She heard him approach and turned around. The headlights shined on her to reveal deep blue eyes.

He rolled down the window "Ma'am? Do you need a lift?" She didn't react.
"I could call a tow truck if your car broke down somewhere" he tried to look down the road to see if there's a disabled vehicle somewhere.

The woman smiled, almost shy. "A lift would be amazing; I'm on my way to Maple Springs when I ran into some trouble. If you can give me a lift there or a hotel, that would be great!"

"Sure, hop in".

"You're a good man Javier; you're doing the right thing" he told himself.

The woman opened the door and climbed in, bringing in some cold air. She settled in the passenger seat and buckled up. She put her hands to the vents to feel the warm air from the truck's heater.

"There's a hotel up ahead, maybe forty minutes out" Javier said as he pulled back into the road "Westland Park, I think. They'll have phones, internet, everything you need to get help from there."

"I really appreciate it" she said then extended her hand "I'm Claire".

"Javier" they shook hands, her hands were cold and had a firm grip. "So, if you don't mind me asking, what brings you out here this late at night?"

Claire reached for his thermos without asking, unscrewed it and took a sip. Her lips touched the rim where his had been. She made a soft sound like "mmm" and licked the coffee from her lips slowly.

"Hope you don't mind" she said, her eyes on him now. "It's funny when you think about it, drinking from the same cup. It's almost like stealing a kiss."

Javier smiled and felt some heat spreading across his chest and thought to himself "Don't read too much into it, she's just being friendly, that's all".

Claire ignored his question but asked him the same "So, what brings you out here? Business or pleasure?"

"Business. I'm heading to a job site outside Big Bend. Pipeline work. How about yourself?" he asked again.

"Pleasure. Must be hard" she shifted slightly, resting one hand between her legs. The leggings left nothing to the imagination, the curve of her thighs, the way she pressed her palm against herself as if warming her hands. "are you married? Kids?"

The question hung in the air. There was only one right answer. Javier's mind flashed back to the rearview mirror, to Maria holding Sophia while Diego and Marcus looked on while their dad pulled away.

There is only one right answer, tell her the truth.

"Nah, no family, just me. Yeah, living my best life, day to day, town to town".

The words came naturally, easy, smoothly. Too smooth, as if he said them before.

Claire smiled widened.

Why? Why did I say that?

"Good" her voice was lower now "I think a big, strong man like you shouldn't be tied down by just one woman. Or a family. Or obligation. Men like you need to roam".

Javier's throat was dry. He reached for his thermos, but Claire was already drinking from it again, maintaining eye contact over the rim. When she lowered it, she licked her lips again, slower this time.

"You want some?" she asked, offering it back.

Their fingers touched as he took it. That same coldness from her handshake but now it felt different, more electric.

He drank from where her mouth had been, he felt a pulse between his ears. Claire shifted closer to him, resting her hands between her legs again. The cab of the truck felt warmer. Smaller. He could smell her now, her perfume was something floral and sweet, real sweet.

"How much further to the hotel?" She asked.

"About twenty to thirty minutes now".

"Good" She leaned her head back against the seat, eyes half closed. "I really appreciate this, Javier. Not many guys go out of the way for someone like this".
I'm not going out of my way; I'm being decent, he wanted to say.
But he was going out of his way. Westland Park wasn't on the route to Marathon. It was a forty-minute detour. He was already calculating how he'd explain this to Travis; road construction, an accident, he took the wrong exit, something.

The lie about his wife had taken seconds. This one was already forming just as fast.
Claire kept drinking from his thermos. Kept shifting closer. Kept resting her hand between her legs, fingers moving slowly. As Javier kept driving in the dark, the temperature kept dropping, the road stretching out ahead like a hook pulling him forward.

It was another thirty minutes on the road, and they pulled into Westland Park, a little hideaway tucked into the maple groves and canyons of the Lost Maples area. The motel was one of those old roadside operations: single story, twelve rooms in a horseshoe shape around a gravel parking lot. An old neon "Vacancy" sign buzzed in the office window.
It was past 11pm but the office light was still on.

Javier parked his truck and got out with Claire. He wanted to make sure she was settled before he got back on the road. Get her checked in, say goodnight, and back on the road.
They walked into the office, a clerk in his mid-to-late fifties with a bored expression looked up with some interest.

"One room?" he asked. Claire patted her jacket pockets. Checked her back pockets. Her eyes widened.

"My purse!" she said, turning to Javier. "My wallet, my phone, they're gone. I must have dropped them somewhere on the side of the road before you picked me up."

She looked genuinely distressed. Embarrassed. Her cheeks flushed. "I got this" he said. He pulled out his wallet and used his company purchase card "It's my treat, just for tonight. You can sort things out in the morning".

It's fine. This is what the card is for. Customer relations.

He'd seen the line item in many expense reports before. Everyone in the company knew what "customer relations" meant: when field hands or salesmen needed a discreet room. The accounting department never questioned it. They just booked it and moved on.

The clerk ran the card and handed a set of keys "Room 12. End of the property, thataway".

They walked across the gravel lot, their breath visible in the cold. Claire walked close to him, close enough that their shoulders almost touched. Room 12 was the last door, tucked against the tree line.

Javier unlocked it. The room was small but clean with a king-sized bed, desk, chair, and bathroom. Generic landscape painting on the wall. The heater kicked on as soon as they stepped inside, pushing warm air into the cold space. Javier sat down in the recliner by the window. Just make sure she's okay, then leave. You've already lost too much time.

Claire took off her jacket and beanie. Long brown hair fell over her shoulders. She turned to him, and smiled.

"Let me freshen up," she said. "I'll be right back."

She disappeared into the bathroom. The door didn't close all the way; she left open just a crack. Javier sat back in the chair. Heard the water turn on. Then steam began curling out from the bathroom.

Is she taking a shower?

She didn't have a bag. No change of clothes. So, she was just... showering in that motel bathroom? Heat spread through his chest again. Lower.

You should leave. Get back on the road. This is crazy, leave before you find yourself in trouble

The water shut off.

Javier stood up, preparing to say goodnight, preparing to walk out the door and pretend this was all just Good Samaritan charity.

The bathroom door opened.

Claire stood there wrapped only in a white towel, hair wet and dark against her shoulders. Steam rolled out behind her like fog. She walked toward him slowly. Each step was deliberate. "Can't you stay and visit with me for awhile?" she asked.

"I shouldn't," Javier said, but his voice sounded weak even to himself. "I don't want to impose."

Claire pressed up against him. He could feel the heat from her shower, smell that floral perfume again: too sweet, almost cloying. "I think," she whispered, "you're the only thing holding up this towel." She stepped back.

The towel dropped.

Javier's breath caught. She stood there naked in front of him, skin flushed from the hot water, curves that made his hands ache. He didn't hesitate. Stepped forward and kissed her, one hand on her hip, the other sliding up her back. She tasted like coffee and something else, something mineral, almost metallic.

He pulled back to take off his shirt, but she stopped him. Her eyes locked on his, those deep blue eyes that didn't quite look right in the dim light. "Tease me first," she said, her voice lower now. "Show me what you got."

Javier kissed her neck, her collarbone, his hands moving across her body. She was warm and wet from the shower. The room got hotter. His blood pounded in his ears.

He unbuckled his belt. Kicked off his boots. Pulled off his shirt.

"Yes," Claire said, stepping back toward the bed. "Let's get comfortable." She sat on the edge of the bed, ran her hand through her hair…

…and with a sharp tug, tore the skin off her face.

"What the FUCK!"

The sound was like wet canvas ripping. The skin came away from her skull in one piece, peeling from hairline to jawline, revealing something underneath that made Javier's brain seize.

Blue-grey flesh. Not skin: something thicker, rougher, covered in tiny scales that caught the light like fish scales. Her eyes! Those beautiful blue eyes shifted, the pupils elongating into vertical slits, the irises turning yellow and reptilian.

Pustular liquid oozed from the tear-line where skin met scale, thick and grey like infected pus. "No," Javier stammered, stumbling backward. "No, no"

Claire: the thing that had been Claire, smiled. Thin lips pulled back to show teeth that were too white, too sharp, too many.

Her forehead began to bulge.

The sound was worse than the skin tearing. It was the sound of bone cracking, cartilage grinding, something inside her skull reshaping itself. The skin over her forehead split horizontally, pulling apart like an oyster shell opening to reveal pink-grey meat underneath.

Something emerged from the split.

A pearl.

Perfect. Luminous. Beautiful.

It grew from her forehead like a grotesque third eye, swelling to the size of a golf ball, held in place by fibrous tissue that pulsed with her heartbeat. The pearl began to glow soft blue-white light that filled the room like moonlight through water.

Javier couldn't look away.

The light entered his eyes and went deeper, pushing past his optic nerves and into his brain. He felt something shut down: the part of him that controlled his legs, his arms, his ability to scream. Just... turned off like a switch being flipped.

Run. RUN. MOVE.

His body didn't obey.

He stood there, frozen, as the thing that had been Claire stood up from the bed. The light from the pearl pulsed gently, rhythmically, like a heartbeat. Like a lure dangling in deep water.

"Come here," she said, but her voice was wrong now — layered, wet, like words spoken through water.

And Javier's body obeyed.

His legs moved forward against his will. One step. Another. Walking toward her even as his mind screamed at him to run, to fight, to do anything.

Maria. Diego. Marcus. Sophia. Oh God, what have I done?

The thing's jaw began to shift. He heard the click and pop of tendons releasing, bones unhinging. Her mouth opened wider than any human mouth should open—: wider, wider, until the jaw hung loose and dislocated.

Inside: rows of teeth. Thin, needle-sharp, angled backward like an angler fish. Hundreds of them gleaming wet in the pearl's light. Javier stood in front of her, paralyzed, aware, watching his own death approach. The pearl pulsed.

Her mouth opened wider. Her hands reached out to his neck and pulled him closer. He couldn't resist, fight back and the only thing he kept telling himself as he remembered the last image of his family in the rearview mirror was, *I'm sorry. I'm sorry. I'm so sorry.*
Three days later.

Sheriff Hildebrant toured the scene at Westland Park, Room 12. He'd been a lawman for twenty-three years and thought he'd seen everything. He was wrong.

The bed was soaked through with dried blood: black now, oxidized, the mattress sagging under the weight of it. Chunks of flesh scattered across the floor, some the size of steaks, others just scraps. Ribbons of tissue hung from the headboard. The smell hit him like a wall: copper and rot and something else, something briny that reminded him of dead fish on a beach.

A man's torso lay on the bed, or what was left of it. The ribcage was cracked open, ribs splayed outward like a grotesque flower. Most of the organs were gone. The face was... partially there. Enough to ID from dental records, maybe.

"Good Lord," Hildebrant muttered.

Deputy Collins approached, his face pale. "Poor bastard was either eaten by a wild animal or met one fucked-up serial killer." Hildebrant crouched near the bed, examining the bite marks on what remained of the body. The teeth that did this weren't from any animal native to Texas. Too many. Too uniform. The pattern was wrong.

"This was no wild animal," Hildebrant said. "Wild animals hunt for food, not sport." But this: this was orchestrated. Methodical. Like a hunter.

He thought about female coyotes luring domestic dogs into ambush zones. The female would go into heat, lead some horny neighborhood dog away from safety, and let her pack devour it. Same principle here. Lure. Isolate. Kill.

"Our killer lured the victim with promises of sex," Hildebrant said. "Any ID?"

"Javier Torres, out of Hornet's Nest," Collins said. "Wife and boss both filed missing persons about a day ago. He was supposed to be at a job site in Marathon, never showed up." Hildebrant looked at the ruined body on the bed. Javier Torres. Married. Had a job. Took a detour he shouldn't have taken. "Damn fool," he muttered. "If you'd only stayed on your path."

"You want me to make the call to Mrs. Torres?" Collins asked.

"No." Hildebrant stood up. "This is my county. My responsibility. When's the forensic examiner getting here?"

"Hour, maybe less."

"Get this place secured. Collins, a word outside."

They stepped out into the cold morning air. The sun was just coming up over the maples, golden light filtering through bare branches. "What does this remind you of?" Hildebrant asked quietly. Collins, an older deputy, been around longer, thought for a moment. His face went pale.

"McFlagg. '78."

Randy McFlagg. 1978. The old Bearlund Estates Hotel. Same MO. Same bite patterns. Same impossible anatomy to the wounds.
Cold case. Unsolved.

The locals had their own explanation: old superstition about creatures called Anglers. Legend said they lived by coastal cities originally, but one got brought inland. Old Randy McFlagg caught something off the Gulf in '78. Brought it back to Bearlund Estates as a trophy. Thing wasn't dead.

It killed McFlagg and escaped to the rivers. Locals say it spawned there and some of the offspring adapted to hunt on dry land. They call 'em Anglers. The females hunt while the males…well, nobody's sure they seen a male and those that did, didn't live to tell about it.

The locals believed Anglers still prowled the back roads, fishing for food. Or mates. Hildebrant had always dismissed it as folklore. Small-town ghost stories.
Until now.
"Don't say anything yet," Hildebrant said. "But work this case like it's connected to '78. I've got a suspicion."

He walked back to his cruiser, lit a cigarette, letting the smoke calm his nerves. He got in and started the engine.

Back to the station. An hour drive. He had a phone call to make to Mrs. Torres. Had to tell her that her husband was dead. That he'd been found in a motel room, torn apart, miles off his route. Hildebrant pulled out onto the highway, heading west.
That's when he saw her.

A woman on the left side of the road. Pink beanie. White and brown fleece jacket. Black leggings that showed every curve. She turned around as he passed. Those bright blue eyes.

Hildebrant's foot eased off the gas. His hand moved toward the door lock, unlocking it. Just pull over. See if she needs help. That's what you do.

He pulled onto the shoulder.

The woman walked toward his cruiser, smiling.

The Sovereign Cut

The following day, it was decided that everyone should go with Roxy to Jake's Apartment so she can pick up the rest of her things. The next task would be to go to the Devil's Maw and ask Jake if he knows where the Kingsmen took the Atrox Stone.

Bruce and Chris rode together in Bruce's jeep. Bruce took the long way to Jake's apartment; giving her and Kira a chance to talk and bond. It was good to have another woman in the group. While driving down Ocean Park Boulevard, Bruce saw a blonde woman walking alone. Blue beanie, black fleece jacket, tight white leggings showing off her curves. Her ass bounced as she walked. She turned around and made eye contact: stunning light green eyes, pulling him closer...
"WATCH THE FUCK OUT!"

Chris grabbed the steering wheel and yanked Bruce's jeep back into its proper lane, narrowly avoiding a head-on collision with an 18-wheeler. The truck's horn blared. The driver cursed at them. "DUDE! What the fuck is wrong with you?!" Chris clutched his chest.
"What? Hey, man, I'm in a dry spell here. I'll take any chance I get..." Bruce said. He couldn't believe what he saw, not just the nice ass but those eyes...they had had him like an angler fish luring in its prey.

"I don't want to die because you want to get your dick wet!" Chris's voice cracked with anger. "Look, let's focus on what we have to do. And I promise you; I promise once we save the world, if you still can't get any, I will personally jerk you off. So please, don't kill us!" Chris paused for a second. "I think I peed a little."

Bruce made a face but couldn't get mad. It was his fault. Good thing about a jeep, it's easy to hose off any messes. Chris turned around and leaned back in his seat. "She does have a nice ass. But not worth dying for."
Broadway Street Kira's VW Beetle

Kira drove while Roxy shared an elaborate story. She told Kira about her strange dreams, each one heavier than the last. "No way! He took your top off? Like, In front of everybody?" Kira's eyes were wide. "Yeah. In my dream." Roxy's face flushed with embarrassment. "I couldn't help it. And the fucked-up part? I wanted it. Like, really wanted it. My body was responding and I couldn't stop it. Is that wrong?"

Kira thought for a moment. "Not really. I mean, it's tough being locked down in one relationship for a long time. It's normal to want to explore. Hell, sometimes you just want to feel wanted again, like you still have the goods, you know what I mean? Not comfortable. Not safe. But wanted. Desired. Like you're the only thing in the world he sees."

Kira smiled, but it faded quickly. "I like being able to come and go as I please. Someday, if the right person comes along, I'm sure I'll settle down. *Maybe.* My grandpa wanted to stick around long enough for me to..."Kira fought back tears. Roxy reached over and rubbed her shoulder.

"I'm okay," Kira said, composing herself. "Continue with the dream. Tell me about this guy."
Bruce's jeep with some streaks across the driver's side.

"Dude, you did the right thing," Bruce said. "But it's complicated. She broke up with him yesterday. But I know she still has feelings. I don't know..." Chris trailed off.

"Hey, man. You two have known each other for a long time. You both spend so much time together. It's natural. Nothing to be ashamed of." Bruce waited to make a left turn. "You said it yourself; she didn't push you away. Didn't reject you. Maybe this is something you both needed. Getting the anxiety out. If I may dare to say it: you two would make a good couple."
"She's got Jake."

"Things change, my friend. Things change." Bruce raised his eyebrows and made a snarky grin. "Listen to us. Our friend is probably possessed, and we're talking about me stealing his girlfriend behind his back. There's no way the universe won't punish us for this." Chris's face was heavy with guilt.

"First of all, we're going to save our friend. The change in his behavior; I'm sure he's possessed. So, we'd better find out our options. Second: you feel what you feel. It's natural. People fall in and out of love all the time. You can't help it. If it's meant to be, it's meant to be. Don't fight it. Just let it be." They arrived at Jake's place first. Chris unbuckled his seatbelt. "I don't know if I can do that." Bruce got out. "Hey. I'm not trying to tell you what to do or how to feel. Just know my words haven't changed. I've got your back."
"Yeah?" Chris looked at his friend.

"Always." Bruce looked around. "Jake's truck isn't here. Lights are still on. Let's take a look around and wait for the girls." Chris began looking around, nerves fraying. Then he felt the coin in his pocket. That big brass challenge coin. He took it out and looked at it. A sensation spread through his gut. Warmth. Confidence. It'll be alright. You've got this.
Kira's Car

"Damn, girl. I thought I was the only one with those dreams," Kira said. Roxy folded her arms. "You had a similar one? Did your nails turn purple from shock or possession?" Roxy wiggled her fingers in a ghostly fashion. "No. I changed the channel before it got that heavy." Kira held up her right hand to her ear and made a twisting motion.

"You what?" Roxy scoffed.
"Changed the channel. That's what my grandpa used to tell me whenever I had bad dreams. Just change the channel."
Roxy leaned back, waiting for Kira to tell the rest of the story. "You had a dream or two? Was it the same guy as mine?"

"I don't know! I haven't seen your guy, but I'll admit: my guy acted a lot like yours. I even tasted that damn drink. Obsidian Ember. There's nothing like it anywhere."
Suddenly, both women realized: that drink; with its addictive, infectious taste, wasn't made from anything in this world.

"Look, in the spirit of sharing, I'll tell you about my dream." Kira's voice softened. "It was three years ago. I'd started college late; took some time off to travel, really get to know myself. I was still living with my folks in Neon City. I had this dream. It felt so real."
Roxy listened carefully.

"I dreamt I was in London. Maybe Paris. Could've been Rome. Europe, definitely. I was taking a subway, and got lost. So many people around. Guys kept 'bumping' into me. If you know what I mean." Roxy raised an eyebrow. Guys could be horny savages. "I ended up wandering the streets. Hard to tell where I was. Suddenly, there was this nice plaza. Lots of lights.

Beautiful night sky. That's when he saw me. The man with the smooth voice. Salt-and-pepper hair. Strong build. Handsome. With the strongest bedroom eyes, I'd ever seen."

Roxy knew that look. Possibly the same man that seduced her. "He came over. I didn't want to talk to him at first. Thought he was looking for a sugar baby. I wasn't interested. Until he spoke." Kira's eyes glossed over. Her hands gripped the wheel, driving on autopilot. "His voice. I couldn't resist. I just wanted to hear him say anything. For hours. Then he offered me a drink." Kira licked her lips.

"Obsidian Ember," Roxy said quietly.

"Yes. I had one taste. It made me feel warm. Glowing. Like every nerve just... woke up at once. I felt it everywhere." She paused. "He got closer. Put his hands on my waist. And girl, the way he looked at me. Like he wanted to devour me. His hands started sliding lower, and I felt everything just heat up. Everywhere. And as his hands kept moving..."

Kira made the ear-twisting motion. "Changed the channel. I woke up in a sweat. Then I noticed my lips were stained purple. Took forever to go away. I'd only had one sip."

Kira had the thousand-yard stare.

Roxy looked at her nails. "Did you... did you want to go back? To the dream?"

Kira's grip tightened on the wheel. "Every fucking night for a month. I'd try to fall asleep and find him again. That's how I knew it was wrong."

"Do you think it's the same guy? The Cosmo monster?" Roxy asked as she wrapped her arms around herself. Kira took a deep breath. "Probably. Yes." She pulled up to a stop.

"Listen. I don't have all the answers. But I know that whatever did this to you has done it before. I feel it now. We must try to stop it. We will reclaim our lives. Our future. Everything. We'll avenge our loved ones. Avenge ourselves. We are not pieces of meat made solely for the pleasure of some cosmic being."

"Let's get your things. Then we can talk some more about Jake. The changes in his behavior. Mood. Everything." Kira turned to face Roxy. "I can't help you if you don't tell me everything." Roxy smiled. "Your grandpa said the same thing to me."

"It runs in the family." Kira winked, parked the car and got out. Bruce and Chris joined them. Jake's not there so it was safe for Roxy to get her things. Bruce and Kira spoke while Roxy and Chris went inside to get her things. "Hey" Bruce said.

"Hey yourself" Kira said. "Your buddy's got a nice place. I couldn't afford an apartment like this." Bruce nodded "Yeah, ol' Jake got several grants and scholarships. Mostly from private industries. He was going to be a geologist someday. He's probably gonna work for one of the bigger oil companies." Kira looked around. "If Grant Kingsley is involved, I can see how your friend can afford a place like this but people like that don't give their money away unless they want something."

"Isn't that just capitalism?" Bruce snorted back. "Maybe, or maybe it's selling your soul" Kira said. Bruce nodded and said to himself *Capitalism, just like I said.* "Well, for somebody who is going into accounting, I am sure you will avoid the mega-firms and stick to the smaller ones, more fulfilling right?" Kira gave Bruce a look, the look that most women give to men, when they make a good point. Chris and Roxy were coming back with a few boxes. Everyone knew once Roxy got her things in Kira's car, they would have no choice but to go to Jake's office. Chris was nervous, he had a bad feeling about driving out to the Devil's Maw. "Let me call him first" Chris suggested. Nothing.

Bruce tried no luck. After some hesitation, so did Roxy. Nothing. Kira tried in the off-chance Jake would answer but that was the third strike. Roxy remembered that she got Jake a step-counting device so Jake can track the number of steps he takes in a day. Chris was able to use the corresponding phone app, and it says that Jake is offline. "So, either he is underground, out of town, or his phone is off". Chris said.

All four of them knew going to the Devil's Maw was a bad idea. "Let's just wait a while and see if we can call him." Bruce said.

On the road towards Coralyn Bay Airport.

"That was easier than I thought." Mr. Suit sat in the back of a limousine, sipping tea. Things were finally looking up. He could send Mr. Kingsley the news he'd longed to hear: the Sovereign's Cut had been found and was on its way. He waited for his call to connect to Mr. Kingsley's private line. "Excellent news, sir. I have the Sovereign's Cut in my possession" Grant Kingsley's voice came through. "Perfect! I'll have all the arrangements made. Go directly to my private airport, hangar seven. I'll be waiting for you on Maranoa Island. Well, done."

Mr. Kingsley went to a mirror and admired himself. Soon, very soon, he would make an announcement. The discovery not of the year, or the decade, or even the century, but of a lifetime. Mr. Suit had time before arriving at the airport. He reorganized his thoughts, tying up loose ends. Dr. Chalmers. She'd stolen the Sovereign's Cut. He knew it. The jewel emitted a strange, unique signal. Did she really think they wouldn't notice?

Mr. Suit wasn't a violent man. He had other people commit violence for him. But in this case, it had been a warmup. He remembered that night well. The spotter had painted Dr. Chalmers's car. They'd redirected her GPS to lead her off the main road. The path to Devil's Maw could be treacherous. Funny how it took one little tap to run her off the road.

Funny how, for all her brilliance and demeanor, it all crumbled when the collectors fetched her and brought her to a discreet warehouse in the port district of Caillou Bay, thirty-five miles from Coralyn Bay. Dr. Chalmers thought she was tough. Refused to say a word. Refused food and water. A smile crept over his face. He loved this part. He'd walked in wearing mirrored sunglasses, holding a blank piece of paper. "This is great. Beautiful. Perhaps the greatest prose in human history."

"What are you babbling about?" Her defiance had been impressive. He'd tossed her the paper. Dr. Chalmers had picked it up and checked both sides. "It's blank." "No, it isn't. Check again."

"It's blank. Maybe you should take off those stupid glasses and see for yourself." She'd tossed it back. "No, no, no." He'd leaned forward. "I assure you, it has content."

She'd given him a look. It hadn't worked. "That paper you carelessly discarded, and will pick up, will have the greatest confession ever written in human history." Mr. Suit had removed his glasses. "Because you're going to write it." Dr. Chalmers had seen his eyes and privately wished he'd put the sunglasses back on. That way, he would've looked human. He loved it when they resisted. When they fought back. So much more pleasurable.

She'd been strong in her own domain. But the flesh was weak. Physical strength was the first to go when pressure was applied. Even a strong spirit could break with finesse. But Mr. Suit had to hand it to her; Dr. Chalmers was a strong one. However, if the flesh is strong then the heart is weaker. This next moment will last in Mr. Suit's memory for a lifetime. "I don't want you to be lonely here, I brought you a guest. Do you remember her?"

Mr. Suit pressed a button and one of the stainless-steel panels by the wall recoiled and in the other room was "Elisa!" Dr. Chalmers called out. She'd crumbled immediately. "I will tell you everything, just don't hurt her. Please!" Mr. Suit pointed to the blank paper. Dr. Chalmers wrote down everything. She admitted her guilt in the theft of company property. She wrote down the exact chain of events. The people involved.

But sometimes, a lesson must be taught. He had Dr. Chalmers restrained and allowed her to watch as a few of Mr. Kingsley personal morality officers came in to meet Elisa. "Leave her alone! I told you everything. LEAVE HER ALONE! punish me, I was the one who stole it, it should be me, it should be ME!". Dr. Chalmers tried in vain to move but her restraints wouldn't allow it. She had to watch…everything. The look on her face as the morality officers gave the winged lady a lesson. *Ah, memories.*

Mr. Suit continued to unpack the recent events. All of this could have been avoided if the first set of collectors hadn't screwed things up. Good thing they were dead. At least they saved him the trouble of having to deal with their failure. And that insidious man, Jake

Dawson. The handpicked puppet was supposed to play ball, lead them to the jewel. Not be complicit in its theft. Mr. Kingsley had promised Mr. Suit a reward: the capture of Jake Dawson, to be brought to Maranoa Island. As sport. *His head will look lovely in my trophy case,* Mr. Suit thought.

The limo pulled up to Hangar 7. The jet was prepped and fueled. Mr. Suit boarded with his briefcase. In time, the jet received clearance and took off. High in the sky, Mr. Suit looked at the jewel, *the Sovereign's Cut.* Beautiful. Dark obsidian purple with magma flowing in the center. So clean. So pure. It's a pity that it would never see the light of day again. Unless Mr. Kingsley wanted to flaunt it. Pity about the cracks. Perhaps Mr. Kingsley could get someone to fix them.

Five Hours Later Maranoa Island

The plane landed as expected. Mr. Suit jumped into a waiting car that drove him to Mr. Kingsley's private estate: Crownspire. A blend of modern and classic aesthetics, Crownspire was a marvel of architecture and engineering. It was made of diamonic glass and TerraSteel and built to last. Impervious to earthquakes and hurricanes. It was located just outside the Caribbean and Atlantic Ocean. Maranoa Island had unique status in the international community. Technically located in international waters, no government could lay claim over it.

Maranoa Island was protected by the best mercenary fleet and garrison that money could buy. Nobody came to Crownspire uninvited and lived to talk about it. At the highest level, Mr. Kingsley awaited. The elevator ride was always pleasant. As soon as the doors opened, a lovely blonde woman escorted Mr. Suit directly to *Mr. Kingsley's main conference room.* Grant turned around with impatience. "Show me."

Mr. Suit removed the cuff and placed the briefcase on a glass table. Mr. Kingsley opened it. He held it in his hands, imagining he could feel its power. "Exquisite. Simply exquisite."

The orange light of the magma flashed across his face. There was no need for magic. The Sovereign's Cut had unique properties of its own. It could put the mightiest of people under its spell. "My friend, you have done well. Now, let me show you something I added to my collection." Grant held the Sovereign's Cut in his hand and walked with Mr. Suit to the other side of the large conference room.

"Have you ever seen such a lovely pair?" Grant asked. Mr. Suit smiled. "Once, when I caught it for you, sir". In a large glass display case, two large amber wings were pinned against a black velvet backboard. The sign read "Nogwyn, female. Circa 2026." Grant Kingsley went over to a monitor at his private desk. "Look at this, a warmup before tomorrow's big hunt." Mr. Suit looked over at the monitor. Suit had a genuine smile as he thought, *Ms. Reyes, there you are.* "She has been drugged, so she would be good for practice, sharping up the old trigger fingers" Grant said. "Now, your promised reward, as requested" Mr. Kingsley said with a crooked smile.

Two huge men in black masks entered, dragging a third figure wearing a hood. They removed the hood. Grant stepped forward with a glass of brandy in his hand and pointed at "Jake Dawson, I presume?" Mr. Suit looked at his prize and thought, *not so brave now. Look at him, practically going to cry, to wet himself. This was too sweet.*

"Where am I? Mr. Suit?" Jake was trembling with so much fear, he looked like he was wobbling like a mound of gelatin.
THUD!

"Here, you speak only when spoken to." Mr. Suit pistol-whipped Jake at his left temple. The young man fell, holding his face. "I promise you, this will not be clean or gentlemanly. This is personal." Mr. Suit smiled. "Get him ready. Tell the processing center I'll bring in fresh sport. Use a mahogany base when they stuff Mr. Dawson's head." Jake started to cry. To tremble. To curl into a fetal position. Mr. Suit had a large grin, *this is lovely. Maybe I should record this.*

"Enjoy your prize, my friend," Grant Kingsley said. "Take him to the hunting grounds. Mr. Suit and I will be there shortly. But first, a toast! To success!"
"No! No, no! For God's sake, somebody help me!" Jake kicked and screamed as the two huge men grabbed him.

"God won't save you now. Nothing can." Mr. Suit smiled with pleasure as he watched his prey squirm in fear. Jake grabbed a pistol from one of the guards. His sweat allowing him to slip away for a moment. He pointed the gun at Mr. Suit and Grant. *Click.*
Click, click, click.

The room burst into laughter. Grant looked at a frightened Jake. "Stupid pleb. Do you think we'd allow you near a loaded gun? Like this one." Grant immediately produced a large caliber pistol. BAM! BAM!

"HURRY UP, GODDAMMIT! HE'S BLEEDING ALL OVER MY FLOORS!" Grant barked to his staff as he holstered his gun. Jake dropped to his knees, bullets hitting him in the left thigh and right shoulder. "Sorry, Suit. Had to hobble him, but he'll still make great sport either way." Grant smiled. Mr. Suit raised his glass. "A toast".

POP! POP! SPLAT!

Grant and Mr. Suit turned around expecting bottles of champagne, but it wasn't.

"LOOK WHAT YOU DID! FUCKING BASTARDS! THIS WAS MY NICE SUIT! MY ONLY SUIT!"

The two guards lay dead on the floor, heads burst open, as if dynamite had exploded inside their skulls. The skin and muscle were slipping off Jake's body. A dark aura leaked from his orifices. "You know how long it takes me to find a suit? To skin it, preserve the muscles and nerves? DO YOU?!"

Grant and Mr. Suit's eyes widened. They dropped their glasses. Both men immediately pulled out their guns and unloaded their clips into Jake's torso. Stray bullets tore through his arm and leg muscles. Mr. Suit got off a headshot, a sickening crack as the bullet shattered Jake's skull. Jake fell to the floor. Grant reloaded and aimed his gun between Jake's legs.

A dark mist came out of Jake's body, and it began to form into a horrid yet human shape. It grabbed Grant's arm and twisted it until it broke at the elbow. Then it ripped off his forearm and watched as Grant went into shock. Then it tore the remainder from the socket just to watch him suffer. Mr. Suit tried to run to the elevator. "YOU'RE NOT GOING ANYWHERE!" A sinister voice shouted as something strong grabbed him before he could reach elevator. Mr. Suit could feel something penetrating his skin and muscles and grabbed his spine. Suddenly, his spine snapped in half!

Mr. Suit laid on the floor, losing feeling below his chest. He saw Jake's body a few feet away. There was no blood coming out of it. Mr. Suit was still alive but in great pain. The horrid shape began to form a tar-like substance, a horrific symphony of flesh, rotten organ meat, and bones. Its eyes glowed like magma.

"You're right. This is personal. It would be a pity for me to deny myself some pleasure. A little taste of what's to come" The screams were legendary. Nobody on the top floor lived to tell about it. And for those who died, their nightmare was just beginning.

Coralyn Bay

"I called his mom, she hasn't heard from him in a while. It's like, he dropped off the face of the Earth or something" Roxy said. Chris was thinking loudly. "Atrox is missing, Jake is missing. Anyone else see the connection or is it just me?"

Kira leaned against her car. "I don't know this guy, but I don't think we have a choice. We must go to his office." Kira turned to Roxy "You don't have to go unless you want to." Roxy wanted to say something, but Kira picked it up immediately. She walked over to Roxy to reassure her that she doesn't have to be alone facing whatever troubles are coming her way. Chris saw the pain and anxiety in Roxy's eyes. It was his time and he stepped up. "I'll go, Bruce! You drive!".

Bruce raised up his hands in a *what the hell!* expression. "Be careful" Kira called out as Bruce and Chris jumped into his jeep. Roxy was visibility shaken. "Hey, let's get a drink" Kira suggested. Roxy nodded and they jumped into Kira's Beetle and took off. Roxy kept her eyes on Bruce's Jeep as long as she could and she muttered something to herself and hoped Chris could somehow hear it "Don't be a hero."

Crownspire

Ammuzol picked up the shattered remains of his suit, examining the holes and fractured skull. This would take time to regenerate. But he needed to return to Coralyn Bay and bring back the Atrox so Jake's friends could find it and complete their mission.

There was a new member in their group. Another sapling for his collection. He'd almost tasted her before. Once he was freed from his prison, he would taste her again. Ammuzol knew he spent some of his strength and there were no living supernaturals in this island.
It took some energy to manifest a physical form and more to repair one. But with so much raw material lying around, Ammuzol had an idea.

To save some of his power, he collected materials from all the dead bodies around him to fix his suit. He found a semi-usable skull to replace the original. "Not bad" he said while examining his patched suit. He took some clothes from Grant's closet. He would pass by most people unnoticed, but his ornament will find out sooner. No matter, the next time he tastes his ornament, it will be in his own skin so he can savor the flavor even more.

Ammuzol closed his eyes for a second and scanned the island again. Damn! Nothing, not even a fairy, a gnome, or goblin. Too bad the Nogwyn wasn't here he thought to himself as he admired her severed wings. Supernaturals had potent magic in their systems. Humans, blah.

He remembered a time when humans practiced magic like a religion. They separated themselves into castes. Some even had the stupid idea that pure blood was stronger and more sacred than others. It wasn't. Just tastier. And easier to kill.

Ammuzol discharged its physical form to slip back into the suit. He found a cracked mirror and checked his handiwork. "*Not bad*" as he smiled. His suit still had some scars from the bullet holes, but the new clothes could cover most of them. The replacement skull was a little off. *It doesn't matter, by the time my ornament figures it out, I will be tasting her sweet fruit with my own lips* he told himself.

Jake picked up the Atrox and put it in his pocket. He needed to think for a moment. *What is the best way back to Coralyn Bay? Ah, yes. An excellent idea.* He'd take care of two tasks with one act. Save some power for later. He can feed when he gets home. His thoughts went back to his ornament and her feisty companion; they would test him. They could delay but not stop his plan or alter his fate.

The feisty one...

Yes.

Ammuzol's eyes glowed hot.

She was related to one of his new "guests." The wise one. The brother who stayed.

Ammuzol walked to the center of the island, leaving burnt footprints behind. It was a pity he wouldn't be able to witness his actions directly, but he could sense them. He took out the stone and held it in his hand. Not taking any chances now. He raised the Atrox above his head. And pulled into the fabric of reality itself. The island began to shake.

Mark's House

"Alright, you two get back here as quickly as you can, I got a bad feeling, you two don't want to be out there at dark. Okay, bye!" Roxy hung up the phone and rejoined Kira in the kitchen. "The boys didn't see Jake or his truck. The Kingsmen guards were missing too, probably out poaching some poor animals" Roxy shook her head in disgust.

Kira turned on the TV "Maybe there is something on the news. Let me see if I can find a news channel or something on demand…let's see…jackpot!"

"This just in: Maranoa Island, owned by multi-billionaire Grant Kingsley, has just suffered a massive earthquake, so strong that some scientists claim it may have ruptured the Earth's crust. The entire island has plunged into the Atlantic Ocean. A large sinkhole has developed, and all commercial sea and air traffic is being diverted until further notice. Search and rescue operations have been suspended due to…"

Kira and Roxy looked at each other. This is not a coincidence. "Holy Sh.." they wanted to curse out loud but stopped themselves out of respect for Mark's house. About an hour later, the guys came back and heard the news. "Fuck." That is the best answer any of them could come up with as the news of Maranoa Island is flooding all news channels.

"Hey, not to sound insensitive but is anyone else hungry?" Bruce said. Kira turned around and held up her hand as if she was about to lecture Bruce "I could eat" she said. "Why not? This could be our last meal together, let's go out with a bang" Chris said as he looked at Roxy. Roxy looked back, so much they must do, so many things they need to sort out. She wanted to find Jake but something inside her said "There's nothing you can do".

"There is only one place that can handle all of this" Bruce said while twirling his hand around his friends: "Julie's".

"I have never been" Kira said. Everyone looked at her as if she was insane. "What? I don't get out as much anymore. Quit it."

"Well, we can take care of that right now. Everyone lets go in my Jeep. Let's feast and be merry for tomorrow, the whole world could be coming an end."
Downtown Coralyn Bay, Financial District.

Harry Kessler was getting ready to leave work. He noticed it was still getting dark sooner as winter was still hanging around. He never liked daylight savings time. Regardless, Harry was a hard-working man and one of the country's best financial analyst out there. He had an unmatched insight into trends, business forecasting and customer psychology never seen before. People joked he was a time traveler who came back in time to make a fortune for his future-self to enjoy. Everyone wishes.

Harry preferred to work late afternoons to early evenings. Since most firms preferred their analysts to work in the office during the day, Harry started his own firm and sets his own hours. Normally, this wouldn't work in the finance industry, but Harry has a good track record of making lots of money. Tonight, Harry decided he wanted to play and took the night off to go to Julie's and see what was new on the menu.

Bruce pulled up to a parking lot a few blocks away. The gang got their usual table. "The last time, we were here, it was with your grandpa!" Bruce said. Kira looked surprised. "Yeah, your grandpa knew how to party!" Roxy said. Chris nodded as he ordered his usual Shirley Temple.

"So, while things have changed, let's try to keep to some of our traditions. Drinks, appetizers, then whatever you want. Don't be shy. Eat hearty. Let's enjoy ourselves before..." Bruce trailed off. A weight hovered over them. "Before we get to work and kick some ass!," Kira finished. "YEAH!" Chris shouted with his newfound confidence.

First round: rum shots.

Second round: tequila slammers.

Third round: free-for-all.

Wonderful hot food came in. Everybody ate and drank like there's no tomorrow. Lots of laughter. Everybody shared the loaded potato wedges, cheeseburger sliders, onion rings, chicken tenders and hot wings. Kira was surprised her grandpa had shown them how to make a Martinez Slammer.

She looked at Bruce and stared at him for a moment. He turned, and almost made eye contact. She quickly looked away. He caught her. She'd been staring. *Nice.*

Chris and Roxy sat across from each other, sharing food, sometimes feeding each other. Acting like an old married couple. Kira noticed and signaled to Bruce that they should get some fresh air. Let them work things out. While Bruce and Kira decided to step outside. Another patron was having a good time as well. "You're the first Vicki that I ever met" Harry said as he tapped on the bar so the bartender could refill their drinks. Vicki, a young woman in her twenties, soft auburn hair, green eyes, and fair skin with a body made for sinning.

Vicki could put back those whiskey shots. Harry didn't mind, he found what he was looking for, after a few more shots, Harry asked Vicki if she wanted to go back to his place. Vicki seemed tipsy but she agreed. Harry ordered them a ride and they took off. *Outside Julie's at the party deck.*

The night air was crisp. The weather in Coralyn Bay didn't obey the laws of nature. It was a late pre-spring evening, and it was a brisk 68 degrees. "I've got to tell you something," Bruce said. Kira brought her drink with her. She didn't believe in wasting good alcohol.

" What?" she said with a loud confidence.

"Your grandpa tried to set me up with you on at least two occasions." Bruce smirked.
"Ah, ha ha. Yeah, that's my grandpa. Only twice? My grandma would try to set me up with any man with two legs. Sometimes one, if she finds one. Get it? Ha,ha,ha."

Bruce took a step closer. Kira started playing with her hair. "I'm serious. He did. Twice." She made eye contact "I know. He told me. He showed me a picture. See."

There it was. The final group shot. All smiles. Full of love and joy. There he was. Mark. Bruce looked at the picture for a second, but it felt longer. How they could use his help right now but also, everyone missed him. Life goes on, but the void we leave behind never goes away. Like a hole made in the ocean, eventually the hole refills with sand. Water will always be above it, carrying the memory of the loss. But water always moves. Even when still, the memory remains. "Wow. Mark was a hell of a guy. I miss him." Bruce's eyes glistened. "Me too." Kira put her phone away.

They were closer to each other now. Any closer and they'd be standing on each other's feet. Behind them, a band finished setting up. "Evening, folks. This is the Lonely Cats Club. Tonight, let's start with an oldie." The lead singer quickly chatted with his band. Kira turned to Bruce "I didn't know they have live music here." Bruce kept admiring Kira "Yeah, this place is about to get jumping. Do you dance?"

Kira was coy. "A little." The music started, a good dance number from the 1980s. Bruce extended his hand. "I don't, but fuck it. We only live once!" Kira expected Bruce to sway back and forth or do the tennis-pro hip thrust side to side. But to her surprise, this guy could dance.

The Lonely Cats Club played another oldie with an updated beat: "*Do You Love Me?*"
Bruce knew all the moves. The Twist. Mashed Potato. All the classics. Lights turned on the main deck; bright but not enough to distract from the natural beauty of the night sky.

The band switched tempos and played a ballad. Kira let Bruce put his hands on her waist. He moved them higher, out of respect. They were both light on their feet. He had a firm grip but nothing too macho, but reassuring.

They made eye contact. He brushed some hair from her face. This wasn't planned. This wasn't their intention. But the feelings started to flow. He told himself: *Breathe.*
Breathe. Kira told herself the same thing.

Kira squeezed his hand. Bruce squeezed back. Kira moved Bruce's hand lower to her waist. She wanted to see if she could trust him. His hand stayed there. He never tried to go lower. The ballad filled the night air with magic. A special harmony that would make Cupid jealous. "I don't know what it is that I said. If I could remember what it was, I would say it again."
Those lyrics.

"The stars brought us together. Destiny weaves our future together in her loom."
Bruce saw Kira in all her glory. Her beauty, inside and out. Never afraid to take chances. She could fend for herself. She is intelligent and caring.

Kira saw Bruce in his splendor. He is kind, caring and generous. Always willing to help. He made her grandpa feel alive. He's never afraid to show his emotions.
This can't be.

But it is.

Can two people who just met fall in love so fast? Bruce leaned in. Kira stepped up on her toes to reach him. Their lips moved slowly closer...

The song finished. The band took a break. Couples left for their tables or the bar. Bruce and Kira stayed there, holding each other. If only the song had played for a few more seconds. If only the notes had carried a moment longer. They looked at each other. They lingered for a moment before taking a step back. Both acknowledging what had just happened. Kira turned to ask something, but Bruce answered with his eyes: To be continued.

Harry Kessler's Condo

"Well, here it is, my humble abode." Harry said as he led his date into this condo. It was subtle, a few bland paintings, expensive looking furniture that is rarely used. A freshly made bed. Vicki seemed to slowly lose consciousness. "Do you want another drink? Or maybe something to help you relax?"

Vicki nodded no. Harry sat next to her and started to touch her knee. She was losing her strength, but she tried to make eye contact as often as she could. Harry began to undress her; she did not resist. Harry looked to Vicki's eyes and told her, "Come to me, let me have a drink." Vicki leaned her head back and Harry revealed two large fangs and bit into her jugular. Vicki gasped and her grip loosened.

Harry gently lowered her down as he began to drink her blood. Then suddenly, Harry pushed her away. "It burns! IT BURNS!" Harry couldn't look into a mirror, but he could feel that is jaw was melting and his two longer fangs fell off. "What are you?" he mumbled. Vicki's head snapped and turned towards him in an inhuman manner. Her scalp slid off and her skull cracked to reveal a hideous elongated face with a strange appendage coming out like a glowing lure. She shrieked as her glowing green eyes pierced Harry's eyes and caused them to melt.

Vicki reached out with a scaly, taloned hand and ripped off Harry's lower jaw. She proceeded to feed on him until she had her fill and then felt something coming into the nearby beach. She didn't bother to put her face back on. She shrieked as some strange cosmic power caused her body to glow and then melt as it drained her very essence. "Be proud of me, father" she said before her vocal cords were melted.

Deep in Barracuda Harbor

A strong wave rushed through, moving every ship so violently that cargo containers dropped into the water.

North Point Beach Five Miles from Downtown Coralyn Bay

A body washed ashore. A few drug-addicted vagrants went to check it out. They wanted to see if anything valuable was there. "What's this? A crystal?" Suddenly, the bloated body stood up. For a second, a purplish-orange light flashed then with unnatural strength, it grabbed the vagrant who'd taken the crystal by the neck and twisted their head around. The corpse dropped the crystal into the mysterious man's hand. The rest of the vagrants fled as fast as their drug-riddled brains would let them. Jake was back home. He looked around. Necrosis hadn't set in yet. "I'm home."

Sunrise Hill

In Coralyn Bay, there is a hill that overlooks the entire downtown area with breathtaking views of the bay. In springtime, locals gather there to admire the beauty but often to make declarations of love. Many people got married there. Many of them proposed. And sometimes, couples break up. The Widow's Branch, the only tree on the hill, is where couples who broke up or separated due to misfortune would carve their names. A monument to lost loves.

The night went by so fast. Bruce and his friends knew there was a lot of work to do, but time was slipping through their fingers. One moment, Bruce had met the girl of his dreams; a woman he wanted to know better. A woman he wanted, if he should be so lucky, to build a life with. Bruce walked with Kira by the path around Sunrise Hill. Their magical night transitioned into a warm, glowing morning. They both knew this majestic bubble they'd stepped into was temporary. Once they left this place, things would change. Whether they wanted to or not.

A few hundred feet away, Roxy and Chris walked together, strong emotions running through them. Bruce and Kira kept their distance. They sensed those two needed space.

Chris and Roxy walked up the hill and looked at the bay. The sunrise made the ripples in the bay look like shiny diamonds or twinkling stars. Roxy took a few steps forward and turned to face Chris. "Tell me. Tell me why."

Chris looked at her. Her beauty. Her soul was too good for this world. "What do you want me to say?" he asked. Roxy took a step closer. "Why you never asked me out." Chris searched for the right words, but he knew the truth would have to do. "I was scared. I mean, look at you. You can have anyone you want. I figured you'd let me know. Give me a sign. But ever since we were kids, it felt like we had this brother-sister thing happening. I mean, I tried once."

Roxy's face showed surprise, skeptical surprise. Her back was to the bay, so the sun was slowly rising behind her. Chris summoned his courage and continued "We were in eighth grade. Right before school let out for the summer. Last dance of the semester. The following semester, we'd both be in high school. I remember it well. I spent the whole day working up the nerve to talk to you." Roxy started to recall that day. "Yeah, you were acting weird. Your voice kept cracking. I thought it was just puberty."

Chris's expression turned sullen. "No. I'd never been to a dance. All I knew was how to waltz, my mom taught me. It was my only move. I worked up the nerve to talk to you. I asked if you were going. You said yes. I asked if you wanted to go with me."

He paused. "Do you remember what you said?"

Roxy shook her head. It was so long ago. She'd had countless conversations with Chris. "You said maybe." Chris's eyes reddened. "You said you were waiting to see if Derek Johnson would ask you first. If not, then we could go." Roxy couldn't believe it. But it was true. She'd never thought about it since. She'd meant no harm. They were kids.

"I know you didn't mean to hurt me. You always took care of me. Looked out for me. But it was then I knew: I wasn't your type. You had eyes for other guys. I was your friend. Your brother from another mother. That was my place, and I respected it ever since."

Chris looked up, tears streaming down his face. Roxy had this heavenly orange glow behind her. They stared at each other, holding hands. Then, as the sky changed to blue, Chris pulled his hands away. "I will never forget the other night. But…there are things we need to sort out." His voice was steady and confident. "I am nobody's silver medal."
"No," Roxy said. Against her will and feelings, she took a step back. "You're not."

"We have bigger things to worry about. When it's all over, let's sort it out." Roxy held back tears. She knew he was right. "No matter what, you will always be special to me. A friend. A lover. My Roxy. I will always support you, tell you when you're wrong, and be there when you need me." Chris said with all the warmth in his heart. With all the meaning in his soul.

"I know." Roxy said and she lunged forward and hugged him. This time, she let the rain fall.
So did Chris.

Bruce and Kira watched from a distance. They didn't know what had just happened, but they could tell that whatever it was, it needed to happen. After a few minutes, Roxy and Chris walked down together, but with a little distance between them. "Are you two alright?" Bruce asked. "Fine. Just needed some fresh air. Whew!" Chris gave Roxy one last glance.
She returned that same glance with a faint echo of longing. But this wasn't the right time. "Yeah, you know me and Chris. BFFs."

"Hey, let's get some breakfast. Am I the only one starving?" Kira asked.

"Yeah, let's go. Get our strength. Let's hit the Pancake Hut; it's on the way to school. I figure we can use one of the meeting rooms to strategize." Bruce thought for a moment. "The one in the old Geology wing."

Everyone was full of joy and could feel their souls in harmony as the morning light washed over them. Until…**BUZZZ…. BUZZ……**

Roxy looked at her phone. *It was Jake.* She froze up, it took a lot to scare Roxalyn Dominguez, but this one call scared her so bad that her hands were shaking. Chris snapped up the phone from her hand. "Jake! Oh no, Roxy went to the bathroom. Huh? Pancake Hut, you wanna join us? I got Bruce and his new girlfriend here. Un-huh, yeah, it's about time he got his…thing wet." Chris made an apologetic face to his friends. Bruce looked on while Roxy took a few steps back, she wrapped her arms around her waist. Kira went up to her "Hey, it's okay. I've got you."

Chris went blank for a second. "Sure, I'll tell her. Yeah, see you in a bit, yeah bye." Chris ended the call. "Jake wants to see you. Says you left your keys behind." Roxy patted herself down. Her keys were missing. Bruce looked at his friends. "I'll drop you off at Mark's then I will go over there and get your keys, I'll settle this man to man."

"No, Mr. Hero. You'll make this worse. I'll go" Chris said.
"The hell you are!" Bruce snapped back "Let's all go together. Strength in numbers". Kira held on to Roxy. For the first time in their friendship, Bruce realized something is seriously wrong with Roxy. She is afraid. She is trembling and her courage is hanging on by a thread. Bruce wanted to drive over there and kick Jake's ass. Bruce recognizes the signs of abuse. He's seen it in his mother when he was younger. He wasn't strong

enough to protect his mom then but now; he can at least protect his friend.

He took the keys out of his pocket and held them tight. He saw Kira holding on to Roxy. Then he saw Chris. Not the slubby IT guy, not the gonna-be lawyer. But a man who can get things done. They needed answers and Chris was right. Bruce paused and put his keys back in his pocket. If he went over there, a fight would break out but if Chris went over there, alone, he could find out the answers. Chris turned to Bruce.

"Look, I know everyone thinks I'm just this pudgy guy who tinkers with computers and can quote the law, but I can handle this. Trust me." Chris said with fresh confidence and new strength. Bruce walked up to him. Roxy and Kira looked at them. Bruce put his right hand on Chris' shoulder and squeezed. Without words and just a look:

Bruce: *are you sure?*
Chris: *No, but it has to be done. I can do it. I will do it. But you have to let me go. I will call you if I need help. But this is my cross to bear. Alone.*

Bruce: *Okay, do it, find out what you can and get out of there, quick.*

Chris nodded. Bruce patted him on the shoulder. Roxy and Kira didn't know what happened but Chris half-skipped over to Roxy and planted a kiss on her. "I'll be right back." Chris stepped out and ordered a ride. A small sedan pulled up and whisked him away. Roxy looked as the car took Chris away.

Kira said first "Let's go back to my place. We can go over my grandpa's notes. I'm sure we will find the answers there." Kira took Roxy by the arm. Roxy wanted to shrug Kira away as she was afraid to let Chris out of her sight. Roxy always protected him but now, Chris has to do what he has to do.

Crystal Valley, Devil's Maw Muster area.

Kathleen Davis noted all of her personnel and equipment before today's expedition. Today was going to be a beautiful day, inside and outside the caves. The Kingsmen security team were quiet today, probably had to do with the recent events. The news reported that Miranda Kingsley, Grant's wife, assumed control of the company. In fact, she authorized today's expedition.

Kathleen looked over the charts: "Starwound" is currently being mapped by CaveScan drones and today her team is going to the second antechamber "Obsidian Vorun". She wondered who came up with those names. Today was a small group with herself and two other experienced spelunkers. A gentleman from the Tri-Coastal History Commission was supposed to be here later and she didn't want to disappoint him. "Okay everyone, by the book and by the numbers. We're using scanning equipment only. We have no idea how deep that antechamber really is, okay? Let's go".

"Oh, Hi Mr. Dawson!" Heather, one of Kathleen's cave divers said as Jake Dawson walked over to his office. He had a slight limp and looked a little unwell. *It has to be stress. Poor guy is under a lot of pressure. Let's leave him alone until we finish our work.* Kathleen thought to herself as she saw Jake enter his office without acknowledging anyone. Into the caves they went, and it wasn't long before the lights were gone and all they had to go by was their flashlights and some of the Noctilium paint on the walls. Kathleen was amazed how someone was able to reach the ceiling like that, but she couldn't figure out how.

The tunnels seemed narrower and now there was a bend that wasn't there before. At least, Kathleen believes it wasn't there before but maybe the charts were wrong. That's why they are there to map, to explore and to discover. Despite all the advancements with AI science, even machines support humans in the loop. The tunnels were warm and wet. The rocks were rough and felt like they were pushing against her and her team. Kathleen could hear the humming of a CaveScan drone already in Obsidian Vorun. "Huh!!".

Beautiful. Simply beautiful. Glittering crystals, lava stone, shale and are those…gemstones?

Heather looked around while Wally, the rescue technician, carefully followed the drone as it made its scans. "Watch out, something is dripping in here, making the floor slippery" he continued to follow the drone. Kathleen wished she had a bigger light. "What is that? Ms. Davis come quick!" Wally shouted. Kathleen carefully walked over and saw there was another opening "Is there another antechamber?"

Heather continued to follow the natural pattern of the cavern wall and then saw something peculiar, was that a fossil? She kept going and found herself at the end of the wall but there was an opening, big enough for someone to crawl inside. She looked around to see where Kathleen and Wally were and decided to crawl in. "Whoa!" Heather was able to find a hidden chamber and inside a literal closet full of skeletons.

Some were prehistoric life forms such as starfish and other marine mammals. Another looked like a mermaid or something like it. It had to be real as there is no way someone could have known about this chamber to set up a hoax. Another strange skeleton, humanoid, with impressions of wings but its skull, traumatized by some sharp weapon. Then Heather smelled something rotten in the chamber, she turned her light in its direction and saw a recently deceased man wearing a Kingsmen uniform.

"AAAHHHHHH!"

Kathleen and Wally found something awesome and terrifying, a vast underground lake but they couldn't tell if that was water or something else. "Could it be oil?" Kathleen asked. Wally got closer to it and touched it with his gloved hand. "I don't' think so, oil companies are pretty good at finding this stuff and with its proximity to Miller's Quarry, someone would have found it some time ago."

A scream!

"Heather" Kathleen said as she began her ascent to the Obsidian Vorun above and Wally turned his back to the mysterious lake. Something crawled out of the lake and immediately grabbed him. A scarred being stuck a makeshift hand into this throat and filled up his vocal cords with the sludge. Kathleen got up and immediately followed the sounds of Heather's scream. "I can't get out! I'm stuck!"

"Hang on, help is on the way! Wally over here! WALLY!" Kathleen turned her flashlight around and didn't see Wally. Then, a figure emerged from the hidden antechamber. Kathleen sighed in relief "Wally, quick, Heather is stuck…."

Heather looked up as the crawl space entrance was closing on its own. She tried to look through the narrowing tunnel and saw something pull Kathleen away. The tunnel started to open again without hesitation; Heather began crawling through the tunnel. She was halfway through when she felt a slimy hand reach in and grabbed her foot. Heather panicked and tried to pull herself out. The tunnel started to contract again. Heather screamed, she cried and she begged for her life. The tunnel collapsed on her and sealed her in. *Mark's House.*

Kira opened the door and saw a note from her dad. She read it and checked her phone. "My folks are headed back to Neon City this week but are driving to Austin to see one of my aunts. They will be back in a day or two." Bruce checked on Roxy, she is a nervous wreck. "I'll be okay, let's do something otherwise I'm likely to pull my hair out" Roxy said. Kira nodded and led them down to Mark's library. "I am sure my grandpa had notes, something. Let's dive in."
The Devil's Maw, Jake's Office.

Chris pulled up in his mom's van. He took a ride home, changed his clothes and summoned his courage as best he could. He felt Mark's Challenge Coin in his pocket and said to himself; *I can do this...I got to do this...*Chris stepped out and noticed three more cars parked in the lot. They had this layer of dirt and grime as if they were parked out here for weeks, but the tire tracks looked fresh.

"Hello! Jake, are you here?" Chris said. Then a door opened from one of the trailers in the Kingsmen area. "Hi, I am looking for Jake Dawson. I'm a close friend and I..." Nobody came out. Chris walked over to the trailer, and he could see boot prints. Everything seemed abandoned yet seemed as if the Kingsmen people left in a big hurry. "Over here Chris!"

Chris turned around and saw Jake at the other side of the big trailer in a makeshift portable office building. *Damn, Jake looks horrible.* "I got your text, I thought we were going to meet at your place" Chris said as he reached for his phone so he can try to text Bruce on his whereabouts. *Damn, no signal.* "I have a meeting with the Tri-Coastal Historical Commission in an hour. Come here, it won't take too long". Jake smiled.

Jake welcomed Chris and motioned for him to sit across from his desk. The office was a mess and looked like it hadn't been cleaned in weeks. "Any word on Dr. Chalmers?" Chris asked as he tried to relax. Jake sat down and casually remarked "I think she ran away with an old girlfriend or something, probably to Acapulco or Barbados, who knows, who cares." Jake reached into his pocket and tossed some keys on the desk along with Roxy's Prism. "Seen Roxy lately?"

Chris took the keys and prism into his hand. "This morning, at breakfast, remember?" Jake looked out in the distance. "Oh yes, of course, I forgot. So, how was it?" Jake had this sinister aura surrounding him.

"Breakfast, you mean?" Chris said, the prism still in his hand.
"No, how was she?" Jake's eyes were accusatory. "I can smell her scent on you. You would be a fool not to; I wouldn't blame you if you did. You know the expression: while the cat's away the mice will play? You saw her new body art, I made it myself, looks good on her, doesn't it?"

"I don't know what you're talking about. Roxy and I hug each other all the time, you were always cool with that" Chris said. His instincts told him to leave but his mind told him to wait…the prism is in his hand. Jake seemed to hiss "Not anymore. I think cosmic obsidian looks good on her, but you know that, don't you! Don't lie to me." Jake stepped closer. Chris thought he saw steam coming out of Jake's nose and a strong menace in his eyes.

Chris tried to gulp but his body froze while Jake put his hands on the desk like a tiger ready to pounce. "Tell Bruce that he can come down whenever he's ready to see the caves."

A car pulled up. *Dr. Everous Scratch is early.* Jake looked over and walked to the window. Chris immediately looked through the prism at Jake. *Holy Mother of Moly!*
"Tell Bruce to come down later and tell him that I have this" Jake pulled out the Atrox Stone. Chris noticed little cracks and one in the center that looked like it was deeper. "You can go, I have other business to attend to now but Chris, I will see you again, real soon."

Dr. Scratch got out of his car and Jake stepped out to greet him. Chris sprang up and waddled to his mom's van as fast as he could and took off. "Dr. Scratch, how pleasant of you to join us." Jake shook his hand. *Dr. Scratch noticed how rough Jake's hand felt but it is probably due to all the time he spends in the caves.* "Likewise. I am anxious to hear about your findings and perhaps take a tour?".

Jake escorted Dr. Scratch to his office while struggling with a limp. *Jake knew it would take time to fix, but it was of no consequence.* He sat down and closed his eyes, allowing the darkness to seep in. *Drawing strength.* "My, you have a booming voice. You should be on the radio or something." Dr. Scratch took a few cautious steps into Jake's office.

"Charming. I'll keep that in mind. Please, make yourself comfortable. Would you like a drink?" Jake adjusted himself in his chair to appear more imposing. "Yes, thank you. Tea, if it's not too much trouble."

"Not at all." Jake got up and went to his mini fridge. He pulled out a small box and turned on his portable kettle. "Now tell me, what did you find? I'm certain you found something." Dr. Scratch asked while the kettle was warming up. "Actually, it's extraordinary. This cave system might be much older than we thought. We believe a pre-industrial society existed here: probably at the same time as the Roman Empire." Jake said while watching the kettle.

"You don't say." Dr. Scratch was skeptical. Jake walked to the kettle and poured hot water into a cup along with a black tea bag. He watched as this special blend began to dilute in the hot water. Dark. Like tar. Jake handed the tea to Dr. Scratch, who instinctively took a sip. "Oh, that's got a nice punch to it. Unique flavor. What is it, if you don't mind me asking?"

"Plum tea." Jake sat down. "Drink. Enjoy. And I will tell you about our discoveries." Jake punched a few keys on his keyboard and activated the projector. "My team has transcribed as much as we can and arranged the story written in the cave in a more cohesive way. It talks about great beings; kind and gentle. And another being, not so gentle. My team and I have different interpretations of the story. I was hoping you could look at the data and decipher it for yourself." Jake said.

Dr. Scratch drank his tea as he looked at the projections. "What I find fascinating is that the story is written on the walls, the ceilings, some even on the ground. But some of the story seems to have been lost to erosion." Mr. Scratch took bigger sips of his tea. He looked into the cup. Dark swirls. Very hypnotic. Little crystals or like stars. "Did you put any sweeteners in this?"
"No. It's all natural." Jake smirked.

"It's funny. If I didn't know any better, I would have thought that some insects made some of the carvings. Like spiders crawling up and down. Funny, if you think about it." Dr. Scratch smiled as he took another sip of his tea. Jake did not find that comment humorous at all. "Again, you are very charming." Dr. Scratch finished his tea. It was the best tasting tea he ever had.

"I can take a deeper dive into the data. You know, it could be a case of sour grapes, maybe one god did something bad to another, you know how the Greek Gods fought with each other like a dysfunctional family." Dr. Scratch finished his cup. "May I have another? Sorry to impose."

"Not at all." Jake took the cup. With one look, it refilled.

"Are you a magician?" Dr. Scratch asked.

"Not exactly." Jake stood and handed the cup back. He made sure the door was closed. Dr. Scratch drank the tea. His mind was swirling. Drifting away. "Where did you buy this tea, may I ask?"

"A secret family recipe." Jake watched as his potion began to take effect. Dr. Scratch's eyes began to narrow. His mouth began to droop. His arms went limp. "Good. I'm glad you like it. I want you to listen very carefully. I will tell you the story written on those walls. You will remember. You will tell the story exactly as I describe it. Share it with everyone."

Mark's house.

Kira, Bruce and Roxy were all crammed in Mark's library. Nobody wanted to be alone even in a safe place like Mark's house. Bruce read some books about geology, Roxy read about folklore while Kira read the books on her grandpa's desk. A van pulled up and they could hear someone approaching. They got up and walked out to the kitchen when they heard someone knocking frantically on the front door.

"Chris!" Roxy said and immediately hugged him. "He knows…. he knows…" Chris tried to speak but his nerves are getting the better of him. "Calm down man, take a seat, come inside, quick!" Kira said. Bruce went to get Chris a glass of water. Chris sat down, his pulse racing. He looked at Roxy. "He knows" and he handed her the prism. Roxy looked at and felt that it was cold, whatever power was in it was gone.

"Take small sips" Bruce said as he handed the water to Chris. Chris tried to take sips, but he gulped the water down in one shot. "I saw it, IT!' Roxy put her arm around Chris. "That thing…is not Jake." Bruce put his hands on the top of his head as if he wanted to yank his hair out. Kira had nothing to say. Roxy's mind was all over the place. *So, all the remarks, the pinching, the groping, the sex…. oh god…*Roxy looked up to Kira. "Tell me everything, when Jake found the Atrox, when you noticed the changes in behavior, depending on how it's been, there is a chance, we can bring him back." Kira said.

Starwound

Roxy told her friends everything. The changes in Jake's behavior along with the physical changes in her body. The dreams, the secret desires, Roxy held nothing back. Kira took note and understood best. Kira had her brush with desire and temptation and deep down; she wanted to give in as well. "You did nothing wrong" Kira said as Roxy looked up "I would've done the same thing, in fact, I would have done more".

Bruce looked at them and then at Chris. "You said that Jake invited me down to the caves at any time. Well, I think we should prepare, arm ourselves, come up with a plan of attack." Roxy's mind was away for a moment then she added "He's coming for you." She turned to Chris. "You touched his ornament. He's coming for you; there's no time to waste." Chris slumped into a chair. "I know, he made it very clear. One way or another, he's coming for me. I don't think I have much time."

"So, he has the Atrox with him. It's simple. We go over there and blast it to pieces. Roxy, I know you own a couple of guns, surely, you have something that can do the job, right" Bruce said. "Wait, hang on. Think about it, that's exactly what it wants" Kira said. "I went over my grandpa's notes and all the stories that he and my grandma told over the years. I don't think my granduncle was trying to destroy it. I think he was trying to hide it." Kira let Roxy go and went back to her grandpa's desk. "It all lines up. Chris, you said the Atrox has cracks on it and that it looked fresh, that is the seal on it weakening. It can't break it by itself; it needs something or someone else to do it."

"I read your grandpa's notes. He knew it was protected by spells. Look" Bruce pointed out in a worn journal. "Right there in his handwriting: Unweave. Trueform. Sunderlight!" Bruce was angry. "There is no way, Mark would have been wrong." Kira opened another page in a different journal. "Well, Mr. Smart guy, he was my grandpa longer than he was your friend. I was the one who heard all the stories. I was the one who carried the flame when everyone in my family told me that my grandpa was nuts and that I shouldn't believe everything I heard! Don't you dare!" Kira shouted in such a fierce voice that it would have scared even the bravest of knights.

"Did he tell you what happened to my granduncle? How they found him?" Kira said as she approached Bruce with an aura of dread around her. Kira looked at everyone, tears in her eyes. "In pieces…. that's right…in pieces, something tore him to shreds and they never found his head!"

The room was silent. Nobody dared to move or speak. Kira collapsed in a heap on the floor. Bruce felt ashamed. He loved Mark so much that he would never allow anyone to slander his name. But Kira, that is his granddaughter. The true keeper of the flame. He was only a pretender, a placeholder. He never verified anything Mark said, not after the dragonfly wing incident. He took Mark at his word. Deep down, he knew that she was right.

Roxy got up and extended a hand to Kira. She looked at Roxy's hand and saw the purple nails. Kira took it and Roxy hugged her. "Hey, we all loved your grandpa. He was our family too, we believe you, we believe you." They cried, Roxy motioned for Bruce and Chris to join in. Chris hugged Roxy and had a hand on

Kira's shoulder. He looked up at Bruce. Bruce hesitated and then joined in; Kira hugged him back hard. "I'm sorry!" she cried out.

"No, it's me. I'm sorry. Mark meant the world to me.... he was.... he was the father I never had....". Bruce said. Kira looked at him and buried her head into his chest. Bruce thought of something he read a long time ago: *Through pain and trauma, the survivors reached the shore, bounded by tragedy, forever in each other's debt. Let no power, on Earth or in the heavens, break this bond, a bond they wished they never had yet a bond they will always treasure.*
The Devil's Maw.

Dr. Scratch had left after a long day. He had so much material to review, a whole new narrative to write and all the evidence he needed to back it up. Jake waved goodbye and then half of his face began to slide off. "Damn. I need time to rest before I pay lover boy a visit. Nobody touches my ornament. Nothing tastes her nectar but me." Jake went back to his office. He took the Atrox Stone in his hand, feeling the pressure escaping from it. *Strange,* he thought. *All the power in existence, yet I can't break this simple thing.* He walked back to the Devil's Maw and into his domain, the gateway to oblivion. Starwound.
Kira's House

"Okay, so we need to seal the cracks and place new spells, sounds easy but it isn't.... isn't it?" Chris said. Kira used a series of books and notebook paper, as she explained her plan. She placed the appropriate references for all to see. "No. The Atrox is a cosmodial artifact, but it has its own power. Magic alone won't seal it as the Atrox can kill Earthly magic as easy as we can swat a fly."

"So, there are other supernaturals beings out that can help? Not just snogs and morgrins? Aren't there any friendlies like elves or gnomes that can help us?" Bruce asked. "Yes, but the risk is too great for them. Ammuzol can kill them just as easily, but he will use their blood as "fuel". It is more potent so that's why nothing magical or supernatural is coming to help us. We are on our own." Kira said. Chris slapped himself in the forehead "Fuck, and this Ammuzol guy wants to kill me." Roxy looked up "It all makes sense. Mark did mention something, on the original plan, that we would need science and magic on the Atrox so whether we try to break or seal it, it has to be a combination!"

Bruce looked over Mark's notes "Unweave…Bind, Trueform….so the reverse must be Conceal, Sunderlight…Shield." Bruce held Mark's journal. Kira was right. Mark jotted them down, just in case he was wrong. "Okay, so we know we have to seal this thing. We can look around the garage and see if we can find some epoxy, glue, something but the magic? Do we need to find a sorcerer or hot goth chick?" Bruce continued.

Kira scolded Bruce for his *hot goth chick comment* with a look. "No, Hot pants, I can handle the magic spell. I need to check around grandpa's stash and…what's this?" Kira found a wooden box by the desk. Kira opened it to find a glass vial with holy water from the Dead Sea, a small box with consecrated ash, and a piece of silver. Grandpa knew. Or suspected Jake was under some evil influence. He was going to help, but something got to him first. Kira traced the edges of the wooden box "Oh, Grandpa, why didn't you tell me?"

Everyone saw the contents and realized that Mark was preparing for a confrontation. Bruce got up "Let's check the garage and see if we can find something to seal the physical cracks." Kira put down the box. "Let me check my grandpa's room, maybe, he left something I can use to apply the spell." Kira said. Bruce, Roxy and

Chris went to the garage while Kira went upstairs to her grandpa's bedroom.

Kira realized that most of her grandpa's stuff was gone as her Dad had begun donating many of the personal items in the house. Kira checked the drawers, the closets and under the bed. Kira was at a loss on what to do when she heard a voice say "KayKay". Kira turned around and didn't see anyone. Then Kira felt a warm gush of air pass through her and then saw a shimmering light. "I don't have much time, listen to me".

"Grandma?" Kira said.

"Take this, it is made with real silver thread, it will bind the crystal." A silhouette handed Kira the silver scarf that belonged to her grandma Janet. Kira took it in her hands. "Seal the crystal and look away...look away." Kira noticed her grandma's voice was gentle yet devastated. Before she could ask her anything, her grandma's presence was gone.

"Found it!" Chris had a handful of industrial glue. Bruce and Roxy found tape and an epoxy resin, but it would have to be mixed before it would be useful. Chris was about to hand it to Bruce when suddenly he cried out "ARRGGHHH!"

"What's wrong?" Kira shouted from downstairs. She ran into the garage as fast as she could and she saw Bruce and Roxy trying to comfort Chris. Chris's hand was burnt and the skin started to boil as if something corrosive was poured over it. They took Chris to the kitchen and applied first aid.

"We should take him to the ER" Bruce said. Chris looked up. "NO! You saw it! This wasn't no accident! It was that thing, that thing that's possessing Jake!". Roxy looked around but she sensed nothing. Kira looked on while holding on the silver scarf. "We don't have a choice. We have to go the Devil's Maw. We have to seal the crystal now." Chris said. *This thing burned him, is probably torturing a good friend and is trying to harm the love of his life, this is personal.*

"Fuckin' A we do" Bruce said. Roxy checked her purse. She nodded in agreement. Bruce gathered the few supplies they had and put them in his jeep. "No going back, either we come back or that thing does." Kira said.

"Hang on, it's getting dark. Shouldn't we wait until morning?" Roxy asked. Chris held up his burnt hand. "See you real soon, I don't think I'll last till then". Kira thought for a second. "This is the right time to strike. Ammuzol is weak, for now". Bruce closed the driver's side door. "What do you mean? He burnt Chris' hand from wherever he is".

Kira took out her phone. "Look, my dad gave the Atrox to Grant Kingsley. Now his island is destroyed. This thing literally sank an entire island back into the Earth. Jake is there with the stone. If he was able to, Ammuzol would have killed Chris not maimed him. He is weak, he spent too much power. We have to strike now, by tomorrow…"

"By tomorrow, he would have recovered and we would have no chance at winning. He's tired and he knows it. Kira's right. We have to do it now." Chris said. The four of them stood silently for a moment. "Let's go" Bruce said while exhaling out all his doubt. The four of them got into his jeep and drove into the evening, towards the *Devil's Maw.*

The drive felt long. The temperature was slowly dropping. The path to Devil's Maw was treacherous and felt even worse at night. No county infrastructure. No street lights. No signs. Nothing. Chris checked his phone. Roxy checked hers, as did Kira. No signal. Bruce kept his

Jeep steady, but the road was bumpy, as if they were riding on skulls.

Nobody talked. The radio was off. Everyone was quiet. Their nerves fraying. The parking lot had cars, but as they drove past, they looked abandoned, as if they'd been sitting there for years. Jake's office had the light on. But as soon as they pulled up, it turned off.

Roxy checked her handbag. She had Final Verdict locked and loaded. She checked her ankle and found her revolver there. She took it out and handed it to Bruce. She wished she'd brought something heavier, but firing a rifle in an enclosed space like a cave probably wasn't the best idea. "No matter what, stick together. Strength in numbers. Stay sharp. Let's go." Bruce said as each of them nodded in agreement. Bruce popped open the back of his Jeep. He handed Chris a baseball bat and took a steel pipe for Kira, but she turned it away. Kira had her grandpa's spell book and exorcism kit.

They moved together, checking the compound. Keeping their eyes open. They went to Jake's Office, but nothing was there. The only lights were at the mouth of the cave. There was no other way in. No other option. They had to heal the crystal. They had to hide it and keep it away from the Grant Kingsleys of the world. Bruce walked in first, followed by Kira then Chris and Roxy.

They walked past the muster area and could see piles of discarded backpacks and equipment. They approached with caution. Chris looked around and saw bits of plastic and electronics. He took a deep breath. All the drones were destroyed. He found a handheld device with an incomplete map of the cavern system. He scrolled through the data and shared the information.

"It seems like Jake was pushing his team to this point: an antechamber labeled 'Starwound.' This device provides a partial map. So, the question is: do we think Jake would take the Atrox Stone there?"

"Fuck that! I mean, come on. Are we seriously thinking about going to a place called Starwound?" Roxy said. Kira took out a small compass with a scorpion encased in amber. She held it out. Its tail moved to indicate a specific direction. "I think the Atrox is located in the other chamber, Obsidian Vorun". Chris looked at the strange compass. "What is that?"
Kira smiled. "An old birthday present. Now, I think we should go that way, my compass is picking up a strong energy field that way, it has to be the Atrox." Kira nodded. "Ammuzol probably set up a trap for us."

"Yeah, he doesn't realize we have a true wizard in our ranks. I say let's go to Obsidian Vorun. Starwound feels like an obvious trap." Roxy said. The group agreed and headed left towards Obsidian Vorun. They only had two flashlights and were saving their phone batteries for an emergency. Kira looked up. "Hey, look. Noctilium." She shined her flashlight to the ceiling. "It's made from glowworms and fireflies. Usually a good omen."

None of them were prepared for the descent down to Obsidian Vorun. The floor was slick and wet. They could hear the distant dripping of water, and the light was dimming faster and even their flashlights had a hard time shining in such deep darkness. The Noctilium was fading as if whatever put it up there had either run out or been taken out.
Kira could feel something. A strong presence pulling her toward it. She moved carefully. The descent was steep. Getting out would be a challenge.

"Where are we?" Roxy asked. Chris put down the bat and took out the mapping device to check their location. "We're getting closer." He reached back down to find the bat. It was gone. Chris turned on his cell phone light to find the missing bat, but couldn't find it. Kira touched the wall of the cave, feeling its energy. It was cool to the touch, but the air was getting warmer. She took a deep breath. "Closer. You are getting too close" a sad yet gentle voice told her.

Kira turned her head. She could barely make out her friends in the darkness. "We're almost there. Get ready" she said. Bruce was checking around and thought to himself *too bad we didn't leave any trail markers*. He could barely make out the other tunnels. Some of them looked big enough for a person to walk through, but that could be misleading.
"Roxy, help me."

Roxy turned around. She could barely see anything. Her senses were dulling due to darkness surrounding them. Bruce shook his head. Nothing was behind him. "I thought I heard Jake," she said.

"I hope not," Bruce said. "At least, not yet."
Kira continued to lead the way now. To her, the pull was getting stronger. she was walking a little more casually yet quickly than her friends wanted. Sweat beaded on their foreheads. Even Roxy's palms were getting sweaty. She re-holstered Final Verdict. It wasn't time yet, and if something came at them, she didn't want to fire with sweaty hands. Roxy heard Jake's voice:
"Closer."

"Closer, I said" the strange voice told Kira as she moved forward but slowed her pace. Chris, Roxy, and Bruce surrounded her and looked around in awe.
Obsidian Vorun

The stalagmites jutting from the floor and ceiling made it look like the jaws of some horrible creature. The darkness was so absolute that their senses struggled to adjust to the pure absence of everything. In the center of the antechamber was a stone table and resting on top of it was a shard of obsidian shale, carved to look like a hand of some sort. Resting on top of it was the Atrox Stone.

"Guys, I think we made a big mistake," Chris said. Suddenly, Kira was struggling as if fighting some invisible foe. She started to lash out in the air as if to hit some invisible foe then she began to faint. Bruce immediately caught her. "Are you okay?! Kira!"
"Consecrete Undar. Oblivien Vor. Illumina scarvor"
A sinister voice from the void spoke.
"Welcome to Starwound!"
The ground shifted and caused everyone to slip. Deep crevices formed and something tried to pull everyone down in the deep recesses of Starwound. Everyone tried to hang on to something and pulled themselves up. Roxy was able to unholster Final Verdict but her handbag with the extra clips was gone. She had one spare clip in her back pocket. The tunnel behind them started to close as if it was contracting like a blood vessel. Chris was able to run up to the stone table and grabbed the Atrox Stone. He used all his physical strength to bring it back to his friends.

"We have to begin the ritual. NOW!" Bruce said. Kira was fighting to regain her senses. "Apply the sealant." She muttered. Chris reached into his pocket to grab the industrial glue, but it was gone. Chris started to panic did he leave it behind at the house? In Bruce's Jeep. The tube of glue was on the floor; he saw it and reached for it when something pushed him down. Chris got up and somehow stepped on it, squeezing all the glue out. He tried to collect it with his hands but made more of a mess.

"Forget it!" Bruce shouted as he immediately took out the epoxy resin from a vial in his vest pocket. He motioned for Chris to bring over the Atrox. Roxy stood on overwatch while Kira was fighting another battle on her own. Roxy took a quick peek and saw Kira's eyeballs had rotated backwards. Kira gasped as she struggled. *Hang on girl* Roxy said, feeling helpless.

Chris held the Atrox steady as Bruce applied the resin. Steam seemed to come out of the stone, weakening the bond. Bruce patted down his other pockets. "Shit! My UV light!" He searched in his pockets. His bag. His surroundings. *Shit! Did I forget it? Did I drop it? Where the fuck is it!* Chris tried to wipe some of the glue off his hands on the Atrox, filling up some of the smaller cracks.

"Roxy! How could you? I trusted you." Roxy turned around. From the other side of the cavern was Jake. Chris looked at him. Jake looked better than he'd last seen him. "How could you? I trusted you. You didn't try to help me? Couldn't you feel that I was in danger?" Roxy froze as did Chris.

Bruce thought of an immediate solution. Not perfect, but it would do. "Chris! Hand me the Atrox." Chris looked at Jake. Guilt and shame covered his face. "It wasn't her fault! It was mine! I took advantage of her…don't blame her, blame me" Chris confessed while holding on to the Atrox. Jake looked at him. His face was full of pain, sorrow and betrayal. "I trusted you. I treated you like a brother. And you did this behind my back? You didn't even try to help me…you couldn't wait until I was out of the way"

"CHRIS! The Atrox. Over here. NOW!" Bruce shouted. Roxy looked at Bruce, at Kira, then back to Chris and Jake. "Chris! What are you doing?" Roxy said. Chris was staring at Jake. Bruce said out loud "My phone.

I have a special setup for fieldwork. I can shine a weak UV light for a few seconds, but it should be enough to trigger the epoxy. Dammit, Chris, give me the stone!" Jake kept his eyes on Chris. Chris could see tears in Jake's eyes. He was begging them to help. Kira was in a half-squat, recovering from some sort of spiritual attack. Suddenly, Chris turned and pushed her down. He grabbed her exorcism kit and ran toward Jake. "WHAT THE FUCK ARE YOU DOING? CHRIS! CHRIS!" Bruce shouted.

"AHHH!!!!..." Kira's breath left her body as the attack on her renewed. She tried twisting her ear, but the attacks were getting stronger. Bruce held her. He could feel the struggle. Her temperature rose and fell. Kira was in a fight, and he couldn't help her.

Roxy followed Chris toward Jake. Kira mumbled something. Bruce didn't understand, but she was struggling to speak to her friends. She was in no condition to help. Kira's back arched in an unnatural way. Bruce was stunned. He didn't know what to do.

Chris ran over to Jake and dropped the Atrox Stone. It chipped off some of the resin. Some of the hairline cracks widened slightly. Jake looked at the crystal, then back to Chris. "Please…help me. I don't know how much longer I can hold him back." Jake said as his voice trembled. Chris' eyes widened "Let me see what's in here. Hang on, Jake!" Chris went through the exorcism kit, then in a panic turned it upside down, dropping everything to the floor. He grabbed the vial of holy water and opened it. He splashed Jake with it. "By the power of Jesus! Demon, be gone!"

Jake stood there for a moment, pausing as if thinking what would be the appropriate move. Then he screamed "Argh! Ahhh!" Jake held a hand over his face but left a gap so he could see out of his left eye.

Chris kept walking forward, splashing Jake with holy water, repeating various chants he'd heard from horror movies as a kid. Jake lowered himself into a fetal position. Kira was struggling. Levitating in the air. Still mumbling something Bruce couldn't understand. Then suddenly, she dropped. Bruce tried to catch her, but they both fell hard. Kira struggled to breathe. She looked at Bruce. Her eyes full of awareness. Desperate to say something.

Roxy followed Chris and heard him shouting various "Demon, be gone!" chants at Jake. As soon as she arrived, Jake slowly stood from the fetal position. His eyes glowed bright orange. He licked his lips. "Welcome home, my ornament."

Kira struggled to her feet. Her lungs working overtime to get air back. "Breathe. Easy now," Bruce said. Kira reached for her brown bag. "We... we... must hurry."

Roxy looked at Jake. Chris ran out of holy water. He ran up to Jake and shook him with all his might. "Come back to us! We love you! I'm sorry!" Jake kept his eyes on Roxy.
Chris slapped Jake in the face, trying everything to bring his friend back. Jake looked at Chris with the side of his eyes. Roxy's mouth dropped.

This is not Jake.
"Get back!" she shouted at Chris and then shot at "Jake". She unloaded a few bullets into him. 'Jake' looked at her. He grabbed Chris by the throat and choked him with his left hand, lifting him up into the air. Chris's feet swung wildly. "You rejected my offer before. Now you want to save him? Give me... everything. Anything..." Ammuzol's eyes pierced through as he licked his lips. Roxy emptied

all the rounds that Final Verdict carried. "How about… nothing!" She fired the last round right between Jake's eyes.

Jake dropped Chris. Roxy ran over and held Chris' head up. "Chris! Chris! Are you okay?" Chris struggled to breathe. Roxy knelt next to him. She wanted to move him away from Jake, but Chris was in no shape to move, and Jake wouldn't be getting up anytime soon. Chris coughed as he struggled to breathe. Roxy looked over at him, tears running down her face. Her hair dangled over his face.

Chris started to breathe. He looked at Roxy to reassure her he was all right. He laid eyes on her and knew that whatever life he had left, he wanted to spend it with her. His guardian angel. His Roxy. He smiled at her and then caressed her cheek. She kissed his hand. Chris took a deep breath…. then suddenly, something pulled him into the void.

Roxy looked up and screamed at what she saw. She immediately reached for Final Verdict and put in its final clip when two grotesque hands grabbed her by the wrists. The "skin" was burning her. It lifted her off the ground. Two glowing eyes, like lava, stared at her. "It's time for my little ornament to shine."

Kira regained her strength. Bruce struggled to hold on to his phone. "We have an epoxy resin on the Stone, I need to shine this light to seal it, then it's up to you" Bruce said while Kira summoned as much energy as she could. Kira's mind was foggy, but she knew what to do. She still had her personal travel bag on her. She peeked: spell book and her grandma's silver scarf. They crossed over to the other side of the cavern.

"CHRIS! ROXY!" Bruce called out. Kira was a step or two behind him. Bruce had his phone in his right hand and the revolver in his left. The cave felt cold and then by some twisted mockery, the Noctilium shined to reveal the horror… the sight stole all their speech. It paused all of their senses. It stole all their will to fight. Chris was on the floor. A hole punched through his chest. He was bitten in half. His guts and part of his spine exposed.

Bruce made out different pair of severed hands on the floor. One of them held a special large caliber pistol. Final Verdict. They saw Roxy…

Roxy was naked and her feet were planted into the ground. A dark tar-like substance ran up her calves and stopped below her knees. Tears ran down her face, like broken starlight. Her lips had this rough purple hue and her arms stretched up with branches growing out of the stumps where her hands used to be. There were signs her branches bore fruit that was picked off before the fruit was ripe.

Bruce froze…everything he saw in his nightmare, the foul feast…it's happening. He grabbed the revolver in his free hand and pointed it at that thing pretending to be Jake. He pointed it at Roxy. He could see her suffering, but he didn't have the strength to end it. Instinctively he shouted to Kira, "Seal the fucking stone!"

Jake appeared and grabbed Kira as she picked up a piece of silver and the rosary from the floor. Jake started to squeeze Kira's throat while Bruce emptied his revolver into Jake's back. This gave Kira time to place the rosary on him. Now the reaction was real. Jake reacted to the purity of the rosary. Kira placed the silver in his mouth and closed it with force. Jake swallowed the silver. She placed a St. Michael medal on Jake's forehead and finished a quick prayer. The body of Jake convulsed. The exorcism was working.

Fucking Silver! I hate that BITCH! Ammuzol thought as he was forced out of Jake's body. Out of spite, he "returned" Jake back to his friends. To their horror, Jake was only a desiccated corpse. Jake was gone there was nothing to save. Bruce, his eyes filled with tears, his heart pounding, he had one shot left. A strange mist formed around Jake's body. It began to take a solid shape, so Bruce pointed the gun at it. He fired but hit the crystal by mistake. The crack began to grow.

The cave began to shake. The stalagmites began to fall. Bruce and Kira had to dodge them. The entire cave began to distort and pull them toward Ammuzol, who discarded any human form. As the crystal broke, his true form began to take shape. Ammuzol looked at Bruce "A reward for my savior."

Ammuzol spit out a spear from his mouth that stabbed Bruce in the shoulder. Bruce fell backwards and hit the ground headfirst. His vision was blurred; he felt the blood pouring out of his wound. His strength left him, but he tried to get back on his feet. Ammuzol took steps towards Kira. "You. Another ornament for my collection."

Immediately, Kira began to chant the three spells. Bind: "By the loom of the great goddess, I spin her webs upon you!" Ammuzol smiled then snarled by the mention of his hated enemy. Conceal: "By the spirits of the Earth, may your key be unfound!" Ammuzol laughed. He took another step. The cracks of the Atrox were getting larger. Shield: "A sacrifice must be made; a price shall be paid! May the goddess protect us from you!"

Ammuzol got closer and reached out to Kira. His fingers were close enough that Kira could feel her skin burning. "I remember you, the ornament that got away…It's not too late…ask me and you shall have it…Anything…Everything or Nothing…"his orange eyes glowed and he started to drain the life and spirit from Kira.

"It's not working…. what did I miss?" Kira said as she felt her breath leaving her body. Bruce couldn't get up but he had enough strength to make one move…*one move left*…he took out his phone and pressed a purple button. The UV light shone on the Atrox, and the epoxy began to harden.

Ammuzol felt his grip loosening, he was almost free. He turned his head and saw Bruce shining a weak light on the Atrox. "Foolish boy, that won't work now." Ammuzol laughed and it echoed throughout the chamber. Bruce's phone lost power, the UV light drained the battery and Bruce dropped his phone. The concussion was sinking in.

Ammuzol stared at Kira, undressing her with his eyes. Kira was frozen in place. It didn't matter what she said now. He was going to take anything he wanted from her. Everything she had and leave her with nothing. Kira's feet were getting wet as a dark fluid was filling up the cave. The void began to take shape. In the distance, Kira could see a crooked mountain. A turbulent sea surrounding it and a howling wind. Kira could see shapes twisting in the water, strange creatures with bright lures on their heads, were pulling these shapes into the darkness below and their screams made the wind howl.

Beyond the crooked mountain, Kira could see a great and terrifying palace and in the courtyard were a few shimmering trees, all making a mournful howl…among them was Roxy! Many brave warriors that shared her spirit also suffered her fate. Kira saw a great storm over the sea. The sea thrashed and, in the waters, Kira heard Chris. Ammuzol turned to admire his work.

He kicked the crystal as he continued towards Kira. The crystal was by her feet. Ammuzol reached out and touched Kira.

"NO, LEAVE HER ALONE!" a lone figure fought its way out of the sea and leaped on Ammuzol's back. He wrapped an arm underneath his chin and with his other arm, tried to pull back the hand that was touching Kira. Kira snapped out of it when she heard her savior's voice. "Grandpa!"

Kira froze, she couldn't move or think clearly…the seal! She looked down and pulled out the silver scarf out of her pocket. Her grandpa was struggling with Ammuzol. Kira picked up the Atrox. Sensing her actions, Ammuzol reached out and pulled the crystal to him and held it in his left hand.

Bruce struggled. He had one eye open. His mind struggling to make sense of what was going on. Is that Mark? Bruce shouted to himself "Dammit, man. Feel pain later. Your tribe needs you." He cursed himself as he was unable to move. Unable to act.

Ammuzol began to distort itself. It grew multiple tails and swung them at Kira and her grandfather. Kira could see the fear in her grandpa's eyes.

Then it hit her: the strange beings twisting in the sea….Roxy….Chris…..her grandpa….they're here…in the void, trapped. Ammuzol kept his victims' souls as trophies. A soul couldn't die, but it could feel pain.

Mark was losing his fight with Ammuzol. He was struggling. Spending all his strength. It was all in front of her. She couldn't bring herself to do it. To cast the seal. The magic she placed on the crystal called out to her. Now, she understood what her grandma's spirit had warned her. *I can't do it…I CAN'T!*

Screams. The howling wind. Ammuzol's glowing orange eyes. He was coming closer. Reaching out to her as if to pull her into his twisted domain. To condemn her and her family to eternal torment as he freed himself. "PLEASE! HURRY! I CAN'T HOLD ON MUCH LONGER!" Mark shouted. The tails had spears on their ends. They impaled her grandpa. Blood. Arms. Flesh. Chunks of one of his legs flying in the air. Yet, Mark kept fighting with all of his might....until suddenly...the pain.....he cried out "KAYKAY!"

She tried to look at him. Her eyes filled with tears. With fear. She saw past the ancient cosmodial being and looked at her grandpa. He shouted "KAYKAY! PLEASE! HELP ME!"

Finally, her voice broke free from her fear. "GRANDPA! ABUELITO!"

She reached out to him. To pull him away. Ammuzol's head turned around unnaturally and shrieked at Mark. His dark, taloned hands gripped Mark's neck and started to twist it like a pretzel. Kira's eyes were blinded by tears. All she heard was the snapping!

Kira froze in horror. Her soul was leaving her body. Then the seal left her hand. She couldn't tell if the wind pulled it away. If she let it go. Or if someone behind her pushed her arm to let the seal cast.

Ammuzol turned away to face Kira, realizing too late: the seal was cast. The silver threads from the scarf wrapped around the crystal. The Atrox began to close itself. The silver thread binding it like a spider's web. Ammuzol roared; a bone-chilling roar. He pierced Kira's mind, her heart and her soul. She knew…her friends were gone. Her grandpa was gone. They are never coming back…she will never see them again, in this lifetime or any.

Ammuzol was pulled in, toward some massive black hole in the center of the universe. *The Oblivion Maw.* The last of him to leave was the glowing but vengeful stare of his eyes. The seal was placed. The Atrox Stone was healed. The portal and the distortion in the cave was closed.

Kira's eyes were wide open. Her mouth locked. Her hand still outstretched. She could see the final image of her grandpa…. she couldn't save him. She could save the world but not the people who mattered to her most. Finally, Bruce found the strength to get up, ignoring his own pain. He walked up to Kira. Blood was clotting on his wounds. He'd made an emergency patch on his left side, but he still needed medical attention.

The cave was dark. The temperature was dropping and by luck or instinct, Bruce led Kira upwards towards the light. They heard water dripping. Kira was in shock, her mind was fractured and she was moving on instinct alone. Bruce felt his brain was swelling up but something helped him to find the silver lining in the cavern ceiling that finally let them back out. Bloodied, bruised, and broken, Bruce and Kira stumbled out of the cave and collapsed outside. The wind blowing past them.

"Light!" Bruce weakly said. To him, it was relief…to Kira, a reminder…of what she had to do…what she had to live with…light will always be a reminder of the people she'd lost and forever condemned.

Epilogue

Weeks passed.

Bruce stared out his window from his nearly empty apartment. He thought about the events that happened at Starwound for weeks now. His mind wouldn't stop thinking of those final moments. Chris, Roxy, Kira and Mark. Local and State officials closed The Devil's Maw for good.

Investigators found multiple dead bodies and ruled it an accident due to exposure to toxic gases. The same excuse they gave back in 1990 when the bodies of Frankie Martinez and his friends were found.

The parents of Chris, Roxy, and Jake were told that their children died inside the cave by a series of tragedy events. One of them got stuck in a deep ravine, then two of them went to help but a sudden rupture of noxious gases caused a cave-in which trapped them. Investigators "found" the remains of several people using special scanning equipment. The surviving families were told their loved ones died in inaccessible passages as well. The families decided to destroy the caverns to let their loved ones rest in peace. If they only knew the truth.

It was a lie. A lie told by the same people who knew the truth. That monsters are real. Ancient evil walked the Earth. The world was not ready to accept it. Not ready to believe. There were many inquiries, so many unanswered questions but Miranda Kingsley escaped scrutiny due to the disaster at Maranoa Island. The University faced sanctions for safety violations. Dr. Chalmers was never found.

Bruce had gone through so many interviews. He answered so many questions. Nobody believed him, but the evidence supported him. Neither he nor Kira had played any part in their friends' deaths. Investigators detected a strange energy variance inside a deep chamber. They concluded that to be source of the toxicity. Conveniently, they "omitted" that fact in the official report when they made The Devil's Maw off limits. Bruce knew what laid down there. *Inside Starwound.*

Lt. Davis and Detective Meadows helped tie up any loose ends for Bruce and Kira. Bruce was able to recover from his physical wounds. Kira on the other hand, remained in the hospital. Her physical wounds had healed, yet she was unable to sleep without medication, and she hasn't spoken a word in weeks. The doctors said it was due to trauma. The trauma of seeing her friends trapped in the cave and knowing she was unable to save them.

Bruce stopped by every day to see her. He wanted to be there for Kira. He remembered the only time he was able to see her; it didn't go well. He saw her for a moment, she was having a nightmare…she kept reaching out…. she tried to scream but nothing came out. Her parents blamed him for everything. Everyone did…except Jake's mom.

After Jake's funeral, Jake's mom told him, "I knew you did everything you could, I'm glad that Jake has such good friends". Only a handful of people came, Jake's dad didn't bother to show up.

Roxy and Chris' families were not so forgiving. They needed someone to blame, and Bruce, as the only other survivor, took the brunt. Kira's parents were the same way, until they realized: maybe what Kira needed was to see a friend. Someone who'd made it out with her.

"You can see her now," the nurse told Bruce. Bruce needed a moment to collect himself. He dropped out of college. His mind was too distracted to finish his studies. The life that he knew was gone. Kira was all he had left. Thomas told him that he was taking his daughter back home to Neon City. He sold Mark's house; now, all the Martinez family would be gone from Coralyn Bay.

Kira's doctor determined she was fit to travel. He advised her parents to take her away from Coralyn Bay. She needed to be far from the traumatic environment. Bruce walked into Kira's hospital room. Her dad was leaving with her bags. He nodded and lowered his gaze at Bruce. A sad recognition. A silent admission: it wasn't his fault. It wasn't anybody's fault.

Kira's mom: her makeup a little messy from crying and hugging her daughter, looked at Bruce. "We'll give you two a moment." Kira's mom put her hand on Bruce's arm and squeezed it. He understood. Just a moment, nothing deep but make it count. Bruce nodded. He was alone with Kira, at last.

"Kira, I..." Bruce looked upon her. *Shakira Karae*…the strong, confident and beautiful woman he met was gone. Her skin, hair and eyes were pale, they lost their glow, their passion for life…Kira left something at Starwound…or something was taken away…

Bruce took a step towards her. She didn't move or even acknowledge him. Bruce sighed, lowered his head to fight back tears *"Not now, she needs you…be strong"* he told himself. Bruce looked up and Kira trembled then quickly hugged him, burying her head into his chest. Bruce held her tight. Her skin was cool, almost cold. For a second, it felt like Kira was trying to steal Bruce's warmth. Bruce smiled as he said to himself *Go ahead, take whatever you want…. whatever you need…you deserve it* he was hoping she could read his thoughts.

Bruce wanted this moment to last forever but he would give anything…anything to have his friends back….to have Kira bust his balls, even if it meant she had to leave his life and find happiness elsewhere….he just wanted her back. He looked down at her and brushed some of her hair away from her face and she said, "I did what I had to do," then she looked down at the floor. "I had to….I…"

Bruce didn't know what to say. He wished he was the one who had to make the choice….to face the true horror…the impossible choice….to be damned for all eternity. He wished to take away all of her pain. Despite all of his knowledge and strength, he knew, he could never do that….so he held her closer and squeezed a little more.

Bruce rested his chin on top of Kira's head and softly told her "No…We did what we had to do, all of us…" he could feel Kira's tears slowly running down her face as she held on to him tighter.

There was so much they wanted to say to each other. So many things they wanted to share. Things they needed to share with each other but neither one of them had the strength to do so. So much was lost. So much was taken…

One last time, they made eye contact. They both remembered the smiles. The laughter. The warmth of their friends. Slowly, they felt a trickle of light surrounding them as they remembered that one beautiful evening on the deck outside of Julie's…the music, the glow…. then Kira leaned up on her toes, pulling Bruce towards her…he didn't resist…. but…

Bruce felt an intrusion into their space…. no..not now….it was her parents…
"It's time".

Time. The one thing they needed and never had enough of…time. Bruce hugged Kira once more…. "Kira..I" then she looked up and whispered "KayKay". This was it. This was all they could offer each other. Their future, their potential, the lives they would've had together was gone.

She had to leave. He had to stay.

Kira's parents walked up to them. Thomas put his hand on Bruce's shoulder while her mom put a soft hand on Kira. It was time to go. Bruce escorted them out. He saw Kira one last time in the backseat of a robo-cab. She looked at him and placed a hand on the window. Bruce put his to hers…he could feel her faint glow…he saw in her eyes, an echo of the woman she once was…as the car pulled away…the echo was gone….

He followed them to the airport. He watched them unpack their car. A security officer told him that he couldn't stay in the unloading lane, so he quickly parked. But by the time he made it back, Kira and her family were through the gate. He could only see a glimpse of her. Her mother was holding her arm escorting her away.

Bruce stayed inside the lobby as long as he could, tracking her flight status. When it was time for the plane to take off, he watched from the parking lot as it left. He hoped he could see her out one of the windows. He was hoping she could see him as her plane took off.

He stayed in the parking lot for hours. He stared out into the star-filled sky. A cool breeze swept by him and for a moment, the sky seemed to show him wonders beyond his imagination. Yet, his mind was empty…then his thoughts came back like a flood. He had to leave. He couldn't stay in the parking lot forever. Bruce paid for his parking tab and left. Alone, he drove out into the cold night.

City lights streaked by as he drove by the museum. By the university. By familiar haunts where he used to meet his friends. Bruce stopped by Sunrise Hill and walked over to the Widow's Branch. He took out a pocketknife and carved "BB & KK" into the bark. He thought about staying to watch the sunrise over the bay, but he knew in his heart, the magic was gone.

He drove all night and made his way out to Grand Madre Island. He walked along the shoreline, tossing seashells into the bay. He was alone…. the world felt emptier yet a whole lot bigger…. he wondered…

What do I do now?

What kind of a life can I live now?

How can I go on living, knowing what's out there? Knowing I can never truly be safe?

Look what happened to Mark….to Kira.
Evil never forgets. Revenge has no expiration date.

The Atrox Stone was buried. *For now.* Who knew how long it would take before someone, or something, found it again? Perhaps… it wanted to be buried. Deep in the cave. Closer to darkness. It would wait until its enemies died and it would find someone new to tempt…or possess…Bruce knew there was evil out there that lived in the shadow. In dreams. And it was real. Coralyn Bay had nothing for him anymore. No future. No present. No life. His heart ached for Kira…if only they had more time….

He remembered the stories Mark had told him. The stories that older people had told him. There was a time when a person would literally get up and go. Go far away and start a new life. There was nothing for him here…all the beauty, the wonder, the magic…was gone. People would always talk about him…Coralyn Bay, so large yet so small…. Bruce knew what he had to do.

He checked his bank account on his phone. Alone in the forgotten sands of Grand Madre Island, the gateway to the sea and to faraway roads. Bruce reached inside his vest, into one of the pockets and pulled out the lighter. Mark's gift…he knew Bruce didn't smoke but it was meant to light the way…to shatter darkness…to find hope.

Bruce remembered the last time he saw his friends, together in Mark's house, they huddled together…those words he thought out and wished he shared…

Through pain and trauma, the survivors reached the shore, bounded by tragedy, forever in each other's debt. Let no power, on Earth or in the heavens, break this bond, a bond they wished they never had yet a bond they will always treasure.

Bruce looked out in the bay towards the horizon…hearing the water splash back and forth as sea gulls flew overhead. The sky was a dark blue slowly changing color…the light was leaving the bay and heading west. He got into his jeep and drove away. His mind was made up. He was leaving everything behind. The sun was setting in the west.

He didn't know where he would go. If Ammuzol wanted his revenge, then it would have to find him. He drove toward the sunset. He would remember, even if the world chose to forget. Someone had to carry the story. Someone had to keep the flame burning, to hold the shadow at bay. Evil killed a noble torchbearer and wounded his heir…the true keeper…

"KayKay" Bruce whispered one last time.

It was up to him now to remember. To keep the light shining in the darkness, alone if he must. He held the lighter in his right hand and then put it back in his vest, close to his heart.
Evil wins when good forgets.
Tears streamed down Bruce's face as wind whipped through the Jeep. He drove west, toward the sunset, toward the unknown.

Appendix

Dr. Everous Scratch, Professor of History and Ancient Languages, was able to translate several passages of hieroglyphs found inside Devil's Maw. The story was carved into various parts of the cave from the walls to the ceiling in the area known as Starwound.

The Silver Thread

Ages ago, before Earth was born, there was another universe with its own history. A place of utter darkness, silence, and harmony. Its sole inhabitant lived for eons alone, but in truth, may have been the cause of the lost universe's destruction.

In its isolation, the cosmodial entity rested. Its power began to spread throughout many planes of existence until it entered one plane and concentrated on the planet of Andar.

The people of Andar resembled the men and women of Earth. They had similar but different languages and lived under the dominion of various cosmic beings, whom they called gods. The Gods of Andar demanded tribute. Each year, the Andars gathered their best crops and most precious treasures to pay for divine protection. Until one year, the crops grew weak. The treasure was scarce.

The people of Andar put aside their differences and gathered at the Sacred Temple of Serlene. There they prayed and beseeched their gods for help. Their world had been ravaged by a strange creature, awoken when a great asteroid crashed into the vast forests, unearthing this savage beast.

They named it Phyr.

Phyr burned the lands. It ate all the crops and beasts. And once its horrible task was done, it began to eat the great nations of Andar.

The messenger of the gods took the tribute without a word.

Aurelion, The King of the Gods, heard of his people's tribute and their troubles. He looked down from his palace by the edge of the stars and decreed that none of his subjects leave to help the people of Andar. Some would say he was afraid of the great demon Phyr. Only one did not listen.

The noble Atheniferr, Protector of Plants and Animals, descended to Andar. She brought with her a sack filled with glowing jellies, medicines, and silver seeds, which she used to replant the land.

Many noble warriors were sent to kill Phyr. None of them returned.

The last queen and two kings of Andar gathered their full strength and marched to fight the demon. The Army of Three Crowns fought with all their might but were defeated. The last sovereign, King Thessan of Summerish, begged for mercy.

Distracted, the great demon was ambushed by Atheniferr and her brothers, who defied their king to fight alongside their sister. By dawn, Phyr was dead, along with all of Atheniferr's brothers.

Atheniferr was made mortal from her wounds.

Thessan, the last sovereign, took dominion of Andar and claimed Atheniferr as his bride. Banished from her own home, Atheniferr accepted and became queen.

The Andars rejoiced and celebrated their savior. The name of Atheniferr was loved, and many children bore her name.

Thessan, however, was shunned.

Time passed. Andar was rebuilt.

The gods returned and demanded tribute, but the people refused.

Where were the gods during the Great Crisis? Where were the gods when Andar was burning?

The gods threatened war. Andar refused to pay tribute. The gods threatened punishment. Still the people refused.

Thessan, sole ruler of Andar, made his own vow: any god who set foot on Andar would be executed. He ordered the head of Phyr, the demon that had scared the gods themselves, to hang in his courtyard. He adopted the image of Phyr as his new crest.

Despite his bravery, Thessan remained in the shadow of his queen. Atheniferr, the cosmodial who had lost her own brothers and sacrificed her divinity to protect and nourish the people, she was loved by all.

In secret, Thessan visited the ruins of Phyr's lair and learned forbidden knowledge. Knowledge that even the gods feared.

A great tree grew in the king's courtyard. At first, it was pleasant. But later, as the king's envy and madness grew, its fruit became bitter.

The gods sent a new messenger to arrest Atheniferr. She was taken to face trial for disobeying her king's command and for influencing the lesser beings to rebellion. Thessan used this as a rallying cry and led his people to the very steps of the gods' realm. A great battle was fought on the footsteps of heaven. The stars grew faint. The skies of Andar turned red.

The great King of the Gods begged for mercy.

As Thessan lifted his sword, it was his wife, Atheniferr, who begged him to show mercy. Thessan spared the god-king and took him prisoner.

Thessan returned home a hero, but word spread: the gods were weakened by lack of tribute. They needed Andar, for there is no food in the heavens. Many gods begged for mercy and received none.

Atheniferr's actions were praised by many, yet many grew sour. Thessan's influence began to spread among his people. Many Andars began to spread rumor and hate towards the queen and her cosmodial heritage. *She is one of them. Of course she pleaded for gods' lives. She will steal tribute, the fruits of our labors to give to her true family.*

One year passed. A bountiful spring was predicted.

Queen Atheniferr had great news for her husband. She asked to speak with him, and he insisted on seeing her in the courtyard, in front of the Tree of Phyr.

It was there that the Great Betrayal began.

Thessan beat his wife, despite her love and loyalty. She tried to speak, but her husband refused to listen. He revealed his terrible power. He slew Aurelion the god-king and the other gods. Now, Thessan demonstrated his new abilities by forcibly changing the queen into a great spider.

He uprooted the Tree of Phyr. A dark chasm lay below. He tossed his forsaken wife into the abyss and covered it with the tree, whose roots planted deeper.

As she fell, out of instinct, she spun a strong web at the base of the tree. Atheniferr descended into darkness. She spun her web until her body ran dry. She held on, alone in the darkness.

Alone in darkness, she cried. She only wanted to share the news that she was with child. Her body, transformed against her will, now bore an egg sack. She clutched it close so she could shield it from the darkness. Her warmth and love provided nourishment to her eggs. Then, sometime later, they began to hatch.

In the darkness, she could not see, but she could feel: her children, many of them, were born. She worried if her husband's curse had passed to them, until she felt their soft hands. Hands of children, not spiders.
She recoiled, afraid of scaring her own children.
But they spoke from a power of their own.

Mother do not recoil. We love you as you are. Tell us, why do you cry? She could not speak. Only tears flowed. She wanted to raise them as best she could. Would they truly know this monster was their own mother?
Do not cry, Mother. Stay with us. Do not leave!

They pleaded, and Atheniferr's children formed a circle around her. They showered their mother with warmth, understanding, and the innocence from a child's unconditional love. A mother's tears became starlight. As light returned to this place of darkness, so too did Atheniferr's true form.

In her last moment as a spider, she anchored her web to a star. Its light shimmering on the web made it look like a giant silver thread.
She told her children never to disturb it.

Years passed. Atheniferr and her children explored their new home, creating many magnificent things: stars and planets, made from imagination and not sorrow. Soon the entire area was littered with starlight, save for a few dark spaces.

Atheniferr watched her children grow and taught them many lessons, how to be good shepherds, to give without expectation of reward. Alas, the day came when someone or something tripped the Silver Thread. Its vibrations were subtle, felt only by two.

Fearing the reason, Atheniferr left her children to return to the web's source. Her children were grown and strong. She promised to return but demanded that none follow.

Up the thread she climbed, sensing more darkness, yet something less divine but more horrid. A fracture in space. A strange light leaking through. While Atheniferr was away, another being woke from its slumber, angered by the trespassers. It watched them tinker with their creations, violating its sanctity.
But it watched two in particular.
Bruelius and Nayia.

Bruelius, Guardian of Strength, was always bested by his sister, Nayia, Weaver of Songs and Harmony. While Bruelius was strong, Nayia could outpace and outthink her brother at will. Never to harm, but to tease. In truth, Nayia's gifts were meant to temper her brother's boldness.
Bruelius loved his sister, but he was jealous of her gifts and abilities.

One day, a great crashing of thunder on the mountaintops of Cardan, one of Bruelius's worlds, crushed many of the planet's villages. Bruelius struggled with a great boulder until Nayia arrived. She used a few sticks and ropes, and with her cleverness, moved it. In anger, Bruelius left Cardan. His mind filled with shame, envy, and hate toward his sister.

He traveled deep into the heavens, toward the edges of known space. He cursed his sister and his own weakness. His anger created dangerous radiation that seeped into the empty spaces of the heavens. Now the

children of Atheniferr and their creations could no longer pass safely. Sensing his error, Bruelius left to right his wrongs and ask forgiveness from his sister.
But a voice in the darkness spoke to him.

"You are the God of Strength. You are the Guardian of All. No one should make you bend. No one should make you feel shame. Bring her to me, and I will teach her humility."
Blinded by pride, Bruelius agreed, but he did not trust the voice. He asked it to give him speed so he might best his sister in a race around the boundaries of heaven. The challenge was made. Brother and sister raced throughout the heavens, leaving twin streaks of light for all to see.

Nayia bested her brother. She reached the edge of heaven and looked out into the void. Bruelius, in his anger, pushed his sister toward the darkness. Bruelius realized his error and called out, but he saw only darkness. No sound was heard, Bruelius stayed for days, calling out to his sister.
Nayia never returned.

Ashamed of his sin, Bruelius leapt into the darkness to find his sister. To his horror, he found her chained to a rotting stump. Her mind hollowed. Her spirit void.
Her arms had been twisted upward, reshaped into gnarled branches. From these branches grew fruit: strange, luminous, wrong.

Ammuzol, the Great Devourer who feasts on innocence and sin, had claimed her as his eternal harvest. He would plant his seed and consume the fruit before it could ripen. An endless cycle of violation and hunger.

Bruelius challenged the violator, but Ammuzol was already moving as dark mist, surrounding him. The

cosmodial horror took shape and tore Bruelius limb from limb, saving his head as a trophy.
Nayia remained at the center of Ammuzol's domain. Her legs bound to that rotten stump. Arms reaching skyward as twisted branches. She would forever bear fruit that would never be allowed to grow.
Forever his ornament. Forever his feast.

Ammuzol knew others would come to steal his prize. So, he decided to take shape, an unnatural mirror of his first opponent, and returned to the bright heavens, beginning his rampage.

Many of Atheniferr's children died, never knowing how to protect themselves. Many innocents were killed. Creatures great and small. Many voices. Many songs lost forever.
One warrior rose from the haze of ashes and blood. She bore her mother's courage and her father's anger. Behold! *Valkaia, The Guardian of Hearth and Land.*

Valkaia forged a mighty sword with help from one of her brothers, the Guardian of Fire and Steel. She rallied her siblings to make a stand on a lonely world whose star system bore no other life.
The world, Terra, lay bare. Its fires, used to create it, had yet to cool.

There she faced Ammuzol in a fierce battle that lasted for days, until she was able to score one hit: a slash across his face, sending chunks of flesh, bone, and a sinister eye away toward the magma.
Ammuzol took offense. No other being could give him pain. He lied to himself and called his pain pleasure.

He outlasted Valkaia. His strength kept growing. He grabbed her sword and shattered it. Valkaia had one last weapon: a spell only her mother knew. The Light of Creation. Mirroring her lost sister's gifts, Valkaia sang the spell. A light began to glow from her hand. She reached out to subdue the Great Terror.

But to her horror, the truth came out: the source of Ammuzol's strength was not natural. He could never bend. *Nayia!* The brave warrior called out, the truth caused a break in her concentration. Valkaia dropped her guard and it was all that Ammuzol needed to end her life. Valkaia, her hands and her heart removed, became another ornament for his collection.

Ammuzol, weakened by this battle, took a knife made from the bones of his victims and carved his flesh. From this vile act, he created his sons: the Seduul.

The Seduul went out into the universe to continue their father's work. Each had a personality, but each was in fact their father, who could recall them at will. If a Seduul was killed, its body disintegrated, leaving its father with a hideous scar, a scar he wore with pride, as it further intimidated his victims. The Seduul would violate, destroy or distort many beings, their gravest sin, the violation of mermaids and sirens, which lead to his unintended and unwanted daughters, whom he called anglers.

Then, as the last of Atheniferr's children cried out, all their own creations dead or dying, a great light appeared.

The Silver Thread snapped.

Atheniferr returned.

She was older. Wearier. She had completed her great task in her former home and returned to her family. She returned to find death, pain, horror and despair. She could sense the helplessness. She could hear the cries of her children, searching for their mother, wondering why she did not protect them.

There, waiting for her was her enemy, Ammuzol.

Ammuzol snarled. He assumed Atheniferr was just another trespasser. He attacked her and began to overpower her. In his great palace, he dragged Atheniferr by her hair. She saw the horrible ornaments; she felt their violation and pain. Ammuzol claimed his latest prize. But then Atheniferr used her mighty nails to tear off most of her locks and stood free.

She looked upon her foe as he mocked her. She closed her eyes for a moment. The universe revealed Ammuzol's horrors and his actions, the memories of pain, fear and despair began to overwhelm her. The cries, the screams…the pain.

It is in this moment of grief, anger and revenge that Atheniferr committed either the greatest act of justice or gravest sin. Ammuzol had to be stopped. Atheniferr only knew one way, but she didn't realize the heavy cost that had to be paid and the sacrifices that would have to be made…

She pulled at all of creation and made herself big, beyond recognition.
Atheniferr held the very universe in her hands. She compressed it.
Then she released it.
A great thunder of sound and light.
All the universe was undone and remade.
Ammuzol was gone.
But so were her children.
The weight of her actions; the loss of her children, Atheniferr faded from existence.
Such memory, of love and loss, doesn't simply fade. It is ingrained.
In the center of the universe: a great prison. In it, the Great Horror itself: Ammuzol.

But he has such strong and terrible power; he did not enter alone. He brought his victims. His trophies. And his favorite ornament, the Lady Nayia, remains with him.

It is said Atheniferr made the prison and made the door without a key. But in truth, the prisoner made his own key.

Lost in the wilderness of space, if the key is found and broken, it will unleash its prisoner. Atheniferr can never return. In her anger and grief, she damned her children into the great prison: the Oblivion Maw. They can never be at rest. They exist with their tormentor. To free them is to release him. And that is something she can never do.

Dr. Everous Scratch was last seen entering Devil's Maw on March 9th. His family has posted a reward for any information regarding his whereabouts. Mrs. Miranda Kingsley will match this reward tenfold. **Are you in?**

Recommended Soundtrack

The following is a suggested soundtrack to listen while reading *Remember the Shadow*, for readers who want to stay in Coralyn Bay a little longer.

The Dream
- *Sunrise*, Norah Jones
  - When Mark meets Janet

Before the Storm
- *Tripping Billies*, Dave Matthews Band
  - Bruce's Theme

Opening the Door
- *Dance Hall Days*, Wang Chung
  - Julie's Bar & Grill
- *This Girl*, Kungs & Cookin' On 3 Burners
  - Roxy's Theme

Losing Control
- **His Eyes**, Pseudo Echo
  - Jake's possession theme.

Through the Fog
- **Kokomo** or **Chasin' the Sky**, The Beach Boys

Obsidian Ember
- *Come to Me*, Brad Fiedel
  - Both instrumental and song. Start when Roxy begins her dream and let it play.
  - Alternative: *The Dance*, Tangerine Dream
    - Legend 1985 Soundtrack

The Morgrin
- *Smooth Operator*, Sade
  - Mark's Ringtone

The Soul Jackal
- *Number One*, Chaz Jankel
  - o   Any of the library scenes
- *Burnin' in the Third Degree*, Tahnee Cain & The Tryanglz
  - o   Jake's entrance in Big Ray's Bar/Ammuzol's General Theme until Starwound

Fractures
- **Starálfur**, Sigur Rós
  - o   Mark's farewell theme

Hello KayKay
- **Woman**, Doja Cat
  - o   Kira's Entrance

The Sovereign Cut
- *First Day of My Life*, Bright Eyes
  - o   Bruce and Kira's final dance (in lieu of the fictional song)

Sunrise Hill
- *Use Somebody*, Kings of Leon
  - o   Chris's Theme song
- *Holocene*, Bon Iver
  - o   Sunrise Hill's Theme song
- *Alternate Sunrise Hill Theme*: **New Sight,** Jerry Goldsmith from *Star Trek Insurrection* Soundtrack-play at beginning of the chapter and stop at 4:00 in the song.

Starwound
- *Blue Room,* **Tangerine Dream (Legend 1985 Soundtrack)**
  - o   Descent into the Devil's Maw

- ***Darkness*, Tangerine Dream (Legend 1985 Soundtrack)**
    - Ammuzol's theme

Epilogue
- ***Teardrop*, Massive Attack**
    - Beginning, stops when Bruce meets Kira
- ***First Day of My Life (reprise),* Bright Eyes**
    - Bruce and Kira's moment alone
- ***Aphex Moon: A Place to Drift Beneath The Moonlight,* Future City Music**
    - Play when Bruce goes to the airport until the end of the chapter

View the playlist on YouTube: @MaxVarrow
- Remember The Shadow

About the Author

Max Varrow spent years mastering the craft of storytelling, whether it be dark fantasy, horror, science fiction or comedies. Max enjoys peeking into the unknown areas of the universe and regularly visits the distant corners of imagination and the darkness beyond. Max also speculates in Artificial Intelligence and imagines where it will go in the future. Joining Max in his literary escapades are his dog, Stewie and cat Bindi, who go on their own misadventures. Max lives in Central Texas.

www.maxvarrow.com

Visit my YouTube channel: @MaxVarrow

Amazon: Max Varrow

Good Reads: Max_Varrow

TikTok: @max.varrow

Visit my Threadless Store: varrowshop.threadless.com

Other Works and Future Releases

The Angler: Extended Edition
Pocket Change (Comedy)

Future Releases

The Adventures of Zero:
- Shadow of Veldrath
- The Crimson Blade

Beyond the Shadow: Stories from The Silver Thread
Digital Echoes (AI Anthology)
Light Tracer (Sequel to *Torchbearer* by Ruben Lopez)
Serena and The Ajax
The Angler 2

Prelease Stories
- The Angler (Standalone preview from Remember the Shadow)
- Upload (Preview for Digital Echoes)-*Coming Soon*